CRIES
FROM THE
COLD

Bernadette Calonego

CRIES
FROM THE
COLD

Translated by Gerald Chapple

Previously published as *Eisiger Kerker*, by Calonego Media Inc. in Canada in 2020. Translated from German by Gerald Chapple.

Published by Calonego Media Inc., Gibsons, B.C., Canada, bernadettecalonego.com

Paperback ISBN: 978-1-9992302-8-9

Ebook ISBN: 978-1-9992302-9-6

Cover design by Vila Design: viladesign.net (Photo Depositphotos, rybarmarekk)

Interior design by Inca Vogt, inca-vogt-autorin.com

Editing by Lindsey Alexander of Reading List Editorial: readinglisteditorial.com

For Cheryl and Wayne

PROLOGUE

Scott has been watching the pack for some time. The coyotes come across the ice toward the beach, about a kilometer away. Six of them. The lead bitch in front, a sly beast. He shot the male, her life mate, a short while ago. You don't usually see the pack during the day; coyotes hunt in the dark. Don't want to be seen. Like him.

But today something has compelled the coyotes to come out in broad daylight. He hasn't a clue what it was.

The pack heads for Savage Beach. That's where he's going, too. He considers the beach his territory. You could find driftwood here even in winter. He's hitched a carrier sled to his snowmobile. Today he's going to fill it.

The pack has gotten to the beach. Not much snow there, he's pleased to find when he comes closer. Even the ice on the North Atlantic is pretty snow-free.

The coyotes will make for the nearby woods—they're full of rabbits and mice. He cuts back his motor, waits. Those fuckin' critters, what are they up to now? Crowding onto the beach, running back and forth, excited. Like they smell blood.

If those damn beasts don't get out of here soon, he'll have to fire a shot into the air. He could also shoot the bitch, but she's too far away. Besides, he doesn't want to take on the whole pack.

He just wants to get at the fucking wood. It doesn't cost anything. He's short of cash. His business isn't going too well now. Government's fault. Went and legalized marijuana. That wrecked his revenue. It's harder with coke and crack. The cops are keeping a close eye on him. He doesn't want to get nabbed a second time. Eight months in the slammer was more than enough. Next time the prosecutor will hit him with years.

What the hell . . . ? Did someone dump a carcass on the beach?

He takes his binoculars out from under his coat. Holds them up to his eyes. Jesus! What's that? Looks like a crate. About as long as a coffin. And the coyotes smell something. They're really going at it. Claws scratching.

He stuffs his binoculars under his coat and gets out his rifle. Bang! Bang! The pack scatters. Just so long as they keep away, the damn animals. He straps on his rifle and drives cautiously toward the beach. Not a coyote in sight. Clever, those critters. They've learned what shots mean. Coyote kill, state sponsored. The government pays twenty-five dollars for one dead animal. To protect a few caribou from predators. How idiotic is that! Maybe there'll be a bounty on pests like him sometime.

He drives hard onto the beach, up to the crate. The thing's built with solid boards. In good condition; a lot of firewood for the taking. But first he wants to know what's inside.

He's stowed an ax under his snowmobile seat. He scans the forest edge once again. Feels watched. Okay, no animal dares to come out. The ax whips downward. The corner of the crate splinters from his heavy blow. The hole is big enough for a look inside. He leans over and peeks through the opening. His gaze hits a skull. He staggers backward. He's a hard-nosed tough, but right now he's horrified. He's seen a swatch of hair.

He looks into the crate again. Wrinkles his brow. Something

dawns on him. What he sees is shocking and crazy. His heart is hammering.

Now he sees it. The symbol.

A sign stamped in the wood. Almost faded away.

Three intertwined triangles.

He stares at the symbol. He knows it. Knows it well.

Holy shit!

He circles the crate the way the coyotes did before. It can't be true. He trembles as he puts away his ax underneath the seat. Looks at the crate again. Thinks a little more clearly.

Things don't look so bad. Nobody can pin anything on him. He was in the clink at the time. Maybe this is his chance.

Something catches his eye. He shoves two fingers through the gap between the boards. Carefully pulls on something. Until he has it in his hand. He quickly pushes down on the splintered wood. Closes off the gap.

As he climbs onto his snowmobile, he sees a coyote by the edge of the woods. He pulls down his visor and heads off.

1

"When are you meeting them?" my doctor asks. "When are you going to be dissected?"

I like that about her. She talks like me. I can be completely upfront with her. She's not going to get upset easily. Even the sight of me when I was brought in didn't unsettle her. Blood everywhere and broken bones. She didn't see until later what my head had suffered. That was one year and six months ago, and I still don't know who wanted to beat me to a pulp. A professional dogwalker saved my life. Or the four pit bulls he was walking. They saw to it that the masked assailant took off.

I used to think, too, that I was nearly invincible. Until I was knocked down with a crowbar during my evening jog.

"Don't let anybody talk you into anything. You're cleared for combat, Gates."

I asked her to call me that, not Mrs. Gates or Detective Sergeant Gates. Or Calista. I call her Dr. Ironman, although she has a different name.

"You will certainly have to send them a report," I say. About the pain in my leg. The medicine for these attacks that my injured brain orchestrates. About my right hand, which sometimes prevents me from lifting heavy things. Handguns are no problem.

but machine guns are chancy. I never know whether my hand can take it or not.

The doctor certainly won't put *that* in her report, but my bosses at the Royal Canadian Mounted Police can read between the lines.

"Obviously that shouldn't surprise you. I see no reason to leave you on the sidelines any longer. But you have to believe in yourself as well, Gates."

The doctor is about forty, five years older than me. She's ingested wisdom by the truckload, not by the spoonful. It definitely couldn't have been easy for her in the hospital's hierarchy.

She moves me to the large wall mirror where I practiced making faces for months. A macabre ballet of facial muscles.

"Look at yourself closely, Gates. Phoenix out of the ashes. Like being reborn. Only stronger and harder."

She's got her own jargon. Built me up with it. Not like the RCMP psychiatrist who was constantly poking around in my past. Time and again he wanted to talk about that summer night when I was twelve. When I heard screams outside my window: *Stop! You're hurting me!*

He wanted to know everything. All about it, and what happened afterward. He rooted around, drilled down—so I threw the words in his face again: "Stop! You're hurting me!"

That's when he smiled. Smugly. I can see him today, right before me. As if he'd discovered Troy, the mythical ancient Greek city. Nothing's mythical about me, Mr. Psychiatrist; it's other people who are screwed up. Like that person who went after me with a crowbar.

"Tell me what you see, Gates." Her voice comes from behind me. I'm myself again, at least on the outside. Most of my healed injuries are concealed by clothes. The scars. Nothing visible on my face except for a small white streak on my hairline, above my forehead. That's from the operation. I mustn't hide anything under bangs or unruly curls. My hair is combed tightly back and tied in a knot—my RCMP look. You can tell immediately that I've got Greek ancestry; my parents took care of that. Eyelids like parachutes and eyes that sparkle like marbles. An aura of tragedy. I'd be great in the Prisoners' Chorus in the opera.

I'm suppressing something. There's one more scar. On my lower lip. I did it to myself when I bit my lip from the pain. The attacker destroyed the prettiest part of my body. My well-formed mouth. Now I wear lipstick when I have to. I never needed it before.

But not this afternoon. I'm showing my scar. Makes me look tougher. Or banged up?

The doctor keeps at it.

"Do you see how far you've come?"

I want my job back. I want my job back.

"I see anger," I reply.

"No, you're not seeing that; you're feeling it. And that's good. Anger's going to help you with your appointment today. Chin up!"

I can't get any food down at noon; adrenaline's keeping me on my feet. I don't put on any lipstick. I'm not ready to get kicked out of the RCMP without a fight. Not like a colleague of mine who was shot in the back and is now twiddling his thumbs in a trust company office.

Three men are seated across from me. My former boss from the Major Crime Homicide Unit; the deputy head of Human Resources, and—this puzzles me—the deputy commissioner himself. Why is the top man in the Vancouver RCMP at this meeting?

"We have looked through the medical report and would like to give you a chance," my old boss begins.

Give you a chance. Earlier, they would have scrambled to get me.

He doesn't mention the psychiatrist who hovers like a ghost over the proceedings. Although he isn't even in the room.

"We think it would be best if you test your muscles in a less stressful environment than Vancouver."

His language! *Test your muscles.* He means my brain injury. Doesn't want to say it. Vancouver's my hometown. I'm familiar with everything here. That's not stressful, I'd like to say. Mustn't, though. They're giving you a chance, Calista, did you hear? Better than disability insurance.

He continues. All I hear is "Labrador." God, that's the end of the world. Ice-cold in winter and swarming with ravenous mosquitoes in summer. I saw it on TV. And there's a city with the complicated name Happy Valley-Goose Bay.

They're all looking at me. Did I miss something? Did I black out for a moment? I feel hot. That must not happen here, not in front of these people.

"You can decline right now, Detective Sergeant, then we don't need to go any further."

Is that a warning? Of course it's a warning. The RCMP can send you where they want to. You can give reasons why someplace might not be a good idea. Maybe once, but not twice. And there's no way I can do that now, in my situation. That's as clear as a sunny day. I hope the sun shines in Labrador now and then.

"A posting to Happy Valley-Goose Bay? For how long, sir?"

There's an airport, I remember. Two airports. One civilian and an international military one. That's where pilots from different countries do their low-flying bomber training over the endless tundra. The Inuit protested against it. That's what the TV program was about.

"Three years, Detective Sergeant, in the vicinity of Happy Valley-Goose Bay. The town's called Port Brendan."

I freeze. Three years. Where the heck is Port Brendan?

"The Port Brendan post covers southeastern Labrador. Four men are stationed there. We want to reinforce them."

I hold off answering. I don't want to agree before I know the whole truth. My boss is kind enough to offer me the truth piecemeal. He doesn't want to hit me with it all at once—got to give him that.

"Port Brendan is three hundred kilometers from Happy Valley-Goose Bay. There's a road to Port Brendan; they've started to pave it. The next, rather small airport is in Blanc-Sablon, to the west, and from there it's about three to four hours by car to Port Brendan, depending on weather conditions."

I suddenly have a hunch. A newspaper report on the *Toronto Star* website.

When was it? Going on two weeks ago?

The skeleton of a young woman who'd been a friend of an American fighter pilot. It had unexpectedly turned up in Port Brendan, where she was from. When she disappeared two or three years ago, it was in the headlines. The government in Washington protested when the RCMP interrogated the pilot in Happy Valley-Goose Bay.

"Is this about the girlfriend of the American pilot?" I ask.

Now the deputy commissioner comes in.

"We can only discuss details with you if you accept the reposting."

They don't even give me time to think it over. Because they know I've got no alternative. Labrador or nothing. Three years. I can get through that. Heavens, I've survived the hell of the last eighteen months. And I get a controversial murder case. And it must be that murder—or else the DC would reveal more.

"Sir, I accept your offer."

Nobody says anything for a moment. Are they all surprised that I agreed? Or relieved?

The deputy commissioner brushes his hand over the file before him. I see the name *Lorna Taylor* on a white label.

"I can tell you this much for now, Sergeant. You will keep the rank of detective sergeant, but don't be offended if your colleagues in Labrador address you as Constable."

That's the first surprise he drops on me. The second comes just before I sign the agreement.

"It would be good if you could fly out in three days."

Three days. I'm speechless. Sign anyway. The Lorna Taylor case is waiting for me.

"Learn a few phrases in Inuktitut," my ex-boss advises before I leave the room.

Of course: I'm being sent to Inuit country.

2

It's snowing like mad; planes can't take off. I'm stuck in Montreal, have to spend another night in the hotel because the plane can't land in Happy Valley-Goose Bay. A storm. But what do you expect at the beginning of March?

They gave me three days to pack. Just time enough to say goodbye to all my siblings. I've got six. All of them felt sorry for me—that was the worst part of it. I've really had it up to here with pity. They also sympathize because I—unlike them—haven't got any children. My parents tried to make me change my mind. They never understood why I signed up for the RCMP. Mom told everybody what a good dancer I was. Years of expensive ballet lessons for nothing. I was even better in math, but Mom never talks about that. All because of Becca Heyer, she complains whenever she gets the opportunity to. She thinks that's the reason I chose my profession. Right she is. That's where it all began.

I woke you up when I heard a girl scream—I wanted to throw the words in Mom and Dad's face—*at night, outside, and you two did nothing.*

Stop! You're hurting me!

I was twelve when I heard Becca's scream, and her body was found three weeks afterward. Beaten, raped, tortured. I read the detailed reports later when I was with the RCMP. It was then that my anger at my parents' indifference really came to a head. Their failure. They simply didn't believe me that the scream I heard meant something really awful. I was an earwitness to the crime. I know the screams of a child being raped. I don't have to imagine it. I heard it with my own ears. I'll never forget it. Never.

But let's move on.

In the hotel café in Montreal, I contemplate Lorna Taylor's case, as Céline Dion sings a ballad in the background. The pain in my limbs is only gradually going away; I've discovered that flying feels like hot tongs. I know what's in the Lorna file. I've practically devoured it in the last few days. I work systematically. Or I used to before the assault. That was the case even when I was a child. I could solve hard puzzles fast. Pictures of monochrome desert landscapes or of similar-looking wine corks in a thousand jigsaw pieces.

Lorna disappeared in December three years ago. She had a job in a furniture store in Happy Valley-Goose Bay; she didn't sell furniture but worked in the newly opened interior decorating department in the same store. Good to know that there was something like that in Happy Valley-Goose Bay. It was comforting for me to read that about eight thousand people live there. But Labrador in its entirety averages only one person per eleven square kilometers. The inhabitants call it the Big Land. It surely didn't take much imagination to come up with that name.

Back to Lorna. When her work was over at five, she wanted to meet her boyfriend, Guy Stravitz, the American Air Force pilot, at a restaurant. She never arrived. It was a beautiful day in Labrador, which means no storms, no snowfall, moderate winds, and very cold. Stravitz told the police later that he didn't pick her up at her workplace because it wasn't very far to the restaurant and Lorna wanted to avoid her boss's prying eyes. When she didn't show up, Stravitz texted her several times. The two had known each other for four months, and a friend of Lorna's said they were very much in love.

I study Lorna's file picture. A young lady laughing, with smooth black hair, probably shaped with a hair straightener. A pretty, pert face, eyeliner, and a lot of black mascara, a small tattoo on her neck.

I rummage around for a photo of Stravitz. In his pilot's uniform, he looks like an all-American boy: a military haircut, an innocent face, an optimistic gaze. Twenty-eight—five years older than Lorna. He waited in the restaurant for an hour before asking the owner to help him find Lorna's parents' phone number. Which shows he didn't know anybody in her circle of friends he could contact. Her parents in Port Brendan reacted to his phone call with caution: they had never met him. Lorna's closest friend, Grace Butt, knew the young couple's plans for the evening, but she, too, hadn't heard anything from Lorna. Nobody knew where she was. Her parents informed the police at midnight.

My parents would have done that sooner if they'd been in the Taylors' shoes, but they're Greek. Mom and Dad get worried fast, but only if their own children are involved, and they assume the worst right away. Lorna's parents certainly knew the dangers lurking about there. You can freeze to death so easily. And there are wild animals—bears, moose, lynx, coyotes, wolves, for all I know. Labrador is pretty much a closed book for me. And with about a thousand blank pages.

My eyes meet those of a man sitting at another table. He's young, probably early thirties. I've forgotten how it feels to be checked out by a man. For eighteen months I've avoided being looked at in public. Even when I appeared to be "normal" again. Fake it to make it, my older sister coached me. Act as if. I can't tell her how strenuous it is to act as if everything is perfectly all right.

Guy Stravitz has an airtight alibi. He was already in the restaurant when Lorna left the store. The RCMP in Happy Valley-

Goose Bay were able to question him twice before he was recalled to the States. The case hit the headlines in Canada, and even the American media found out about it. At the time I was still the ambitious, fearless researcher in Vancouver's Major Crime Homicide Unit. And happily married. So I thought.

I avoid the stare of the young man at the bar table and concentrate on the report in front of me. Somebody killed Lorna. I order a tomato juice with Worcestershire sauce when the waitress passes by.

"Pardon my boldness, but may I ask you a question?"

I look up, surprised. The man from the bar table is standing in front of me.

"Yes?"

"Are you perhaps the new person joining the RCMP in Port Brendan?"

I'm hearing for the first time the accent everybody spoke of. The unfamiliar cadence sounds friendly, calming. Hard to imagine that people who talk like that can be evil. Nonetheless I'm annoyed. My ex-boss assured me that my posting to Port Brendan would be officially announced only after my arrival.

"How do you know that?"

He smiles an excuse.

"I was standing behind you in line when they changed your flight. My in-laws own the house the RCMP is renting for you."

Now, I could be angry and dismiss him, or I could riddle him with questions. I decide to riddle.

"Do sit down," I say. "Detective Sergeant Calista Gates." That rank is still mine.

"Ernie Butt. I work in the Transportation and Construction Office in Happy Valley-Goose Bay, but I grew up in Port Brendan. Was just at a conference in Montreal. You're from Vancouver?"

Ernie Butt. The first man from Labrador I get to know. He has a dark moustache, and his two front teeth are long and narrow.

Doesn't look like an office type, but that's probably because of his clothes: a heavy lumberjack shirt and ski pants.

"So you already know that, too." I smile, not wanting to seem huffy.

He nods.

"As I said, I was behind you at the Air Canada counter. I must warn you. Labrador is a vast region, but it's a small world. We don't have many secrets. People always want to know what's going on."

I drink some tomato juice in response. Céline Dion keeps singing in the background. I don't have to encourage Ernie Butt to go on talking; he does it all by himself.

"Did they send you here because of the bones?"

"Because of the bones?"

"The bones that were discovered—Lorna's bones. Lorna Taylor. They told you about that for sure."

I furrow my brow automatically.

"The identity of the bones is not yet officially confirmed."

"I know. Everybody thinks it's Lorna."

"Why?"

"She disappeared three years ago." He leans forward. "I really hope this case is cleared up. It's not good for the tourist industry."

"What do you mean?"

"We want to attract more tourists. Single women, too. Women tourists have to feel safe in Labrador."

"The cause of death hasn't been determined."

He gives me a look of concern. "It must have been murder."

"What makes you think that?"

"The bones were in a wooden crate. My cousin found them on Savage Beach. He was looking for driftwood."

"He was looking for driftwood in winter?"

"Sure. It's washed up in the fall. Free wood for the stove. My cousin knows where to look. He does it summer and winter."

"And he found a crate there? In the snow?"

"There's not much snow on the beach. My cousin saw it from far away. A pack of coyotes were sniffing around it. He wanted the wood and chased them away. That's when he discovered the bones and the skull."

Where are the bones now? I would really like to ask, but I don't want to give myself away that much.

Ernie gets up.

"I've got to get to the airport; I rebooked via St. John's so I can go visit my sister." He looks down at me almost like a father. "Lots of luck in Port Brendan. We'll certainly meet there during the Winter Games. By the way, my wife was friends with Lorna. You must definitely talk to her."

I remember: the friend who knew about Lorna's restaurant plans. Grace Butt. Ernie raises a hand in farewell and leaves.

I stare at the pile of papers in front of me. I wish I'd pumped Ernie some more, but he's gone. I open my iPad and hit pay dirt. *Wooden Crate with Skeleton Found on Labrador Beach.* The article confirms everything Ernie told me. The cousin. The search for driftwood. A coyote pack. Coyotes in Port Brendan—well, that's wonderful. The crate. And the information that there's a reconstruction of a Viking house near Savage Beach. Did I read that right? Vikings in Labrador? Something else for me to research. A sentence at the very end: *Police do not want to say at this time whether the crate was washed up in the fall or whether somebody recently placed it on Savage Beach.*

3

Seventeen hours later, I'm standing in Inspector Peter Allen's office in Happy Valley-Goose Bay. I might as well be on the moon because I've seen practically nothing of the town. My plane landed just before a thick pea soup of a fog covered the place. A bush plane was supposed to take me to Port Brendan, but that's out of the question for today, Inspector Allen informs me. They've reserved a room for me at Hotel North. I feel dead tired. Haven't slept much in the past few nights. I'll simply have to suck it up. Getting over things was no problem before. The victims, the violence, the crimes, jealous colleagues, long hours at work—all of it no big deal. And now I'm crumping because I've missed a few hours of sleep.

My one consolation: Inspector Allen seems to be as tired as I am. It's Saturday, and he's working instead of being with his family. A solid man, barrel-chested, beefy face. And huge bags under his eyes.

"We had three suicides this week. All youngsters under sixteen. It's an epidemic."

I've heard about the wave of suicides among young Inuit and Innu Indians.

"In Port Brendan?"

"No, in communities up north."

My eyes wander to the map beside Allen's desk. There is an Inuit settlement on the north coast of Labrador, and an Innu reserve half an hour from Happy Valley-Goose Bay. Port Brendan is farther away. Four hours on a half-paved road through the wilderness.

I'm too tired to be patient.

"What can you tell me about the crate with the skeleton?"

Inspector Allen rubs his face as if that will put thoughts of the dead kids from these communties out of his mind.

"Somebody put the body in the crate and weighed it down with stones. Then he tied it up with a rope and sank it somewhere in the ocean."

"It's Lorna Taylor?"

"Pretty sure. We'll have the dental report today. Lorna had a small gap up front and a Maryland bridge in her upper-right jaw. We know that from her parents."

The parents, who finally find out that the dead woman is their daughter. And that she was discovered not so far from their house.

"You're assuming it's murder?"

"That seems the most probable hypothesis."

A crate in the ocean. Something crosses my mind that I read some time ago. A dead humpback whale washed up in Newfoundland. People wanted to put the skeleton on display. To rid the bones of fat and flesh, they put them in a wooden crate, loaded it up with stones, and left it in the water for a while. In no time at all, fish lice had eaten all the tissue; only the bones were left.

"Do you think the perp left the body in the water so fish lice would strip it and the bones would be completely clean?"

For the first time, Inspector Allen looks at me as if he doesn't have a clueless city slicker before him.

"We've thought of that possibility."

"So the perp wanted to preserve the skeleton right from the start?"

"Looks like it. And he wanted it to be discovered."

"How was he able to sink the crate in the water? Isn't the ocean frozen in December?"

"Not three years ago. The water didn't freeze until the end of December. Happens sometimes. That year was an exception. The road was quite passable for many days during the first half of the month because heavy snow didn't come until January. Which means that many people went back and forth to Happy Valley-Goose Bay, to buy Christmas presents, for example."

"How many people have been questioned in the last several days?"

"We've spoken to many people here in Happy Valley-Goose Bay—to Lorna's coworkers, her superiors, friends, people who knew her. Your new colleagues have been active, too, in Port Brendan. You'll find out when you get there. Unfortunately not much has come from it all as yet that can help us move ahead."

"How's it possible that nobody ever saw the perp doing whatever he or she was doing? His or her actions must have been conspicuous."

The inspector raises his eyebrows.

"You'll find out for yourself that there are many secluded bays along our coast. And people have cabins everywhere, out there in the bush. No problem doing things unnoticed."

"Do you think the perp planned on having the crate wash up on a beach somewhere?"

"It didn't wash up. Someone deliberately placed it on the beach so it would be found. It didn't break loose. The rope had recently been cut with a knife."

"Do you know how long the crate was in the water?"

"Probably three to four months. Because the cartilage hadn't disintegrated yet."

Several months. Until Lorna was only a skeleton.

"Then the perp hid the crate somewhere. Where could that have been?" I'm talking to myself more than to the inspector.

"Best you discuss it with your colleagues in Port Brendan. But as I said, isolated, hidden hunting shacks are all over the area."

"Can a person transport a crate like that in a boat by himself? Or on a sled? The crate was weighed down with stones, after all. Or maybe there were two perps?"

Peter Allen rubs his forehead. I hope he doesn't lose patience.

"Oh yes, you can do it by yourself. You can pull it over the ground with ropes. And then tip it into a boat. It's relatively easy to do. It doesn't take many stones to sink a female body to the bottom of the sea. And pulling it out of the water is no big deal, either. The crate is lighter in the water, of course."

"Lighter? I find that hard to imagine. With those stones? And the wood must have absorbed all that water."

"Nevertheless it's not as heavy in the water as you might think. You mustn't forget that after three months there was only a skeleton in there. Besides, the water would give the crate a boost when it was pulled up to the surface. The way water gives a seal a boost when it hops onto an ice floe."

I look at him and process the information. I could think more clearly if I weren't so tired.

"So there's a high probability the perp is from Port Brendan? And he wants us to pay some attention to Lorna's murder . . . But why now?"

"I think he'd already put the crate on the beach in the fall before the snow came. It just took some time before somebody found it."

"Ernie Butt's cousin found it. I happened to meet Mr. Butt in Montreal when our flights were rebooked."

"The man who found it is not Ernie Butt's cousin, not even related to him. What else did he tell you?"

"He's afraid that the unsolved case might hurt tourism in the region."

The inspector smiles for the first time.

"Ernie's always concerned about Labrador's good reputation. Even though there are tens of thousands of tourists in London every year, and there are hundreds of murders there."

He pours himself a coffee from a pot on a coffee machine.

"You really don't want one?" he asks.

I refuse. I want to be able to sleep through the night.

He takes a sip and says, "Jack the Ripper didn't hurt London's reputation, I'd say."

Ernie Butt seems to get under the inspector's skin.

What puzzles me is that Lorna's murderer wants to cause a sensation, if the inspector's theory is correct.

"Where's the skeleton now?"

"With the medical examiner. You can take it with you. It's being flown back to Port Brendan. The family wants to bury Lorna as quickly as possible."

"Has the medical examiner finished his investigation?"

"Yes, Bernard Closs will get the report. I'll give you all the documents tomorrow."

Sergeant Bernard Closs. My new superior in Port Brendan. He gets the report first, not me. I've got to get used to it. More reason to ask questions while I'm here.

"Were there signs of violence on the skeleton?"

"The stones in the crate left traces on the bones, naturally. Everything else is in the report."

He doesn't want to tell me anything more before my new boss has seen the report. Can't he send it to Closs electronically? Or is this only an excuse not to reveal anything more to me? No point now in asking if I could speak to the medical examiner.

The inspector clears his throat.

"The case is now in the Port Brendan RCMP's hands. We'll help where we can, but we have a huge area we must take care of."

Then he says something astonishing.

"In any case we can clear the American pilot of any suspicion.

He never lived in Port Brendan. He also never went there. His alibi is solid."

I can hear the obvious relief in Allen's voice. At least the jobs are clearly distributed. Port Brendan is in charge of the investigation. That's good.

Still, I'm surprised. Why is the Happy Valley-Goose Bay RCMP so ready to pass on the case to their colleagues in Port Brendan? Especially at this time, when there's a good chance of solving the murder? That would be a success for Peter Allen, who must be familiar with every detail in the case. He certainly wouldn't want to let that opportunity slip away. Strange.

The inspector stands up.

"I wish you every success in Port Brendan. Good weather for flying tomorrow. You're staying at the Hotel North, aren't you? You'll be called when the plane's ready. Go have a big steak at Jungle Jim's—it's today's special, good price. Steak Night."

I don't have any desire for a steak, not even at a special price, but I thank him because he probably divulged more to me than he wanted to.

Something crosses my mind at the door.

"How do you actually bury people here in winter? The ground's frozen solid, after all."

His face adopts a good-natured expression. I've taken on my proper role again: the ignorant policewoman from Vancouver.

"With ice axes," he replies, "or with a jackhammer if need be."

4

The hotel phone wakes me up at six a.m.

"A taxi will pick you up in an hour. Your flight is at eight," an unknown man's voice informs me. "The weather turns bad again around noon."

That's one of my first lessons in Labrador. Weather determines everything.

I've had an unexpectedly good sleep and feel rested. And hungry. The breakfast room is filled with men and women in work clothes. They must be using this window of good weather for a flight somewhere, too.

I'm way too warmly dressed for the sweat-inducing room temperature. As if they're trying to overcompensate for the cold. My taxi driver, a bearded man with thick fingers, comes a little earlier than agreed.

"It's always good to have some wiggle room," he explains.

We're out of Happy Valley-Goose Bay so fast that I only get a fleeting impression of the town. The car window is fogged up. I see commercial buildings with vinyl facades, a Chinese restaurant, and a pub. The taxi driver engages me in conversation about the military base.

"The Americans pulled almost all their people out some years ago. They think they aren't needed here because the Cold War is over. The Yanks used to leave a lot of money here—that helped the whole town. And then the Yanks got furious because the police accused an American pilot after his girlfriend disappeared, and that was the final straw."

"Nobody was accused; the police only interrogated the pilot," I correct him.

The driver gets upset.

"They should have left him alone. He was in the restaurant and had nothing to do with it. It was somebody from Port Brendan. They found her last week. And what do we get out of it now? I used to drive Yanks around all the time. This thing has totally wrecked my business."

I can't control myself. Ignorance always does provoke me.

"The police were only doing their duty. If it had been your daughter, wouldn't you have expected them to be fully committed?"

My words throw oil on the fire.

"My daughter would have had nothing to do with a Yankee," the driver hisses. "But the local men aren't good enough for a lot of women. Before that, when Yanks were stationed all across Canada, the girls were crazy about them. You know how many women from Newfoundland and Labrador crossed the border with their American boyfriends? Thirty thousand—can you believe it? Thirty thousand or more."

"From when to when?"

"What do I know? Twenty years maybe."

If he's right, then that was a big hemorrhage. Especially in Labrador. There aren't even thirty thousand inhabitants here, total.

"Did Lorna Taylor want to go to the US with the pilot?"

"No idea. Wouldn't surprise me. A lot of girls move away from here. My daughter lives in St. John's on the island."

He must mean Newfoundland. If he likes to talk so much, well then, I can pump him a little bit.

"What could have happened to Lorna, in your opinion? Have you heard anything?"

"If you ask me, she definitely had a jealous boyfriend somewhere, a pretty girl like that. Yeah, some guy went nuts."

There's no mention of that in the files. Lorna had a previous relationship, but it was over before she moved to Happy Valley-Goose Bay five years ago. Her ex-boyfriend was already working in Alberta, where he has a new girlfriend today.

A gray rectangular building comes into view. The taxi spits me out. My body shrinks like a snail that's been touched by an ice cube. Cold, so cold. I feel I'm in a freezer. My one thought is to escape the cold as quickly as possible.

The bush plane is already waiting on the snow-covered tarmac. It's equipped with skis. I watch some men carefully pushing a metal box onto it. Lorna Taylor's skeleton. A man comes up to me. The inspector. I don't recognize him at first because a fur cap with flaps covers his ears and half his face. By way of a greeting, he hands me a brown cardboard box. I can only hear the words *documents* and *dentist* when the propeller begins to roar.

Minutes later I'm sitting on the plane. So this is it: I'm on my way to Port Brendan. My post for the next three years. My stomach nerves are vibrating. What I see down below doesn't make me feel very confident. An unending, white vastness. I can spot forests, then plains buried in snow, among snakes that are probably rivers, and lakes like frozen dinner plates. An inhospitable no-man's-land. Everything's quite flat at the beginning; then the mountains come into view. The pilot doesn't say much, drops a name sometimes that I don't remember. Only Mealy Mountains sticks in my mind. Mountains of flour. They really do look white, as if coated in flour, but the name comes from an explorer, the pilot says. It's a national park now. I came across the indigenous name of the park on the internet, a name I couldn't pronounce that was cobbled together from the Innu Indian and Inuit languages.

Lorna Taylor was already dead when the park was officially established. Her remains are flying with us, and I send a plea to the Great Goddess that we arrest her murderer so that she and her family finally find peace. The pilot drops the word *Wonderstrands* into my thoughts. I read something about that as well, before going to sleep. A forty-kilometer-long sandy beach, mentioned in reports by the ancient Vikings. In a flight of optimism I saw myself wandering barefoot on the sand, sandals in hand, the sun on the sparkling water, my loose hair down past my shoulders— until I read about the madly biting horseflies in summer and the wolves that often turn up on the beach. Seen from the small plane, the snow-covered beach mocks my naïve desire for the joys of swimming and summertime frolicking.

Ah, Calista, whatever is waiting for you?

The houses of Port Brendan appear on the horizon half an hour later.

They look as if somebody at one time tossed them onto the rocky coast, and now they are desperately clinging to it. I can make out bay after bay with some effort, as if the ocean has regularly breached the coast. It looks rocky everywhere, in spite of the snow cover; only the surrounding forest gives a clue that there is soil here, too. The most unearthly feature is the ice that lays siege to the coast like a frozen lava flow. The North Atlantic. The Arctic begins not so far from Port Brendan, as it shows on the map. It's a mystery to me why people want to live here at all. What kind of foreign, unforgiving world have I gotten myself into? Suddenly I have trouble swallowing.

Three figures are waiting near the runway. The plane roars toward them on its skis and fortunately can stop in time. When I hop into the snow, a long drink of water of a man comes toward me. In a matter of seconds the cold nestles into my body again.

Am I wrong, or is it colder here than in Happy Valley-Goose Bay?

"Constable Gates. I'm Bernard Closs."

Constable. My new boss shows me my place right away with his welcome. That's a fine start.

"Are these your bags?" he asks. "We'll go to the office first and then to your house."

Two men put down the metal box.

"That's Lorna's remains," I say. "And this box has the documents from the Happy Valley-Goose Bay RCMP."

He nods and takes the box from me. I can't see his eyes behind his sunglasses. The sun isn't shining now. But the snow is blinding.

"There's enough room for Lorna in here, too."

Closs, Detective Sergeant Closs, opens the rear door of his SUV, a white police car.

Then he threads his way into the vehicle; the motor's running already. I sit down on the passenger seat. The warmth feels good.

"I'll make a loop so you can see something of Port Brendan right away."

Closs has taken off his hat: he has short hair, which makes his head look boney. When he turns his face toward me, he appears less severe. That's how an explorer looks after a successful expedition: haggard, but proud. Like an ascetic marathon runner.

We turn onto a road that is narrowed on both sides by high walls of snow. A white tunnel without a roof. I don't suffer from claustrophobia, but I feel imprisoned.

"We are having a lot of snow this winter," Bernard Closs remarks.

"How long does it take for these walls to disappear?"

"Probably until the end of May."

End of May. Makes me dizzy.

When we get to the village, there are no more walls. Closs introduces me to Port Brendan's infrastructure like a tour guide.

"This is the center of town: gas station, supermarket, post office, funeral home, hairdresser, pub. The building over there is the Office of Fisheries, and the bank is on the ground floor."

He heads for the port, where several colorful boats are pulled up on land.

"Powell Motors sells snowmobiles, and if you're lucky you can pick up a good used car."

On it goes: the Anglican church, Pentecostal church, gift shop, hardware store, the school with a gym. My head is spinning. A modern building with four gables looms up in front of us.

"That's the clinic, the pride of Port Brendan."

It's the only building that makes any claim to being aesthetically pleasing. The other structures are obviously built primarily to be protected from the hard climate. The clinic is an imposing building for the area, I must admit, although my boss's well-intended informational tour is depressing. I've seen only a handful of people and a few approaching cars. I long for a hot coffee.

"What's that up there?" I point to a bulging tower on one of the hills.

"That's the old American radar station. It was shut down in 1968."

"Americans were stationed here?"

"Yes, that was part of the early warning system, the DEW Line, in case the Soviets decided to attack the United States with bombers. The Americans built dozens of these radar stations in Canada's north. This one was built in 1953, as far as I know."

"The Americans built it, and not Canada?"

"The Canadians didn't have the money for something like that, or the know-how. That's why the personnel were American, too." He looks me in my astonished face. "Couldn't imagine it today, eh?"

His lips relax; that's probably his smile.

"But there are still Americans stationed in Happy Valley-Goose Bay?"

"That's a NATO training center. Airmen come there from many countries. The US reduced their personnel to a minimum."

Until now I had almost no idea how strong the presence of American forces was in Canada.

"Did the American pilot really have nothing to do with Lorna's death?"

"I don't think so. He certainly didn't stuff the body into a crate in Port Brendan. Here we are."

He stops in front of a brown brick building that stands out from those around it. All the other houses I've seen are clad in metal or vinyl. We get out. It's wonderfully warm inside. It smells of coffee. A woman is standing behind the reception desk; she has bobbed hair of an indeterminate color and looks at me full of curiosity. Even her age is uncertain. Forty? Fifty?

"This is Wendy, our dispatcher," Closs introduces her without mentioning her surname. And he suppresses my name, too, but I fix that.

"I'm Calista Gates," I say.

"How was your trip?" she asks.

Before I can answer the lady, Closs calls: "Coffee for me and Constable Gates, Wendy," and makes for his office. I smile at the dispatcher and follow him.

"What's with Lorna's box?" I ask.

It didn't escape me that Closs didn't even lock the SUV. He bangs the box with the documents onto the desk.

"I'll wait till the others are here. They'll arrive in an hour. I've got the early shift today."

Besides Closs, there are three other men at this post.

He takes off his jacket and I follow suit. I've become hot. The rooms are completely overheated.

"Or do you think we should check to see if our colleagues in

Happy Valley-Goose Bay palmed off the wrong skeleton on us?" Closs says dryly, and I'm not sure whether he's joking.

"It might be instructive to take a look at the skeleton," I suggest.

"I've seen it. I was at the medical examiner's in Happy Valley-Goose Bay three days ago."

Wendy comes in with a pot of coffee and mugs, sugar, and condensed milk. I feel I'm in an old film. The RCMP in Vancouver has an espresso machine in every office. The personnel brews coffee for themselves. I like mine strong and black, like the Greeks. What I'm drinking now is so thin and tasteless that I almost can't get it down. Doesn't seem to bother Closs.

"Have you read the report?" he asks. "It's sealed."

He shoves the package over to me.

"Inspector Allen is from the old guard. He still hasn't made it into the twenty-first century. I've got all this in the computer."

I lay a protective hand on the box.

"What did the medical examiner say?"

"Lorna was strangled. The lingual bone is broken and the larynx bruised."

I'm mystified.

"All the small bones and cartilage were still in the crate?"

He nods. "Yes, that crate was well built."

I want to inspect it later, but I'm more interested at this moment in the cause of death.

"The perp strangled the victim with his bare hands?"

"So we assume."

That's important. Hate is frequently behind a crime like this one. Strangling with bare hands is a personal contact; the perp wants to be close by as his victim slowly takes her last breath. A horrible death. The primary aim surely wasn't to shut Lorna up. The perp wanted to act out his hate.

Closs puts his coffee mug on the table.

"Otherwise no injury other than the left little finger. It's missing."

"The whole finger's missing?"

"Yes, but it wasn't simply lost in the water. Somebody cut it off. Antemortem."

Before death. Lorna was still alive when it happened to her. That means the medical examiner could tell that the metacarpal had time to start to heal.

Strange. We had a case in Vancouver where the perp cut off all a body's fingertips to make the identification difficult or impossible. We found out anyway. But just the little finger. Was the perp somehow prevented from cutting off all the fingers? Or did he change his mind?

I'm not touching my coffee anymore.

"Are those the only bones that are missing?"

"Yes, the crate was apparently well anchored. There was a tiny opening on the lid that allowed the fish lice to push in."

"How long was the crate in the water?"

"About three months. Everything is definitely in there." He points to the cardboard box.

I'll read that report carefully, but I want information from him directly. The sergeant is used to asking the questions and not being asked himself.

I try to recall everything I've read about fish lice. They're very efficient and quick to clean up bones. Though they're tiny—most of them only two millimeters long—they can make the flesh of a large sea animal disappear without a trace in a few weeks. All that's left is the brightly polished surface of the skeleton.

"Was the crate intact when found?"

Water, even saltwater, can't do much harm to good wood over decades.

"It was apparently intact until Scott Dyson hacked up a corner of it with an ax. "If you can believe him."

"That's Ernie Butt's cousin?"

Closs looks at me questioningly. I tell him about my encounter with Ernie.

"As far as I know, they're not related," he says. "Ernie probably wanted to show you what a big shot he was. Because he's got a government job, he thinks he's something special. Dyson on the other hand . . . he gathers driftwood on the beach. That's how he discovered the crate."

"Is he a suspect?"

Closs empties his mug and quickly pours himself another.

"Sure, as part of the investigation. Personally, I don't think he had anything to do with the murder. He wouldn't want to make a scene with something like that. It's widely known that he often fishes illegally. He for sure wants to let sleeping dogs lie. He used to deal drugs. Served a little time in the slammer for it. Right around the time Lorna vanished. Since then we haven't caught him at anything."

"Wouldn't sharks or other large predators try to break into the crate to get to the body?"

"The crate must have been sunk near the coast. Where the big beasts don't go."

I still don't understand the perp's motive.

"How long did it take for the fish lice to clean off the bones? One week? Two?"

"Ten weeks, I'd guess."

"So the bones are something like a trophy. Where do you think he hid them afterward?"

"In the woods. In a cave. Or in a hunting cabin. There are so many possibilities."

"We could search all the cabins in the surrounding area."

"Yes, that's an approach. Even though it's a hard one. There are probably around eighty homemade shacks around here. And many we don't have any idea about. People are supposed to notify the proper offices about them, but few of them do, and it's very hard to keep an eye on it."

"Maybe we can take a helicopter up over the area?"

Closs says nothing, absent-mindedly drinks his bad coffee. I don't think it's my position to leave him in peace, so I keep asking questions.

"And the crate? Where is it?"

"Still in Happy Valley-Goose Bay with the medical examiner."

I suppress a sigh. So I won't be able to see it all that quickly.

"Has the ME discovered something by now?"

"Rough-cut wood; the perp probably sawed it himself. A lot of people do that here. There's a symbol burned into the wood."

I'm amazed. It's the nonchalant way that the sergeant passes on such decisive information.

"What kind of symbol?"

"A Viking sign."

"Well, what does it look like?"

"Three interlocking triangles. It was burned into the wood."

"How?"

"Probably with a hot iron."

"Is there a practicing Viking cult around here?"

"Viking cult?"

He looks at me as if I've asked him what the capital of the Ivory Coast is.

"There are people who are completely obsessed with Viking culture. They dress like Vikings and get together for Viking rituals. Or what they think the rituals are."

My explanation doesn't help. He shakes his head.

"There's a Viking house here, a reconstruction. Built for the tourists."

"Where is it?"

"At Savage Beach. About three kilometers outside Port Brendan."

At the beach where the crate with Lorna's skeleton was found. Closs stands up abruptly.

"We should get her in here," he says.

I guess right away what he means. We put on our jackets, go to the SUV, and carry the heavy metal box into the office together. An odd way to transport bones. Then it occurs to me why metal was chosen. Inspector Allen didn't want to stick Lorna into a wooden crate again. The thought reconciles me to him.

Closs unlocks the metal box and opens the lid. We both stare at the skull, the pelvic bones, the neatly stacked ribs and vertebrae, leg and arm bones. I'm amazed at how little has been scattered around. Many of them are still marked with a label. Each one has Lorna's name on it, the name of the bone, and the stamp of the medical examiner's office.

I search for suspicious clues on the skull but can't find any. A pile of bones. That's all that remains of a young woman in love who had her whole life before her. That could be me. A skeleton in the ground. My Greek Orthodox parents would have never had me cremated, although they do live in Canada now. What was Lorna thinking during her final minutes? What did she feel? Was everything a dark fog? Or was it terror? Panic? Pain? As I felt? Fear that this was the end?

Closs closes the lid.

"Constable, is everything okay?"

I look at him in surprise. I hope I carried it off all right. Maybe Closs was waiting for a sign of instability, peculiar behavior, a clue that I'm not fit for work. He has surely been alerted.

"Of course. I . . . "

A man comes into the room. He walks so softly that we hardly hear him.

Closs looks up.

"Fred, what is it?"

"The parents are here. They're in the car out front." He glances at me briefly. "They heard that we have the skeleton."

"Fred, this is our colleague, Calista Gates."

"Fred van Heisen."

He shakes my hand, a firm grip, but he looks at me only briefly.

Dark. That's my first impression of him. Dark eyes, eyebrows, hair, self-contained expression. Good-looking.

He immediately turns back to Closs.

"What do we tell them?"

"We don't need the bones anymore. No reason to keep the people waiting."

I intervene before anything happens.

"Can they come in? Maybe they've got some questions for us?" *And we for them,* I add to myself.

Closs has no objection.

After van Heisen turns around, I call: "Wait!"

They both look at me, baffled.

"Do we tell them what's happened to the little finger?"

Van Heisen raises his eyebrows in question.

"Her left little finger was separated when Lorna was still alive," I inform him.

Closs makes a snap decision.

"No, not yet. We won't give out this information for now. We and the perp are the only ones to know."

5

Lorna's mother spots the metal box at once when she comes in.

"Is she in there?"

Closs nods. Van Heisen fades into the background. Lorna's father stands in the room, bent over; his powerfully built wife blocks his view of the box.

"We want a beautiful coffin for her, but I don't want to see her remains. I want to keep her alive in my memory."

Since nobody reacts to her wish, I step up.

"The undertaker can do that for you."

I remember that Closs pointed out the funeral home on our ride.

She looks at me, aware of me for the first time.

"You're the new one, aren't you?"

"Yes, I'm Calista Gates. I'd like to express my sincere condolences. We will do everything we can to find the person who did your daughter wrong."

Lorna's mother starts to cry. I go over to her and put my arms around her. That's a privilege of women police officers. Physical contact.

"Now it will be simpler to solve the case, won't it?" her mother sobs. "Now that you've found my girl."

I can't tell her that the murderer wanted Lorna's bones to be discovered on the beach. That he might have been sending a message that way. Which gives me some hope. The hope he's making a mistake.

I slowly let go of Lorna's mother.

"We're pleased that we finally know more about what happened to Lorna."

"How did she die?"

I look at Closs, and he nods without saying a word. He lets me have the floor.

"She was strangled."

The mother's hand flies to her mouth. Lorna's taciturn father looks at the floor.

"Who'd do a thing like that to her? She's never done anything to anybody."

I've heard those two statements often. They are so true. And so false. There are cruel people. Without pity. Without feelings of guilt.

"We're working to find that out. If you have any information at all that can help us further, please let us know."

"We've already told the RCMP everything. You can't know that—you're new here—but we've told the police everything."

"Time and again there are some details," I say, "that you don't think are important and that are overlooked. That's often been my experience. We need your cooperation in order to better help you."

She nods, wipes her tears away with a handkerchief.

I blurt out a question. "Mrs. Taylor, did Lorna wear a ring?"

"Yes, I think so, more than one. Why do you ask?"

"Because we didn't find any of her rings. Did she wear any other jewelry?"

As long as the sergeant doesn't stop me, I'll keep going.

"Jewelry? A gold chain around her neck. A birthday present from us."

She starts crying again. I put a hand on her arm. Time to end the questioning. We'll pick it up again after the funeral.

"We'll help you bring Lorna to the funeral home if you'd like."

Lorna's father speaks up for the first time.

"We'll do it."

Lorna is with her family once again.

Van Heisen helps him carry the metal box. I close the door behind them and stay back.

"Her parents just came by themselves, no sons, relatives. Don't you find that strange, Sergeant?"

They told me in Vancouver that people in Labrador function by clan. Family and relatives evidently play an enormously important role. If that's true, shouldn't Lorna's parents have brought family members or other relatives along at this difficult hour? But they came without any support. I try to figure that out.

Closs shrugs.

"They still have three sons. They work in the Alberta tar sands."

I remember that. The brothers were never under suspicion because they were all away. Lorna was the only daughter.

"Could her parents have suspected that the killer's in the family? Or a close relative? They never said so, I mean. Just a dark thought."

"Maybe. But they've never talked about it."

The sergeant doesn't stop me. That's a good sign. But he doesn't contribute much to the conversation. For him it's an old case that he's been dragging around for three years. Still, he should be happy that the investigation is moving ahead again.

Noise and voices in the hallway. Seconds later two men are in the room.

"Since when do we close the doors around here?" one of them shouts. "Is that what they do in Vancouver?"

The second man holds out his hand to me.

"I'm Frank Delgado. Don't pay any attention to my friend Sullivan; he's got a reputation all over for his big mouth—am I right, Austin?"

"Do I have to be politically correct now, or what? Are we going to have to paint rainbow stripes on the walkway to the supermarket for people of whatever sex it is?"

"Shut up, Austin, or there'll be trouble."

Austin Sullivan, I already have the feeling, will be my opponent for a while. His blond hair is longer than usual for the RCMP; it falls over his forehead, giving him the aura of a pirate.

Frank Delgado, short, but muscular, might be the type who secretly enjoys Sullivan's transgressions. Been there, seen that. Why should it be any different in Port Brendan?

Closs defuses the situation.

"Now that everybody's here, we can begin the morning meeting."

Sullivan grins.

"Morning meeting. All of a sudden we're so formal, Sarge. I'll have to write with a fountain pen from now on."

"A gold-tipped fountain pen," Delgado adds.

Closs ignores the two.

"Constable Gates, I'd like an outside view of the Lorna Taylor case. What are your initial impressions?"

Now he's showcasing me. And I've just arrived. Some kind of speedy reversal! I feel all eyes are on me. *Come on, Calista, you know the drill. It's a piece of cake for you.*

"As you can imagine, I'm not yet familiar with all the facts in detail." *Eye contact with all those present, Calista!* "I've read up on the case documents. But I don't know as yet what's in the medical examiner's report "

Closs breaks in.

"Initial impressions are sometimes the best. Shoot."

"I'm assuming that the victim knew the killer or killers. How well is hard to say because everyone in a small town knows

39

everyone in some way or another. But it's possible that she got into the perp's car on her way to the restaurant. Maybe simply to have a brief chat with him—"

"Or her." That was Sullivan, naturally.

"I mean to say a male or a female perp—or several. To talk to him or her because it was so cold that day, and it wasn't very pleasant to be standing around. I can imagine that Lorna was murdered in Happy Valley-Goose Bay and her body was brought to Port Brendan. Inspector Allen told me that the road was passable for several days in the first half of December. Many folks apparently went shopping in Happy Valley-Goose Bay at the time. The perp is probably from Port Brendan; at least he knows his way around here; he knew where to sink a wooden crate in the water without being seen. Or if he were seen, people would think nothing of it. He wasn't conspicuous."

Delgado stirs his coffee noisily. I see out of the corner of my eye that he's drowned three heaping spoons of sugar. Three.

Since nobody has any remarks, I go on.

"There's probably a personal element to this murder. Lorna was strangled by someone's bare hands so that her tongue bone and her larynx were injured. Strong feelings were a motivating factor: hate, jealousy, rejection, bruised ego . . . revenge. Under these circumstances, Lorna could also be a surrogate for something the perp hates."

I notice the door's ajar. I must speak to my colleagues about that. The reception area where Wendy works is within earshot. I lower my voice a little.

"I think it's noteworthy—and I'm sure I'm not telling you anything new—that the killer wanted to preserve her bones. As a trophy or . . . " I hesitate, searching for the right word. "Or as a means of extending his revenge. Maybe he returned to the hiding place again and again to look at the bones. Until a few months ago. Something must have happened at that time that caused the perp to relocate the crate to the beach. So that it would be found.

What that might mean . . . right now I can't even hazard a guess."

Van Heisen clears his throat.

"Maybe his ego isn't so hurt anymore. Maybe he's received some gratification because of some event or change in his life."

Van Heisen surprises me; that's an interesting theory.

Before I can answer, Sullivan barges in.

"Fred, you're getting ahead of yourself. And you're feeding your partner her lines. Good teamwork."

I look at Closs. He hasn't revealed that Fred and I are partners.

Closs pays no attention to Sullivan, keeps his eyes on me.

So I go on.

"One aspect has me puzzled. Maybe you can make some sense of it since you know the area. There was a Viking symbol burned into one of the crate boards. Three interlocking triangles."

I haven't had time to look up the significance of this on the internet, but Delgado does it now on his iPhone.

"Odin's knot," he announces, "a symbol for slain warriors. Odin's a god in Germanic mythology."

"Gates asked me if there's a Viking cult here," Closs interjects.

Sullivan pounces on it.

"A cult? With orgies and sacrifices to the gods or what?"

I shake my head.

"Many people dress up as Vikings and celebrate feasts with specific rituals."

"We have some locals who dress up as Vikings," Closs explains. "For the tourists in summer. Like in L'Anse aux Meadows in Newfoundland."

I know about L'Anse aux Meadows. A tourist magnet. There were excavations in the sixties. Archeologists discovered that Vikings had built a temporary settlement there about a thousand years ago. It's now a UNESCO World Heritage Site.

Delgado makes a dismissive gesture.

"The symbol doesn't have to mean anything. People hawk Viking stuff in the supermarket and gas stations, for tourists."

I don't think his argument holds water. But nobody contradicts him, including me, and he gathers steam.

"My dear colleague, you're right to say it's all conjecture, speculation. In the final analysis, it could also be a sexual crime. Lorna was raped, and the perp murdered her. To cover his tracks, he deposited the body in Port Brendan."

"We can't exclude that; you make a good point." My standard answer, to signal flexibility. "We only know that the killer didn't strangle her with a scarf or stocking or some other instrument. He did it with his bare hands, so brutally that even her larynx was injured. It takes a lot of strength and rage to accomplish that."

"Believe me, colleague, there's a whole slew of men here that can exercise that much force," Delgado says with a laugh, and Sullivan joins in.

I'm about to say that the question isn't whether they can do it but if they are prepared to when Closs intervenes.

"Thank you for your input, Gates. We'll keep up the questioning in the town and surrounding area. I'm redistributing the assignments. Gates, you read the new documents and create a situation report with all the important facts. But first I'll take you to your house."

He gets up.

"One question, Sarge," Delgado says, "about that situation report. I'm a bit confused. Is Constable Gates leading the inquiry?"

Ah, trench warfare has already begun. I hope it lasts only for a few weeks and not the whole time I'm here.

Closs doesn't bat an eyelash. The man keeps his nerve.

"You're confused? Well, that's a new one, Delgado. None of us has ever seen you confused. And another thing: some of us should go to the funeral and keep our eyes and ears open."

"Let's send our new colleague," Sullivan retorts. "That'll give folks something to gawk at."

I'm keen to see if the sarge lets that one go. Straightaway he gets off the hook with the reply: "If that's the case, then it's more suitable for you and Frank. We want to watch the people in mourning and not the other way around. Don't forget that."

Delgado is already at the door.

"Will do, Sarge. Funerals are a big event around here. Even bigger than Netflix."

I have to give Delgado credit: he's not easily offended. But I'm not so sure about Sullivan.

I glance over at Fred van Heisen. He's the only one still seated and acts as if he didn't register the exchange. He has a serious look on his face. Maybe that's the only expression at his disposal. Or maybe he doesn't think there's anything funny about Lorna's fate. Heaven knows what's going on in his head. There'll be plenty of time to find out.

Closs says we should get going. I discover on our way through Port Brendan that the town is divided into small clusters of houses in several coves. The sarge explains that three hundred years or so ago each fisherman chose a cove and settled there. Only the center of town, where the police station is, lies on a rather elongated stretch of coast. It turns out that the rocky point of the bay, where my new home is, juts out into the ocean like an index finger, so you can see the center of town from there. I'm relieved. At least I won't feel cut off from the rest of the village.

The road to the bay is plowed. We stop in front of a little house with an olive-green vinyl facade and red window trim. A spot of color—that's nice. The other four buildings are closer to the shore and white or gray; they're just partly visible behind huge piles of snow.

We climb the red wooden stairs on the left side of the house, where the main entrance is located.

Closs opens the door and hands me an old-fashioned key,

saying: "Nobody locks their front door here, especially during the day. It's the custom for people to simply drop in without knocking. I'm telling you this so that you won't be scared if somebody's suddenly standing in your kitchen. That's the way it is here. I'll go get the report."

I'm only half listening because I quickly scout out the four rooms. With each one, I grow happier. Someone has had the house renovated. Tastefully renovated. Modern furniture, neutral fabrics, nice color accents with vases and cushions. The kitchen is not new, but sparkling white. That's always a good sign. The interior seems bright and airy, though the windows are small.

When I go back to the kitchen, the sarge is standing in front of the open refrigerator. It's full. I see eggs and cheese, butter, milk, and vegetables, apples, orange juice; there are packages of meat and a boxed pizza in the freezer.

"That was my wife. She's stashed coffee, bread, and things like that around here somewhere."

I open the kitchen cupboards and discover all sorts of food: coffee, sugar, tea, flour, salt, pepper, spices. Selfless help from a perfect stranger. I must attach the importance to these gestures that they deserve. Or else human cruelty will get the upper hand in my world. I close my eyes for a few seconds.

"Everything okay?" Closs asks.

"Yes, everything's okay," I respond. At this moment it's actually the truth, although I know that this moment won't last for long. "Give your wife my thanks; that's awfully kind."

The sergeant quickly says good-bye once he's explained the wood stove and the hot water tank to me.

"Somebody will drop off a police car and a snowmobile. And there's a street map of Port Brendan on the table," he shouts back over his shoulder.

A sudden silence. The house will be my safe haven in Port Brendan. I find there's a guest room with bunk beds in the basement. I can't imagine that my mother or siblings will turn up in this place. They'll be deterred by the cold. And the mosquitoes in summer. I repress all that. First things first: I've got to make it through the winter. Closs held out the prospect of a car and a snowmobile. I've never been on a snowmobile.

Even before I can unpack my suitcases, the phone rings. The landline. Probably it isn't for me; I don't even know my house number.

I pick up the receiver and look at the display.

Ernie Butt.

When I press the answer button, it's a woman on the line.

"I'm Grace. You met my husband in Montreal, Ernie Butt. My parents are renting you the house. How do you like it?"

Several thoughts shoot through my mind: She knows I've arrived. Somebody must have seen me. Grace Butt. She was Lorna Taylor's friend.

"I like it very much. It's so nicely furnished."

"That was my doing. I love interior decorating." Grace sounds pleased. "I found everything myself, the floors and the new faucets, and all the beds have new mattresses. I actually wanted to make it into an Airbnb, but my parents didn't want that."

I'm not in the mood to have a long conversation about interior decorating and change the subject.

"Your husband suggested I should talk to you about Lorna Taylor."

"Did he? Well, then . . . We're coming to Port Brendan for the funeral. But I don't know when that is. By the way, Rick Stout will plow the snow for you. It's included in the rent. Have you met him yet?"

"Who's Rick Stout?"

"He's the house down from you. You can see it from the kitchen. I know his wife, Meeka."

So it was Rick Stout or his wife who saw me go into the house. The bush telegraph works fast. But it's good to know that I don't have to shovel snow myself.

"He has a duplicate key to your house. He'll bring it over."

"Fine. Your husband's coming to the funeral as well?"

"Yes, of course. I don't like to travel all by myself in winter. It doesn't bother him."

"Something I'd like to know, if you can tell me. Did Lorna wear any rings on her fingers?"

"Yes, one on her left ring finger. I'm sure of it. She showed it to me. And one on her little finger next to it."

"What sort of ring was on the little finger?"

"Hmm . . . it was silver—Lorna wore silver jewelry. With a little triangle on the front that was raised a bit."

"Did the triangle have any special meaning?"

"A special meaning?" Grace stretches out her words, and her voice becomes hesitant. "I . . . don't know what you mean. I think Lorna wanted to cover a little tattoo with it."

"What kind of tattoo?"

"Oh, something ugly. I really don't think tattoos are pretty."

"Can you remember what the tattoo was of?"

"Sort of a Viking symbol."

My breath catches in surprise.

"What did it look like?"

"Don't know exactly anymore. Something weird."

"Three interlocking triangles?"

"Maybe."

She doesn't sound convinced.

"It wasn't big. I can't remember it very well now."

"Why a Viking symbol?"

"She probably saw it in the Viking house and thought it was cool."

"Did she work there?"

"No. That was of no interest to her. She always wanted to get out of Port Brendan."

I hear a voice in the background.

"Excuse me," Grace says, "but I must head to church. We're

having a Bible reading. We'll see each other when I come to the funeral. And don't forget to turn on the fan on the wood stove. It's the black lever higher up."

I can sense my disappointment growing. I've had to break off right in the middle of the conversation—it's frustrating. Next time I'll make it an official questioning. I found nothing about Grace Butt in the files. But there's a Grace Short in there. That must have been before her marriage to Ernie Butt. She didn't offer anything of substance, as I recall, other than that Lorna was really in love with her pilot and went around with him everywhere.

One more detail sticks in my mind. Lorna's parents gave her a gold chain as a present. But she wore silver jewelry. I make a note of this: *Where are Lorna's gold chain and rings?*

My two suitcases are still standing in the living room, unpacked. I don't feel like tidying up. I see the box with the medical examiner's report lying in the kitchen where Closs put it. I grab it.

All of a sudden I hear somebody open the front door.

Without knocking.

6

A man is taking off his snow boots in the vestibule.

"Hello," he calls. "I'll show you how the wood stove works. Grace probably thinks you might accidentally burn the house down."

I hurry into the vestibule. The man grins and throws his wool cap into the corner. His face seems crumpled somehow; his eyes look watery below his thick eyebrows. His cheeks round and shiny. His mouth disappears under a thick moustache. I guess him to be in his early forties.

"You're my neighbor?" Quick, what's his name?

"You bet, that's me."

He tramps firmly in his wool socks in front of me into the furnace room where the stove is, and where the walls are lined with stacked wood. Now the stove is explained to me all over again. The man doesn't think a formal introduction is necessary.

"What's your name?" I ask.

"Rick Stout." He points to a stack of wood. "Start at this corner, where the wood's the driest."

He opens the stove door and shoves some pieces of wood in. Then he crumples up some nearby newspaper and piles a few milk cartons on top. He lights it all with a gas lighter.

"There are more cartons for burning over there. When you're out, I can get more at the Moose Market."

"Thanks so much, but there's no need. I can do it myself," I say quickly. "I'll be getting my police car soon."

Although Rick looks friendly, I don't want him to come into the vestibule in the future without being asked. My home is my castle.

The fire blazes up and he closes the stove door.

"Turn the lever firmly; that's the only proper way," he instructs me. "And then push this button—that's the fan. Right now, only the oil furnace is running, but once the stove is heating, it'll stop. Wood's cheaper."

Grace apparently gave him orders to drive the point home. It strikes me that Rick seldom makes eye contact. Even now he looks away as he asks: "Did they send you here to find Lorna's killer?"

"If you tell me who it is, I'll arrest him at once."

"There are all kinds of rumors going around. I don't want to say anything definite."

I don't feel comfortable standing here with him in the furnace room, but as long as he's talking I don't move.

"What sort of rumors?"

"That Lorna was pregnant and had the baby aborted. That rubs a lot of people the wrong way. Don't tell anyone you heard it from me."

There's no indication of a pregnancy in the police report. Nobody's told the police anything about a possible abortion—except Rick Stout today.

"Pregnant by whom?"

"That's the big question," he replies mysteriously.

"By the American pilot?"

"Ask around at the clinic. The doctor there's supposed to deal with that sort of problem."

"Do you mean a problem like abortion?"

49

"I've only heard rumors. I don't know anything more."

He still won't look at me. He doesn't have the courage to come out with it.

"Which doctor do you mean?"

"There are only two, a man and a woman. Dr. Perrell and Dr. Cameron."

Dr. Carl Perrell. I shiver in spite of standing by the stove. I know that name. I have to check in with him regularly. Orders from my Vancouver bosses.

"You'll get used to the temperature here," Rick remarks, who misinterprets my shivering.

"Grace said you'd bring me a second key to the house."

"Right."

He takes it out of his pocket. It's always good to have a backup key. I'm terrible about misplacing keys.

I hear my cell phone ding. Somebody's texted me. So the house has reception. Another load off my shoulders. I turn to the stairway.

"I have to unpack my suitcases now," I say, waiting until Rick has put on his boots again.

"Phone me, or pop over if you need any help," he says by way of good-bye. I must get used to the cold as well as the people's willingness to help. And the wicked rumors in a small village.

I read the text on my cell. From Wendy, the dispatcher: *Warning from the sergeant. A coyote pack sighted near Crow Point. Stay home.*

Where the hell is Crow Point? And what does this have to do with me? Probably the animals are in my neighborhood. As if I had time to stroll around and get attacked by coyotes.

In the bedroom I avoid looking at the big bed. Don't think about Martin. Or about the many nights in our marital bed. The intimacy and the passion. Our Sunday morning conversations after making love. All gone.

I spread out the Port Brendan street map on the kitchen table.

Well, now, I do in fact live on Crow Point. I trace my finger along the coast, going north. And stop. Savage Beach. Where the crate with Lorna's skeleton was found. Three bays over from here.

I have a Google Earth picture of Port Brendan. It's a jigsaw puzzle. A going-away present from my youngest brother. He had it made within two days by a friend whose company owns a puzzle cutting machine. My kid brother always has the best ideas for gifts. My heart suddenly turns to jelly. Jigsaw puzzles are one of my favorite pastimes. I can get completely lost in them. Forget everything. My doctor recommended doing puzzles to retrain my injured brain. I get the puzzle out of my suitcase and study the image on the box. Port Brendan in summer. I recognize Crow Point by the crooked finger sticking out into the North Atlantic. Savage Beach. Somebody traveled to it and unloaded a box, undetected. Only the perp knew that a skeleton was in it.

I put the puzzle box down on the living room table and look out the window. Three houses, one directly in front of me. That must be where Rick Stout lives. Below that house is an unending whiteness. Ice, as far as the eye can see. An ocean, trapped beneath a frozen blanket. I was born in Canada but have never seen sea ice. Never had any desire to. It comes across as hostile, inhospitable.

The view of Port Brendan from another window appears like a ray of hope in comparison. A picture of normality. There are houses in which I imagine TVs, toasters, pajamas, nail polish in the bathroom cabinet, dental bills, normal things. Just like in homes in Vancouver.

I make a coffee in the pod machine on the kitchen shelf. I should have brought an environmentally friendly French press with me. Can you buy one like that here?

I sit down at the table and continue reading the medical examiner's report. The guy did good work. He's probably not as overworked as the MEs in Vancouver. I'm annoyed that I didn't have an opportunity to speak to him in Happy Valley-Goose Bay.

In Port Brendan everything goes through Closs. Damn bureaucracy! Anyway, I can glean some insights from the documents. The carpal bone clearly shows signs of healing. The ME concludes from this that Lorna was still alive a few days after the perp cut off her little finger. The murderer most likely held her prisoner for several days before killing her. He ran a considerable risk in doing so. Doesn't necessarily fit my theory that massive hatred lay behind the deed, hatred so great that the killer strangled her with his bare hands. He would have had to put up with his hate for several days without taking any further action. Maybe he tortured her in a different way. Torture that couldn't be detected by looking at the skeleton. I exhale slowly to calm myself down. The house is getting warmer. Too warm even for my liking. I take off my sweater. On my white T-shirt are the words *Don't mess with me. My mother's Greek.* Another present, but from a sister.

A murderer's mind doesn't always work logically, as I've learned by now. Not as methodically as I'd like. And not predictably, like in the mystery series on the internet. I drink my coffee in little sips; it's better than expected; that makes me happy. Now I'm even warmer, feel my forehead sweating. Heavens, I'm in the middle of all this ice and I'm sweating. Life's full of surprises.

No ring found in Lorna's crate. It might also be that the murderer tried to take her rings, and the one on her little finger was too tight, so he couldn't. Enraged, he simply hacked the finger off.

I try to visualize the situation. To do that, he must have tied Lorna up. Her fear. Her screams. The pain. Not knowing what was coming. My stomach tightens up. *Not knowing what was coming.*

Did he give her anything to eat while holding her prisoner? Or did he let her starve? I've never been able to switch off my emotions completely. Not like other investigators. I've rarely used gallows humor to let off steam. Don't want to. Horror is my driver, my motivating force.

It was already that way when I was twelve and went to look for Becca Heyer. *Stop! You're hurting me!* My parents didn't want me to know afterward what happened to Becca.

Impossible. The headlines were everywhere. Sexualized brutality. Brutish. And after all that torture, the murderer tied Becca to a tree in the torrid summer heat of the Okanagan Valley, where he'd dragged her off to. Desertlike. Rattlesnake territory. He gagged her with duct tape. When hikers found her, she had died of thirst.

How long had Lorna's suffering lasted?

It's especially important for me to get a handle on my emotions right now. Otherwise they will be counted against me. *Can Calista Gates still perform? Can she still serve as an investigator?*

You bet I can perform. You'll see. I throw the pen in my hand onto the floor in anger. I pick it up immediately. That's exactly the kind of reaction I must avoid.

Are the neighbors watching me through the windows? There aren't any curtains to block their curious eyes.

Then I see them. Half a dozen coyotes. Lounging near the shore. They seem skinny to me. Their fur must be warm in this cold. In Vancouver I once saw a coyote in the city, but never a pack. Some movement to the right. A man with a rifle. I can't see his face. The coyotes haven't sensed him yet. The man suddenly turns and disappears from view. A police vehicle stops in front of the house. Someone gets out. Fred van Heisen. The other half of my team.

He knocks and opens the door.

"I've brought your SUV," he says when he catches sight of me. He seems even more somber under his fur cap.

"Do come in. I'll make you some coffee."

I almost expect him to refuse; he doesn't exactly exude sociability. Bad guess. He peels off his parka and takes off his cap. And boots. He comes into the kitchen in stocking feet. A custom I'll have to get used to.

"You scared off the man with a gun. He was after the coyotes."

I fumble through the coffee pods.

"Strong or weak?"

"Espresso, please."

He takes a seat and passes a hand through his disheveled hair. There's something Eastern European about him. Or what I think is Eastern European.

"Can you hunt coyotes here?" I ask.

"Yes, the provincial government has a twenty-five-dollar bounty on them. But shooting inside the village limits is not permitted." He rubs his hands to warm them up. "The bounty won't bring in much. Coyotes often stay near where people are; they know how quickly they can get to safety. They're not easy to hunt."

"How many people here have guns?"

"There's probably a hunting rifle in just about every home. It's not hard to get a gun license. Most people hunt moose. That means meat for the whole winter."

"Have you got moose meat in your freezer?"

The corners of his mouth twitch inconspicuously.

"My neighbor gave me half a cow. Somebody will certainly give you some, too, as a present. Just wait. People are generous."

I put two steaming cups on the table and sit down. My leg's hurting again. I must learn to live with pain.

My colleague takes his coffee black. Just like me.

"Are people also generous with information?"

He frowns.

"Do you mean about Lorna's case? Did you read the files?"

"My impression: either people don't want to be forthcoming, or they really don't know anything."

"Probably both."

"We have to systematically question all the boat and snowmobile owners some more. Where were they when Lorna disappeared; did anyone see anyone behaving suspiciously for any reason; who owns a sled? Who was staying in the woods? Who was in a hunting cabin for some length of time . . . ?"

"We did that immediately after Lorna was found. You mustn't forget we live on the edge of a wilderness. You can hide in the bush around here better than maybe anywhere else on earth."

"But a boat on the ocean can't hide itself!"

"Gates, have you seen the outline of this coast? One lonesome cove after another. And almost all of them have a fishing shack or an old cabin."

"The perp must have returned to his hiding place again and again. The medical examiner's report says that Lorna was alive for several days after her finger was cut off."

"Believe me, we'll do everything we can to finally get the perp. And we'll track down other possible hideouts and search them."

"I'm trying to picture how it was feasible in practice. Where could the perp have sunk the crate? And how did he find it again?"

"Probably not very far from shore. He tied one end of a rope to the crate and left the other end floating on the water. Why do I think that's possible? Poachers do that when they steal lobster traps or nets or baskets of whelks and hide them in the water."

"Could it have been a thief with a criminal record?"

"We've checked out everybody in the area with a record. No hits, unfortunately."

"What's with the Viking house?"

Van Heisen clasps his hands. I don't see a ring.

"It was put up four years ago. It's a copy of a sod house. For tourists. There's something like it at L'Anse aux Meadows, on the northern tip of Newfoundland. Very famous. Lots of people go there in the summer. They hoped the same thing would happen here, but the great boom didn't come."

"Did they dig something up here, too?"

"No, there are only ancient reports of Vikings being here—it's all very nebulous. You'd have to ask an expert."

Other questions were more pressing at the moment.

"Grace Butt phoned, Lorna's friend, the one who renovated this house. She said Lorna had a tattoo under her ring on her little finger. A Viking symbol."

Van Heisen likes his coffee; I can see that. He gulps away at it. Gives him time to think.

"Doesn't have to mean anything. You saw symbols like that everywhere when the Viking house went up. New souvenirs in the shops. Mugs and table settings and pendants. I think it's a bit overblown."

"Why?"

"They've never found any Viking things here. Nothing like the bronze brooch at L'Anse aux Meadows. No sign of a settlement."

"So you think the perp hacked off her finger for another reason?"

"Maybe."

I wait for an explanation. But nothing comes.

"What might it have been?"

He keeps turning the mug around in his hands. He doesn't want to walk out onto thin ice.

I push him a bit. "I had to speculate in front of everybody today. Now it's your turn."

That helps.

"Getty's ear crossed my mind. You know the story?"

I nod. I saw the film on Netflix recently. The millionaire Jean Paul Getty's grandson was kidnapped by the Mafia in Rome; I think it was in 1973. And when Grandpa didn't want to pay up, they sent him one of his grandson's ears.

"You think the perp sent the finger to Lorna's family? To get ransom money?"

He raises his dark eyebrows. "Maybe it wasn't about money."

"What are you thinking about?"

"Revenge, possibly."

"Her parents never mentioned anything of the sort."

"Maybe they've got their reasons to keep it quiet."

"Why this theory?"

He puts down his mug.

"Gates, you wanted me to speculate. You shouldn't simply scrap any one theory."

"Something else. My neighbor just told me about a rumor that Lorna had an abortion here in the hospital."

Van Heisen shakes his head.

"We followed that up and asked Dr. Perrell about it. The rumor wasn't confirmed." He looks up. "Can you take me back to the station? A bit of a trial run with the new car."

We climb into the SUV, a Ford Edge, five minutes later. I keep an eye out for coyotes but can't see them anymore. And the man with the hunting rifle has made himself scarce. He might have got one coyote at best; the others would have taken off right away.

The motor starts up at once in spite of the cold. A good omen. Hopefully we'll become friends, this vehicle and me. And maybe the man next to me, my new partner, will become a friend as well. If he relinquishes his defense mechanisms. And I mine.

We have to hunt as a pack to find the killer.

There's no other way.

7

He senses how cautiously his new colleague is driving on the snow, though the road is plowed and sanded. There's hardly any snow in Vancouver, unlike Regina, where he comes from. Fred would like to know whether Calista Gates has ever been to his home province of Saskatchewan but saves the question for later. For the moment he'd rather be quiet and keep his eyes open. His worst fears haven't been realized. Gates is not one of those loud, aggressive female police officers who desperately want to signal how tough they are. He's aware that a woman can't be a shrinking violet if she wants to survive in the RCMP. Better not show her feelings or, worse, fear. Gates last worked in the Major Crime Homicide Unit—that much he'd learned from Closs—and had made a name for herself there as an expert in profiling perpetrators. Why they transferred her to Port Brendan is a riddle. He'd heard of the brutal attack on her, of course. He can imagine how much it took to patch her up. But Labrador? For a highly qualified woman from Vancouver? He has only one explanation: The people in Vancouver haven't found her attacker or attackers. Haven't cleared up who severely injured someone from their ranks. It must have really stung the honor of the RCMP. They don't want to be reminded of it on a daily basis. Better to shunt the colleague in question off somewhere so they didn't have to deal with the matter anymore. Out of sight, out of mind.

He asks himself what the sarge might think of it. Closs didn't say anything about the reasons for Gates's transfer; he instructed his team not to bring up the attack on her. There must be some kind of deal between him and his RCMP superiors, about which Fred can only speculate. As a matter of fact, Closs is supposed to be replaced after four years, but he's here right now, and nobody's talking about him moving to another position.

"Right?" Gates asks, as they came to a fork in the road. Port Brendan may be small, but it's not easy to figure out. All those inlets and convoluted side streets.

"Right, and then left at the next intersection."

He thinks Port Brendan is underrated. What goes on here is not taken seriously enough elsewhere. Small, isolated communities are in danger. Nobody wants to talk when you come right down to it because they don't want to step on each other's toes. Nothing's out in the open; they only stab one another in the back in secret.

Good thing Lorna's remains were discovered at last. When she disappeared without a trace three years ago, there was hardly a soul in Port Brendan who didn't think the American pilot was responsible. That attribution of guilt was an easy way out. The Americans wanted to leave Happy Valley-Goose Bay. That meant the town lost an important source of income. The US president acted like he was no friend of Canada, rather an opponent you can't trust for a second. An American as the suspect was the ideal scapegoat for the locals.

Lorna's boyfriend had a solid alibi, however, and nothing indicated that he had something sinister up his sleeve or anything to do with Lorna's disappearance. But he remained a suspect in the eyes of many, particularly when he was suddenly recalled to the US. Fred feels the anger rising within him. Anger and satisfaction. He feels validated because three years ago he thought Lorna's family and acquaintances should be scrutinized more carefully. In most cases, the victim knows the killer. It's something you learn early on in your training, dammit. Gates mentioned it in the office today. Why wasn't that done more carefully in Lorna's case? Every day he can observe mutual dependencies in the small community. One example leaves a sour taste in his mouth: Sergeant Closs's wife is a nurse in the clinic, and Lorna's father is the administrator. Her supervisor.

"Were you ever up there?" Calista points to the outlines of the old radar station that can be seen from the street. A few ruins, their shapes vaguely emerging from the snow. She obviously has a sharp eye.

"Yes, I go jogging there in the summer, on the abandoned access road."

"Hard to believe our government simply invited the Americans in. I mean . . . hard to imagine that from today's perspective."

"You didn't know about it?"

"No, I don't remember ever being concerned about the American military presence in Canada. Maybe because all the radar stations are in the North, and I was never there."

"You were never in Northern Canada?"

"No, I was more attracted to the southern parts. To where it's warm."

"Then Labrador must be a shock for you."

She slows down and turns onto the main street toward the village center. Only then does she answer, without looking at him. "I prefer the word *chance*."

He glances over at her. Not a trace of sarcasm on her face. From the side, she looks more decisive than from the front. More chiseled. Nonetheless a pretty profile. She probably thought up her answer back in Vancouver. He recalls that morning in the office. How Closs lured her into an uncomfortable situation.

Constable Gates, I'd like an outside view of the Lorna Taylor case. What are your initial impressions?

What a damn circus. Gates certainly didn't want to show off as the know-it-all expert from Vancouver—and least of all on her first day. Closs set her up. She couldn't very well refuse, couldn't brush off the sergeant's request. Sullivan and Delgado exploited it, naturally.

Fred has wanted to knock Closs off his pedestal for a long time. Hopefully Gates will dig where the sergeant left the ground undisturbed.

"What's that?"

She brakes so abruptly that the car begins to skid.

"Don't brake!" he shouts. She does what he says, to his great relief.

They stop in the middle of the street. Gates glances in the rearview mirror. Unfazed.

"Is that a sawmill?"

She stares straight at him. Eyelids like half-moons.

"There are cars out front. Why don't we take a quick look inside?"

Now he gets it.

"Because of the crate? Nothing there. The locals saw their own lumber and cut down the trees themselves. They don't buy anything in the mill. All their stuff's for export."

She drives on and looks for a place to turn around.

"Who built the Viking house?"

"A local businessman. Gerald Hynes."

"And who financed it?"

"As far as I know, the provincial government. To boost the tourist industry."

"They might have bought their wood here, don't you think?"

"Your job doesn't start until tomorrow."

He can't believe he's unable to come up with something better.

She makes the turn and stops in front of the sawmill.

"Fair enough. You're the lead, and I'm coming with you. These guys work on Sunday?"

"They work here whenever work comes in."

He doesn't stop her. Be interesting to see how the employees respond to the new RCMP woman.

Inside the workshop there's the smell of freshly cut wood. A saw screams. Gates heads with a firm step toward the source of the noise. He can see that she's all police officer: erect, shoulders back, feet not too close together, chin up. She must have been on street patrol at the start of her career. He'd noticed her right leg was dragging a bit when they left the house. It's not noticeable now.

Two men watch her come closer. She raises her hand and the screeching saw stops.

"Good morning, I'm Sergeant Gates, new with the RCMP here. Can I talk with you for a minute?"

Sergeant. Not constable. Good that Closs doesn't hear that. The men take off their gloves and look at her with curiosity.

"Is either of you the owner of this sawmill?"

One of them steps up.

"That's me."

"Do you have a minute?"

He nods and doesn't take his eyes off her.

"Don't we have enough cops at the station?" he jokes. "Are we in Chicago or what?"

"There are about twelve thousand law enforcement officers in Chicago." Gates's retort is like a pistol shot.

Wrong answer, my dear colleague. In Port Brendan, that's an invitation to a tit for tat.

The other man seizes the opportunity.

"Won't you have to build an addition on the station now? Maybe a sauna for the lady?"

The two men grin.

Gates hesitates for a second, but then ignores his remark.

"Can you show me some of your products?"

The owner is taken aback.

"Our products? I'm not sure I understand why you'd want to see our products."

"Do you put a stamp on your wood before it goes out?"

She has to ask twice because the man apparently doesn't understand her Vancouver accent.

Fred hangs back, although the owner repeatedly tries to make eye contact, as if expecting him to intervene. Hell if he's going to get involved.

"A stamp? Yes, we do."

"Can I see it?"

"Sure."

He takes a board from a stack against the wall and places it in front of her. A small, but clearly visible, black symbol at the lower end.

Gates reads the writing.

"*Hanson and Sons.* That's burned on everything that leaves this place?"

He can see that the mill owner hasn't yet guessed what she's driving at. He's hesitant when giving information.

"Yes. Unless a customer doesn't want it."

"Did you sell the lumber for the Viking house?"

He nods.

"Was there a stamp on it?"

Now it seems to dawn on the man.

"Yes, but that was different." He gets a long-handled stamper from a shelf on the wall. "This one here."

Fred recognizes the symbol, although he's two steps behind Gates. Three interlocking triangles.

The man's smile is wiped off his face. "Does this have anything to do with Lorna Taylor?"

"We're following up on all possible leads," Gates replies.

The other worker looks at his boss. "I always said those heathen markings would bring bad luck."

"For God's sake don't bring up that old crap again. Your pastor's nuts."

"They weren't heathens; the Vikings believed in their gods," Gates says. She reaches for the stamper. "May I take this with me?"

"What's that got to do with Lorna?" the owner asks.

"We can't say anything about that because there's an ongoing investigation. But thank you very much for your information. It's very helpful."

Fred holds out his hands. She gives him the stamper and takes the men's names in the notepad she took out of her jacket pocket. This woman doesn't waste any time. He smiles to himself. Calista Gates will be the talk of the town. She put the heat on those guys and didn't even need a sauna to do it. Sullivan would say that out loud and laugh. But he's not Sullivan, and he no longer has to go on patrol with him. Now he's got Gates.

"Will we get our stamper back?" The owner has nervousness written all over his face.

"Yes, once we no longer need it."

Gates says good-bye and walks to the exit.

He brings the stamper along after her. In any other situation he'd have felt downgraded to a lackey. But his satisfaction with the fact that certain people aren't treated with kid gloves anymore is greater. And he doesn't even have to answer for it.

Arriving at the station, he's not surprised that the sergeant immediately confronts Gates. She's completely dumbfounded that Closs already knows about the interlude at the sawmill. He's not at all astonished; news flies around here at the speed of a rocket.

"These questionings have to be coordinated, Gates," Closs rants.

"I feel I'm always on the job if I happen to hear something important, Sergeant. Then have someone else ask Gerald Hynes why a piece of wood with this stamp on it"—she waggles the stamper back and forth—"turned up in Lorna's crate."

8

Using her binoculars, she peers through the window at the white expanse of the bay. Now she can't see it anymore. Whatever it is that's lying on the ice. The wind is blowing billows of snow around.

The voice on the radio says a snowstorm is brewing. A blizzard with sixty- to seventy-mile-an-hour winds. Ann's whole body cramps up. This is already the third storm since the middle of February; the two previous ones knocked out the electricity for days. Surely it's punishment for her coming to Labrador two months earlier than usual. She convinced herself that she had no other option because of the fundraising campaign for the hospital.

She's never seen the North Atlantic the way it is now. A never-ending desert of ice. In past years, she's come after the ocean's begun to thaw. The landscape out the window is scary. She can make out the horizon just vaguely.

On land there are towering drifts of snow everywhere, some as high as a three-story house. The streets are like tunnels, with thick walls on either side. How do you avoid claustrophobia here? She has no idea how people in Labrador manage to survive the winter. Normally she's no longer here by the first snowfall. But there are good reasons for coming back to Labrador again and again. There's no other choice this year but to fight her way through.

The swirling, drifting snow denies her a view of the shimmering ice outside. A white barrier will soon drop over it like a theater curtain. She will still be able to make out Shannon Wilkey's house across the bay, sad to say. She can't make it go away, even though she's constantly furious about it. There was nothing on that spot before. Just a rocky shore and undisturbed bush. Until Shannon Wilkey went and plunked down an architectural monster and ruined the view. It spoiled the joy of living in Port Brendan in the summertime. The village is just the right size to her. Two thousand inhabitants, and she's made friends with some of them. She loves the Mealy Mountains in the distance, and she loves one of the most beautiful beaches nearby—twenty-five miles of sparkling white gold. A legend tells of the Vikings who were said to have landed there. Ann knows all of them, those legends.

She finds peace and security in Port Brendan. Keeping her private life private is difficult, however, because the locals are so curious. She skillfully reveals only what she wants to. She knows folks are puzzled by what a young woman from far away is doing in Port Brendan. But nobody can pry her secret from her.

Every spring she looks forward to flying to Deer Lake, traveling for five hours up the breathtaking west coast of Newfoundland and taking the car ferry over to Blanc-Sablon. It's still a good three hours to Port Brendan after that. A long trip—it's not for impatient people—but she doesn't mind. It's where she's found her second home.

And then Shannon Wilkey discovered her bay. Ghost Bay. When she got wind that the American woman intended to build a house catercorner from her, Ann didn't believe it at first. Nobody would build there. Too rocky. Too exposed to the brutal winds. And where could you put the septic field the village stipulates? Certainly not on that bedrock.

Had she known Shannon better, she wouldn't have been so naïve. Now she knows that if that American woman wants something, she'll go and get it. What a monster that house turned out to be! The buildings in Port Brendan have small windows to keep the warmth of the wood stoves inside in winter and the wind outside in summer. Like her cozy little frame house. In Shannon's villa the windows go from floor to ceiling. Like in an aquarium. A shark tank. How often has she pictured in her mind's eye the villa going up in flames! Red-yellow tongues blazing up into the dark sky. In her revenge fantasy, she doesn't see anyone flee the house. It's always too late to escape. Sometimes she even manages to shock herself with her fantasy.

She aims her binoculars at the ice again. A dot of color in front of Shannon's villa catches her eye. The American drives a silver SUV. But now a red pickup's parked there. Ann saw it a week ago Friday, too, and then again on Tuesday. Her eyes go back to some movement on the ice. Suddenly a hot rage seizes her. It's stronger than her sense of caution. Ann has never thrust herself into the public eye in Port Brendan. Until now. She puts down the binoculars fast and reaches for the phone.

When Wendy answers at the police station, Ann says in a trembling voice: "I think there's an injured animal in a blue garbage bag out on the ice."

9

Well, that's a fine start to the day. I open the front door, and what do I see before me? A white wall. I can clearly recognize the door's imprint in the snow, the indentations and protrusions. I fetch the broom and try to hack holes into the wall with the handle. Abject failure. Some snow falls into the house, but the wall stands firm.

The wind had all night to plaster snow against the side of the house. Where's Rick Stout, who's supposed to plow it? I wouldn't mind if he burst into the house—only he can't because that wall is in the way. I have to get to the office early today so I can speak with Closs before the others show up. Closs is on the early shift. It's a quarter to eight; I hope that gives me an hour alone with him. To stake out some territory. I drew up a situation plan for him, a list of people that we ought to interrogate in the Lorna Taylor case, and also some hints where we might need to begin the questioning. And what does Closs do? He assigns the men to be questioned to my colleagues, the women to me. Better to talk woman to woman, he seems to think. Baloney.

Of course, I was hoping to be able to decide which people to question. Stands to reason, after all: I'm a fresh pair of eyes on the case; the others can't see the woods for the trees anymore.

I hack away again at the wall of snow. I get nowhere. Except that my right wrist hurts. Could be the result of injuries from the attack, though. I can never predict when something's going to hurt again.

There's a balcony door in the kitchen, but the balcony itself is missing. I tear it open, and I squint until I can see again. Gusts of snow blow in my face. I take a look down. It should work without me breaking a leg. Everything's padded with snow anyway.

I slip on my winter jacket, put on my toque and gloves. The wind has turned more bearable—only forty miles an hour, says the weather report—but it's supposed to get worse soon. I take a deep breath. Cold, cold, cold. Then I jump. Land in a snowdrift, break through, deep. Up to my chest. Half my body is stuck in a freezing vise. Didn't count on that.

I rotate my arms like a windmill. My ski outfit doesn't help; I can't get any friction. My slippery gloves are useless. Shoot! I've got to get to the office! This threatens to wreck my beautiful plan.

Then I hear a snowblower. The machine slowly makes a path to my house. Rick Stout sees me stuck and turns the machine off.

"How the heck did you get there?"

I look up at the open balcony door; he does, too. Grins.

"We call that the mother-in-law door."

I don't ask why. Can figure out the answer myself.

"There used to be a wooden porch around the house," he explains, "but they took it down, it was so rotten."

Looks like the door isn't an emergency exit for heavy snow days. Who knew?

"Can you get me out of here?" I ask meekly.

"Sure."

Stout shovels me to freedom.

"It was just a bit of snow," he jokes.

His throat is uncovered in spite of the cold. Doesn't seem to bother him. He looks around as if seeing his surroundings for the first time.

"Pretty soon we can export igloos."

My feet are starting to freeze.

"I need my car. It's in the garage."

Rick sticks his shovel in the snow.

"You'll have to wait for the snowplow. Hasn't come by today yet. The street's blocked."

But the guy's got a snowblower! Stout points to the sky.

"There'll be more snow this afternoon. Where's your Ski-Doo?"

"In the shed."

I point to the left side of the house. A new machine, Closs emphasized. As if he was afraid I'd smash it up first thing.

"That's what you'll need."

Stout starts up the snowblower, and it eats through the snow up to the shed. Then he digs out my front door.

Before leaving, he returns to the shed and looks at my snowmobile. Bits of ice hang from his moustache.

"Must have been darn expensive. Have you driven it yet?"

I nod. I made three little circles with it yesterday. And was constantly afraid of tipping over. I don't want to come to my final resting place under this monstrosity.

Stout gets moving.

"I've got to dig my uncle out. His arm's in a sling because he slipped on the ice."

I suddenly see my neighbor in a new light. First he helps me, then his uncle.

"Thanks for digging me out," I shout after him.

All he does is raise an arm in response.

Keep your distance from the local population—that was drilled into me in Vancouver. That'll be hard to do here. In Port Brendan you're continually dependent on other people. And they're so terribly helpful. When you fraternize with them, staying objective is difficult. The entire RCMP team in Port

Brendan comes from different provinces, so none of us has grown up with the locals or is related to any of them.

That's not a problem in Vancouver. I shake the snow off my ski clothes and boots. In Vancouver—that's where I want to be now. No snow there. I can jog and bike every day. Or roller-skate. I don't mind the rain. I'm a water animal. You don't go swimming in Labrador. The North Atlantic is far too cold. The lakes, too. In Vancouver I start swimming in March. And now I'm stuck in this icy hole. I've only been here for three days, and every waking hour I pine for the Pacific. Most folks in Port Brendan have probably never even seen it.

Then I hear Stout's voice again. He's stopped on the unplowed street.

"What kind of a name is Calista?" he shouts. That must really be important for him.

"It's Greek."

My mother explained to me when I was little what it means: the most beautiful. *Because you're the most beautiful one to me.* But she only said that when my sisters weren't around.

I didn't tell Stout that my father's Greek. After he fled to Canada, he changed our family name from Galanis to Gates. As if it were something to be ashamed of.

"My name's Rick," Stout shouts as he walks away with his snowblower. He told me that yesterday.

I take off my ski clothes in the house and call the office. Wendy, the dispatcher, answers. She is the mother of four children. She calls my male colleagues by their given names; to her, I'm Constable Gates. A subtle division of the sexes.

"Constable Gates? I was just about to call you. We need you. Something peculiar was spotted out on the ice. We have to check it out. Austin and Frank are on their way to Mary's Harbor. Fred has to see the doctor."

"What's on the ice? A person?"

"We don't know yet. Maybe an injured dog, but Sergeant

Closs wants you to go and check it out. We got a phone call about it."

Closs has no desire to go look for himself, apparently.

"The snowplow hasn't come yet," I say. "I can't take my SUV."

"You need the snowmobile for the ice. You've got to go out on the ice. In the bay."

She sounds as if she's being a little gentle with me. I'm the new person from Vancouver, and I don't have a clue. Wendy's been working at the station for eleven years. My throat feels slightly irritated.

"Where on the ice?"

"In Ghost Cove."

Appropriate name. I've seen it on the map. Not far from here.

"Who's coming with me?"

RCMP officers are never allowed to go into a dangerous situation alone. Strict orders from above. The ice is considered a risky zone.

"We've scared somebody up. Gerald Hynes. The chief of the volunteer fire department."

Great! The volunteer fire department. Closs's broad hint to me that Port Brendan plays by different rules.

Then something crosses my mind. Gerald Hynes. The contractor who built the Viking house. Now I can grill the guy without asking Closs's permission.

"Gerald's waiting for you at the fire hall," Wendy says, concluding our conversation.

10

Gerald sees her coming from a long way off. A bright green blur on a snowmobile weaving its way among Port Brendan's houses. Like a green grasshopper on skis. Her Ski-Doo swerves now and then. An unskilled, delicate little city girl who's still got a lot to learn. He doesn't understand why they sent a Vancouver Mountie to Labrador. A woman who doesn't have the physique or the toughness.

He'd spotted Calista Gates yesterday in front of the supermarket. Even in her ski outfit she looked like a deer, petite and lean. Gotta have meat on your bones in Labrador; it's no place for somebody skinny as a reed who can be blown down by a gust of wind. A gust like this one right now.

Doesn't the RCMP have any physical requirements for their personnel? How can such a delicate flower incapacitate a man, a man like him, for instance? Maybe she thinks the gun in her holster makes her invincible. *I bet she'll soon be giving tickets to drivers without their seat belt on.* Half the people in Port Brendan don't fasten their seat belts, for Chrissake. After all, this ain't Vancouver, it's the wild North. Freedom's still king here; they know nothing about that in the cities of the South. The woman's got to try to make herself a bit liked. Those guys, her colleagues are more laid back about it.

But that's the way it's always been. The RCMP sends people to Port Brendan from far away. Everybody knows that a posting to an isolated place nobody wants to go to gets you more money because of the bonus pay for the higher cost of living in the North. That's how it is with newcomers. It's the dough that brings them here. They even lure doctors to the hospital with a big fat raise so they can justify the move.

He's heard other rumors about Calista Gates, though. That she's being tested in Labrador to see if she's still suited for the police. Unfortunately he hasn't been able to find out anything more yet. Those guys in Vancouver evidently think they can use Port Brendan like a research lab. And people here like guinea pigs. As if it doesn't matter one bit who's unleashed on the population.

At least she's amazingly quick. He wouldn't have thought her capable of getting dressed and getting the snowmobile in gear in so little time. And she's attired properly for the storm that's already raging. Her Ski-Doo looks new, an elegant machine with a windshield; she no doubt got it from the RCMP.

She stops six feet in front of him and takes off her helmet.

"Gerald Hynes?"

Her question is a bit muffled because of her thin ski mask. She hasn't learned yet to pull the thing down to speak. With that black skintight headgear that leaves only her eyes uncovered, she looks like a Ninja warrior. Her eyes are watering.

"Do you know where we're going?" she asks, in full emergency mode.

Gerald is convinced that the call to the police is a mistake. Ann Smith sounded the alarm. A stranger from Ontario who's not usually here in the winter. She hasn't got a clue what's normal and what isn't.

But it's a good opportunity for Gerald to meet the police-woman from Vancouver. His adrenaline starts to pump.

"Always stay right behind me!" he shouts. He can't hear her answer over the noise of his howling motor.

He speeds down the snowmobile path. He would go even faster, but he's towing a wood sled. You never know. When he looks back, he sees how bravely she's taking the humps of snow. He could have gone around the bay on firm ground but goes quickly onto the frozen ocean instead. The surface is as rough as a pebble beach. The air has turned whiter. Gates is clearly traveling more slowly. He looks back repeatedly. Must keep a steady eye on her. This excursion should make her just a little more humble. He sees her swerve to the right. She's found a track that's not quite as bumpy and accelerates. Smart kid.

Gerald heads for the rocky outcrop at the end of the bay. He mustn't push it too far, or the Mountie will wind up in a snow squall. They're moving side-by-side now. Ghost Bay lies before them. In better weather you'd see the villa he and his men built for Shannon Wilkey. On the opposite shore, his late grandfather's old fishing docks cling to the rocks. Ann Smith lives in his house. He's never understood why Shannon wanted to build right here. On the rocks. There were much better places. How can you figure these people out? An eccentric American with too much cash. From Texas. When her husband comes to visit—rarely—they both put on cowboy hats. Otherwise Shannon shows off her blonde mane. Who the heck knows why she's here so early, in March, and not in Texas. And before this year Ann Smith has never come until May.

Ann thinks it's an animal that's on the ice out here. She feels more for animals than for people, the way he sees it. When old Helen's house burned down in November, she phoned him up to inquire about the fate of Helen's cats. Never said a word about poor Helen, who managed to escape with only the clothes on her back. He almost hung up, with an obscene word. But since he and

Melissa separated, he has to worry about his reputation, or else the girls will think he's a misogynist. The selection of potential girlfriends in Port Brendan isn't large enough to afford that.

He doesn't see anything blue on the ice. He doesn't see much of anything at all; he's got the feeling he's under frosted glass. Suddenly Gates waves her arm.

What does she want now? She makes a circle in the bay, goes along the coast and over the ice, then makes a smaller circle. Concentric circles. She forces him to do the same. He swears under his breath. They'll still be out on the bay at nightfall if she keeps up like this.

As he turns his snowmobile, he can see the sled he's towing out of the corner of his eye. And there's something else—he brakes and peers at it more closely. Then he makes his motor roar like a bull moose in rut until the Mountie looks over. He lifts his arm. A blue bundle on the ice. They head carefully for it from different directions, their paths forming an arrowhead.

A large blue plastic bag. The wind pulls at the loose corners but can't lift the bag because something heavy keeps it on the ice.

Gerald gets off his snowmobile and is about to bend over it, but Calista—ever the investigator—stops him with a hand gesture. All this fuss about a garbage bag, he thinks to himself.

She takes off her helmet, then her bulky gloves. She has thin gloves on under them. She's really thought of everything. He watches her approach the blue plastic bag and lift a corner. Something hairy looks out. A dog's head.

The thing looks dead as a doornail. And frozen stiff. He's upset about it. *Oh no, I wasted my time for this.* But the RCMP woman isn't deterred. Of course. She thinks she's on the trail of some crime. Even if it's only a dog. As if there weren't anything more important. It was definitely killed by a coyote. Happens all the time. People shouldn't let their dogs run around loose. But where's the rest of the beast anyway? A heavy chain appears out from under it, a weight that fishermen use.

"Can you lift this thing with your gloves?" she shouts, bracing herself against the wind.

He holds the chain high, and she pulls out a piece of red material. It flutters in the wind, but he recognizes the writing in spite of that. *Animals Are the Better People.* Every soul in Port Brendan would recognize the hoodie. Lorna Taylor owned a sweatshirt like that before she disappeared three years ago.

Calista digs some more. A cap from the winter Olympics with a logo, *Vancouver 2010.* And an ax. Good heavens! It's getting better and better. Or worse. A piece of wood. She turns it over, stares at it, then at him. Holds what she's found right in his face. He recognizes the stamp at once. Same wood as for the Viking house. Holy shit!

She points to the sled. He helps her load the bag and its contents onto it. Then he lifts the seat of his snowmobile and takes out a long bungee cord to lash the load down.

Visibility is getting worse by the minute. Calista nevertheless insists on making a few more concentric circles. He finally convinces her that it's pointless by now. He must bring her back to Port Brendan unharmed. Her and the sweatshirt and the cap. The chain. The ax. And the board with the stamp on it. How did all that get into a garbage bag that somebody weighted down with a chain and put out on the ice? He represses the image of the dog's frozen head. With good reason.

He takes Gates to the police station. She wants him to come in with her. The hell he will, and he lets her know it.

"I've already lost too much time—and money."

"You're a witness," she points out.

A witness to what? Better not get involved in a discussion. He deposits the blue bag in the driveway and roars away, towing the sled behind.

11

I haven't even known my boss for a week, but I can read his furrowed brow. He moves the wrinkles like an accordion. He's listening to me, half interested, half skeptical, studying the red sweatshirt.

"Was this really Lorna Taylor's?"

He should know better than me. He's the expert on the case. His memory's never been destroyed by a clubbing, either. Back then, after the attack, I could remember almost nothing. My long-term memory worked tolerably well; short-term memory was gone. It came back slowly after several weeks. And that was just one of the problems with my damaged brain. I would read something and not understand a thing. I couldn't recognize some words anymore. Couldn't speak coherently. Words came out of my mouth I had no intention of saying. Where had they been hiding? Didn't know how to use a laptop anymore. Couldn't work my laptop keyboard. Had no idea what three times twelve was. And how much I had in the bank. What a guy on the phone wanted from me, and how to make sense of the people on TV. It was all confusing and chaotic.

But that's a thing of the past. I want it to be past. I know the Lorna file backward and forward. And I let Closs know it.

"It says in the file that she owned a sweatshirt like this one, but it wasn't found with her clothes. There are lots of these sweatshirts in Port Brendan; members of an animal rescue group ordered them over the internet."

"Then let's find out how many there are and where they are."

The wind's howling outside, and the building groans. I've thawed out thanks to the hot tea in my stomach; I've switched to it from the awful coffee. The room is still too warm for the arctic clothing, but I cannot get rid of the thermal underwear that makes me sweat.

"I wanted to question Hynes about the stamp on the board, but he refused to come in. Simply took off. We must bring him in as soon as possible."

"That can wait until later," Closs disagrees. "Fred, what do you think about what we've found?"

He turns toward van Heisen, who's standing quietly in the corner. He came back from his doctor's appointment half an hour ago. He looks noticeably pale, though he's normally tanned. He's from Regina, in Saskatchewan, where it's very cold and icy in winter, almost as bad as in Port Brendan. Except the wind never stops here. That much I've been able to worm out of Fred. He's often calm, like now. Doesn't say a lot. Especially about personal things. Still, he shared with me that he's not all that unhappy in Labrador because he likes the higher salary in the North and can save up for a house in Regina. He told me this in the car, where he couldn't avoid talking to me.

He clicks his tongue.

"Might be a warning."

"To whom?"

"No idea."

Closs is disappointed by his answer.

I break in.

"A warning sounds plausible. I'm of the same opinion. And here we have a piece of wood with the same stamp we found on the crate with Lorna's skeleton. A blood-red sweatshirt like the victim's. The ax. A severed dog's head."

"If the murderer's behind it," Fred remarks, "then he really laid it on thick."

Exactly, Fred, that's what I think, too.

"Almost overkill. A hint like a ton of bricks. Have we got a case of cruelty to animals here? And what's happened to the rest of the body?"

Closs again seems skeptical.

"The dog was dead for sure when its head was cut off. Maybe it got into a hen house somewhere, and somebody shot it. Wouldn't be the first time."

"But that wouldn't be legal," I mutter. I can't conceive of anyone raising chickens in this climate.

Closs is already thinking ahead.

"And the cap?"

"Maybe Lorna had one like it?"

It's lying before me on the table, in an evidence bag. The ice on the webbing has melted. A red-and-beige cap with the words *Vancouver 2010* on it. These hats were sold at the winter Olympics in Vancouver and Whistler. And now, ten years later, one of them turns up in a blue garbage bag on a frozen bay in Port Brendan.

"Somebody weighted the bag down with something," Closs states. "With a chain like the ones fishermen use on their boats."

He spreads out his fingers—a gesture I've seen him make before. "Let's take the dog first. It must belong to somebody. Any ideas, Fred?"

"No. Never seen one like it."

The head is in the small kitchen freezer. Closs doesn't ask me, but I speak up anyway: "I think it's a Labradoodle."

"A what?" Once again those prominent furrows on his forehead.

"A cross between a Labrador retriever and a poodle—very fashionable these days."

Closs is seated, while Fred and I are standing in front of his desk.

"What did Ann Smith see, exactly?" he asks for the second time.

"She thought it was an injured animal."

At that moment I get a text message. It's a reply from the local animal rescue group. I inquired about any missing dogs and left a description.

The lady from Texas complained a couple of days ago that a black-and-white long-haired dog was running loose on her property.

I read the message aloud.

Closs makes a decision.

"Fred, you follow up on the sweatshirt story. Find out who's worn an Olympics cap and where the chain's from. And blue garbage bags—nobody has them around here. The bags in the stores are green or black. Gates"—he looks at me smugly—"you ask around in Ghost Bay to find out who's seen what."

Sarge assigns me the women again: Shannon Wilkey and Ann Smith.

"And the dog?" I ask.

"We'll send everything to the lab in Happy Valley-Goose Bay. Then at least we'll know how it died."

I suppress a sigh. How miserable it is here! No lab, no medical examiner, no tests. Everything must go to Happy Valley-Goose Bay. It could take days for us to get the results. But no use complaining.

I put on my ski jacket.

"Don't take the Ski-Doo back, Gates," Closs warns me. "All hell's breaking loose out there. Fred can take you home. Take the pickup with the plow, Fred."

That's our boss for you: fatherly all of a sudden.

A little later Fred is driving down the main street, the snow-plow mounted on the front of the truck. We can see about fifteen feet ahead and crawl along at a snail's pace. A single car is following us.

"There are always the crazies," Fred mutters.

"Do you mean the driver behind us or the guy who left the garbage bag on the ice?"

Fred fumbles around the controls for the heater before answering.

"It looks rather calculated to me."

"So you don't think it's a coincidence?"

"Coincidence? When someone decapitates a dog?"

"The perp wants to challenge us," I mutter. "A mutilated animal. That can only mean *You're next*. But *who* does he mean?"

Fred doesn't take his eyes off the road. The plow shoves the snow to the side, where white snowbanks are already piling up.

"And why out there on the ice? So far from any houses."

That has me puzzled. Why not on a doorstep? And why when a blizzard's coming?

I'm itching to interview Ann Smith. And the lady from Texas after her. But I can forget it for today. This damned weather. I must sit at home twiddling my thumbs. Or get the puzzle going.

I think about the peculiar blue bag.

"I can't make heads or tails of the chain, either. A clump of ice could have weighted it down just as well."

Fred says nothing.

I vent my frustration some more. "We didn't even see any tracks on the ice. The wind was blowing everything away immediately."

Fred turns onto the narrow road to my house. Snow has barricaded the entrance again. Fred clears it off with the snowplow so I can enter the house. Then he disappears into a nebulous soup.

The stove's gone out. Luckily, I can also heat with oil. I undress and take a shower. Who knows how long I'll have hot water. Or light. Power failures during a storm are said to be routine here. I really must buy myself a gas generator for emergencies.

It's unusual for me to be all by myself. Many people took care of me during rehab. But Martin, my ex, up and left me six months after the assault. He couldn't stand seeing me weak, injured, clumsy, drooling down my chin, sometimes as helpless as a small child because my brain wasn't with it. More than anything else, it was my anger he couldn't take. That anger. It came when it was least expected. From one second to the next. I didn't have a good grip on my emotions anymore. If I tried to concentrate, my head would start hurting like crazy. I took out my frustration on Martin. I swore and raged and screamed.

My brain let me down. My neural pathways and neurons and receptors didn't work together properly anymore. It drove me insane. No, it *might* have driven me insane if I hadn't had help. I often didn't want any. Because it made me feel like a child. Dependent, controlled, at everyone's mercy. Like an illiterate.

Martin's a veteran cop. Very busy with his work. Not the nursing type. He'd almost always known me to be strong, stubborn, successful. Maybe he thought I'd never recover. That I'd never be myself again. He wasn't totally wrong. I look like I did before, but otherwise everything's changed. The one person who really understands me is my doctor, but she's on maternity leave for a year and thinks I can manage without her.

I boil a pot of water on the stove, add some spaghetti, take the tomato sauce from the cupboard. I miss my kitchen in Vancouver. My apartment's empty. I didn't even find time to sublet it. Another reason I want to get back as soon as possible.

A noise. I listen hard. Again. A crunching sound. Then something's dragging. It seems to be coming from the basement. I go to the stairs and listen again. Nothing. I turn on the light switch and go downstairs. I feel a cold draft. The door is open. I'm convinced I locked it after me. I shout hello. I can't see or hear anyone. I go get the key. This mustn't happen again. Visitors—so what? They'll have to knock. Suddenly I see a bag on the floor emitting an unpleasant smell. I take a peek inside. Dog shit. Who the hell threw this into my house? Maybe not all my neighbors are as nice as Rick Stout. Or are some kids playing a trick? I did worse things as a kid.

My cell phone rings. Birdsong. I programmed it just before my departure. So that the summer arrives more quickly. First come sounds of rejoicing, then some loud, squawking birds. I don't want to miss any calls.

"I've tried to reach you several times," the voice at the other end says. I sit down. This conversation will be difficult.

"You can't get reception everywhere out here; I warned you about that. I was out on the ice, on the frozen North Atlantic. In a blizzard."

Maybe that will make an impression on the psychiatrist, who's in his office by the warm Pacific.

But he ignores it.

"How's it going with the medications?"

He actually means: How's it going with my brain damage? But he'd never put it like that.

"Good."

"Are you still having seizures, Mrs. Gates?"

"No." Good God, I've only been here a few days.

My monosyllabic answers irritate him. He hesitates with his next question: "How are you sleeping?"

"Good, if the wind's not howling around the house. I use earplugs."

Once again the pregnant pause.

"I'm not your adversary, Mrs. Gates. You know that, don't you? I'm trying to help you."

Yes, and you report to the RCMP.

"What about your feelings?"

I don't want to discuss them. But he does.

85

"Today, for example, were you aware of strong emotions?"

His turns of phrase. Typical shrink.

I try to shock him.

"I was angry today because we found a severed dog's head, and I was furious at whoever did it."

That doesn't shock him, of course, and now he's got me on the hook.

"How did you manage your anger?"

"I put the energy from it into my investigation."

This is the sort of thing he wants to hear, so I give him what he wants.

"That is good, Mrs. Gates, that is progress. Everything will slowly settle down, which was my prediction for you."

But I didn't just feel angry. I was also thinking about clues and how we can nab the killer.

"You're writing in your journal regularly, aren't you?"

"Yes."

I write whatever you wish to read about me.

"When's your appointment with Dr. Perrell?"

"I'll attend to that tomorrow."

"Good. I'll call again."

I look at my watch. One thirty p.m. Nine a.m. in Vancouver. The day is just beginning for him. I press the red button to end the call and stand there listening. The storm drives the air with powerful blasts against the walls of the house, like mighty waves breaking on the rocky coast.

Closs's voice rings in my ears. *All hell's breaking loose out there.*

Question is, which hell?

12

The police are here. Ann watches the slim person from her small kitchen window laboriously getting her leg across the Ski-Doo as she dismounts.

She should have known better. Whatever you do, don't get involved in things when you can't foresee the consequences. Actions can get out of hand and lead to personal tragedies. To brutal turning points that can't be reversed. She regrets that she cleared the snowdrift from her doorstep. Shoveling doesn't bother her; she likes to work her muscles. The cold air is invigorating. Compensation for her daily work at the computer. But at that moment a snow barrier in front her door would have been fine by her. To keep visitors out.

On her way to the main entrance, she looks at the mirror in the vestibule. She's put her makeup on carefully, as she does every morning. She never shows up for anyone with a bare face; that was hers alone. It's fun to look glamorous in these wild parts. It also makes her popular with the local women who sell makeup as a sideline; they were recruited by a cosmetics company promising them "woman power" and self-liberation. They earn a cut from each sale. Ann supports these women by buying everything possible from them. She also helps people with their computer problems. Looking for a computer store in Port Brendan is a waste of time; the nearest one is in Happy Valley-Goose Bay. But who's going to drive four hours through the wild tundra when your printer's on the fritz?

Ann hears a knock at her front door. Locals never knock, they simply walk in. Everybody here does it. She sometimes locks the doors when she doesn't want to be disturbed. A big sin in rural Labrador, a serious breach of local custom. But she's from else-where, so she's considered eccentric anyway. An eccentric who spends the summer and fall in Labrador every year, alone, without a partner.

She's not surprised that the RCMP has sent a woman to her.

"Sergeant Calista Gates," the officer introduces herself when Ann opens the door. "I'm here because of your telephone call."

"Please come in."

The Mountie takes off her boots and her down jacket. Ann escorts her to the living room. Calista Gates sits down on the brown leather chair that is nowhere near Ann's taste, but in Port Brendan's only furniture store you can't be choosy.

"Would you like a cup of coffee? Tea?" she asks.

"No, thank you."

Calista Gates takes a peek around the room, stopping at a wall hanging. It shows a dog team with a sled. Ann doesn't miss a thing. The officer's face glows in the warmth of the wood stove. Dark, almost black hair, tied at the back. Big, melancholy eyes, a regular face that hides nothing. Not even the shadows under her eyes. Or the scar at her hairline.

Ann can't pigeonhole her. Not yet.

The Mountie looks at her in a friendly way.

"It's nice and warm in here; this constant wind is brutal. I'm going to freeze my nose off."

Okay, she's making small talk before the tough questions. So Ann strikes up a chatty tone, too.

"Unlike you, I have the luxury of staying inside and simply waiting for the weather to improve."

"Wendy, our dispatcher, told me you're not here normally in the winter."

"Yes, this time I came a little early because I wanted to help with a fundraising event for the hospital. I promised Dr. Perrell."

"When does the event take place?"

"During the Winter Games, March eighteenth to the twenty-third."

"What's the money for?"

"It's going to computer tomography."

"Do you know Dr. Perrell well?"

Careful, Ann!

"Who doesn't know him? Dr. Perrell is very committed and really wants to help people here. I think he must be supported."

"What brought you here originally?" The Mountie puts her notepad on her lap.

Ann hesitates, although the locals often ask her this question. Or tourists she happens to meet while hiking. It may mean something quite harmless.

"I read a book about Mina Hubbard, who went on an expedition to Labrador shortly after 1900. I found it completely fascinating and wanted to see the region for myself. That was four years ago. And then I got hooked on Labrador."

"Mina Hubbard?" Calista repeats.

It doesn't surprise Ann that the Mountie from Vancouver doesn't know the name. Women of extraordinary achievement often find it difficult to receive recognition.

"Mina Hubbard was a Canadian," she explains. "She came to Labrador in 1905 because her husband Leonidas had died on an expedition here. He starved to death. She wanted to carry his plan through to the end and so explored huge areas."

She could tell her visitor so much more about Mina's adventures or show her one of her books. She could describe how a

89

companion of her husband's on the first expedition left him high and dry, and wanted, after Leonidas's death, to finish the trek successfully on a second attempt. And how Mina won the race with this man in Labrador and, after six hundred miles, reached the finish line before her rival with seven weeks to spare. But she doesn't want this Mountie in the house any longer than necessary. She can't read the officer's notes, but it appears she's jotting down Mina Hubbard's name.

The officer looks up from her notepad.

"When do you normally return to warmer climes?"

Warmer climes? *She must have got that from Wendy.*

"Beginning of November."

"You work at home?"

"Yes, I design websites." *Don't reveal more than is necessary.*

Calista Gates sighs.

"You're lucky. I'm from Vancouver. In my city, we have maybe four or five days of snow in a year, and that's it."

A smile of longing plays around the Mountie's prettily shaped lips, and Ann feels reminded of her own unfulfilled yearning for a familiar place that is still out of reach. She feels a sudden bonding with this woman, with her open face that she presents in such a vulnerable way. People's eyes are sure to dwell on her mouth, on her straight nose, on her dark brown eyes. Ann wonders how the men at the station are reacting to the new arrival. The Mountie looks graceful, but not fragile.

Ann blinks. Her flight of fancy has passed.

The touch of sympathy Ann just felt evaporates when the officer continues: "You know why I'm here, don't you?"

Because of an avoidable blunder of mine, Ann thinks to herself. Too late.

"Can you describe for me once again what you saw on the ice yesterday?"

Ann shifts around in her leather chair.

"The first thing I saw was a snowmobile."

Calista Gates raises her eyebrows.

"Have you given us this information before?"

"No. It crossed my mind afterward that I should have mentioned it. There's a snowmobile track across the bay. I see a vehicle go along it now and then."

"Go on."

"I didn't think anything of it. I saw some movement afterward. Something colored on the ice. When the movement didn't stop, I went and got my binoculars so I could get a closer look. A blue plastic tarp. When the wind blew it upward, I could see the hairy head of an animal."

"How much time had elapsed since you saw the snowmobile?"

She pretended to think about it and responded: "Maybe twenty minutes . . . or half an hour."

"Did anybody stop there?"

"I didn't see anybody."

"What did the snowmobile look like?"

"Nothing conspicuous about it. Maybe black or gray. It was difficult to make out." She crosses her long legs in order to relax. "Sergeant, I saw someone else out there yesterday, later on. Was that the RCMP? Did you find anything?"

"I'll get back to that in a minute. Didn't you see us as well through your binoculars?"

"No."

Ann knows that it must sound odd. She watches the Mountie as she writes. Those thin, feminine fingers. The small nails. She'd like to know how Calista Gates manages to get along in the male-dominated world of the police. She doesn't look sexy, but she's attractive in spite of her bulky winter clothing. She must be a little older than Ann, midthirties probably. Has a pleasant, soft voice.

"How many people were on the Ski-Doo?"

"I can't say for certain."

"What would you say off the top of your head?"

"One person."

Calista Gates looks out the window onto the bay. She sees what Ann has to put up with every day: Shannon Wilkey's grotesque palace. Ann secretly hopes that Calista Gates is as shocked as she is.

But the officer doesn't let on a thing.

"Rather lonesome here," she remarks. "Do you visit your neighbor sometimes?"

Ann chooses her words carefully.

"I like it lonesome, which is why I'm here."

"So you haven't talked to Shannon Wilkey about what you saw?"

"No." Has she questioned Shannon already?

Calista Gates strokes her cheek and then speaks frankly: "We searched the bay yesterday and found a blue plastic bag that was weighed down with a big iron chain. In the bag there was a red sweatshirt with the words *Animals Are the Better People* and a cap like the ones sold during the Olympic Games in Vancouver in 2010. There was also the frozen head of a black-and-white dog and an ax. And a wooden board with a Viking symbol: three interlocking triangles."

Ann feels a chill creeping up inside her as if someone has injected ice into her veins. The officer keeps talking, but she has trouble following the Mountie's words.

Calista Gates watches her with interest. Too much interest.

"Mrs. Smith, do you know that dog? Do you know the owner?"

"No," she replies. "I . . . I have no idea."

13

I stop the snowmobile in front of Shannon Wilkey's villa. The driveway has been plowed and the snow on the patio behind the house has largely been cleared. Shannon must have a private snow removal service. No neighbors like Rick Stout to come by with a snowblower every so often. No, this is the work of a professional snow remover with a huge plow. The space looks deserted; not a car parked anywhere. I can't see a garage, either. Strange.

Ann Smith's house is easy to spot from here: a traditional little house like so many in Port Brendan. Ann adapted to this place. Unlike Shannon, whose residence dominates the surroundings. The American can overlook the entire bay from this location.

For some reason Ann didn't phone Shannon to discuss the blue garbage bag on the ice. She loves her solitude, as she says. In my opinion, her style of self-presentation doesn't go with that. The elaborate makeup, lavish but not excessive, tasteful but Hollywood-esque. Jennifer Lopez couldn't have done it better. Who in Port Brendan sticks on false eyelashes on a normal day? And her stylish clothes caught my eye. Does Ann want to step out today? I'd like to know where to.

She'd sought out this modest house on a lonely bay. And then they drop this concrete colossus in front of her nose. Shannon could have built on another bay, where it would be flatter and simpler to build than on the rocks here. Wendy told me that parts of the bluffs had to be dynamited. She also told me that tons of earth had to be spread on the coastal rocks for the septic field. A bit extravagant for Port Brendan.

I hear a droning sound. Not a car but a snowmobile out on the bay. My binoculars reveal a silver Ski-Doo with a wide, green stripe. Even if it were gray or blue, I wouldn't recognize it. I'm annoyed at myself for mentioning the ax to Ann. As soon as I did, she clammed up and turned very pale. Might be that she's an animal lover and was horrified. But she did know already that a dog's head was involved.

I take off my helmet and glide from the machine. From up close the Texan's house is even more imposing than when seen from Ann Smith's living room window. A monument to modernity. A white concrete facade with gigantic windows. I'm not an expert on buildings, but the windows must be at least triple glazed, given the wind storms around here. The roof rises boldly on the ocean side, like a billowing sail. The front door appears to be made of oxidized copper.

There's a doorbell that I press firmly. With a house like this, nobody's going to burst in just like that. No response. I push the doorbell again. Nobody's moving. I work my way around the house in my snow boots. The front of the house has as much glass as the Museum of Anthropology in Vancouver. Nothing that would stop curious eyes like mine. Trendy furniture, large paintings on the walls, cathedral ceiling up to the gabled roof. Everything looks expensive. Imported from a long way off for sure.

I want to question Shannon about the stray dog on her property. And now she's not in. So much time lost. The air smells like more snow, but the gray sky over the iced-in bay radiates peacefulness. I can see a tiny island off the coast. It sticks out of the ice like a lump. The only eye-catching spots are Ann Smith's ochre-colored house and the ochre-colored fishing sheds on the bank.

I hear a motor again. Only much closer. I tramp quickly around the corner. A Ski-Doo. The driver stops and reveals his head. A young man. I'd really like to put on my helmet, that's how cold I am already. Next time I'll pack a fur-lined cap.

The man comes closer. An Inuk.

"Hi, anybody home?" he asks and glances over at the house.

"No, I haven't seen anybody."

He's wearing a dark-green winter jacket. He looks good in it. Besides, I like green. He's someone who takes some care with his outward appearance—I can see that immediately.

"I'm Sergeant Calista Gates of the RCMP. And you?"

His face clouds over. I know, I know. Not everybody loves the police.

"Kris Bakie."

"You want to see Mrs. Wilkey?"

"Yes, she's organizing a culinary evening for the hospital fundraiser."

That comes out pretty quick in spite of his mistrust. His neck and head are exposed to the ice-cold air. The people here treat the cold like an insect that's best ignored, although it bites.

"Are you involved?"

"I'm the chef de cuisine. I'm cooking a seven-course menu."

Wow! Seven courses. And in Port Brendan.

"Are you from here?"

"Yes. But I live in Happy Valley-Goose Bay mostly. I'm the owner of the Eider Duck restaurant. And you?"

"I'm from Vancouver."

Now the penny drops. That restaurant in Happy Valley-Goose Bay. Fred mentioned it recently. The pride of the region. The jewel of Labrador. Two Michelin stars. And a prominent chef. A young Inuk who's gone far in haute cuisine and in Canada. In Vancouver, for instance. And who then returned to his native home. Shannon, the rich Texan, had hooked the illustrious chef for a fundraising gala in Port Brendan. Look at that! Maybe I'm not living so deep in the boondocks after all.

"You used to work as a chef in the Hyatt Hotel on Burrard Street?"

His face lights up.

"Yes. Until a year ago."

"I once had an excellent caribou tenderloin there. Was that one of yours?"

Now he smiles in delight. I'm finding the guy simpatico.

"I introduced some new dishes from the Arctic there. They were very well received."

"I can imagine. We Vancouverites are real foodies."

My nose tickles. It will start to run now. I fumble for my handkerchief while not letting him out of my sight.

"Please, don't leave the area. I'll eat at your place every week when the road opens again."

He eyes me with amusement.

"Labrador must be culture shock for you."

"Thanks for your sympathy. I've only been here for a few days. Is there another season in Labrador besides winter?"

"Early winter, winter proper, late winter, mosquito season, and winter again."

I join in with his laughter and am surprised at myself. Better get serious again.

"Did you make an appointment with Mrs. Wilkey?"

"Sort of, but she couldn't say for certain when she'd be back."

"Back from where?"

"No idea."

I think for a minute. Should I wait? She can't have gone far.

Bakie scuffs the footprints in the snow with the soles of his boots.

"What's the RCMP want with Shannon?"

Now that he's identified himself, he's become bolder.

"She complained about a stray dog."

"A dog? Isn't Lorna Taylor a priority for you?"

I can't tell him that the dog might have something to do with Lorna's murder. Or maybe not. I must find out both of those things.

"Yes, it is, absolutely," I answer, then add my litany. "If you have any information that might help us, then please, do let me know."

He doesn't say anything, just shrugs. We're both cold, but he suppresses it better.

I follow up.

"Do you perhaps know whose dog it is? It's black-and-white with a curly coat. Looks like a Labradoodle."

"No idea."

He turns around slowly and walks back to his snowmobile. Helmet in hand, he shouts: "We'll see if the Brown Man has got Shannon."

"What's this about a Brown Man?"

He laughs. "An old legend. Way back, they say a man roamed the area wearing brown buckskin clothes. And attacking people. But you don't have to be afraid of him, Sergeant. Good luck on your search."

He turns his machine around and goes off. I fish out my cell phone with my ice-cold fingers to inform the head office about what I'm up to. A year ago, that wasn't expected of me. I would have considered it controlling.

Then I see a new text message from the animal rescue group: *The dog probably belongs to Melissa Richards in Port Brendan or her boyfriend, Kris Bakie.*

I swear out loud.

Then it occurs to me who Melissa Richards is, because Wendy told me when it was hot off the press.

Gerald Hynes's ex, the man who was with me on the ice.

14

Hello.

Shannon?

Yes.

Is this connection secure?

Yes.

I've got some info for you. The new policewoman.

Good. What have you got?

I don't think you have to worry about her.

Okay . . . What . . .

She's from Vancouver, that's right. She was a detective sergeant in the Major Crime Homicide Unit until about a year ago.

But I want to know why—

I know—let me finish. She was in the hospital for weeks. Then she was transferred. Probably to be tested to see if she's still fit for service.

But that doesn't tell me why she's in Port Brendan of all places.

We mustn't get paranoid. It can simply be by chance. A new position opened up in Port Brendan.

That doesn't make any sense at all. Why can't she stay in

Vancouver? Surely her doctor's there. And the whole infrastructure in case . . . in case something happens.

Maybe she picked Fort Brendan herself.

Good God, do you know what you're saying? If she did, then she must have a reason. She's not just anybody.

I get your cautiousness. But it doesn't give us the slightest bit of evidence that anybody knows anything about the person we're watching.

I can only hope you're right. But it wouldn't surprise me if she soon turns up at my door with some awkward questions. Then we'll have to talk again, seriously.

We have a plan. For whatever happens. Don't forget that.

15

Bernard knows immediately that something not good's going to happen when Fred van Heisen shows up in his office. He sees the indignation writ large on his deputy's face, and that doesn't happen often. He takes the bull by the horns and asks straight out: "What's the trouble, Fred?"

Van Heisen fires away without hesitating.

"It's everywhere on Facebook: the sweatshirt, the dog's head, everything. And they're speculating wildly all over the place and spreading rumors. That should have been better controlled."

Bernard's already aware. His thirteen-year-old son told him about it over breakfast. Fred doesn't have children who operate as secret informers. Probably he's a "creeper," someone who looks for info on Facebook under a false identity. Bernard doesn't think that's wrong, because Facebook is a veritable gold mine for the Port Brendan police. Folks talk about everything on Facebook; most people don't have the slightest inhibition. His son once drew his attention to pictures of a grandmother displaying her Christmas presents; among other items he spotted a voluminous bra and personal lubricant. Closs knows the woman; she works in the kitchen at the nursing home. Georgina, his wife, once told him that a local woman openly confessed on Facebook that she cheated on her husband with R. G. (everybody knows who R. G. is, naturally). That she deeply regrets the affair and is now working on her marriage. Closs recently caught his daughter giggling with a friend as they were looking at a tablet. The cause was a young fisherman on Facebook who was sitting bare-assed on a bucket on his boat and doing his business.

Bernard takes Fred's last words—"That should have been better controlled"—as a very clear accusation aimed at him. Fred usually holds his tongue, unlike Sullivan and Delgado. He has to admit that Fred is right. Calista Gates ought to have sworn Gerald Hynes to silence after the garbage bag was found. But people in Port Brendan play by their own rules. Sooner or later the details would show up on Facebook—sooner rather than later, in his experience.

"Gates comes from the big city and hasn't got a clue about the small world we're in," Bernard retorts, justifying the situation. "Her mind-set is probably still back in Vancouver."

His voice is more condescending than is appropriate for the faux pas. A concession to Fred. Bernard has to keep his deputy in a good mood. His superiors had planned to send Bernard to Edmonton. He's been in Port Brendan for four years; usually after that long, the RCMP moves personnel around. Bernard was ready to move on, but his wife wasn't. And neither were his two kids. His family had grudgingly moved from British Columbia to Ontario and then to Labrador, but by now they felt very comfortable here. His wife had found a good job in the clinic; his son was on an up-and-coming hockey team, and his daughter had made half a dozen friends in her class. Bernard's family threatened him with open rebellion.

Then came the phone call from Vancouver. It led to a secret deal. Bernard's transfer had been postponed for two years. And Fred had to bury his hopes of becoming the boss in Port Brendan. All because of Calista Gates.

"None of us knew how the world in Port Brendan worked

when we started here," Fred replied. "It's up to us to explain that to Gates."

By "us" he means me, Bernard thinks to himself and changes the subject, as he finds himself doing whenever the conversation turns to Calista Gates.

"The dog owner has been found: Melissa Richards."

Fred is not so easily diverted.

"That's already on Facebook."

"Anything about the red sweatshirt?"

"Apparently there's a dozen of them. The animal rescue group ordered a bunch. Lorna was only one of several group members to get one. The sweatshirt in the garbage bag could have belonged to anybody."

Lorna Taylor. Bernard has sensed the locals' mistrustful frustration over the last three years. They can't understand why the police aren't able to solve the case. But there's a spark of hope now. In him as well. It has to do with the skeleton but also with Calista Gates. He doesn't come right out and say it, but a new investigator sees old crimes from a new angle. Unexploited possibilities. He just has to ensure that everybody on his team gets credit and that Gates, whenever necessary, gets put in her place.

He stands up behind his desk.

"We must find out where the ax came from, and whether it was used to cut the dog's head off. And we'll want to find the rest of the cadaver."

"Not to forget the Olympic hat."

For a second he thinks Fred means it ironically. But his face looks serious as he leaves the room. Nevertheless, Bernard is left with a bad feeling.

No sooner has van Heisen left when an unfamiliar woman's voice hits his ears. Wendy appears in the doorway.

"Melissa Richards is here about the dog."

Wendy had filled him in on Melissa's clan. Because having background on someone's clan is de rigueur in Labrador.

"Melissa Richards, from Port Brendan South; they're the Richardses who came over from Newfoundland years ago, from St. Anthony. They bought the old orphanage—the building with the blue metal roof. You've surely seen it. Melissa's mother raises flowers in her greenhouse in summer. She cleans in the clinic two days a week."

He presses his lips together.

"I can't worry about her now, too. I have other things to deal with. Is Gates back yet?"

"Here, sir," somebody calls, and Calista Gates pops up behind Wendy. She has her helmet under her arm. Strands of hair from her ponytail have come loose everywhere. The cold has turned her face red. "I'll take care of Miss Richards."

"We can question her in here," he suggests, changing his mind on the spur of the moment. When he writes his report for the Vancouver RCMP, he can say in good conscience that he's observed her doing an interrogation.

She throws him a look. He can tell by her expression that she sees right through him.

Melissa Richards is wearing white, tight-fitting stretch pants and knee-high boots. He can't recall ever seeing pants like that in Port Brendan. Or colored hair that shines like copper. He suspects her red bomber jacket with a Canada Goose badge is a knock-off. These illegal imitations have been making the rounds in Port Brendan for some time now. Even his daughter wanted to buy a cheap imitation from China, but he vetoed it, promising her the original for Christmas. It will cost an arm and a leg, yet the girl sulked for days.

"Why did everybody know and I didn't?" Melissa gripes as she's brought over to Gates.

"We wanted to be absolutely sure where the dog came from so we wouldn't frighten any children unnecessarily and let them think it was their dog," Gates explains in a reasonable tone of voice. "Please have a seat over here."

Melissa sits down and keeps on bellyaching.

"Everybody knows our dog, the only black-and-white whoodle here, so you didn't need to ask too many questions."

"What's a whoodle?"

Gates takes off her ski jacket. Closs watches Melissa eye her up and down. People in Port Brendan all shared a common characteristic: curiosity.

"A cross between a Wheaten terrier and a poodle. It's the only one in South Labrador," Melissa adds proudly.

Gates writes something on the pad in front of her.

"Gerald Hynes was there when we found the dog, and he didn't recognize it. He's your ex, is he not?"

Melissa shakes her copper mane.

"Gerald knows the dog very well; he's lying like a mink. Maybe he's behind it."

"So the dog's yours?"

"It belongs to both of us. Kris bought Arrow for me."

"Kris Bakie?"

"Yes. Can I see Arrow?"

"Unfortunately not. We've sent him to the medical examiner in Happy Valley-Goose Bay. Can you hazard a guess as to who might have killed your dog?"

"Maybe somebody who's jealous. Everybody here begrudges everybody everything. It's a hoot."

"Do you have any suspicions?"

"No, not really."

"Can you give us some names of people we might interrogate?"

"Names? Good heavens! If I'm wrong, then folks won't ever look at me again."

Melissa tugs at her skintight pants and stops looking at Gates.

"Kris will be devastated. Arrow followed him around everywhere."

"You haven't talked to him about this yet?"

"I've tried to get him on his cell phone, but he doesn't answer."

Closs sees clearly that Gates hesitates briefly. Why doesn't she follow up on the Hynes clue?

"Kris is your partner?"

"Yes, we're engaged. He asked me six weeks ago."

Melissa raises her hand to show her ring.

"Congratulations," Gates says in a friendly voice. "Your fiancé is participating in the charity event for the clinic, so I've heard."

"Yes, he's going to do seven courses."

"He's on the organizing committee, with Dr. Perrell, is he not?"

"Yes. The ladies are making such a to-do about this fundraiser. My goodness! We collect money every year for the Youth Club and don't puff ourselves up like those folks do."

"Which ladies do you mean?"

"Shannon and Ann."

"Ann Smith and Shannon Wilkey?"

She nods.

"And Meeka Stout is part of it. She lives right below you; the gray house with the white shed."

Interesting, Bernard thinks, that Melissa Richards swapped Gerald Hynes for the prominent chef. Kris Bakie is definitely the reason she hasn't moved away from Port Brendan like many other young women, to Newfoundland or Ontario, or wherever there are more options. Bakie's an Inuk, but one with prestige. That's important to Melissa for sure. In Labrador, whites and Inuit have often intermixed. It was mainly white men marrying Inuit women. He'll point this fact out to Gates, who hasn't got a clue about such things.

Melissa has hit her stride.

"They're doing it for Dr. Perrell; that's why Shannon is here so soon and Ann Smith, too. Nobody can refuse a request from Dr. Perrell. It didn't take him long to persuade Kris."

"Are you or were you active in the local animal rescue group?"

Melissa regards Gates in surprise. "No, I mean . . . I haven't saved any cats or dogs. I've sometimes taken part in the group's online auction on Facebook. Why do you ask?"

Gates continues, impassively. "Do you have any tattoos?"

"Yes."

She takes off her Canada Goose jacket and rolls up the sleeve of her body-hugging sweater. Four butterflies flutter in a dance on her lower arm. Bernard can see them, because Melissa shows her arm for him to admire the tattoo.

"That's the only tattoo you have?"

"I have a caterpillar here."

She points to the top of her breast and grins.

"That's all of them?"

"Yes. Why are the police interested in tattoos all of a sudden?"

Gates ignores the question.

"Did you ever have anything to do with the Viking house? Did you work there or dress up like a Viking for tourists?"

Melissa shakes her head and knits her eyebrows.

"Did you ever buy a cap from the Vancouver Winter Olympics or receive one as a gift?"

"No. I used to have a T-shirt but threw it out a long time ago."

"Do you happen to know if anyone in Port Brendan owns a cap like that?"

Melissa rolls her eyes.

"Man, that's ten years back! How am I supposed to know? What's that got to do with our dog?"

"Those items were found together with your dog. We're trying to establish a connection."

"A connection? Don't you want to find the person who killed Arrow?"

She grabs her jacket and gets up to leave.

"I met your fiancé today in front of Shannon Wilkey's house," Gates reveals.

Melissa's attractive face immediately tenses up. "He was at Shannon's again?"

"Didn't you know?"

"He was at her place two days ago to talk about the fundraiser. I thought . . ."

She doesn't finish her sentence.

"I asked him about the dog because I . . . because I thought he might know something about it. He told me he didn't have any idea whose dog it was."

"Did he say that?" Melissa's voice sounds less cocky. "And Shannon? What did she say?"

"She wasn't home."

"Where did Kris go afterward?"

"I was hoping you could tell me that."

"Sorry, I can't." She throws her hair back. "Is that everything? I've got to go; my mother is sick."

"Yes, of course," Gates replies, as if unsurprised by her sudden departure. "We'll keep you informed about the dog. Here's my card and phone number in case something else occurs to you."

Bernard waits until Melissa is gone. Then he leaves his corner and closes the door. He's experienced enough to guess at least one of Gate's conclusions.

She immediately says: "She didn't even ask what happened to her dog. Whether it was a cruel death. Weird."

He nods and waits.

She folds her arms. "At the beginning, she accused Hynes, but it was a halfhearted try, and she didn't come back to it. Strange that both men claimed they didn't recognize the dog."

"That's really odd." He wants to know why.

Gates seems lost in thought about Melissa. "For instance, she didn't ask, who could have done such a terrible thing to my dog? She didn't even shed a tear."

Gates shakes her head as she ponders. "She was upset when she heard that her fiancé was at Shannon's place again, and she didn't know about it. And she still can't get him on his cell phone."

"Maybe jealousy's involved," he adds. "Shannon is supposed to be an exciting blonde."

He's glad his wife doesn't hear him. Georgina wants a politically correct father for her adolescent children.

"Maybe something other than jealousy," Gates says.

"What are you thinking of?"

"Don't know, exactly. It's more of a hunch."

He doesn't think much of hunches. He goes to the door and opens it.

Gates gets up slowly, pointedly.

"Is Melissa in danger? Is the blue garbage bag a warning to her?"

"You should work Hynes over," he replies, surprised at himself.

16

Dr. Carl Perrell strides into the room, bursting with energy, a folder in one hand, the other reaching out toward me. A pleasant handshake, winning smile, mellifluous voice. Tall, strong shoulders back, and a very short haircut that makes him look athletic. A youthful, college-football-player look. What's a man like him doing in Port Brendan, for heaven's sake? He could fit right into a Netflix series about a popular doctor—and the entire hospital staff would give him the shirt off their back.

I've dreaded coming to the clinic. What will I have to reveal in this small hospital? And who'll see my data? It already started badly at the reception desk. An employee behind the glass looked at my card from the Ministry of Health and called out, as loud as she could: "Your birth date is June 17, 1985?"

As if this information wasn't on my health card.

The waiting room was filled with people who now knew the date. As I stared at the woman, appalled, she opened her mouth again.

I intercepted her: "Wait!" I whipped out my notepad and wrote: "*Please do not announce my private data to the whole world,*" and shoved the note under the glass partition.

She read it and was annoyed. "We have to do it in case the information on the card is incorrect."

Then she directed me to take a seat in the waiting room. I evidently alienated her, and all Port Brendan will learn how arrogant the new RCMP officer is.

Dr. Perrell knows nothing about this intermezzo, but he's studied my medical file from Vancouver. My history seems to fascinate him. He wants to pump me for all kinds of facts, though they're in my file. Maybe he thinks he'll find out something my brilliant doctor at Vancouver General missed.

"Brain injuries can be complex," he declares, as if I didn't know. He has a British accent. "Every injury is different, every brain responds differently. That's why research is pretty much at the beginning stage."

Even that tells me nothing new.

"I get brain damage cases time and again," he says. "So many accidents with Ski-Doos: the head hits the ice; it can be severe even with a helmet on. The ATVs are bad, too, especially because people don't wear helmets."

I don't inquire what happens to these injured people. I'd love nothing better than to not discuss a thing in my medical history with him.

Dr. Perrell rubs his chin. And then comes a sentence I don't ever want to hear again: "You're apparently very lucky. Very few people recover so quickly from such a serious brain injury."

Rapid recovery. Rapid for the experts. For me it's been an eternity. A year and a half of tests and then more tests and rehab.

But I must secretly admit he's right. I've read enough to know that I've been fortunate in the midst of misfortune. For example, I sleep quite regularly. The only thing that keeps me awake sometimes is the pain in my leg and my head. Most people with brain damage can only sleep for a few hours and then only by taking pills. But most notably it's my memory that's working much better again. I still can't remember the details of the assault, and sometimes I can't recall other events in the past, either. But my brain has responded very well to the intensive memory training I do every day. Different brain cells have gradually taken over from dead ones. New receptors and synapses have formed.

"It's a small miracle," my doctor emphasized again and again.

I still have trouble with those damn numbers. It's hard to do math. Algebra was once my favorite subject, but it's now an incomprehensible chaos for me.

"Puzzles, wow! You're still good at puzzles. Baffling."

Dr. Perrell looks at me as if elephant ears were growing out of my head. "Almost every person with brain damage has huge problems with spatial orientation."

I stay silent, furious. As if there aren't enough problems to deal with. My stabbing headaches when I have to concentrate for a long time. My loss of libido. I'd love to finally get the hots for a man again. I can't distinguish between red, purple, and orange anymore. I have to sleep for at least ten hours to feel rested. I can still smell, but I can't say for certain what I'm smelling. Of course, I don't rub his face in all that; the less he knows, the better.

"Have you had any seizures since coming here?"

Oh, yes, the seizures. When I suddenly fall down.

His eyes show concern. This man must have charisma if Ann Smith and Shannon Wilkey come here to assist him in his humanitarian work in spite of snow storms. His British accent must certainly charm some women. For me he's a potential threat. He'll have a say as to whether I'm capable of fulfilling my police duties.

"No, I feel pretty good," I assert. "The medications help."

"Problems sleeping?"

"No."

"Ever spaced out?"

I know exactly what he means by that. That's something I can't let him think happens to me.

"No, never."

"Problems concentrating?"

I shake my head.

"Panic attacks?"

"Everything's normal since I've been on the medications."

I am worried, however, that I found my basement door open again yesterday. Something's not right. I'll have to change the lock.

To my astonishment, the doctor smiles at me and announces: "Well, continue taking them regularly, and come back in three weeks if nothing's changed."

I've heard rumors that it's easy to get a sick note from Dr. Perrell. Maybe he's happy to have somebody who absolutely wants to work for a change.

"Do you like it here?" he asks as he renews my prescription.

"I need to get accustomed to it." Then I respond to his questioning glance: "I'm a city person."

"I know Vancouver a bit. I was there for the Olympics, as an emergency doctor. I have very fond memories of that time."

"Do you have a hat from those Olympics?"

He's taken aback. "A hat?"

"As a memento of a beautiful time," I quickly add. That was a little too direct. A disruption in the hospital hierarchy. I'm the patient, he's the doctor.

He answers nonetheless: "No. But I still have a jacket with the logo somewhere."

I want to keep him in a good mood; he controls my health records. "And you, how do you like it here?"

"I've found my mission in life," he says, almost solemnly.

Nevertheless, I'm cold. As if I'd have to stay here my whole life long, too. Dr. Perrell gives me the prescription, then shakes my hand again in farewell. I'm dismissed.

Once outside, I take the air deep into my lungs with relief, but it's too cold. Heaps of snow lay siege to the sidewalks. The pharmacy is right across the street. I walk over to it. Salt has softened the snow, but not everywhere. I slip on a frozen spot, row with my arms, and manage to catch myself at the last second. One thing I know: I mustn't take a blow to the head ever again or everything will get exponentially worse. Fred van Heisen comes toward me in the pharmacy. He quickly sticks a pillbox into his jacket pocket. He seems almost embarrassed, as if I might guess what medications he's on.

"Were you able to talk to Gerald Hynes?" he asks.

"No. He's at a gun-safety course today."

We are in a corner where nobody can hear us.

"How far did *you* get?" I ask.

"You can't buy a blue garbage bag in Port Brendan or anywhere else around here. But they've got them at Critch's in Corner Brook. Worth seeing if anybody can remember who bought something like that. What's new with you?"

"Shannon Wilkey is on deck today. I've tried calling her but only got her voice mail. So I'm on my way there now."

"I'll go with you." It comes out like a shot.

I take note of his sudden interest. Maybe Closs told him something about an exciting blonde as well. As far as I know, Fred has a girlfriend back in Saskatchewan.

"Sure," I agree.

The pharmacist is behind the counter. I'll give him my prescription another time. I don't want Fred to witness it. A teenager pushes his way past us and heads for the front door.

The girl on the cash register shouts at him: "Don't forget to pay, or the Brown Man will get you!"

Something clicks in my brain. Kris Bakie used this expression yesterday.

"What's with the Brown Man?" I ask the cashier.

She looks surprised at first, then she laughs.

"Oh, it just a saying. Old people would try to scare us with it.

'Don't go to Savage Beach, or the Brown Man will eat you.' Of course we'd go anyway. It's kind of a superstition."

"Why is he called the Brown Man?"

"Because he wore clothes made of animal skins. Like brown suede."

"Why did old people not want anyone to go to Savage Beach?"

"As I said, superstition. Although the Viking house was built close by; it is made of earth and sod, like in Newfoundland. For the tourists."

The pharmacist pushes himself into the conversation, a man of imposing size.

"There are a lot of superstitions around here. My great-uncle was always searching for buried treasures. Somebody told him that blood had to be spilled in order to find it. Cut off a man's head, or a cat's."

I'm all ears. Fred listens with a frown.

The pharmacist is in his element. "I think my great-uncle was a little bit nuts. But he finally did find something in the ground. An old coffin from the French period." He grins. "In the old days, nobody bought a broom in May because it was always said: 'Never buy a broom in May, or tomorrow will be your final day.'"

I want to know more.

"Did your great-uncle cut an animal's head off in a search for treasure?"

"Knowing him, yes, probably. He had a screw loose."

"We've got to go," Fred urges.

I thank them both and go with Fred out into the cruel, cold air. He pulls a cap with ear flaps over his head. He doesn't look happy.

"Now we've solved the puzzle: somebody wants to find treasure, so they decapitated an animal to spill some blood. And we're wasting our time."

I squeeze my nose shut briefly because the cold hurts. "Does that mean you don't want to come along to Shannon Wilkey's?"

Of course he wants to come, in spite of the superstition. Thought so.

"Let's take the route over the ice," my enigmatic colleague decrees.

That means a ride on the snowmobile yet again and not in the heated SUV. I feel like an astronaut on Mars, with my ski outfit and the helmet on my head. It's definitely warmer there than down here.

"All right. But I'd like to see the Viking house first."

"Are we sightseeing today, or are we working on an investigation?" he asks.

"Aren't I supposed to know my way around this place?" I retort. "In my duty manual it says I must make myself thoroughly familiar with the area. Besides, the crate and the skeleton were found below the Viking house."

I take his incomprehensible muttering as agreement.

It's not even ten in the morning when we speed over the rough icy surface that's no longer recognizably the North Atlantic. Fred takes the lead; his snowmobile is probably twice as heavy as mine. A moist film covers my visor in no time because I forgot to push the helmet's ventilator button. I flip the visor up but am almost immediately blinded by all that whiteness. I have to stop to put on my sunglasses.

At that moment the cloud cover tears apart, and the sun's rays shoot like streams of fire onto the ice and the coast. I blink hard. The landscape is transformed into a fantastic backdrop. The coast looks like a black-and-white-sprinkled icy wave that blissfully froze as it withdrew into the sea. The blue sky glorifies it all; even the white powdered forest seems harmless, an endless ocean of miniature trees. Port Brendan looks almost beautiful from afar. What a transformation!

Just as I'm about to start up again, I discover a striking

outline of something on the shore. It must be the reconstructed Viking house. I get my binoculars out of the compartment under my seat. The glass steams up, and I have to keep rubbing it clear. I hear Fred call but ignore him because, in my field of view, there's a silver Ski-Doo with a broad green stripe parked beside the Viking house. I just keep standing there until Fred has no choice but to come back. He stops and takes off his helmet.

"What's the matter?"

"Kris Bakie's Ski-Doo is over there."

I stopped speaking of instinct long ago. When men with the police speak of it, they're hailed as having magnificent observational skills; if it's a woman, people smile her concerns away as esoteric gut feelings.

By way of an answer, Fred puts his helmet back on. The nearer we come to the Viking house, the more it looms up as an astonishingly big, elongated building. A pointed, grass-covered roof juts partway out of a snowdrift; low chimneys grow like pinnacles out of its ridge. The wind has swept the roof clear of snow but has piled it up on the south wall. We circle the building. There are two entrances at the back, protected by small gable roofs. The wind didn't pack this side with snow; the doors are practically clear. Only the silver snowmobile lies a little ways off, half buried in snow.

Impressed, I swing off my Ski-Doo. So that's how the Vikings lived a thousand years ago on the edge of the North American continent. I don't know much about Viking history, but as I see it, the copy of the sod house looks authentic.

"Do you know anything about the Vikings, Fred?"

He shrugs. "Not much. They called Labrador 'Markland.' They came from Greenland. And . . ."

He's carefully inspecting the snowmobile.

I give up trying to learn about the Vikings from him. "I'll take a look around inside."

The first door is stuck. I push against the wood, but nothing gives. I try the second entrance. The door opens at once.

It's pitch-black inside; my eyes adjust slowly to the dark after the glaring white. I stuff my gloves away, get out my phone, and illuminate the windowless space. The light beam reveals a crudely carved low bench against a wall of dried clay; stripped tree trunks above it support the roof. Casks and woven baskets are lying around with a smattering of small wooden buckets. Thin reeds seal up the sloping roof.

I grope my way forward, tumbling over coils of rope. Suddenly I see a pair of boots on the floor. My pulse races. The small beam of light wanders over a human body. A dark-green jacket. Large spots on it.

"Fred!" I yell.

A man is lying on his stomach and not moving.

Fred is at the entrance; he hesitates for a moment, then catches sight of the lifeless body and rushes to it. I kneel. The dark-green winter jacket is torn in three places. Probably knife wounds. Blood encrusted on it has darkened. Fred mutters something beside me. We turn the body over carefully. An Inuk. Face smeared with blood, but I recognize him instantly.

Kris Bakie.

I feel for a pulse. Nothing. The man's hand is ice-cold and rigid.

Fred touches Bakie, too. He shakes his head. "Can't do anything."

The head injury looks bad. I feel dizzy.

Somebody wanted to bash in his skull and almost did.

Fred gets up. "I'll call the station."

I take a deep breath. Stay calm. Think. Stab wounds in the back. Somebody probably knocked Bakie down with a blow to the head, then attacked him with a knife or some such weapon. I hear Fred outside requesting help over the police radio. I lean over the dead man.

"Who did this to you, Kris? Who was it?"

We'll see if the Brown Man has gotten Shannon.

Fred's at my side again.

"The boss is coming with people from Emergency. They're sending a Cessna from Happy Valley-Goose Bay. They think it'll take an hour."

An hour. Happy Valley-Goose Bay is more than three hundred kilometers away. But the weather's good. If it doesn't change from one minute to the next. Just like death changes everything from one second to the next.

Kris Bakie and I were talking together just yesterday: a self-confident young man with a splendid future ahead of him. An award-winning, nationally known chef, who wanted to help the people in his homeland. Melissa Richards was so much in love with this Inuk that she broke off her relationship with Gerald Hynes for him.

After all these years with the RCMP, I've still not gotten used to the finality of death. Gone. Finished. Forever. Kris Bakie is not coming back.

I caress the dead man with my gaze because I can't stroke his hand. Mustn't wipe out any evidence.

"I think he wanted to meet Shannon Wilkey here," I whisper.

17

My knees hurt. I stand up.

"Can you take over? I'll go get my flashlight."

My phone battery drains much too quickly in the cold.

Fred nods, and I go outside. The glistening brightness hits me like a spotlight. I put my sunglasses back on in a hurry. In front of the door, I can see my footsteps. And Fred's. But there are even more tracks. Boot prints. They must be the victim's and the perp's. The wind blew away the soft new snow during the night, uncovering the footprints. That means Kris Bakie has been lying here since yesterday. I photograph the prints with my cell phone. Then I discover snowmobile tracks. They go uphill to the edge of the woods. Snow is really good for leaving a tell-tale trail.

I turn my head toward the iced-over ocean. Somebody came from there to here. I noticed these tracks when we approached the Viking house. We'll compare them to the profile of Bakie's machine. I can already guess what we'll find. Yesterday I watched Bakie ride from Shannon's house down to the ice-covered bay. The attacker must have come from the woods so that he wouldn't be spotted out on the white ice from a distance. I keep snapping photos until my fingers are stiff from the cold. Suddenly I hear Fred shout. I take the flashlight out from under the seat of my snowmobile and rush into the dark house. We'll have much more light now.

He points to a corner.

"I believe that's the murder weapon."

I crouch down and stare at a stained metal blade.

"What is it?"

"A Viking knife. There are more tools hanging on the wall."

"Then the attack wasn't planned very well," I think aloud. "If the killer took the knife from here."

"Or he knew what he'd find inside."

I put on latex gloves. Closs will be pleased when he learns that we probably have the murder weapon. One of the murder weapons. We go searching for an object the perp could have used to hit Bakie on the head but don't find anything that looks suspicious. We find a small flashlight instead that neither of us owns.

We hear Ski-Doos on the bay. Closs appears with two paramedics, who attend to Bakie right away. It takes no time for them to confirm he's dead. Closs orders Fred and me to secure any evidence before the body is taken away. I show him my cell phone photos of the tracks in the snow.

His face brightens for a second. "Well done, Gates."

The compliment makes me happier than I'd like to admit.

"Fred van Heisen discovered the possible murder weapon," I tell him.

Closs scrutinizes the Viking knife Fred hands him. The dark spots on the blade look like dried blood. Closs turns to Fred.

"What are your conclusions?"

"Bakie arranged to meet somebody he knew here; they argued and the dispute ended violently. Or somebody waited for him here and then killed him from behind."

"Have you got any thoughts on this, Gates?"

I ignore his phrasing.

"I share Fred's assessment that the assailant waited for Bakie and then attacked him from behind. I can't find any scratches or wounds that indicate Bakie was able to defend himself. We also didn't find any signs of a struggle."

Fred says nothing, so I continue.

"Maybe the attacker lay in wait for Bakie in here. Bakie opened the door and was knocked to the ground with an object before he knew what was happening to him. He falls on his face, and the perp stabs him in the back."

I hesitate again, hoping Fred will pick up where I'm leaving off.

Now he bites.

"Just three badly placed stab wounds in the back—that's odd."

I nod.

"Really strange. I suspect that none of the knife wounds were fatal. None are near the lungs or the heart or close to the liver and the kidneys. As if the perp suddenly aborted his attack."

"Aborted?" Closs frowns. "The man's dead."

"Because he was lying in here all night at five below. His head wound is the worst of his injuries, in my view."

She'll never recover from those blows. Her head is half bashed in.

I'm cold, and it's not even nighttime yet. I pull down my thin headgear to cover just half my face. I must look like a criminal in this ski mask.

Closs puts his hat back on as well.

"Maybe the murderer was interrupted?"

"Out here?" Fred is skeptical.

"The tracks point to only two snowmobiles," I concur. "Except for ours."

"We really must first search the surrounding area properly in order to know that," Closs lectures me. "Tell me once again why you two came here."

I explain everything to him obediently, mentioning Bakie's remark about the Brown Man in front of Shannon Wilkey's house. And that I spotted his Ski-Doo at the Viking house today and wanted to ask him why he lied to me about the whoodle when it actually belonged to him.

The roar of motors mingles with my words. We step out of the house. The two paramedics are waiting to put the body on a sled. Sullivan and Delgado get off their snowmobiles.

"If Bakie thought he was meeting Shannon Wilkey here, then we'll just have to go listen to what she has to say." Closs directs this to me and Fred. "What are you waiting for?"

"We're not finished securing the evidence," Fred responds.

"These two can take over."

I think of something else.

"Shouldn't we first notify Bakie's next of kin?"

Closs reacts impatiently.

"You guys get going. Just tell Shannon about the dog's head; leave out the murder for now, if you can steer clear of it."

An order. I'm pissed off. Why is he shooing us away from the crime scene when it was Fred and I who discovered the dead man? We're important witnesses. He could have had us secure the evidence and sent the other team away. He knows my reputation. But maybe it's worthless now.

Fred reveals nothing. We're already way out on the ice when we hear the Cessna.

18

When Rick hears the hum of the motor, he lowers his chainsaw and searches the sky.

"What's that doing here?" his brother asks as he stacks the sawed-off branches in the crate on top of his homemade sled.

"Maybe politicians are already flying in for the Winter Games," he mutters.

They both follow the flight of the plane as it loses altitude.

His brother frowns.

"Is it landing on the ice?"

"Near Savage Beach, if you ask me. Maybe it's something to do with the Viking house."

Rick was one of the workers employed in the construction of the sod house. As far as he was concerned, they could build another one like it. The pay was good, and he could go home after work. Jobs like that are in short supply in the south of Labrador. He could have looked for work in the north, in the nickel mine in Voisey's Bay or at the new dam at Churchill Falls. But he doesn't want to be separated from his family for weeks at a time. He needs his wife, and he needs frequent sex. He prefers to fish a little in summer and see to it that he's employed now and then by a government job-creation program. He's proud of the new

Viking house, as are most of the locals. Port Brendan now has a tourist attraction. Maybe he can work on a second sod house next summer. He hopes to, for Meeka's sake. His wife can perform in the Viking house as a throat singer on festive occasions. She also has an engagement for the Winter Games, beginning in two days. She'll perform in the arena during the opening and closing cere-monies. He's proud that he's married to the prettiest Inuit woman far and wide. He fell in love with her early on, but she first had a child by a man whose name will never cross his lips. A white man like himself. The guy deserted Meeka because their child has Down syndrome, and Meeka, after a hysterectomy, can't have children anymore.

For Rick, little Dulcie is a gift. He'd always known that he'd not have Meeka if he didn't have her child as well. To his surprise, he'd give his life for Dulcie today. For Meeka, too. Chil-dren are the salt on his fish. Sometimes Meeka takes care of Inuit children from a community up north that social workers take from broken families. That's fine by him. It keeps Meeka busy. She doesn't want to constantly travel around anymore to do her throat singing.

"Are we done here or what?" his brother asks.

It apparently hasn't escaped him that Rick is only cutting down the skinnier trees, halfheartedly.

"Yes, that's enough for today," he answers.

He sold a good part of his firewood to some old people. Now he's got to restock his supply. That doesn't bother him. It's a plea-sure to take his snowmobile into the woods on a sunny day. Espe-cially after a snowstorm. He feels the freedom out here. Only him and the universe. He always goes out with his brother. When you're cutting down trees, an accident can happen just like that. They take a break from time to time in the trapper's cabin in the forest.

Those are moments of total well-being for him. It's almost like lying in bed with Meeka. But she doesn't want to sleep with him so often these days. Maybe she doesn't feel that she's a complete woman on account of her hysterectomy. Poor Meeka. As a young girl, she'd surely never dreamed that would happen.

The new policewoman hadn't paid a visit to their place. Probably they don't do this as spontaneously in Vancouver as they do here. She's reserved, not as effervescent as Meeka. He's happy that Calista Gates has rented the house on the slope above them. Before her there were troublemakers in there who drank all the time and harassed his wife. Now there's peace and quiet.

The noise from the plane has cut out. The politicians certainly don't want to miss the Winter Games. It will be a huge spectacle for a village like Port Brendan. Dulcie will be part of the mummer group. She likes dressing up from head to toe in the Labrador tradition and dancing and singing. Meeka sewed a new costume together with her and made a new mask. The weather was much too bad at Christmastime, when the mummers normally go from door to door. The kids had to stay at home. His daughter was inconsolable. But she'll be able to make up for it in two days.

"I don't think it's politicians in that plane," his brother suddenly notices, a bit out of breath from bending over and loading wood. "It's landed at Savage Beach." He leans on the sled. "Maybe it's got something to do with Lorna Taylor. Or with the dog's head."

Rick ties down the chainsaw to the fully loaded sled with a rope.

"What's that about a dog's head?"

"Didn't you see it on Facebook? They found a severed head from that funny poodle out on Ghost Bay."

"What funny poodle?"

Rick had heard about it, naturally, but acted as if he didn't have any idea. Perhaps his brother can tell him something new. He wasn't able to get into Facebook this morning because he uses Meeka's iPhone to do it—a present from him, by the way—but she'd left for occupational therapy with her daughter and the iPhone was gone.

"Kris Bakie's dog."

Rick drops the rope.

"Is that true?"

Often the most absurd rumors make the rounds on Facebook. Too many people butt in who would be better off keeping their mouths shut. Everybody's everybody else's friend. But that can't be a good thing. Meeka has about two thousand Facebook friends.

"Gerald found him. Gerald Hynes. And your new neighbor. They found the dog's head on the ice. And Lorna Taylor's sweatshirt."

His brother brushes sawdust and bark from his old winter jacket, which is covered with resin. Then he says darkly: "That's a bad omen."

His brother is extremely superstitious, the opposite of himself. But in this case, he doesn't think he's overreacting. Who would cut off a dog's head? Kris Bakie's dog. And Lorna Taylor's sweatshirt on top of that. Did Bakie have anything to do with Lorna's disappearance? He'll discuss it with Meeka. He suddenly wants to hurry home.

He makes a loop with the rope and lashes it down to the sled with a sailor's hitch.

"C'mon. We're leaving."

19

Fred pushes the bell on Shannon's door. We wait, then I ring. Nothing. I look around. Just see tire tracks, no parked vehicle. Without a word, Fred trots over to a shed painted white like the house. He rattles the black wooden door. Locked. He peeks through a tiny window on the side.

"An SUV," he shouts.

Why didn't I get the idea earlier that a car could be hidden in there?

"Someone must be here," Fred says, coming back to hammer on the front door.

"Open up! Police!"

I wade through the snow to the front windows on the bay side. This time the enormous glass panes remind me of indoor compounds in the zoo. Looking permitted, touching impossible.

I peer inside. Then I take my right glove off and slap my bare hand repeatedly against the window. Whack, whack, whack. The glass is surprisingly warm from the sun's rays.

Suddenly someone is standing behind the window. A woman in a smeared painter's smock, a bandana in her long hair. Angrily, she's waving her hands around.

"Police!" I bellow through the glass separating us, pull my ID out of my pocket, and hold it up. She makes a vexed hand motion toward the entrance. I stomp back through the snow.

Fred has already vanished through the open door. He's taking off his boots in the vestibule. Shannon is next to him, now looking more befuddled than unfriendly. I take off my jacket and head-warmer and introduce myself. She points to her smock as if saying to ignore it.

"I was painting, so I had my earphones in as always. I block everything out, listen to music, and paint and paint. I mustn't be interrupted, or the euphoria is gone instantly."

The sunlight flows in behind her so that her face is in shadow. She's older than I expected, probably midforties. Patiently she waits for us to finish with our boots and clothing, then she takes off her bandana and removes her smock. In the twinkling of an eye, she's transformed into the seductive blonde Closs spoke of. She wears a soft, mohair sweater, and color-coordinated stretch jeans that emphasize her long, slim legs.

Her blond hair is "cascading over her shoulders," my youngest sister would write in one of the romantic novels she churns out for a publisher. Actually, not far off the mark. Shannon Wilkey's emergence from her chrysalis takes but a few seconds.

I glance sideways at Fred. He's visibly charmed.

Shannon takes us into her sun-washed temple. I absorb the space in silence and must secretly admit: this is a place I'd like to sit in every day. So much light and lofty space, and a harmony of color and proportion. The lady hasn't just got money but taste as well. The icy wilderness spreads out in front of the glass wall, as if the frozen ocean lay at the feet of the lady from Texas. From here, the scenery looks different, like a movie set.

I take a look around. An impressive collection of art unfolds in front of my eyes—and this in isolated Labrador! On the extra-high walls there are paintings everywhere, some huge, others no larger than a serving tray. All of them depict unspoiled meadows in bloom. Shannon evidently likes contrasts. I'm probably the last person to hang flowers on the wall. I like African carvings and black-and-white photographs. But Shannon's colorful meadows are exuberant. They sparkle with a zest for life. Her colors burst like little bombshells that make you want to take cover.

"Can I offer you something to eat? A sandwich?"

I'm so hungry that, contrary to my habit, I accept. I'd never have done that in Vancouver. Fred is just as receptive as me. While in her supermodern kitchen that opens out onto the living room, a relaxed Shannon chatters away in her Texan singsong. She talks about her fascination with contemporary design. She acts casually, as if she's in the dark about recent events here. As if she knew nothing about Lorna's skeleton or the dog's head.

"It was a nightmare, getting those Italian tiles delivered. And the cooking stove. It's from Germany. I'd planned all the built-ins; I'm a perfectionist, really obsessive. I'd never have made it without Gerald Hynes; the man really runs a tight ship as far as his workers and craftsmen are concerned."

And on and on in the same vein. The floors of long-lasting bamboo. The cleverly designed lighting. The choice of a Finnish fireplace.

At some point I remember the seriousness of the situation and sit down on the barstool beside the kitchen counter. Fred lets me run the interview.

"Mrs. Wilkey, have you wondered why we're here?"

She looks up briefly and lays asparagus on smoked salmon. And dill and capers. My mouth is watering.

"I suppose because of the license for the fundraiser. We've found the solution in the meantime," she replies.

I'm surprised.

"What's the problem?"

"You're new here, aren't you?" She smiles, almost conspiratorially, flashing her perfect teeth. "Somebody complained to the police that we don't have permission from the tax department to fundraise. Which was true," she confesses airily. "We thought we could simply do it through the hospital. We were mistaken. But now we're going through the Rotary Club, which is a nonprofit organization."

She nods and pours the coffee.

"People here are great, but also a bit small-minded. And jealous. They don't want anybody to get all the credit."

She laughs like someone who's really enjoying herself.

I wonder if Shannon Wilkey is aware that her flaunted wealth must stir up different emotions. There are many who are unemployed in Port Brendan. Maybe the Texas lady is one of those well-heeled people who regard their money as a deserved privilege. Nevertheless, she's helping with the fundraising. She doesn't have to.

We bring the cups and plates with the smoked salmon toast over to the living room area, which includes three huge divans. Fred has been glued to the cushions in silence since we came. So it's up to me to drill down.

"Why do you live here off and on?"

"Oh," she says, holding her coffee cup elegantly, like a hovering object. She waits for a few seconds before explaining: "I came here four years ago on a cruise. It was a voyage to the Arctic. Five hundred tourists on board; so many fascinating people. They came from all over the world. What an adventure. We saw polar bears! And so many icebergs. It was fantastic. But I was in a personal crisis. Very bad. I couldn't paint anymore. I had a total block."

She pushes back her blond mane again and again. A gesture I cannot stand. It forces the person she's talking with to observe it. Looks affected. Maybe it's a diversionary tactic, too.

"Only artists understand how existential a crisis like that can be. Labrador cured me. Our ship couldn't put in anywhere because it was too stormy. That's why I came back the next year. To see Battle Harbor. And Red Bay. You certainly know that Basques from Spain fished there five hundred years ago and built summer houses. I rented a little abode in Port Brendan and began to paint again. It was a release."

Just as I'm about to ask a follow-up question, Fred butts in.

"You complained about a black-and-white dog?"

She's taken aback, her big, blue eyes directed at Fred.

"Complained? That's not the right word. I saw the dog running free. The poor animal. It's so cold out. But"—her hand brushes away some invisible thing in the air—"I then learned it belonged to Kris. Kris Bakie, the chef. The dog had run away."

I want to know what sort of a person she is, so I hasten to speak up: "Does your family come to visit when you're here?"

Her eyes wander back to me. I ignore Fred's surly look as she speaks: "My husband comes sometimes—not often, he's very busy. He has a huge corporation. He's the CEO. He understands that I need peace and quiet to be creative. When I'm in Dallas, I must forever invite people over or go to receptions. Here, nobody disturbs me." She laughs. "I simply tell my friends that in Labrador they'll be eaten alive by mosquitoes in summer and that there are a lot of bears. So they're never tempted to visit me."

"Is that right about the mosquitoes?" The question escapes my lips spontaneously.

"Don't be afraid. If there's a wind, it's not a problem. It almost always blows along the coast in summertime."

She winks at me. Shannon is not only attractive; she also has considerable charisma.

"I'd like to come back to the dog because it was found dead," Fred says.

"Oh, no!" Shannon's smile disappears. "Was it run over?"

"We've only found the head, out there on the bay." Fred points to the ice.

"Just the head?" A vertical line appears on Shannon's forehead.

"Yes, did you see anything unusual on the ice?"

"You mean, did I see the dog on the ice?"

"Yes, or people with the dog."

She shakes her head.

"I'm often in the studio, painting. Then I'm totally absorbed and won't let myself be distracted."

"Did you see a blue garbage bag on the bay, either yesterday or the day before?"

"No. Why . . . The blizzard surely blew it away. Why do you ask?"

Is it slowly dawning on her that it's not only about a dead dog?

"The bag was weighed down with a fisherman's chain and was bright blue. That stands out. Constable Gates and Gerald Hynes drove out and brought it back from the ice."

Shannon's face has suddenly tensed up.

"You think somebody killed the dog? Could it have been coyotes? There are a lot in the area. What did Gerald say?"

"At the present moment we assume that somebody killed the dog and severed its head. But we're still waiting for the forensics report."

Shannon crosses her arms as if she has to protect herself.

"Does anybody want to take revenge on Kris?"

Fred and I burst out with the same question: "Does he have any enemies?"

She purses her full lips. "I can imagine there are some people who'd make short work of a stray dog."

"Would they do it to take revenge on Bakie?"

"I don't know. You'll have to ask people who know him better."

Fred is interested at once and follows up on the lead. "How well do you know him?"

"Just vaguely."

"He tried to come and see you yesterday. Constable Gates ran into him in front of your place."

If Shannon is surprised, she doesn't show it.

"He probably wanted to talk with me about the banquet in the Viking house. I'm organizing it with him."

She stands and gets the coffee pot from the kitchen and pours a second cup. Her hand is trembling slightly.

I think it's time for more information, because Shannon evidently hasn't seen anything on Facebook.

"We also found something else in the garbage bag, a cap from the Winter Olympics in Vancouver and a red sweatshirt with the words *Animals Are the Better People* on it. Apparently a young woman also had a shirt like that—Lorna Taylor, whose skeleton was found on Savage Beach recently."

Shannon sinks down in slow motion onto the divan.

"Can you repeat that?"

I list everything again.

Shannon looks at me, concentrating, and blinks.

"Does Ann Smith know about this? She lives in the house across the bay there. Have you asked her yet?"

"She phoned us because she saw something and thought it might be an injured animal."

At that moment we hear a telephone ring. It sounds like a land line. Shannon gives a start.

"Excuse me, but I must answer that."

She leaves the living room, and we hear her distant voice.

Fred finishes his sandwich. He doesn't respond to my questioning look, just the way I ignored him earlier.

Shannon storms back all of a sudden, her eyes wide open.

"Kris Bakie is dead. They found him in the Viking house. His sister just phoned me. She's talking about murder. Why did you keep that from me?"

We're both speechless. Too dumfounded that Bakie's sister is already talking about murder. Where was the leak this time?

Shannon sinks down on the divan again.

"Are you here because of that?" Her voice grows sharper.

"You ask me all these questions and tell me nothing! How am I supposed to trust you when you aren't open with me?"

I clarify for her that the next of kin must be notified first.

She clenches her fingers together.

"Is it really murder?"

"We're treating the circumstances around the death as suspicious."

"What happened? Who did it?"

"Unfortunately we cannot give out any details because it's an ongoing investigation."

I brush the bread crumbs off my lips with my napkin.

"Now that you know about Kris Bakie's death, I have to ask you some questions. Where were you yesterday at two o'clock?"

She suddenly stiffens up.

"Why do you want to know? Am I being dragged into this business?"

"It's part of our routine; we'd like to get to the bottom of this case as fast as possible."

"I already told you: I was painting in the house. I didn't hear anything."

I modify my tactics.

"Why did Bakie go to the Viking house? Did he plan to meet someone there?"

"How should I know? We wanted to put on a banquet in the Viking house. Maybe he was going to see how we could arrange the tables."

"There's no electricity there."

"Kris has a mobile kitchen in a minibus."

"How was he going to get the minibus out there?"

"On runners. Over the ice."

I still don't get it.

Fred speaks up again.

"Did you leave the house at any time yesterday?"

Shannon looks him up and down.

"Is this an official interrogation? Am I perhaps a suspect . . . ?"

"No, at this point we don't suspect anyone. We're trying to piece together a jigsaw puzzle."

"I can't help you any further. I must digest all of this. It's so awful. I hope you understand."

She reacts as I expected: she doesn't want to talk to us anymore. I ask where the bathroom is. I phone Closs from there and inform him that news of Bakie's violent death has reached Shannon Wilkey.

"Come to the office, and I want to have Fred here, too," he orders.

I blow my nose with a tissue and step on the lever of the shiny chrome garbage pail. A crumpled cigarette pack is lying in the trash. I recognize the brand instantly. Karelia. A Greek brand. I only know that because my father got upset years ago about the name of an actress in a TV soap opera. The character's name was Karelia.

"That's a kind of cigarette!" he exclaimed. "How can a woman be named after a cigarette?"

"But nobody in North America knows that," my mother retorted. Since then it's been a private joke in our family—out of Dad's hearing range, of course. Otherwise he never talks about Greece. He never goes to visit his family there, unlike my mother. Dad forbids her to travel to Greece with me or my six siblings. He must have experienced something horrible in his native country, but he never talks about it, and neither does my mother.

I have a difficult relationship with my father. Dad can't comprehend why I'm working for the RCMP. He can't bring himself to understand why I'm haunted in my dreams even today by the desperate scream of my schoolmate. He won't hear a word about that warm summer night when his daughter, who was lying half-awake by an open window, heard a blood-curdling cry for help. "Stop! You're hurting me!" His daughter, who did all she could to find the girl who screamed out her pain and her fear, but got no help. Dad never wanted to acknowledge that the police-woman in me was born during those weeks. Perhaps my father's stubborn attitude is the reason I've never really been interested in Greece.

And now a Karelia cigarette pack in Shannon Wilkey's bathroom. The brand has become very trendy in Vancouver, at least among dyed-in-the-wool smokers. I'd never have expected anybody in Port Brendan to know it.

20

There is so much tension in the air at the station that you can make electricity out of it. Closs has gathered me and the three others on the team around him. Situation review. Forensic evidence from the Viking house hasn't yielded much. No results yet for the fingerprints on the flashlight Fred and I found. It's a cheap Chinese model and for sale in Port Brendan. Austin Sullivan found that out. I'm still frustrated that Closs put him in charge of the forensic evidence and not me. I think Sullivan's mouth is bigger than his competence. He likes to brag about his time with the RCMP in White Hills in Northern Ontario. He let me know that, compared to then, working in Port Brendan is a walk in the park. All his swagger during murder investigations has to do with physical conflicts and not with sensitive details. One of his favorite topics is his performance in his personal workout room in the basement that he generously invited others on the team to use. He didn't invite me.

Sullivan thinks as Fred and I do, that the murder weapon is the Viking knife. It's being examined at this moment in Happy Valley-Goose Bay, as is Bakie's body. Frank Delgado lets Sullivan do the talking. Didn't he see anything of interest? Closs doesn't encourage him to say anything.

Fred must be also annoyed that he wasn't allowed to keep working at the crime scene. He asks the question that was on the tip of my tongue: "What was the victim knocked down with?"

"We're still looking for whatever it was," Sullivan informs us. "I assume that the perp is a strong man, because I think a single blow rendered the victim helpless."

"Do you know why the perp took a knife off the wall afterward and stabbed him? He could have just kept on hitting him."

"Out-of-control desire for revenge, maybe."

Now I had to disagree with that. "With only three not very convincing knife thrusts?"

I've investigated several knife murders in Vancouver that were committed in a furious frenzy. The medical examiners once counted over twenty stab wounds.

Sullivan shoots back at once. "Now what motive might my dear colleague find in this murder case? An argument about wooden spoons?"

Closs speaks up. "What do we know at this point about the snowmobile tracks?"

"One of the snowmobiles had wide runners," Delgado explains, finally breaking his silence. "It must be a rather large model."

"We'll follow that up immediately. Maybe there aren't many like it in this place."

"I've got one," Sullivan shouts out to the group. The men laugh.

"The murder most likely took place," Delgado continues, "between two in the afternoon, when Gates met the victim at Shannon Wilkey's place, and six in the evening."

That seems plausible to me. Another possibility is that the killer didn't want to miss supper and cause a stir unnecessarily. Supper in the south of Labrador is at five or five thirty. We can work with that until the medical examiner confirms the time of death.

"What about the boot prints?" I ask.

Silence. I think I know why. Probably any traces of those have been trampled flat by now by our people, the paramedics from Port Brendan, and the team from Happy Valley-Goose Bay.

"I thought you'd be able to tell us something about that, Gates. After all, you took the pictures." There's a mean smirk on Sullivan's lips.

"I'm putting the pictures on all the computers," Closs says. I gave them to him earlier.

Sullivan deflects at once.

"We'll go out again right now and take the Mini-CrimeScope with us."

I think there are better forensic light sources than the Mini-CrimeScope, but at least this station has a reliable instrument for making traces of blood visible under fluorescent light. We'll definitely find some on the wood of the walls in the dark Viking house.

It could all be much worse. Just a year ago there wasn't any cell phone reception in Port Brendan, Wendy told me. The government didn't reach an agreement with the phone company until very recently. Hurray for modern technology! It cost over a million dollars. The small villages and settlements are expensive for the provincial government. Damn expensive for the inhabitants who live in them, too. Groceries cost more, and if you order online you pay a hefty surcharge for long-distance shipping. Cars rust out more quickly; frost riddles the streets with potholes; asphalt crumbles. Ice and waves wreck the wooden docks in the port. Maybe I'll become a wreck here as well. But I don't want to stay long enough for that to happen.

Closs takes charge again. "Now get out there before it gets dark."

Sullivan and Delgado trot off.

The sergeant turns to Fred. "What did you get out of Shannon Wilkey?"

Fred summarizes our conversation for him.

"And the dog's head? What did you find out?"

This time Fred says nothing, and I've no choice but to answer for him.

"Shannon found out that the dog was Kris Bakie's, but she claims to know nothing about a blue garbage bag on the ice. She says she was painting in her studio the whole time, listening to music through her earbuds, and so she says she didn't observe or hear anything."

"We didn't see any studio; we'll have to go back and look for one," Fred adds.

"I think it's peculiar that Shannon seems to have had no idea about the contents of the garbage bag, although it's all been circulating on Facebook. I had the impression that it really made her nervous when we told her about it."

Maybe *nervous* isn't the right word. *Alarmed*, rather. But this isn't the place or time for such subtleties. I inform Closs about the rest of the conversation and how at the end Shannon clammed up.

"Let's wait until she's recovered from the shock," the boss advises. "Until now, Labrador was a wildly romantic idyll for this woman; now she's here in winter for the first time and, to make matters worse, somebody she knows has been killed."

"She claimed to know Bakie only vaguely."

Closs picks up his notebook. "You and Fred stay with the dog's head and the ax. They could very well have something to do with Bakie's murder."

"Or with Lorna Taylor's killing."

Lorna is dear to my heart because I don't want her to be forgotten in all the turmoil.

Closs is already at the door.

"Gather evidence for that, Gates. Then I'll gladly agree with you. I'm going to take a look at your photos of the land around the Viking house. I'll bet there are a couple of interesting imprints to be found in the snow."

Fred clears his throat and adds something else of importance. "Shannon has a telescope on a tripod in her living room. It's aimed at Ann Smith's house."

.

21

Gerald fills his coffee mug and stretches his legs in the hallway. One more hour, then the firearm safety course the provincial government requires will be over. Many people at the tables have joked about the course's title: "Gun Safety." He knows; he's taught it for years. The same worn-out gripes every time. Most of them think they took in their knowledge of firearms with their mother's milk. Just because they began shooting when they were kids. He, too, went duck hunting with his father as a little boy. When he was seven, he got a shotgun for Christmas. His father was not a passionate hunter, and his son took after him. But his mother wanted birds for the traditional Sunday dinner. No noon meal on Sunday was complete without the dark meat of murres, seabirds he thought looked like miniature, flying penguins. Sometimes the men also brought ducks home, or a gull, although gulls were protected and were not supposed to be hunted. His father never admitted to others that hunting was no fun for him, and so Gerald feels the same way. Hunting is considered masculine. Although women go deer-stalking, too. Just last year he applied for a hunting license for moose. The meat gets him and his elderly parents through the winter. It's tasty and lean, and his parents will also use it for sausage.

The coffee prompts an unpleasant feeling in his stomach. Not as refreshing as usual. Calista Gates wants to talk to him about the dead dog. She didn't say so directly, but he can imagine that's what it is. Under different circumstances, he'd welcome another meeting. A woman like her doesn't turn up in Port Brendan any old day. Yesterday he'd have had a keen interest in learning more about her, but today he used the course as a pretext to avoid her. He doesn't yet know how to explain to her why he professed not to know the dog. Of course he knows Kris Bakie's dog. And he's certainly not the only one. But he has absolutely no desire to talk about Bakie. The whole village knows Melissa left him for Kris. He told people afterward that their relationship had been strained for a long time. Truth is, it was a total surprise when Melissa suddenly moved out of his beautiful home one day. And it hurt him. He simply didn't see it coming. Nothing could persuade her to come back to him. He would have taken her back, at least at the beginning. But she's crazy about Bakie.

Gerald has never been able to figure it out. He was once sought after in Port Brendan as a man who managed to establish his own construction company. There was a time when women virtually flung themselves at him. Back then, he rarely said no. He regarded himself as God's gift to women. Then he met Melissa, fell head over heels in love, and they moved in together. He worked a lot—he admits it today—but Melissa profited from it. So he thought. She gave up her job in the school office and let herself be spoiled. Sometimes, when he just wanted to watch TV after a long day's work, she'd go to the Humpback Bar or go dancing in the Golden Anchor. He didn't mind—he's not the jealous type—he was sure of himself. But then he was bested by a successful chef who'd been all over Canada.

He hears shouting and excited voices coming from the classroom. It sounds like a very lively discussion. He has gone around a corner in the hallway to take a breather. In the past, he would have immediately joined the others to see what was going on. But since separating from Melissa, he'd sort of become a loner. Maybe he should have gotten out of Port Brendan and moved to Alberta or British Columbia like other young men. He'd once worked in Alberta for three years and made good money. But Labrador has him in its clutches. He finds everything he needs is right here. Except a congenial woman. Even so, when he drove down the main street to class this morning, he felt like a caged beast. The snowplow had cut a one-lane tunnel through the masses of snow. The white walls on either side were easily over twenty feet high. He could only go forward but couldn't turn around.

Boxed in. That's how he feels now.

A man leaves the classroom and tracks him down at the coffee machine. A worker from the fish factory. Volunteer fireman.

"Have you heard, Gerry?"

"What?"

"Kris Bakie's dead. The RCMP people found his body in the Viking house."

"Dead? Are you sure? What was he doing in the Viking house?"

He has barely asked the question when he realizes his response is the wrong one. He should have asked how Kris died. But the worker keeps talking.

"They're saying on Facebook that somebody killed him."

Gerald snorts in scorn.

"You really believe all the hogwash you hear."

Only then does he consciously absorb the news. Bakie murdered. Who did it? he'd like to ask, but bites his tongue in time.

The man is on the point of being insulted because Gerald doesn't want to find out anything more.

"So go ask somebody else if you don't believe me."

Gerald tosses his coffee cup into the trash. He has the feeling that he'll have to pay damn close attention from now on. When he returns to the classroom, all eyes are on him. He anticipates comments like "Hey, Gerry, what do you say about somebody knocking off Bakie?" But nobody dares to say anything; maybe they aren't sure, either, whether the rumor is true. He gets on with his instructing but has trouble concentrating. After the workshop's over, he'll certainly get an earful. Wild speculations.

It gets worse.

Calista Gates and Fred van Heisen are standing at the door as the participants put on their jackets.

"May we have a word?" van Heisen asks.

"Perhaps in there." Gates gestures toward the classroom behind him.

He grimaces instinctively.

"Only if nobody stands outside and listens."

They sit down at a table and wait until all the nosy people have gone.

Van Heisen gets right to the point. "We found Kris Bakie dead in the Viking house today. We suspect his death was violent."

So it's true. He rubs his thumb and forefinger together but stops when he notices himself doing it. "There's already been chatter about it on Facebook. People are talking about murder. Is it murder?"

"That's a possibility. We're waiting for the medical examiner's report."

"The guy in Happy Valley-Goose Bay?"

Van Heisen nods.

Gerald has had a lot to do with the people there as chief of the volunteer fire department. He's feeling hot.

"How'd he die?"

"We can't say at present. We're interrogating a list of people. Please tell us where you were between two and six yesterday afternoon."

Gerald has the presence of mind to keep calm. Of course they're going to question him. How could they not?

"I was at Dr. Perrell's house. I've been putting in a new kitchen for him, and I'm renovating some more. Then I went to my parents' like I do every day. They're both frail."

"Were you alone at Dr. Perrell's house?" van Heisen asks.

"Constable, am I a suspect?"

"No, we only want to be able to rule people out."

Calista Gates doesn't take her eyes off him. He's used to having women study him, but not like that. He mustn't get caught in another lie.

"I was alone at times, but a workman helped me later on."

"How long were you alone?" Van Heisen didn't stop looking at him, either.

"From about twelve to two, during lunch. But my pickup was parked in front. People probably saw it."

"Couldn't you have taken the snowmobile somewhere?"

"It was on the back of the truck, just in case."

"How many Ski-Doos do you own?"

"Two."

"Where was the second one?"

"In my parents' garage."

"Did you take it out somewhere?"

"No."

Gates has been taking notes and now takes over the questioning.

"Why did you claim you didn't know that dead dog?"

"There are a lot of black-and-white dogs around here."

That's an exaggeration, but he can't think of anything better.

"If I'd said it was Melissa's, and then it turned out that it wasn't, she'd have freaked out for nothing."

"According to Melissa, it's the only whoodle in southern Labrador."

Gates's voice is neither loud nor hard, but the message gets through nevertheless: don't you try to fool me.

"I don't know anything about that; I'm not a dog expert.

146

When I . . . when we found the garbage bag, I didn't really concentrate on the dog. I could barely make anything out during the storm."

He looks at the whiteboard in front of him with the main points about gun safety on it.

"The ax struck me. It could be mine. But I don't have anything to do with the dog's death."

His interrogators sit stock-still. He can imagine why. He's spilling the beans, and they want to let him keep on talking.

"There are green paint spots on the ax. Happened on the job. That's how I recognized it."

He looks at van Heisen, avoiding Gates's gaze.

"I lost the ax at some point. It was in the back of my truck. Some of my stuff gets swiped now and then when I leave it somewhere. That's why I keep most of my tools on the seats and lock up most of the time, though almost nobody does that around here. Sometimes when I'm in a hurry, I leave the keys in the ignition. Old habits die hard."

"Do you have any idea how the ax got into the bag?"

"No, that's beyond me. And like I said, I have nothing to do with the dog."

"So why all this secretiveness?" Calista Gates doesn't release him from her claws.

"Because I don't know what's really going on. You want answers from me. Then I've first got to figure out what's going on. It's not every day I find a dog's head and my ax at the same time."

"Can you make any more sense of it now?"

"No."

"And the wooden board with the Viking insignia?"

"What about it?"

"Was that stolen, too?"

He feels he's on solid ground again.

"Not on my watch. But I had to send a delivery back to the

sawmill because the measurements were wrong. What happened to it, I don't know."

"Any suspicion about who's behind the garbage bag?"

Gerald is taken aback. Behind the garbage bag, she asks. Not behind the murder. Where's she taking this?

He thinks about his answer. Does he need a lawyer? First the dog, then Bakie. He sees his world turning dark. Like the twilight outside lying over the houses and the ice in the bay. How swiftly everything can change. Not only for him and Bakie's family. For Melissa as well. And for the people in Port Brendan.

"It might be that somebody's trying to frame me."

"Who?" van Heisen asks.

"Melissa's family. Her brothers. Those people hate me."

"Why?"

Gerald clears his throat. It's disconcerting for him to disclose personal matters, but he's got to save his skin.

"They're furious with me because I didn't marry Melissa, although . . . although I gave her an engagement ring. They're convinced she wouldn't have hooked up with Bakie if I'd gotten her to the altar." He clears his throat again. "The Richardses saw me as a good match. They also think I should have compensated Melissa better because we lived together for six years. But I—she took me to court and I won."

"The family didn't approve of Melissa's relationship with Bakie? Wasn't he a good match? A widely acclaimed chef, a star?"

He's not surprised she's the one who asks that. She's not from these parts.

"He's an Inuk. An Inuk isn't good enough for the Richardses. They came over from Newfoundland, and far fewer Inuit live there than here in Labrador."

Gates exchanges glances with van Heisen. It's the first sign of silent communication between the two that Gerald has observed. Van Heisen strikes him as a lynx, silent, intent, lurking to get something. Unpredictable. Nobody knows much about him. What does he do when he's not on the job? Has he gotten a girlfriend? He doesn't belong to the volleyball club, and he's never seen at the ice rink, like Sergeant Closs and the others. Now and then, he's spotted jogging. Alone.

Gates addresses him again.

"I must ask this question: Was your separation from Melissa twice as hard because Melissa left you for an Inuk?"

At first he is seized with anger, but he quickly gets himself in check. Showing anger would really be bad.

"Why should that be? I've got Inuk ancestors myself, even if it doesn't show. My grandmother was an Inuk."

"Did Bakie have any enemies?" van Heisen asks.

The two of them are now working in tandem. Like he does with his foreman, Randy, who's been with him now for seven years.

"I can't answer that. He was no enemy of mine, if that's what you mean. I can't afford to have enemies. I'm running a business."

While he's talking, van Heisen's cell phone buzzes. He pushes a key and leaves the room. The door closes tight.

Gerald slides both hands down his face. He feels Gates's eyes on him.

"How did Melissa take it?" he inquires.

"Take it?"

"Bakie's death."

"We were at her place and her mother let us in briefly. She said Melissa was too distraught for the moment to talk to us."

"It was hard for me back then when she . . . but I don't wish her ill. Particularly after what's happened to Bakie. I . . . "

Van Heisen reenters the room. The look on his face does not bode well.

22

Fred tells Gerald Hynes he can go home because he allegedly has something important to discuss with me. I'm displeased. Hynes's hard shell was just beginning to crack. We might well have missed our chance.

What Fred reports annoys me even more. It seems Bernard Closs went to Melissa Richards's to seize Kris Bakie's laptop. Melissa refused to hand it over, arguing that it belongs to her as well.

"Now we've got to obtain a judge's approval first, and that can take time," Fred says. "The boss wants you and Melissa to talk, woman to woman, and bring her around to cough up the laptop."

My mouth opens wide, then shuts immediately—a good thing, because I might have let loose with something I'd have regretted afterward. What crap! It really could have waited. I try to stay objective.

"Melissa probably panicked and thinks she's under suspicion. But we told her mother we'd come back tomorrow."

Fred comes to Closs's defense.

"The sarge might be afraid she'd delete information that could help us."

"Does he really think Melissa has something to hide? Then he'd better have very good arguments for the judge if he wants a search warrant."

"He's hoping you can persuade Melissa."

"But she's completely in shock, for sure, and can hardly think straight. All we can do is give her time until tomorrow."

"You'd better work that out with the boss."

"I thought my communicating with the sergeant has to go through you, Fred."

He doesn't miss the sarcasm in my voice. His mouth widens.

"That was surely a . . . an oversight."

Yeah, sure, an oversight. But I don't want to argue with Fred. I've got something on the tip of my tongue.

"What's with Bakie's cell phone? He probably communicated by phone rather than by computer."

"I asked the boss that, too," Fred says tersely and stops. He avoids eye contact.

A light dawns.

"That can't be true. Tell me, please, it's not true."

"It is. It's somewhere in Bakie's inside pocket and went off to Happy Valley-Goose Bay. The sarge wants it back as fast as possible, naturally."

I shake my head. Sullivan and Delgado didn't take it out of the pocket. And Closs didn't ask about it. The phone is off to forensics in Happy Valley-Goose Bay, but we could have had a good look at it first and found important leads.

"So we'll have to just twiddle our thumbs and wait."

Something else occurs to me. All the time we were in the Viking house, Bakie's phone didn't make a sound. That could only mean he'd turned it off. Melissa told us she wasn't able to reach him. He obviously didn't want to talk to her. Interesting.

Fred changes the subject.

"What do you think of Hynes?"

"We've got to check out his alibi . . . and his Ski-Doos."

"Do you think what he says is credible?"

"I still don't understand why he didn't come out with the truth about the ax and the dog right away while we were on the ice. I held the ax right under his nose, and he didn't say a thing. Nada. At least he's a bit more talkative now. Too bad you interrupted my interrogation."

"Won't happen again, Gates. However . . . Hynes isn't stupid. Sooner or later somebody would have recognized an ax spattered with the green paint. His foreman, maybe." Fred puts his jacket on. "Does Melissa's family really hate him so much that they'd pin a dead dog's head on him? And maybe even a murder? And if so, why?"

We stand up and Fred adds: "So you'll take Melissa Richards? I'll take care of Hynes's foreman."

Before leaving the building, I scroll through the text messages on my phone. One is from Melissa Richards: "I want to talk to you alone. Tomorrow at ten?"

Well, that's a breakthrough. She didn't throw away my card.

I phone Closs and tell him about Melissa's text. He's got a reporter on the other line at the moment, and to my astonishment he doesn't insist on my seeing her this evening.

Once I get home, I warm up some soup. As I'm eating, it crosses my mind that I promised my godson, Jeremy, I'd videochat him. I lay the computer on the kitchen table and dial him up. When his innocent face appears on the screen, happiness hormones flow through me.

"Aunt Calista, what are you doing with that?"

He's spotted the snowmobile helmet on the dresser. Jeremy's two sisters crowd into the picture.

"It's my call," Jeremy shouts, pushing his sisters away. Five years old and so possessive.

I tell him about the piles of snow here, and he wants to see my snowmobile.

"It's already dark where we are," I explain to him, "I'll show you some other time. How's the guinea pig doing?"

He disappears, and I see the familiar living room of my oldest sister and her husband in the background; then Jeremy holds the guinea pig up to the camera.

"Mama says it's too fat and shouldn't eat so much."

His words are drowned out by a loud din. Not at his end, but at mine. Wouldn't you know.

"Wait a second, Jeremy, there's somebody at the door. I'll be right back."

I go around the corner and see some silhouettes through the door window. I open it carefully and stare at three little costumed figures before me, their faces hidden by some remnants of fabric.

A child's voice shouts, "We are mummers! Can we come in?"

"Mummers, mummers, we are mummers," a second, wildly excited voice. Kids in costume. I surrender and wave them inside.

"Come in," I say, and they follow me into the kitchen.

Jeremy is bug-eyed when I hold up the laptop to show him the procession.

"Look who's come to visit."

My nephew is momentarily speechless. Then there's a confusion of shouts and chatter, and soon all his siblings are in front of the screen. Even my sister shows her face for a minute.

"It's an old custom in Newfoundland and Labrador, and it's called mummering," I explain to them. "The people dress up in costume and go from house to house and dance; then you must give them something to drink."

Curiosity overcomes my little visitors when they hear voices emanating from my laptop. They take off their masks. They are Inuit children; one of them seems to be Rick Stout's daughter, Dulcie—Wendy told me about her Down syndrome. I don't know the two others.

"Are they going to dance now?" Jeremy asks, excitedly, giving his guinea pig back to his mother.

"Dancing, dancing," Rick's daughter repeats, beaming, and begins to hop around. The two others—they're boys—are probably a little older than Jeremy, and can't tear themselves away from the screen.

"We don't have any music to dance to," one of them shouts.

"Music, music, music," Dulcie sings, in high spirits. She looks seven, but I'm not a good guesser.

"I make music," Jeremy gets his child's guitar and strums it.

All the kids talk at the same time, in Vancouver and Port Brendan. Technology presents no obstacle to them; they've found out how to connect with one another. I watch the spectacle for a while until my sister thinks it's time to end the call.

Jeremy and the girls protest, but my sister promises them caramel corn. Unfortunately the mummers in the kitchen hear her, and I don't have any caramel corn.

I end our call and gaze into three expectant faces.

"Do your parents know where you are?"

They say yes so convincingly that I don't dispute them. I sit the children around the table and melt some chocolate into hot milk. I find some muffins in the cupboard. Georgina Closs really thought of everything.

While the trio are chattering away around the table, I do a futile search for Rick Stout's number in the phone book and on the Internet. Finally I resort to an old trick. I pick a number in Port Brendan at random and ask the woman on the phone for Rick Stout. It works: everybody knows everybody in the village. The woman gives the information out almost instantaneously.

When I dial the number, I get a woman's voice and leave a message. Surely it's Rick's wife Meeka. I sit down on a chair beside the children.

"Are you the police?" one of the boys asks.

"Yes, but I'm not working at the moment, not until morning."

Actually, I'm always on the job, and a lot of work is waiting for me.

The boy gives his and his brother's names, but I can't keep Inuit names in my head.

"Dulcie, Dulcie," Rick's daughter shouts and points to herself.

"Hello, Dulcie. I'm Calista."

A children's chorus repeats my name.

But Dulcie is doubtful.

"Carl, you are Carl?"

"No, Dulcie. Carl is the doctor. The doctor's name is Carl."

Silence around the table. Then a boy shouts: "Dulcie has to go to Dr. Carl."

His brother joins in and the two of them chant: "Dulcie doesn't want to go to Dr. Carl."

Dulcie's smile disappears. Suddenly tears stream down her face. I tell the boys to stop their teasing and caress Dulcie's cheeks and head until she calms down.

I have to think of something, and what comes out is: "Drink your hot chocolate, and I'll tell you the story of Sasquatch."

All eyes are on me while I tell them about the legendary ape-creature in the British Columbia wilds who appeals to the imagination of many Canadians.

Dulcie interrupts me all of a sudden and says, "Dr. Carl hurts the dog."

I stare at her.

"Why does he do that, Dulcie?"

"The dog, the dog," she replies.

The front door opens.

"Hello?" a man's voice calls.

Dulcie beams. "Daddy!"

I go into the hallway. Rick takes off his hat, visibly contrite.

"I'm so sorry the kids invaded your house. I had no idea they'd left. They are allowed to dress up but not to go outside."

"I'm glad you got my message. You certainly must have wondered where they were."

I don't ask him where he and his wife were.

"What message?"

"In your voice mail."

"Oh." He seems surprised and a little concerned. "I didn't listen to it. I just followed the footprints in the snow with my flashlight."

"So you didn't . . ."

His daughter sticks her head around the corner.

"Daddy, I'm a mummer."

"Come along, sweetie, we're going home. Where are the other two?"

"I'm staying here," comes from the kitchen.

Rick laughs.

"Mommy will be back soon, with chicken from Mary Brown's."

Instantly the two other Inuit children appear in the hallway, where little puddles have materialized on the floor.

"We had hot chocolate and muffins," the bigger boy announces.

"Well, weren't you lucky? And you haven't taken your boots off. You must take your shoes off in a stranger's house."

Turning to me he says: "They're always up to something, these rascals."

He opens the door and nudges them into the cold air.

I shout after him: "Thanks for clearing away the snow, Rick!"

He raises his hand as an answer. I watch them out the window going down to the house next door by the bright beam of the flashlight. I reheat the cooled-off soup. The table's covered with crumbs, along with three dirty cups. The kitchen suddenly seems lived in.

Rick might get a tongue-lashing from his wife when she learns that he lost track of the children for a while. Just a few days ago she probably would have laughed it off. But Bakie's murder must really alarm parents in Port Brendan.

And not only the locals. Also the "Come from Away"—that's

what strangers are called in Newfoundland and Labrador. Shannon Wilkey was visibly shocked by Bakie's death. She hadn't counted on something like that in her creative refuge in Labrador. She must have heard about Lorna's skeleton as well, although she's isolating herself. I wonder how Ann Smith is coping with the news of Bakie's murder. The dog's head definitely upset her, as I could easily see.

I clear the table and put the laptop back down. Then I type in Shannon's name in the search window. More than five thousand results turn up. Shannon at exhibitions. Shannon in front of one of her paintings. Shannon at an auction. Shannon as a socialite. Some photos show her with her husband. He looks considerably older than she does and is apparently prominent in the US. Newspaper articles describe him as an important, ultraconservative Republican Party donor. He was on the board of the New Gun Federation for a time.

I study picture after picture until my eyes are tired. Then one of them catches my eye. A photo during the Winter Olympics in Vancouver and Whistler. It shows Shannon at a reception at the US embassy for the American athletes. She's standing with the ambassador and three athletes next to a bear made of ice. I enlarge the photo on the screen. Shannon is wearing a cap with the Winter Olympics 2010 logo on it. A cap exactly like the one I found on the ice.

23

Before my brain injury, I had a phenomenal memory. Now it's merely normal. I've made it a habit to write down anything important immediately. Again and again, I mix up the letters as I write; that never used to happen. I also can't identify some smells anymore. Oddly enough, my sense of taste was preserved. I'm no longer dead-on when choosing an outfit, as one of my sisters observed. I know, it's an insignificant detail compared to other impairments, to my temporary loss of speech, say. It's irritating nevertheless because I used to be proud of my perfect flair for fashion. My doctor in Vancouver kept track of all these changes (she avoided the word *damage*). She admitted frankly that she was a bit confused, because she couldn't discover any pattern, any system to my impairments. But that's often the case with brain injuries, she said, a field that has scarcely been researched.

My doctor is not only confused, she's also fascinated. For instance, because I suddenly possess new abilities. I plan in the evening to wake up at six thirty. In the morning I wake up at six thirty. Yesterday I "programmed" myself for six o'clock, and I was awake at six on the dot. The cat we had when we were children had the same inner clock.

I also have brainstorms that suddenly hit me. Most of them

are very brief. Two days ago the words *coconut milk* clearly appeared before my inner eye. When I inquired about it at the Port Brendan supermarket, the manager informed me that she had recently stocked coconut milk for the first time in the history of the store. Dr. Perrell had asked her for it. Anyway, I can now make Thai noodle soup. Thank you, Dr. Perrell.

Today I'd love to have a vision about who Bakie's murderer is, but my brain won't play ball. It's 6:30 a.m. Time for the Qigong exercises my doctor prescribed. After that, I log on to the intranet, where we gather our office information. Yesterday I told the others about Gerald Hynes and the board with the insignia. His two Ski-Doos. I told them about Shannon Wilkey and the Olympic hat. It is all there. But nobody responded. Are they all still asleep? Seven o'clock. My radio turns on automatically. Kris Bakie is the number-one topic on the regional news, naturally. I hear Closs's voice saying the police are working around the clock to clear up the circumstances of his death. He doesn't utter the word *murder*. Beside Bakie, the public apparently has a burning interest for something else. The Winter Games, that is. They're normally held in Happy Valley-Goose Bay every three years. This year's will be a scaled-down version in Port Brendan because an anonymous, and apparently magnanimous, sponsor insisted on it. There are rumors that Shannon is that sponsor, but she neither confirmed nor denied it.

The mayor of Port Brendan states on the radio that the games will absolutely not be cancelled. He added that Labradorians have never given up in the face of adversity—he probably means Bakie's and Lorna Taylor's murders—and will not be intimidated now.

I butter my bread—homemade because I can't stand store-bought bread. Even the jam is homemade, not by me but by our dispatcher, Wendy. She wants to introduce me to Labrador's berry culture and predicts that, come summer, I'll go berry picking in the tundra like everybody else. Tundra. Me berry picking. If possible with a broad-brimmed hat and mosquito netting. I'll walk on water first.

Birds rejoice. My cell phone.

Closs. He gets straight to the point.

"We've got the medical examiner's report."

Adrenaline courses through my veins. I didn't count on getting the report so fast. Portents and miracles still happen.

"Not Bakie's. The dog's. He was poisoned. Rat poison."

"Why'd they do the dog first?" I exclaim.

"Maybe it was faster—or the ME is a dog lover. What do I know?"

"The ME surely didn't send the report at seven in the morning."

"That's not the point right now."

Oh no, that is the very point. The ME sent the report yesterday evening for certain, when Closs was still in the office. But I wasn't informed until many hours later. Now Closs knows that I know.

But that doesn't stop him.

"Tissue and muscles were cut by a sharp knife, the spine with a bone saw."

I'm startled.

"Why all that effort? It would have been faster with an ax or a chainsaw."

"Maybe the perp happened to have these tools with him. Maybe he's a hunter."

Almost the entire male population of Port Brendan and part of the female population hunts.

"What about the ax?"

"The perp probably put it in the blue bag afterward."

"So you think Hynes is behind it? But why would he have put his own ax in there?"

"Well, it can be any old ax."

"No, he let us know that it is *his* ax. He recognized it by the green paint spatter. Was van Heisen able to talk with Hynes's foreman?"

"Not yet. He's searching for the dog's remains."

"Anything come of it?"

"No, or it would be in the intranet."

Really? A lot of things are missing from the intranet. So much for a well-coordinated team. If this doesn't change, I'll bring it up. And probably make myself unpopular. I'm also aware that Closs hasn't called me because of the dog. He needs me to interrogate Melissa Richards because she gave him the brush-off, and a search warrant takes more of an effort.

He finally asks: "So you're going to get Bakie's laptop today?"

"I'll do everything I can to get it."

"It's urgently needed."

As if I didn't know.

"What do you think of the picture with Shannon and that cap, Sergeant?"

"They probably sold thousands of them during the Olympics. Doesn't necessarily mean anything. But follow up that lead anyway."

I hear a snow blower in front of the house and rush to the window. Rick Stout. Now I can use the SUV.

"I'll be at Melissa's at ten," I shout at my cell, not realizing until later that Closs has already ended the call.

I make a second cup of coffee. So, rat poison. I need to find out if it's sold in Port Brendan's hardware store and who might have bought any. I do a quick search on the internet to see which brands are sold in Labrador. I stumble across a newspaper article where a journalist from Labrador complains that store-bought rat poison doesn't work because rats and mice have to eat it for days until it finishes them off. More efficient are the rat bait blocks sold in Alberta, he writes, which is why there are no more rats there. To get these blocks in Labrador, you've got to put up with a background check and pay $250 for a permit.

The poor dog definitely didn't have to spend days nibbling on the poison. I send Closs a text: "What kind of rat poison?" because there's nothing about it on the intranet. Then I text Fred, telling him about my research and asking about Hynes's foreman.

"Working on it, more later," he replies.

But I don't hear anything from anybody for a long time. Only when I've finished breakfast does a text message from Closs arrive: "Gates, we're patrolling Port Brendan to be more conspicuous. Can you take over until ten?"

That's not a question, of course, but an order. I understand why Closs wants to keep the population calm, mainly because of the Winter Games, but in my mind solving the crime quickly would achieve more than driving around in the village.

At least I can take my heated SUV. I quickly scan the weather report. No snowstorm is predicted for today, which is unusual for March because there are normally several storms this time of year; they occur so regularly that the locals have given them names. "The Lioness" usually arrives at the beginning of March, I see on the weather page, and right now everybody's waiting for "Sheila's Brush" and hoping that this blizzard won't hit until after the games.

My mood picks up when the motor of my Ford Edge kicks in reliably, in spite of the cold. Good neighbor Rick has really done a fine job in front of the house. The small pleasures of a Labrador winter. I patrol between walls of snow and the houses of Port Brendan, drive past six churches with more parking spaces in front of them than the supermarket and the clinic have. Three cars are parked in front of Mary Brown's, the chicken restaurant. Pickup trucks in the village are almost all gray, silver, white, black, or dark blue. The palette of the local Ford and Chevrolet dealer.

The street becomes one-way going down to the harbor, a

narrow breach in a white fort. I have to back up because a pickup is coming at me. I take the road to the red-and-white lighthouse, park in front of it, leave the motor running, and have some coffee from my Thermos. Nothing catches my eye on the ice-covered ocean, not even a seal. I'd hoped to see some harp seal pups, but the mothers brought them into the world far out on the ice, where they're safe from seal hunters because fishing boats can't get out to them.

My thoughts roam over the icy wilderness that's strewn with glassy cubes. I've got so many questions. Why did somebody deposit a conspicuous, blue garbage bag containing a dog's head, an ax, a marked piece of wood, a red sweatshirt, and a cap from the Vancouver Olympics out on the ice and weigh it down with a fisherman's chain? If it was a warning, then to whom? To Kris Bakie? But the perp didn't wait long enough for him to get it. The chef was dead a day later. A warning to Ann Smith or Shannon Wilkey, because the bag was placed within sight of their homes? Could one of them be in danger?

The board with the stamp on it and the red sweatshirt point to Lorna; the dog's head indicates a trail to Bakie. But why the cap and the ax? And the chain?

Shannon was in Vancouver and Whistler the year the Olympics took place, and she wore the same cap. Ann Smith reported the blue bag and turned pale when I revealed its contents to her. But perhaps I'm barking up the completely wrong tree.

A car parks beside me. Fred van Heisen.

He opens the door of my Ford and slides onto the passenger seat.

"Didn't think I'd find you down here," is his greeting. His beaver-fur hat with earflaps makes him look like a trapper. Fred actually fits in, in Port Brendan; with his weather-beaten face, he could easily pass for a Labradorean. A good-looking Labradorean. All he's missing is their sense of humor.

I pick up my Thermos.

"Closs sent me on patrol until ten. What are *you* doing here?"

"I was just trying to turn my car around in this labyrinth when I saw you. Saves me texting."

"Coffee?"

He declines with thanks, and I screw the cap back on.

I have to worm everything out of him.

"What's new?"

"I caught up with Hynes's foreman. Randy. He can't give him an alibi for two hours around noon. But Bakie was alive at that time, of course. I could tell that he was holding something back."

Fred does that, too—holds things back—until I ask him, "So?"

C'mon, Fred, cut the suspense!

"Melissa Richards came to Perrell's house that afternoon, where the foreman and Hynes were hard at work."

"When was that?"

"She got there shortly before four and stayed for half an hour."

"What did they talk about?"

"The foreman doesn't know because they went off to another room."

"Wow!" I have to process that for a moment. "Melissa said nothing about that; neither did Hynes. Why would he keep that quiet? He's not stupid, after all; he knows we'll find out about it."

Fred toys with his gloves.

"He's protecting somebody."

"Surely not himself. Now we're going to pick him apart."

"Protecting not him, somebody else."

"Certainly not Melissa."

"Why not?"

"Because she left him for Bakie."

"People have complicated feelings."

I look sideways at Fred. Is he talking about himself?

He keeps looking at the ice. No sun today, just a slate-gray, overcast sky. My feelings are definitely complicated. Martin left me when I needed him most. Nevertheless, I'm attached to our years of marriage; they were good. At least as I recall them. I still don't understand how he could give all that up. And why, now that I'm a lot better, he doesn't want to come back. He's simply replaced me with someone else. And I don't even know who that is. Don't even want to.

I suddenly realize that my eyes are filling up with tears. Shit, that's the last thing I need.

"You don't think by any chance that Melissa has something to do with Bakie's death?" I ask hurriedly.

Fred turns to me, hesitates. Does he notice my moist eyes? They almost always weep in the raw wind here; he certainly won't pick up on it.

He waits a couple of seconds before answering.

"You can find that out when you're at her place today. I'm going to take a peek at Hynes's two snowmobiles."

"The board with the insignia," I say, "is the connection to Lorna's crate. Not too many people could have known that we found a board like that on the crate."

"You might be mistaken there. Scott Dyson has certainly told everybody what he found. That got him a lot of attention, which he is sure to have enjoyed."

"We'll have to have another go at him. And Grace Butt, Lorna's friend."

"She lives in Happy Valley-Goose Bay."

"She's coming to Port Brendan today for the funeral."

"That's where Delgado and Sullivan are going."

I look at Fred and—dramatically exaggerating—arch my eyebrows.

"My dear colleague, Grace is one of mine. The sarge assigned the ladies to me, or did he not?"

"Please, call me Fred," is his retort.

24

I don't park directly opposite Melissa Richards's house. Not everybody has to know that's where I'm going. Besides, a blue SUV is already there, a shiny, new one. I hope it's not Melissa's mother's. I've heard she guards her daughter like a mother hen. I want to talk to Melissa alone. As I approach the house, a man comes out the door. Dr. Perrell. He seems less surprised by our meeting than I am.

"Constable, good morning," he says as he greets me.

He's wearing a thick, colorful scarf around his neck and a Russian fur hat. He looks very different from the way he looks in a white smock.

I return his hello.

"Are you here as a doctor?"

Hopefully Melissa's able to be questioned.

"As a human being," he says. "As a human being." He stops. "What a terrible business. Kris was a wonderful man. He put an enormous amount of energy into planning for the banquet."

I breathe out white air as I speak, just like him.

"What will you do now?"

"The fundraising event will go on; there's too much at stake, and those involved want to carry on. But we'll have to rethink some things."

He must have spoken with Melissa about it. His eyes are fixed on the RCMP badge on my jacket.

"How's the investigation going?"

"You'll have to ask Sergeant Closs. You've heard about the dead dog and the ax on the ice?"

"Yes, yes . . . that I have. Do you think it has anything to do with Bakie's murder?"

"We're following up on every theory. What do you think?"

"Me? Why me?"

He looks as if my question were an imposition on him.

"I just thought—perhaps you as a doctor hear things that don't make it to the police."

"That's your department, not mine. I have plenty to do with my profession. There is such a thing as a doctor-patient privilege, as you surely know."

He turns to leave.

"Excuse me, work calls."

I play my last card.

"Did a patient come to you recently with what looked like poisoning? Bakie's dog was apparently poisoned. Rat poison."

He walks on as he calls back over his shoulder, "You'll probably find rat poison in every house in this place."

Then he gets into the blue SUV and drives off.

I concentrate on my imminent conversation with Bakie's fiancée. Her house is a little white bungalow, identifiable by a red door. All the windows are covered with fake white mullions, as is the fashion in Port Brendan. Perhaps that artificial lattice is meant to affect Victorian coziness. To me they look like crosshairs. I knock and go right into the hallway.

I shout, but nobody appears. My watch says it's five after ten. I hear water running somewhere. Sounds like a shower. I call Melissa's name several times. The rush of water stops. At last a door opens, and Melissa appears in a fluffy bath robe. Her copper-red hair is wrapped in a towel.

"Grab a seat in the living room," she says, "I'll be dressed in a minute."

The living room opens out from the hallway. Decorative sayings in white gleam from the dark, aubergine-colored walls: "Life is too short to be anything but happy." I ask myself what's she doing now with these pearls of wisdom. "Live in the moment and know there's a reason for everything." The biggest motto is mounted over the sofa: "We're all one family together."

That's where I'm standing as Melissa comes in.

She has tied up her wet hair in a knot. Exactly the way I wear mine. She comes up beside me and remarks bitterly: "He didn't want a family, at least not with me."

I look at her in surprise. She drops into a black leather armchair—dark leather is the height of fashion in Port Brendan—and stares out the window through its crosshairs.

"I so wanted a baby with him, but he was against it. All he was interested in was his career and the restaurant and his own TV cooking show. He said he didn't have the time for kids."

I sit down facing Melissa. She's not wearing makeup; her face is pale and swollen, her blue eyes are red-rimmed. With her hair gathered up, she looks younger. She's wearing comfortable, gray sweatpants and a T-shirt with the phrase *Life's a Beach* on it. Her house is overheated—like all houses in Port Brendan—which lets the locals wear short-sleeved T-shirts in winter. I'm sweating and take off my jacket. Even in the middle of summer in Vancouver I don't sweat as much as in the houses here. I hate feeling beads of perspiration under my clothing. To say nothing of a damp face.

"The Inuit love children," she goes on. "Children are the most important thing for them—but Kris . . . " She shrugs.

It occurs to me that she could have had children with Gerald Hynes. Kris was her second chance, the second lost opportunity.

"How old are you, Melissa?"

"Twenty-eight. Kris is a year younger than me."

She talks about him in the present tense, as if he were still alive.

"Women here used to marry at fifteen and have babies. That was common."

Child brides, I think to myself.

"When was 'used to'?"

"My mother had her first at seventeen. That was normal back then."

"And how many after that?"

"Six. The last when she was twenty-eight."

Which explains Melissa's panic at the last minute.

I tell her that I also have six siblings. My mother married at twenty-one when she was pregnant with my oldest sister. Mom sometimes asks if I don't want to have a baby soon. But I love my work. My children are the children in the world that I want to protect. Martin, my ex-husband (how awful that word sounds!), was happy without offspring. Maybe that's changed now that he and I are divorced.

I sense Melissa wants to confide in me, so I zero in on this opening before it can close up again.

"Was anybody hostile toward Kris?"

She shakes her head slowly.

"Some people are certainly jealous. If somebody like Kris is successful, then not everybody wishes him well. But that's not a reason . . . a reason to kill somebody . . . " Her voice breaks.

"Did he ever tell you about any conflicts he had with people?"

She thinks about it, her swollen eyelids hanging heavily over her eyes.

"A childhood friend of his is a drug addict. Kris wanted to give him a chance, a job in the restaurant as a dishwasher. I told him immediately: no way. But he didn't listen to me. Of course things didn't go well. Kris had to let him go. The guy was on his case for a while about that."

I ask for the man's name and location and write them down. I keep at it, asking for possible enemies and motives, but Melissa can't come up with anything concrete. Or doesn't want to. We need to take a closer look at her family.

I pursue another lead in a surprise attack.

"Why did you meet Gerald Hynes at Dr. Perrell's place Thursday afternoon?"

She sinks farther back in her chair, as if seeking protection.

"I wanted to know if he did anything to our dog."

"That's not how he described it." A bit of a bluff.

Her fingers dig into the leather.

"What did he tell you?"

"You can help us find out who did it as fast as we possibly can, Melissa. We need your cooperation. Please help us."

I watch her face working. Then comes the breakthrough.

"I went to Gerald because I was desperate. I wanted to pour out my heart to somebody. My mother . . . if I tell my mother, the whole family will know about it afterward. And one of my girl-friends—people don't have to know everything."

I wait.

And the confession comes.

"Shannon Wilkey—Kris hoped that she would make him known in America. The two spent so much time together, supposedly talking about fundraising. That's why Kris and I fought on Wednesday. It was . . . bad . . . I shouldn't have said certain things. He didn't come home that night. I first thought he'd spent the night somewhere else." She pressed her lips together.

Before the pain can overwhelm her again, I quickly interject: "What did you say to him that you regret saying now?"

She hesitates.

Just don't drop this thread.

"Melissa, everything's important. I don't judge you for these things. Anything can happen in a fight that you might wish hadn't afterward."

She thinks for a bit, then spits it out. "I threatened Kris and said I'd kill Arrow if he met up with Shannon one more time. But I didn't do anything to the dog."

Now she bursts into tears.

I feel pity for her, I admit. This pain of the heart, this abysmal despair—I experienced it. The terrible knowing that you cannot undo something. But it mustn't cloud my judgement.

Melissa stands up to go get a box of tissues.

When her sobs recede, I move ahead, gently: "Did Kris believe you, that you'd do something to the dog?"

"I don't know," she says in a completely different voice. "He gave me the dog as a present, as a substitute for a child. To divert me. But I don't want a dog. Arrow was his dog anyway. Arrow followed him around everywhere."

Did the killer want to get rid of the dog first, then Bakie?

"The dog was poisoned. Can you think of anyone who might have done it?"

I watch her closely. She gives me a blank stare.

"Many people would get worked up when Arrow did his business in their garden. Kris always let him run around loose. He didn't want to tie Arrow up."

"You told us that Gerald Hynes might have had something to do with it."

"Yes, I said that because he acted with you as if he didn't know the dog."

"So you don't suspect him?"

"No, Gerald loves dogs."

He didn't show it when he was out there on the ice. And denied knowing the dog afterward. I recalled Fred's words: He's protecting somebody.

I repeat the question: "So why did you go see him?"

"I wanted to find out what he knew about Shannon. He built her house. There are rumors that he . . . that he sometimes goes to see her and stays for a rather long time, if you get my meaning."

I play dumb.

"No, I don't quite understand."

"I thought Gerald would be interested in knowing that Shannon was interested in Kris."

"You thought Gerald was having an affair with Shannon and would see Kris as a potential rival and confront him?"

Instead of agreeing, she makes a face that speaks volumes. Apparently I've hit the bull's eye. It's getting better and better.

"You know, of course, that Shannon's married," I say.

Melissa breathes out noisily in disgust.

"Well, that woman is here all by herself, for months on end. So what kind of a marriage is that?"

Not the traditional one that Melissa hoped for with Kris, that's for sure. The one she never had. It's not surprising that many of the locals see Shannon as a suspect. A married woman living alone for months at a time is asking for all sorts of gossip. All the more if she's attractive.

"Many women, especially artists, need solitude in order to be creative," I add.

"But they're just looking for a man!" Melissa exclaims, now more angry than sorrowful. "And that other one, Ann Smith— what's she really doing here? She walks around for miles, at night, too. People often see her with a headlamp, far away from her home. Why does she slink around at night?"

"Why do you think she does?"

"She's meeting a guy somewhere and doesn't want anybody to see her car."

"Meeting who?"

"No idea. But I can tell you one thing: That's the reason Ann's living here."

She's not crying anymore. It's time to ask her about the laptop.

"Thank you very much for your trust, Melissa," I say warily. "Your information is very valuable for me. You can be sure that we're doing everything we can to solve your fiancé's murder. We're happy for any information that can bring us closer to that goal. That's why that laptop can be very useful for us."

To my astonishment, she nods and stands up.

"I'll go get it."

So I take the longed-for trophy without the feared resistance. She gives me the passwords for Bakie's Hotmail account and social media: Arrow1, Arrow2 and so on. Bakie didn't set one for the computer itself. I can't fathom how casually many people treat computer security. I suspect Bakie didn't know that Melissa knew his passwords. Maybe she deleted files last night, but it shouldn't be a problem for our police techies to retrieve them.

The front door opens. Steps in the hallway. A young man is suddenly standing in the room. Melissa gets to her feet and throws herself into his arms; he puts them around her protectively. She starts sobbing loudly again, and the young man looks at me in reproach.

"I'm Sergeant Calista Gates of the RCMP," I say.

Melissa frees herself from their embrace.

"This is my brother, Dennis."

"Are you finished?" her brother asks. "Melissa needs peace and quiet."

His muscles are so monstrous that they look like they've been blown up with an air pump.

"Of course, I fully understand," I mutter, putting on my gloves and quickly slipping the laptop into my rucksack. Her brother casts a suspicious eye on me. Before he realizes whose laptop it is, I'm out the door.

25

My car is unlocked. Not good. I mustn't be careless like that. Is my brain deserting me, maybe? As it did with my open basement door? I turn up the heat in the cold car and take a quick look at my messages. A text catches my eye:

We're still desperately looking for people who can host some athletes in the Winter Games. My husband said you'd offered to put somebody up. Is the offer still on? Two young athletes from Happy Valley-Goose Bay need a room for one week.

Georgina Closs has tracked me down. Can I refuse my boss's wife anything? Shortly after I arrived, Closs asked everybody in the office if anyone could free up a room for one or more of the participants in the games. This was in keeping with the idea that if we help the community, people will help the police.

I've had just one brief conversation with Georgina. In the supermarket. Although it was our first meeting, she knew at once who I was. Maybe she saw my picture when the local paper featured the new policewoman. Two little blond braids peeked out from her pointed cap, which suited her snub-nosed, child's face. The corners of her mouth turned far upward when she smiled, which she did almost continuously. She was awfully nice to me, almost affectionate. I hadn't pictured Closs's wife like that. She was congenial but inscrutable.

Georgina knew about my guest room with a bathroom in my basement. She'd helped find the house when it was decided that the RCMP in Port Brendan needed reinforcements. She's a nurse at the clinic and knows every Tom, Dick, and Harry in town. I'm not enthusiastic about the thought of having strangers as house-guests for a week. Of course I don't let on a word of this to Georgina.

Offer still stands. Have room for two, I text her back.

I let my smartphone sink down in my lap. A man and a woman have been murdered, but life goes on. Everybody seems busy with the Winter Games.

The heat's on, and the car's warming up. I enter Fred's number. He's in a hurry.

"Where's the fire?"

"I've got Bakie's laptop. Have you seen Hynes?" I ask.

"No, I'm on the highway. A pickup hit a moose. Closs sent me."

What a weird way of doing things. We've got two murders to investigate, but our men are going after traffic accidents.

"Good heavens! Anybody hurt?"

My gaze falls on the passenger seat. Some dirt on it. Has it been here long? I didn't notice it this morning. Was somebody in my car when I was questioning Melissa? I even locked my bedroom door last night. Hope it isn't dog shit.

"The moose is dead, but the driver was injured. She's already in the clinic."

My thoughts flash to Perrell. Should I tell Fred what Dulcie Stout came out with yesterday? *Dr. Carl hurts the dog.* I ought to talk to the doctor about it, but I've got other plans right now. I tell him I'd like to speak with Hynes again. Melissa told me she poisoned his mind against Kris Bakie.

"Yes, go see him. I'll call later," Fred says.

I go to Tim Hortons first—I want a doughnut and coffee. As I'm standing in line at the counter, an elderly lady in a pink down jacket speaks to me.

"Is it true that somebody in Port Brendan is poisoning dogs? I have a dachshund. I keep him inside, but sometimes he just runs out the door at a passer-by. He comes back after a half hour or so. I don't want anything to happen to him."

She looks at me expectantly. Completely worried about her dog.

Isn't she worried about Kris Bakie's murder?

"Who told you that?" I respond. I gave Melissa the information just half an hour ago, and the whole village already knows.

"I heard it in the clinic. My niece works there."

In the clinic. Interesting. The lady doesn't give me any time to think; she wants reassurance. And I give it to her; I mustn't make the customers in Tim Hortons nervous. Besides, I assume the poisoning was targeted. The bright blue garbage bag on the ice isn't a coincidence.

I have two cups of coffee in my hands as I go into Dr. Perrell's house. A grand building with a balustrade and a two-car garage. Not many of these in Port Brendan. Music comes from the kitchen. Classical. My guess is Mozart. I wouldn't have expected that from Hynes. He's in a T-shirt and jeans, standing at the kitchen unit and sticking a backsplash of tiles onto the wall. With his arm muscles and tight rear end, he could pass for one of the workmen in the popular renovation series on TV. He's alone. As he was during those two hours on the day of the murder, for which he has no witnesses.

He can't hear me on account of the loud music, but he notices me when I move around. A few steps and he's at the radio, turning the music off.

"You really listen to Mozart?" I ask.

"No, Franz Joseph Haydn."

He smirks because I can't hide my amazement.

"Why shouldn't I like classical music? Because I'm a contractor in Labrador? You probably think everybody around here lives under a rock. Or in igloos."

Something clatters onto the floor next to him. A box cutter with a sharp blade. He picks it up.

"I played the violin when I was a kid. My mother was a teacher in Port Brendan."

I remove my jacket. Icy cold and boiling heat live cheek by jowl in Labrador. I hand him the second coffee cup without a word. He touches my fingers as he takes it. He has the upper hand in this situation, and he's enjoying it. He doesn't thank me. It occurs to me that people here never thank you for a nice gesture. Maybe it's because of the fact that it's a given that people will help one another.

"Do you like the new kitchen?"

He looks around with pride.

"I designed and built the cupboards myself. Dr. Perrell more or less accepted my suggestions."

Hynes astounds me once more. The kitchen is precisely to my taste. Modern and timeless at the same time, in classic blue-gray and white with black accents; the floor is a light color and has a Scandinavian effect. Dr. Perrell must be happy with it. I compliment Hynes and ask where we can sit down. He takes me to the living room, which is less impressive: the same old leather seating arrangement combined with black furniture. Hynes plops into a reclining chair.

"I've been expecting you. You were at Melissa's this morning."

It annoys me that he knows.

"Did Melissa call you?"

"No, Dr. Perrell mentioned it when he took a quick peek in earlier. Melissa surely told you that she came to see me."

I don't disclose to him that it was the foreman who told Fred. I don't want the guy to have any problems with Hynes.

"I'd rather have had the information from you. You must be more open with us, Mister Hynes."

"Gerald, to you, Constable Gates." He drinks his coffee as if it were beer. "I would certainly have told you, but your partner, van Heisen, ended our conversation."

"Are you and Shannon Wilkey together?"

He looks almost scandalized.

"What gives you that idea?"

"Melissa thought you might be."

"Why is this important?" He gets up, furious.

That's the moment I feel it. The tingling in my hands and feet. The tightness in my stomach. Something climbs up inside me, like a thick snake. Dammit. I did take my pill this morning. Or maybe I didn't?

"Can I have a glass of water?" I exclaim, fumbling around in my jacket pocket. Grab the little bottle. Can't open because of the child-proofing; my head's already swimming.

Gerald kneels down in front of me and hands me some water, but I can't hold the glass.

"Open this, please."

I press the pill bottle into his hand. My voice is already very weak. I feel him laying the pill on my tongue and giving me some water.

"No ambulance, don't call an ambulance," I manage to get out.

The shaking begins.

As if a crocodile has me in its jaws. Then I black out.

When I come to, I'm lying on the sofa and Hynes is holding my hand.

I slowly recognize my surroundings again.

"Can you understand me?" he asks.

I nod. Breathe deeply in and out until I can sit up. Now he lets go of my hand. I feel ashamed. How could this happen? How could I ever forget my pill?

"How long was I out?"

"Just for a little while. What's the matter?"

Just for a little while. So not a proper attack. For the moment, I'm relieved.

"I've got low blood pressure. Too little sugar in my blood. If I go without eating for a long time, everything goes black." The words come easily to my lips.

"I'll get a sandwich."

Gerald rushes into the kitchen and comes back with a clear sandwich bag.

"Eat this. And drink your coffee. Should I warm it up in the microwave?"

"Yes, please. Thanks a lot."

He watches me open the bag with trembling fingers. Typical white bread with ham, tomatoes, and mustard. I've got no choice but to eat it under his watchful eye.

Now I've really made a mess of things. I've become his supplicant.

"Please don't tell anybody anything. I don't want to be the talk of the town."

He makes a dismissive gesture.

"Don't give it a thought. I'll be silent as the grave."

He is that already, I think to myself. He says nothing about Melissa and Shannon.

When he comes back with the hot coffee, he has a request to make.

"Shannon Wilkey is an important client of mine. Building her house was a huge contract. It was a big boost for my business. Maybe she'll build something else. I'd like her to come my way again."

That makes sense to me. But is he concerned about his business or Shannon's affections? Maybe Melissa's speculating a little too wildly. She also suspects that Ann Smith is here because of a man. She views every traveling lady as a threat.

At that moment, the lights go out.

Hynes swears.

"Shit. Another power failure!"

It's better I leave. I wash down the mushy sandwich with my coffee and attempt to act in a professional manner.

"We are not aiming to destroy your business, Gerald; we have a murder case to solve. Two murder cases. You can help us with everything you know."

I've scarcely uttered the words when an image appears before my inner eye. Oh, my God! One of my visions. My brain is really going berserk today.

I see a dog's head. And a hand with a scalpel.

26

He logs in to Kris Bakie's email account and searches through it. Bakie was obviously not big on email, which is no surprise to Bernard Closs. Young people prefer to text on their phones. And Bakie's cell phone is still in Happy Valley-Goose Bay, a thought that frustrates him to no end. So for the time being all he has is the laptop. He could have handed this job to Calista Gates as a thank-you for securing the device and the passwords. His survival instinct, however, says no. He wants to keep the reins of the investigation firmly in hand. He'd read the disappointment in Gates's eyes, though she didn't say anything. That's why he told her that Lorna Taylor's funeral begins at three. She wouldn't miss it for the world, and he won't stop her from going, even though he's officially sent Sullivan and Delgado to it.

He'd been immersed in Bakie's laptop content when the power went out. Happens here all the time. They have a generator at the station, but he can't concentrate with the roar it makes. So he takes time to organize his notes. Gates suggested scrutinizing Dr. Perrell more thoroughly. But she doesn't want to take it on herself because he's her doctor. He can't put Fred van Heisen on Perrell because he's being treated by him as well. He didn't ask

Fred what his health problems are. The two other men are on their way to interview members of the Bakie family. He has to wait until they're back and hopes that they aren't Perrell's patients also. Otherwise he'll have to go himself, though he'd like to avoid that since his wife works in the hospital.

The power is back. Wendy brings him a hot tea. She didn't have to, but she's always looking for an excuse to have a little chat. Maybe Gates is right: their dispatcher probably overhears too much about the investigation.

"I've heard that NTV wants to film the funeral, but Reverend Herschell is against it," she comments.

Bernard can't hold it against the pastor. He's just as unhappy with it himself, feeling pressure from the media and the public. There's no talk as yet of sending an outside investigative team to Port Brendan. At least for the present. He knows deep down that he can thank Gates for that. She's the outside team. He must keep her in check and simultaneously let her do her thing. Difficult and nerve-racking.

"As long as the cameras are outside the cemetery, they have a right to be there," he grumbles.

"If you don't mind, I'd like to go, too," Wendy says. Naturally —everybody who's got legs and a cap wants to be at the funeral of the year.

"Go ahead, I'll hold down the fort," he replies, leaning over the laptop again.

Gates told him about an old friend of Bakie's who once worked in his restaurant and had a falling out with him. He remembers that character. A junkie who's registered with the police. He was in the slammer more than once for breaking the law. He apparently leads a drug-free life now and will take part in the snowshoe race at the Winter Games.

The Winter Games. Why is it they must take place now of all times and in Port Brendan of all places? When his team is already up to its eyeballs in work. He's heard through the grapevine that Bakie's murder hasn't made the locals concerned about their safety. The whites apparently believe that a rivalry among the Inuit is to blame. The Inuit, for their part, assume that a jealous white man did away with him. He wonders what people think of Lorna Taylor's murder, then. Not even her death will stop the Winter Games. For the inhabitants of Port Brendan, the games are a marvelous occasion. Even his kids are in them. Georgina drives them to practice. She complains that he, as their father, isn't involved enough. But it's just that right now the murder investigation is taking up all his time and energy. He realizes he'll never get any sympathy from his wife—he knows that from experience. He doesn't meet her expectations, either. He thinks she's unfair. Fact is, they both work full-time. Georgina sometimes takes the night shift, and he works nights and weekends often. It's no easy task to coordinate their working hours. She accuses him of not being home enough, but in his opinion the same could be said of her. Georgina might well have hoped that bringing Calista Gates on board would mean a lighter burden on his shoulders. Bakie's murder has probably destroyed her hopes.

He discovers that Bakie's emails mostly revolve around business deals concerning his restaurant, the Eider Duck. Orders, complaints, communications with other chefs. Particularly with old coworkers from his Vancouver days. Bernard works through the inbox, then he turns to the files. The yield from the photos is disappointing as well: a few snowmobile outings, family get-togethers, and a lot of pictures of artfully arranged meals.

Bernard goes back to the emails. Bakie—or whoever had access to his laptop—might not have been aware that deleted emails don't completely disappear, even when the trash folder is emptied. He presses the restore key, and a good dozen of them do indeed appear.

At that moment Fred van Heisen shows up in the doorway.

"Do you need me for anything, Sarge? Otherwise, I'm going to finish up the accident report."

He nods absent-mindedly, because now things are getting interesting. Bakie quarreled over money with Dennis Richards, Melissa's brother. He reads email after email, and the story begins to take shape. He calls Fred over in his excitement.

"Get Dennis Richards in here. He threatened Bakie over some money. And take a look at this."

He turns the laptop in Fred's direction. Dennis Richards's Facebook page. Pictures of slain coyotes hanging from a wooden gibbet. Melissa's brother posing with a large knife.

"There. On the ground." He points to a spot. "Isn't that a bone saw?"

"Do you want to have Richards brought in right away?" Fred asks.

He can understand that van Heisen doesn't have any desire to bundle up in his heavy clothing again and head out, not after he's been standing in the cold for an hour at the scene of the accident beside a dead moose. But that's Labrador for you.

"I want to take him by surprise," he answers.

Fred gets the address and leaves the office without comment.

Bernard is optimistic. At last a most promising lead. He ponders his strategy.

Twenty minutes later, van Heisen is back with Dennis Richards. The latter has a very sinister look on his face. He's wearing blue jeans, biker boots, and a black quilted jacket with some sort of insignia on it.

"Thank you for coming," Bernard begins politely. "We just want to clear up a few things of interest to us."

"Like what?"

Dennis leans forward on his chair, arms akimbo, as if ready to get up again.

"What did you give Bakie money for?"

"That's nobody's business."

"We wouldn't ask if it weren't important."

Dennis wiggles his biker boots back and forth before he manages to respond. "I invested in his restaurant. The Eider Duck. And I'm probably not the only one."

"How much?"

"Trade secret, Sergeant."

Snotty little shit, Bernard thinks to himself but doesn't show it.

"We know how much. But we'd like to hear it from you."

Dennis spots the laptop and puts two and two together.

"I told Melissa she shouldn't let that go. That Mountie woman conned her. It's not legal."

"Your sister gave us the laptop voluntarily."

"We want it back."

"We found emails between you and Kris Bakie on it. You threatened him unless he gave you your money back."

"Threatened? What a bunch of crap! I've never threatened Kris."

Bernard reads him this passage: *"Either you pay or you comply. You won't get away with this so easily, pal."*

He folds his arms over his chest.

"What did you mean? Bakie won't get away with this, Mister Richards?"

Richards stands up and sits down again.

"Are you trying to pin something on me? You'd better watch it there, Sergeant."

Bernard puts his hands on the table.

"Is that a threat, too? Are you threatening the police?"

"I was just trying to get Bakie to marry Melissa. Is that a crime? I told him if he didn't, then I wanted my money back."

"How much?"

"Fifty thousand."

Bernard exchanges glances with Fred, who's standing behind Richards against the wall.

"That's a nice pile of money. Where did you get so much?"

"I work, Sergeant. Does that surprise you? Unlike many people here who live off welfare. I've worked in Alberta. Three-week shifts, sixteen hours a day. Driving trucks, at minus thirty. That's how you make real dough."

"How long have you been back from Alberta?"

"Six days. I was supposed to fly back tomorrow, but after this business with Bakie—my family wants me to stay."

"Did Bakie repay you?"

"He got engaged to Melissa."

"Bakie wrote you that you'd have to wait a long time to get your money back because he'd have to shut down the restaurant, and that would break Melissa's heart."

"She's got nothing to do with the restaurant, man. She'd run it better than he can—you can bet on it. But he doesn't let her."

Richards speaks as if Bakie were still alive.

"Did you try to force Kris to turn over the running of the restaurant to Melissa?"

"Fuck, no. That's . . . Do you want anything else from me, or can I go?"

Bernard wonders what will happen to the restaurant now, without the gifted chef. If the business is sold, Dennis might not even get his investment back. And so he probably hasn't got a motive to be a potential killer. With Bakie's death, he loses. But Bernard knows the routine well enough to keep all options open for now. People often act irrationally. He continues his inter-rogation.

"Where were you between two and six on Wednesday?"

"I helped put up the podium for the Winter Games—there are plenty of witnesses. And I was home by five, with my mother."

"We'll be checking your alibi."

Dennis's legs twitch.

"You should look into who's got a key to the Viking house.

There are some people around here you should question—not an innocent man like me."

Dennis has struck a nerve. As a matter of fact, keys for both entrances were made and distributed. But nobody seems to have a list of who got them; even the tourist bureau doesn't, something he can't understand. Besides, who sees to it that everybody locks the doors all the time?

"We're grateful for any information that might possibly be connected to the crime," he counters, managing to stay businesslike. "Did Bakie have any enemies?"

"Sure he had enemies. Just ask the fishermen he doesn't buy from. He has his suppliers, most of them poachers, because they're cheaper."

Dennis gets angrier and angrier. He's probably so mad because his sister Melissa won't get married now, even though he's invested fifty thousand.

Bernard is surprised that Dennis doesn't badmouth Gerald Hynes, though Hynes evidently believes that the Richards family still harbors feelings of revenge toward him.

He shows Dennis the Facebook image with the knife and the bone saw.

"Did you kill Bakie's dog?"

Dennis takes a quick look at the photo and laughs.

"You can't fool me, Sergeant. Bakie's dog was poisoned, but I didn't do it. And I didn't cut him up, either."

"Do you own the knife and the saw?"

"Sure, they're mine. Every hunter has things like that at home."

"Not necessarily. Many hunters use a chainsaw when they cut up a dead animal."

"Those are butchers, Sergeant. I don't want to ruin the pelt when I can sell it."

Bernard turns to Fred.

"We'll take a look at his knife. And the saw, too."

He hopes his voice doesn't betray the nervousness he feels. He found a message in the emails that's got him puzzled.

Kris, don't push it too far. Or else it could mean a sudden end for you.

The sender is Ann Smith.

27

The parking lot for the Anglican church is packed. As are the lots for the supermarket, the hardware store, the Salvation Army church—there's not a single spot in Port Brendan that isn't occupied by a parked vehicle. It's a miracle you can even drive down the street and that nobody's left their car in the median.

I've had the wise foresight to take my Ski-Doo and park next to the gas station. It's three hundred meters to the church from there, but I don't care. It's only half past two, but there is already a huge crowd at the cemetery. I've pulled my cap down over my face; I've got sunglasses on to hide my eyes and a scarf over my mouth. I want to be incognito, not cause a stir. And Delgado and Sullivan don't need to know that I'm hanging about at the funeral. After all, Closs didn't detail me for this mission.

I can hardly believe it, but six different denominations have established churches here: the Apostolic Church, the Salvation Army, the Pentecostals, the Anglican Church, Jehovah's Witnesses, and the Roman Catholic Church. Quite a lot for two thousand villagers. People here have more churches than kinds of coffee at the supermarket. The other cemeteries in Port Brendan lie outside the village. One of the old church graveyards is even on a little island off the coast, accessible only by boat. Or by snowmobile in winter. Did people in earlier times want to keep their dead as far away as possible? That won't happen to Lorna Taylor; she'll be put to rest in the middle of the village, next to the cemetery entrance, where a grave has been dug. I can't tell by the shape of the hole whether a pickax or a jackhammer was used.

I push my way through at the rear of the crowd, not as inconspicuously as I thought. I'm one of the few wearing sunglasses. People turn and look and give me the once-over. But they do that to everybody who arrives. A funeral, especially one like this, is an unusual event, after all.

The ground rises slightly, and I place myself at the highest point to survey the situation. I can see the camera team from here, positioned on the side of the street that leads up to the church.

The first person I recognize is the woman who spoke to me at Tim Hortons this morning. A few rows back, Wendy's standing with two teenagers, probably her kids. Ernie Butt is nearby; he's looking in my direction but doesn't see me. I'll meet his wife, Grace, after the funeral; she doesn't want to talk at the police station but at my house. She's not standing beside her husband, who's with three other men I don't know. Georgina Closs catches my eye; she's wearing a pink cap with a pompom on its pointed end and a pink jacket. An interesting color selection for a funeral. She evidently likes loud colors. Her car is bright yellow.

A pathway is cleared for the family and the pallbearers. Lorna's parents are accompanied by relatives; a young man is supporting her mother, who looks devastated. I pick out Grace Butt from the crowd. She's walking arm in arm with another woman, maybe a sister or a friend. The minister begins the service. I avert my eyes to resume my inspection of those present. Gerald Hynes apparently didn't come, nor has my neighbor, Rick Stout, as far as I can tell. I spot some young Inuit women in the crowd, but I don't know if Meeka Stout is among them. Ann Smith and Shannon Wilkey are also absent.

Before the funeral I quickly downloaded the emails on

Bakie's laptop onto a memory stick—without Closs knowing. Purely a cautionary measure. You never know what can happen when a laptop goes for a stroll. I also found more emails in the trash folder. Deleted, but fortunately not completely lost. I'd love to know if that was Melissa.

All of a sudden I hear a quiet voice behind me.

"Your disguise doesn't really work, Gates."

I turn around. Sullivan is thrilled with his discovery.

"I recognized you by your boots," he whispers. "That's my trick right now, looking at people's footwear."

"Well done, Constable," I whisper back. "Are my pictures from the crime scene helpful?"

"I found the key footprint myself."

He takes three steps backward, away from prying ears, and I follow.

"We're mainly interested in one footprint: a rubber snow boot, a popular model, lined with felt. You can get them here in the village."

"So we're looking for a man who doesn't get around much and buys his shoes in the village."

"Or a woman with big feet who's creating a false trail."

Poor Lorna. We're discussing Bakie's murder while her remains are being buried. But her death might be connected to Bakie, and the person who drew our attention to that possibility was the one who left a blue garbage bag on the ice.

"Where's Delgado?" I whisper.

"He's monitoring Lorna's family. Who's here and who's not."

"So you think a relative might be involved? I thought there was nothing to that."

"Now that we've got the body, we hope things can start moving."

Seems to me that the perp is the one who's doing the moving. He put the crate with Lorna's remains on the beach for all to see. I expect him to do something else soon. Hopefully he won't commit another murder.

"I'm pretty sure the murderer wouldn't miss this funeral," I reply.

"Why are you here, Gates?"

"I'm going to interview Grace Butt, Lorna's friend."

"You'll never get anything out of her," Sullivan asserts. "I've tried a number of times."

"Maybe she'll want to talk now that Lorna's been found. She . . ."

I stop because there's a skirmish in the lower corner of the cemetery.

Shouting and screaming drown out the minister's words, and he stops talking when he becomes aware of the commotion.

"It wasn't me," a man shouts over the crowd and the gravestones. "It wasn't me."

I look at Sullivan.

"Who's that?"

"Scott Dyson."

Sullivan takes off in the direction of the turmoil.

Dyson. The man who found the crate with Lorna in it.

Two hours later I'm sitting in my armchair, all keyed up.

Ernie Butt is in my living room and hasn't sat down because he's so incensed.

"If I hadn't broken it up, who the hell knows what they'd have done to Scott," he says. "Scott had nothing to do with Lorna's death; the police have been saying that for a long time. The Taylors are just looking for a scapegoat, probably because they're trying to protect somebody."

Grace is sitting still, her fingers interlaced. It looks like she's fighting back tears. The funeral of her murdered friend has clearly upset her. That's great for me, because when someone feels overwhelmed, they usually start talking. But her husband is still preoccupied with the confrontation at the cemetery. He's already described it for us in great detail: how Lorna's two brothers went after Scott and tried to beat him up, and how he, Ernie, protected Scott, "the poor bugger." I think, though, that Sullivan and Delgado are owed at least some of the credit for helping to drive Scott's attackers off. The minister calmed the grieving family by telling his little flock that they should put their trust in God. He didn't say anything about trusting the police. I hardly remember anything after that, because it was around that time that I spotted Gerald Hynes in the crowd.

"Who's the family protecting?" I ask Ernie, who finally sits down on the sofa.

"The Taylors have been fighting like hell among themselves over land ever since Granddad Sherman died. Sherman would roll over in his grave if he knew about it."

Grace looks at her hands in distress. I've got a feeling she won't say much as long as Ernie's here. Her black, shoulder-length hair has been straightened, just like Lorna's in the file photo. I'll think about this similarity later.

While his wife is silent, Ernie rants.

"That's what happens when you don't have your property surveyed and registered. People live on land they don't have papers for. And do you know why? Because they don't want to spend their money on surveyors and fees. They'd rather buy a new Ski-Doo."

Maybe they have a more urgent need for a Ski-Doo, I think to myself. Ernie has moved to Happy Valley-Goose Bay and found a good job there. He seems to find people in Port Brendan backward, given his new vantage point. I look through the living room window and see Rick Stout coming toward the house. He checks out Ernie's dove-colored GMC Yukon.

"Your car has an admirer," I say to Ernie, who jumps to his feet and goes to the window.

193

"Rick Stout," he tells his wife. "The poor bastard will never be able to afford a car like that." He turns to me. "I always drove a pickup. This is my first SUV. Feels great driving it, I must say."

"But you've occasionally taken my SUV," Grace corrects him.

Ernie throws her a look of annoyance. He obviously doesn't like to be corrected.

"Your old jalopy has nothing on a Yukon. Look at that: Rick's eyes are almost popping out of his head."

Poor bastards and old jalopies apparently don't rank very high in Ernie's world, which doesn't stop him from putting on his shoes and jacket and rushing outside. Men like nothing better than to show off a new car. Rick has done me a huge favor without knowing it.

I immediately focus on Grace. She's wearing stylish horn-rimmed glasses that don't detract from her stunning eyes. They're the same dove color as her husband's SUV.

"I must compliment you," I admit, to relieve the tension. "I feel so good in this beautiful house; it makes everything a bit easier for me."

She tries to smile, and almost does.

"I could decorate homes all the time, I find it's a lot of fun. You can get everything over the internet these days, you know. But doing it my way lets me free up my imagination and dream a little."

"Did Gerald Hynes help you with the renovations?"

"Oh no, I did it all myself. That is, Scott worked for me, but I told him exactly how I wanted it. He did all the carpentry work under my supervision."

Scott worked for Grace. I make a mental note of it.

"You've clearly got talent. Where does it come from?"

"Oh, I've always gone to websites on interior decorating. Lorna was crazy about it, too. She even subscribed to a magazine for interior design."

"I know this must be difficult for you, especially today, but may I ask you a few questions about Lorna?"

Grace nods. Her blue, moist eyes shimmer behind her horn-rimmed glasses.

"She worked in a furniture store in Happy Valley-Goose Bay?"

"In the gifts department. There were cushions and candles and vases and all sorts of pretty things. She knew the latest trends."

"Did you move to Happy Valley-Goose Bay together?"

"Lorna went first. Her parents had no objection. The Taylors . . . they're very nice. It's true there was a fight over a piece of land, but . . . if you ask me, that happens in many families. Ernie's exaggerating a bit there."

I look outside. Four men are standing beside Ernie's SUV and shooting the breeze. For quite a while, I hope. The incident at the cemetery is certain to be one of the things they'll be going over.

"Ernie doesn't like the Taylors?"

Grace blushes.

"I used to go out with Donnie Taylor. Lorna's brother. Before I went with Ernie. Ernie absolutely wanted to get out of this place, and me, too."

I can very well imagine the situation. Donnie Taylor wanted to stay in Port Brendan, and so he lost the girl. Not easy for a man who's attached to his native soil. Or to his piece of the ocean.

"Where did Lorna meet her boyfriend Guy Stravitz?"

"In the Happy Hour bar. Lots of Americans go there. And all the foreigners stationed in Happy Valley-Goose Bay."

"How about you?"

"No. Ernie didn't want me to go out. We were engaged by then."

"But would you have wanted to go out with Lorna?"

She wavers for a second, then catches herself.

"Only with Lorna. We always had great fun together. But my faith doesn't allow it."

195

I ask myself which faith bans bars and hazard a guess. "Are you Pentecostal?"

Grace nods.

"Was Lorna's family against her relationship with an American soldier?"

"At first she only told me. I mean . . . about Guy. But that was because she wasn't sure how serious he was about her. Ernie always said, 'It's not going to go well; he'll get her pregnant and then ditch her.' He worried about Lorna."

"You told Ernie about it?"

Grace turns her eyes toward the stylized bird on the wall. An exotic piece, not from Labrador.

"Yes, you're not supposed to keep secrets from your husband."

Her remark speaks volumes. If she can say that, then she definitely has some secrets. Because she's under pressure to be good. Decent. Free from sin. Apart from her love of interior decorating, what inclinations can this young woman actually live out? Her friend Lorna had fewer inhibitions. And fewer things were banned. Grace must have found Lorna exciting.

"When did Lorna tell her family?"

"Shortly before . . . before she disappeared. Maybe three weeks before."

Grace's fingers are clasped together.

I do a quick calculation. Lorna was together with Guy for a little over three months.

"How did the Taylors react?"

"They wanted to meet Guy at once, naturally. They told Lorna to bring him to Port Brendan. But she wanted to wait."

"Were her parents and brothers unhappy that she fell in love with an American?"

"Lorna never said anything like that. But you know . . . in the past a lot of women from Newfoundland and Labrador married American soldiers. That's really nothing new."

Grace stretches her back, livens up.

"We aren't anti-American. Take my father: he still thinks Newfoundland and Labrador should have joined America and not Canada."

I'm perplexed.

"Was that an option the population could consider?"

"Yes, in a referendum after the war."

"World War Two?"

"Yes, 1948. We joined Canada a year later. It always upsets Ernie when my father gets going about it. He . . . "

We hear the front door open and the rustle of clothing. Ernie's back. Rats. My time with Grace is over.

"Donnie Taylor has to go to the police station," he shouts from the hallway. "That'll teach him a lesson."

I ignore his remark, look at Grace.

"Who do you think might have held something against Lorna?"

She looks at her husband, who kneels down beside her chair and caresses her arm. His voice caresses her, too.

"So say it, my dearest, the police have to know."

Grace sighs and brushes her black hair out of her eyes.

"Kris Bakie."

28

Fred is angry as he steers his snowmobile through the Port Brendan streets. The funeral happened hours ago, but vehicles are still blocking the roads everywhere. Worse than the damn snow-banks. He's in a hurry. The boss has called an important meeting, and he doesn't want to miss it. He curses under his breath. Nothing prevents people here from driving around in the dead of winter so they can be part of the excitement. Especially if it involves murder or manslaughter. Or a fight in the cemetery. He knows he's being unfair, but he has to let off steam under the cover of the noise from his machine.

By the time he makes it to the station, everybody's sitting around the conference table. Closs is really formal. Fred sits down beside Gates and dismisses his fellow officers' mocking comments about his late arrival.

The sergeant begins to speak: "I'll send out a press release so that the media leave us alone for a few more days. Today we'll put together everything we have at the moment. First the shoe prints. I've analyzed the photos from the crime scene; Sullivan found another important footprint there. Pass these pictures around. One snow boot is remarkable because it's not sold in Port Brendan. The make is McCallough, you can see the large *C* on the sole. Rubber sole and rubber shoe with a gaiter and laces. Size nine. Take note of that boot."

Fred removes the picture from the pile. A pretty ladies' boot. That should be easy to trace.

Closs speaks again: "No visible signs of heavy wear on the sole profile; the boots are new, or fairly new. Probably the Seymore SR model."

You've got to hand it to the boss: Closs knows how to get information from the RCMP data bank fast.

"The boot comes in black and beige."

Gates holds up her tablet, on which she's downloaded an image.

"Right, find out who wore these, Gates. But we're more interested in this imprint here." He passes around some more pictures. "Rubber boots—they're sold here. Only this make. Size eleven and a half. Partly worn-down sole profile. I assume that the perp was wearing them."

"Can you tell us why?" Calista asks.

Fred looks askance at her. Her face is somehow different than it usually is: full of energy, but also paler. She must feel she's on firmer ground after six days. She finds her way around in this wasteland amazingly fast for a woman from Vancouver. Two unsolved cases are probably just right for her. No time to reflect on loneliness. Because she definitely feels lonely in these strange surroundings. He knows the feeling.

"Because women aren't stupid enough to leave a sole profile like this one behind in the snow. Do you like that rationale, Gates?" The comment comes from Sullivan, of course.

Closs doesn't follow up on it.

"We should examine footwear from several men very closely."

"I've even seen women wearing rubber boots like those," Delgado says. "They really keep you warm."

"Dennis Richards, for example," Closs goes unblinkingly

ahead as if he hasn't heard Delgado. "Richards says he invested fifty thousand dollars in Bakie's restaurant. That led to friction between the two. Richards claims Bakie didn't want to pay him back. Apparently there's no written agreement between them. We have to take a look at bank withdrawals, but that will take some time. The whole business stinks, if you ask me."

"You don't just give someone fifty thousand dollars without an agreement," Gates remarks. "Perhaps Dennis Richards wanted to launder some money and not leave a paper trail. In Vancouver that's done through restaurants all the time."

Fred doesn't buy it.

"I can't imagine Bakie risking his reputation for that."

"He probably didn't know what the dirty source of the money was," Gates replied.

"Why would Richards launder money?" Fred says. "As far as we know, he's had nothing to do with drugs."

"We'll follow this up," Closs says. "Richards could also have something to do with the dead dog. He had the tools for it. And he worked in Alberta, where it's no problem to get rat poison, unlike here. Delgado, anything else from the crime scene?"

"No footprints inside the sod house, Sarge; the floor's frozen fast. No signs of a struggle. No fingerprints. The perp wore gloves. He evidently planned it."

"And what about Bakie?"

"Also no fingerprints from him. The door must have been open when he entered the Viking house. He still had his gloves on. When are we getting his cell phone?"

"This evening, if all goes well. And then we hope to find out more about the body. Fred?"

He's taking Gates last. As if that isn't a coincidence.

"I checked out the wooden board with the stamp. Hynes told us the mill delivered twenty boards with the wrong dimensions, and that they'd gone back to the mill. I got the wrong dimensions, and they matched the width and thickness of the piece of wood in the blue garbage bag. The stamped board from the crate with Lorna's skeleton was cut to fit. I found out where the wrong boards first wound up—at the children's playground. Some people built a playhouse with them. The sawmill donated the wood. But it wasn't all used up."

"Who built the playhouse?" Delgado asks, who doesn't have any children. Closs is the only member of the team with offspring.

"A couple of fathers. And Hynes's foreman."

"Randy Fillier," Closs says. Fred isn't surprised that the boss knows Fillier. Closs had a large garden shed built.

"Where did the rest of the boards get to?" Calista asks. "The ones that weren't used for the playground?"

"Fillier couldn't tell me. Now I've got to track down the fathers. But I did turn up something about the red sweatshirt. At least one was auctioned off during an online auction run by the animal rescue group. And another was seen in the Salvation Army's thrift store. So it wasn't necessarily Lorna's sweatshirt in the blue garbage bag."

Closs finally lets Calista have the floor.

"Shannon Wilkey was in Vancouver and Whistler during the Winter Olympics," she recounts. "And in a press photo she's wearing the same cap we found on the ice. I discovered the photo on the internet."

They all stare at Gates, until Delgado retorts: "There were ten thousand of those hats sold."

"But not to people in Port Brendan," Closs shoots back. "What else did you find?"

"I had an interesting conversation with Grace and Ernie Butt," she continues.

Then Wendy breezes in with muffins. Calista pointedly stops and doesn't speak again until the door closes behind the dispatcher.

Fred rejoices inwardly: time and again he's advised that

Wendy be kept away from meetings. Closs has done it irregularly so far. Probably because Wendy and Georgina Closs are friends.

"The year before Lorna met the American soldier—according to Grace Butt—she had an affair with a married man who worked for the Newfoundland and Labrador Liquor Corporation. He revealed to her that Kris Bakie's restaurant was serving alcohol without a license. Somebody in authority allegedly turned a blind eye to it until the application came through. That drove Lorna's lover up the wall because he apparently couldn't stand Bakie and his success. Lorna's lover broke off the affair a little later. She wanted to take revenge on him by applying for a job at the Eider Duck restaurant because she was bored at the furniture store. But Bakie chose another applicant. Lorna was angry and threatened Bakie by telling him she knew he'd been serving alcohol for six months without a license. She told her friend Grace about it, who was shocked. Shocked at the affair and the attempted blackmail. The furniture store created a gift department shortly afterward that Lorna really liked. According to Grace, Lorna never again mentioned the Bakie issue."

"I thought we were working on a crime case and not a soap opera," Sullivan comments. Closs taps his ball point on the table.

"Who is this married man at the Liquor Corporation?"

"Grace didn't want to cough it up, but he's supposedly an off-road motorcycle driver, a motocross fanatic."

"Wade Hickson!" Frank Delgado blurts out.

"That's a joke," Sullivan protests. "What's that supposed to mean? Bakie kills Lorna, and somebody kills Bakie for that reason? Can we get serious about this case?"

Closs nods.

"Something doesn't add up here. If it was Wade Hickson—let me emphasize the *if*—then he could have easily busted Bakie over the missing liquor license without getting himself or some naïve chick involved."

"Maybe Wade was drunk when he let it slip." Delgado grins.

"If all this is correct," Calista explains calmly, "then I conclude that Lorna Taylor took some risks. I don't mean to say that she was extorting Bakie. But she seems to have been putting pressure on him. Maybe she threatened Hickson, too, when he dumped her."

Sullivan snorts. "C'mon, people. Knock it off. Lorna was not cagey; she was an impulsive local yokel."

Calista doesn't contradict him. "Maybe that's exactly it—she was impulsive. She talked faster than she thought."

"Why didn't Grace tell us about this earlier?" Closs inquires.

"Because she promised Lorna she wouldn't tell a soul. Grace is religious. After Lorna's body was found and Bakie was murdered, she told her husband. And he advised her to take it to the police."

"Holy Ernie, the patron saint of the Highway and Transportation Department." Delgado can't stop taking potshots.

Fred wonders if he's the only one who's bothered by that.

"A lot isn't clear to me yet," Calista concedes. "The tales of Bakie and the married lover throw a new, less positive light on Lorna; Grace really seems to have liked her in spite of that. Maybe she thinks all of a sudden that this information will help find her murderer."

"And she needed three years to have this insight?" Sullivan literally spits his words out.

"In any case, we'll have to follow up on these new clues," Closs decides.

Sullivan doesn't let it go. "In Happy Valley-Goose Bay? Don't you think we should keep our focus here in Port Brendan, where the action is? The crate was found on Savage Beach. The blue garbage bag turned up in Ghost Bay with all that suspicious stuff. Bakie's murder took place in the Viking house. But Grace's story leads to Happy Valley-Goose Bay. That goes against our working theory."

"I also think that both cases have a strong connection to Port

Brendan," Calista announces. "It seems to me that Lorna's murder looks like a settling of scores with Port Brendan—or with events here. Nevertheless, we have to expand our investigation. It would be good if our counterparts in Happy Valley-Goose Bay could question Wade Hickson. Sullivan and Delgado have questioned some of Lorna's family members twice, and people around them. I know you've already tackled this, but could we go over where the killer might have hidden Lorna for several days one more time? Where could that place be; who had the opportunity to carry out something like that, logistically speaking?"

"After Lorna was discovered," Delgado interjects, "when you, Gates, were still in Vancouver, we easily interviewed three dozen people, beginning with Lorna's brothers and relatives, and fishermen and hunters, men and women. Even the mayor. We've checked out alibi after alibi. Nothing went anywhere. Half the locals own a pickup and a boat, a cabin on the beach or in the woods, or both. Many go into the forest to cut wood; nobody pays any mind. Or they're in the woods to inspect their traps for coyotes or rabbits. Almost all the men are physically strong. And many have built a crate, like the one on the beach, for storing their duck-hunting decoys. To reduce the number of suspects and possible hiding places, we need to first have a halfway-concrete suspicion."

Fred has never heard Delgado talk so exhaustively. He must be frustrated, like everybody else on the team, that things aren't moving ahead. And because now they've got a second murder case to solve.

"Then it would certainly be helpful if we think hard about the killer and his motive."

Gates picks up a sheet of paper covered with notes. "I've tried to generate a profile of the killer. It's probably a man, because a woman carrying out the actions connected to the murder would be more likely to attract the attention of potential eyewitnesses. The perp is proud he hasn't been caught yet. So now he'll grow bolder. At the same time, he's challenged the police by putting the crate with Lorna's remains right on the beach. He feels so safe that he thinks he can risk it. Or he needs confirmation that he's really cunning and clever. Maybe something's gone wrong in his life, and he has to compensate for it. He'd like to build up his confidence with his actions. He feels superior to us. We know from previous murder cases that he's watching closely to see how we react. That gives him a feeling of power. It might mean that he needs to make up for feeling weak in his everyday life."

"And how, my dear colleague, are your insights supposed to help us move the investigation forward?" Sullivan's voice drips sarcasm.

"It wouldn't surprise me if the perp eventually gets so arrogant that he makes a mistake."

"Theories are there to be adapted to new findings" is Closs's rejoinder. "We don't want to fixate on one thing and overlook other information." He casts his eyes around the group. "And we don't want to prematurely release the names of people involved in the case. Or else we'll have another incident like the one in the cemetery."

"Scott Dyson was never under suspicion," Delgado objects. "Three years ago, when Lorna disappeared, he was in the Corner Brook clink."

Fred can easily picture the confrontation in the cemetery. Lorna's brothers must feel like losers for not being able to protect their sister. They'd like to slit the killer's throat, but he hasn't been caught. In their frustration they must find a scapegoat. He's experienced this kind of thing before in small communities.

Calista's voice takes him out of his thoughts. "Did you bring Lorna's brothers into the station?"

Closs shakes his head. "What makes you say that?"

"Ernie Butt says so."

"That's not the way we resolve conflicts here, Gates. Especially at a funeral ceremony. We've gone and warned the Taylors that we won't tolerate anything of the sort."

Closs picks up the pile of papers before him and slaps them into shape.

Fred senses he's about to issue marching orders.

29

It's amazing what nine hours of sleep can heal. I can even better withstand the cold that hits me when I open the front door. I feel better until I discover something under the wiper on my staff car. I immediately turn ice cold. It's a red glove. Thin leather. It's mine. I haven't worn it since coming to Port Brendan. Far too thin and too stylish. Normally I keep both gloves on a shelf in the basement. I sort of remember that. I bring the stiff glove back into the house. Its twin is in fact lying on the shelf. Is my brain playing tricks on me? Or is something else going on? I've got to change those damn locks; I just haven't gotten around to it yet.

I go outside again, carefully locking the front door behind me. A black pickup goes past. Somebody's out and about earlier than me. Looks like Rick Stout's car, with an Inuit woman behind the wheel. Until now, I've only seen Meeka once, from a distance. I follow the pickup to Rick's house.

When Meeka gets out, I shout: "I'm Calista Gates, your neighbor. Can I talk to you for a bit?"

She wrinkles her brow before saying, "Sure."

I take off my boots at the door and follow Meeka in my socks to the kitchen, where there's a large wood stove. The kitchen cupboards look worn, and the yellowish stove seems to be a model from the seventies. Toys and children's clothes are lying around everywhere. I suddenly feel transported back to my childhood. With seven offspring, my mother never managed to keep the house tidy. It wasn't important to her. "Kids are kids," she'd always say when people came over. To make up for it, she had thick Greek coffee and spanakopita ready at all hours of the day.

Meeka takes her cap off. She looks young, with her full face and smooth skin, chin-length black hair, and bangs. Rick must be at least ten years older. We sit down at the kitchen table. Meeka doesn't offer to make tea. She undoes her jacket zipper but doesn't take her jacket off.

"I can't stay long. I just came back to put some more wood on the fire. The stove is our only source of heat. My husband's with the kids at the arena. They're practicing for the opening ceremony of the Winter Games . . ."

"This early in the morning?"

She sighs. "Yes, I could hardly get them out of bed. They have to go to school afterward, and Dulcie goes to occupational therapy."

"There's OT here?" I'm impressed.

"In the seniors' home. The therapist does crafts with the old folks, and Dulcie can join in. She loves it."

Meeka's face softens, though she doesn't smile.

"We'll keep it short," I reassure her. "Maybe you can call your husband and tell him you'll be coming a little later?"

"He doesn't have a phone; I have it. We've only got one in the family. Two phones are too expensive."

"I think so, too; cell phones really eat up a lot of money. I won't keep you long. It's about something your daughter told me when she was at my place recently."

Meeka interrupts me at once. "The kids shouldn't have barged into your place. They were simply delighted to be able to go mummering. They told me about the hot chocolate you gave them."

Now a smile flickers over her face.

"They were no bother," I say. "At least I know now what mummering is."

"You're from Vancouver, aren't you?"

I nod. "There's no mummering there."

"I was invited to a concert in Vancouver once, with a throat-singing group. It was during the Winter Olympics. We played at various locations, in hotels and community halls. We were only there for four days, but I'll never forget it."

I prick up my ears.

"Shannon Wilkey was in Vancouver, too. Did you ever talk to her about the Olympics?"

Meeka's smile vanishes. "Shannon? No . . . I didn't know that."

"Did you get a cap with the Vancouver logo as a souvenir?"

"A cap? No. Why do you ask?"

Meeka turns cautious. I can see it.

"Do you still travel?"

"Not anymore. My husband . . . he doesn't like it when I'm away. I'll perform here now, in the Viking house. For the tourists in summer. That way I can earn a little money. But now . . . " She stops. "It scares me, the murder and all that. Who could do a thing like that to Kris? It's just awful. What's going to happen with the fundraising? And his restaurant?"

Her eyes grow dim, and she looks down at the tabletop.

"What do you think, Mrs. Stout: Who'd want to kill Kris Bakie?"

She presses her lips together for a second. "That's what I'd like to know, too. I know his family. Kris is . . . He went to Vancouver and other places, and he came back with new ideas."

"Are there people here who don't like the new ideas?"

She slides back and forth on her chair. "The Labrador Inuit are industrious and modern. They have their own businesses."

"Kris must have been a role model for them. But did many

people see him as competition, because he was away for so long?"

She hesitates. "Maybe some people want a piece of the cake, but it's not big enough."

"What do you mean?"

"Not everybody makes money from tourism, or from the businesses in this place."

I hope she'll say more, but she gets to her feet, opens the stove door, and shoves in two large pieces of wood.

I wait for her to sit down again.

"What do the Inuit think about the Viking house? I've heard not everybody's happy about it. Because it's not about Inuit culture."

"I don't have a problem with it. Main thing is that the tourists come, for whatever reason. Then we can educate them about Inuit culture."

"Who's got a key to the Viking house?"

And who's got a key to my house?

She's alert again. "Everybody who's involved with the fundraising."

"Dr. Perrell, then?"

She nods.

"Shannon? Ann Smith?"

"And me."

"Can you give me the key?"

Meeka gets up, stands on tiptoe, and stretches her arm to find the key on an old buffet. I take it and thank her.

She doesn't say anything. I must divert her before she clams up completely or even rushes out the door. She's shown an amazing degree of patience with me. Maybe I'm not the only one between the two of us who's curious.

"How does it work, your throat singing? I mean, what's the technique behind it?"

"Technique? I don't know if there's a technique to it. Maybe more of a tradition. Most sounds come from here."

She points to her larynx.

"Can you show me how?"

"Now?"

"Only if you want to."

"Normally I sing duets with a partner."

She thinks for a moment, then sways her head.

"I could sing you a lullaby for a child."

Her lips open slightly, and a song flows from her mouth, the likes of which I've never heard. A succession of scratchy pants, gurgling sounds, a deep, dark humming, a throaty roar, and strained mmmmmhs. It seems as if not only Meeka's larynx but the entire kitchen vibrates. It ends in a soft, purring puff of breath.

When Meeka sees the expression on my face, she laughs for the first time.

"You've never heard that before, eh?"

"Maybe once on TV, but a long time ago. That sounds like . . ." Words fail me.

She helps me out. "We imitate sounds of nature: water, animals, wind, ice. My mother and grandmother taught me many songs, but I also create new ones."

"So you're a composer."

She laughs again. "Maybe you could call it that."

Then her face turns serious. She clicks on her cell phone.

"I have to leave soon. What did Dulcie tell you?"

"The boys teased her because she was afraid of Dr. Carl. That got her stirred up. She said, 'Dr. Carl hurts the dog.'"

"What dog? We don't have a dog."

"Maybe she meant Kris Bakie's dog. You've probably heard that somebody killed the dog and cut off its head. I wonder what Dulcie meant."

My questioning doesn't sit well with Meeka; she jiggles around on her chair.

"No idea. She's never said anything like that to me. I don't have any idea if she knows about Kris's dog. I certainly haven't told her about it. Children don't need to know about that."

"Was she afraid of Dr. Perrell?"

"She needs her shots now and then. She doesn't like it."

"Shots for what?"

"To relax her muscle cramps."

Meeka draws a circle on the table with her finger.

"If I were a nurse, I could give Dulcie the shots myself. That would be my dream job, but things never got to that point." She sighs.

Poor Meeka. It would have been horrible for me not to have a job I loved.

"Might your husband have said something to your little one about the dog?"

"I'll ask him." Meeka looks worried.

I notice something moving outside. Through the window I see a car driving up to my house. I stand up.

"Is something else bothering you?" I ask as we leave the kitchen. A calculated ploy. People often reveal more after a formal conversation than they did earlier. They are less guarded, more relaxed.

"It's just that my husband takes care of everything. The kids, money . . . work. And now this . . . awful death. I don't want to be more of a burden to him."

"Burden to him how?"

"Somebody's sending me stupid emails, and he read them. I don't know who's behind it."

"What kind of stupid emails?"

We're standing by her front door, and I see a heavily clothed figure in front of my house waving to me.

"Oh, kind of slimy things. And then things like, 'I love you,' 'I miss you,' 'I can't wait to see you.' Stuff like that."

I'm staggered. Why is she telling me this so openly?

"I can take a look at them if you want. Maybe I can find out who's sending them."

Meeka's face looks even more concerned.

"That would get my husband really upset. He doesn't want the police . . ."

"You can block the sender. Did you do that?"

She shakes her head. "Rick says he'll find out who it is."

Rick doesn't seem to me to be the sort who knows his way around complicated technology, but maybe I'm being prejudiced.

"The emails are upsetting. You shouldn't read them anymore. Block them. If you don't know how to, I can show you."

"I'll find out how." She opens the door of her pickup. "Somebody's waiting for you over there."

"Yes, I know."

"I think it's Georgina."

Meeka shuts the door, starts the motor, and drives off.

It's a mystery to me how Meeka can recognize that heavily clothed person from over here. But she wasn't wrong. My boss's wife seems rather impatient when I get to her.

"You didn't respond to my text message from this morning. So I thought I'd come right here." Her voice is as girlish as her face, but with an energetic undertone.

"Did Sergeant Close tell you I was here?"

"Oh, no, Wendy told me. Can I take a quick look at the rooms?"

"I haven't got them ready."

"Doesn't matter. I just want to see how much space there is."

How much space there is? I open the door to the basement where the guest room is.

"Yes, this looks very nice," Georgina exclaims cheerfully after sizing up the room. "Bunk beds. If you don't mind, we can accommodate three women here. They're friends."

I feverishly rack my brain to find a way out of this situation while I steer her to a second door.

"The bathroom, how wonderful! That's splendid!"

"Maybe the ladies need a more private space and don't want to be three in a room," I object.

"Nah. People in Labrador aren't as squeamish as Vancouverites."

"And how does it work with meals?"

"They'll be taken care of in the Pentecostal community kitchen. Don't worry about it. I'll bring over three of our sleeping bags today; they're washable. And an air mattress for the floor. You've got enough towels? And how're you fixed for pillow cases?"

This is getting to be a bit much. I prefer to steer clear of type A people with an inexhaustible supply of energy and good intentions like Georgina. They affect me like leeches draining my veins.

"I don't want any alcohol or drugs or loud music in here," I warn her, "and no male visitors." I sound like a den mother in a religious youth hostel.

Georgina stares at me in astonishment with her big childlike eyes.

"They wouldn't dare do that in a policewoman's house—just imagine. They're in the lion's den here."

I feel cornered. How do you give your boss's wife a kick in the shins? You don't.

"When do the athletes arrive? And how long are they staying?"

"They're supposed to be here by late afternoon tomorrow and will stay for six or seven days. They're in the biathlon."

She makes for the door. Maybe she's afraid I'll simply refuse.

"Thanks for being so generous. I've run up against a wall with some other people. Like Shannon Wilkey—but don't tell a soul. She has a huge house and won't take anybody in. She says she's an artist and doesn't want to be disturbed while she's painting."

"And Ann Smith?" Sure, I know her house is too small but can't resist asking.

For the first time, Georgina's virginal face seems peeved, but she catches herself right away.

"That lady is only out to exploit people." She looks at me, with her hand on the doorknob. "My family is taking in three men. That's what we owe the people here after all that's happened."

The door closes, and I watch her drive away.

Only now does it dawn on me what a biathlon is. People on cross-country skis who shoot with rifles.

30

Ann still feels his warm body on hers as she gets into her cold car. These intimate rendezvous are secret, and now, with Kris Bakie's death, they've become even more precarious. No one can know.

This game of hide-and-seek doesn't bother her; on the contrary, she feels free. Hiding has become second nature to her. When safety or even life depends on it, then you quickly adapt. The thought had come to her in her more lighthearted moments that she'd have been well qualified as a secret agent or a spy. But those playful feelings always evaporate quickly.

She mustn't think of his passionate embrace now, the scent of his manliness, the sounds from his mouth when he shares their desire. She must concentrate on the cars behind and in front of her as she turns onto the highway to Port Brendan. Their meetings always take place away from the village, in a remote cabin on a lonely forest road. Never at her place. And never at his. In summer they sometimes make love outdoors if a strong breeze keeps the mosquitoes at bay.

Incredible how lively Port Brendan's streets have suddenly become. Unfamiliar faces, figures in Inuit parkas, colorful head-gear everywhere, logos on ski jackets that say things such as *Team Walbush* or *Labrador City*. A food cart sells hot dogs and hamburgers from the grill. A fuzzy snow hare, the mascot of the games, wanders down the slope and is soon encircled by children.

Her eyes hunt for a place to park, but every spot is taken by vehicles and snowmobiles. Suddenly the nervous, enthusiastic excitement before a sporting event seizes her. She'd love to take off on a pair of snowshoes, heading for the finish line step by step. She'd love to be part of a team feverishly looking forward to the big day, or a team that hopes for victory for their country. But her role in the Winter Games is limited to technical work on the website. The organizing committee asked her to contribute photos. So she maneuvers her car toward the harbor, past pedestrians and vehicles. There's a big parking lot in front of the fish factory.

Her festive mood plummets at once when she discovers the new RCMP woman talking to another Mountie. They're standing beside the police car and talking, looking serious. Ann recognizes Fred van Heisen. Upon reflection, she manages to remember the policewoman's name. Calista Gates. Even close-up she looks pretty beneath her fur hat. Pretty in a natural way, not like Shannon, that Hollywood doll who dresses up to the nines. Calista won't be dangerous for me, she persuades herself. She's not so sure about Shannon.

The two officers look concerned. So would she in their shoes. The RCMP must be worried not only about the games but about solving two murders as well. She notices something else. The way van Heisen looks at his partner. Is she telling him something outrageous or . . . or does she fascinate him that much? Van Heisen has a girlfriend in Saskatchewan, so she's heard. He flies out there at times, but his girlfriend apparently won't come to see him in Port Brendan. As long as the murder investigation is on, he definitely won't be slipping away to Saskatchewan.

Ann isn't under the impression that the killings have frightened the villagers. It could have something to do with the Labrador mindset. They concentrate on what's in front of them, on the everyday, because they can't solve a murder. She's convinced, though, that the seriousness of the situation won't really and truly become clear to them until after the games are over. But she sees herself in a different position. She can't give a reason for her assessment of the situation; it relies on instinct. On the other hand, when she thinks about the garbage bag on the ice, her heart beats faster. Her lover doesn't want to discuss it. That bothers her. She has no one else she can confide in.

Then she does something she wouldn't have thought possible two minutes ago. She parks behind the RCMP car, gets out, and walks over to the constables. Two heads swivel in her direction.

"Constables, hello. I just wanted to ask if there's any news regarding the find on the ice."

"Hello, Miss Smith," Gates responds. "I understand that the incident is of interest to you. We've discovered the dog was poisoned. We're looking hard for the owners of the cap and sweatshirt and are looking into the origin of the bag. Have you heard anything that could help us?"

The constable's voice is full of warmth, and Ann thinks that people could underestimate Calista Gates because of it, which would be a mistake. She's given her just the amount of information she needs to. But not the whole truth. Ann's aware of the fact. Her bare temples hurt in the bitter cold.

"Maybe," she hears herself say, to her own astonishment. "I organized an online auction about three years ago for the animal rescue group to raise money for strays. I remember that a cap from the Vancouver games was offered some time ago. Past auctions were deleted, but perhaps somebody in the group remembers who won the cap back then."

"That's a useful tip, thank you very much," Gates says. "We'll follow up on it."

"Were red sweatshirts auctioned off as well, with the words *Animals Are the Better People* on them?" van Heisen asks.

"I don't remember," Ann answers. She yearns to escape the

cold and says good-bye. Inside the car, she puts on her wool hat and pulls the fur-lined hood over it. A handy camera is in her inside pocket.

On the way to the arena, where the opening ceremonies will be held the next day, children are selling tickets for a raffle. She's seen pictures of the grand prize, a quilt. A masterpiece. An elderly Inuit woman made it over weeks of long, hard work. It shows scenes from the locals' everyday life in accurate detail. She buys twenty tickets, but she'll give them away. They'd never forgive her in Port Brendan if the quilt were to go to someone from elsewhere, like herself. Because that's what she'll always be, an outsider—she harbors no illusions about that. Even if she were to live here for twenty years. At that moment she discovers a person she can give the tickets to.

"Meeka," she shouts, "are you going to the arena?"

Meeka Stout stops. She's wearing a modern version of the traditional parka, with colorful embroidery.

"I've got to go on stage again," she replies, "for the rehearsal. There were problems with the microphone earlier."

"Here." Ann hands her the tickets. "I bought too many and don't want the quilt."

Meeka sees through her ploy and grins. "Yes, I heard it's ugly. Nobody wants it."

She doesn't take the tickets.

Ann sticks them in the side pocket of her parka.

"Where are the kids?"

"Rick took them over to the barbeque. He promised them some Arctic char."

Meeka makes no move to leave. "I saw you with the two Mounties. The new one was at my place this morning. But don't tell Rick."

"No worries. What did she want from you, anyway?"

Ann knows direct questions like this are not welcomed by the locals. But in this case, Meeka brought up the subject and probably forgives her pushiness.

"Who knew that Bakie went to the Viking house on Wednesday?"

Ann is taken aback. "She asked you that?"

"No, I'm asking you. What was he doing there?"

"No idea. I only know that Dr. Perrell thought we'd have to test the acoustics there again. He said in an email that he wanted to go there with you. But that has . . . had nothing to do with Kris."

The sound of drums and singing wafts over them from somewhere.

Meeka responds with astonishment. "Dr. Perrell has never said anything about it to me. I didn't know he wanted to go there with me."

"Oh? I don't get it. It seemed very important to him. You see him quite a lot, don't you?"

Meeka turns her face away so that Ann can only see her embroidered hood. "Now and then, for . . . "

A gang of young people merrily whooping it up passes by. Some words on their backs tell where they're from: *Team Rigolet*. A woman follows them, her child sitting on a sled drawn by a large husky.

Meeka looks back at Ann. "She asked who has a key to the Viking house. Why did she want to know?"

"Maybe because she suspects one of us."

When Ann sees Meeka's stunned look, she regrets her rash answer. "I wasn't serious. We all have an alibi."

Meeka half turns away. "I've got to go now. Thanks anyway for the tickets."

Ann's eyes follow her. She actually wanted to go to the arena, too, but changes her mind. She might well intimidate Meeka even more.

So she limits her plans for the time being to taking a few

pictures of the visitors, of the preparations for the snowshoe race, of volunteers in their green jackets, and of dog sleds. When she turns around to photograph a group of young athletes, she almost bumps into a fast-approaching snowmobile. She saves herself by jumping aside, but catches a glimpse of the woman driving it.

She recovers from the shock only after taking several deep breaths that burn her lungs. RCMP Sergeant Bernard Closs's wife missed her by a hair. Then drove on unapologetically; her snowmobile is already on the ice in the bay.

A passerby who watched the near miss grins.

"That was a close one," he shouts at her.

Ann grins halfheartedly back. Although she in fact sees nothing funny about it. But something entirely different.

31

I see no reason not to ride around on my snowmobile today. There are far too many cars in Port Brendan. It's cold, but the sun's shining, and that makes everything a bit more bearable. Besides, I'm getting a better handle on driving the machine. I'm not afraid of the trail across the bay anymore. My right side isn't hurting. That gives an enormous boost to my feeling of wellbeing.

And that Fred comes along pleases me, too. He's opening up a little more with each passing day. The police car is parked in front of the fish factory, where as a matter of fact we run into Ann Smith. Which surprises us both.

I can't shake off the suspicion that she's keeping a whole lot of things from us. Behind those fake eyelashes, there are probably red herrings hiding away that she's feeding us. Nothing has changed this feeling, even with this brief encounter; quite the contrary. I intend to speak with her a second time.

But Fred and I must first make a quick trip to the shed at the cell-phone tower, where teenagers reportedly drink loads of alcohol. We arrive to find four empty beer bottles but no teens. So it's back to Port Brendan. I'm disappointed that we don't meet Ann Smith again in the village.

I briefly consider phoning her, but I've always been one for surprise attacks.

"I'm going to pop over and see her," I let Fred know. "Can you hold the fort?"

He agrees at once. My respect for him goes up accordingly.

I take the Ski-Doo out on the bay ice. When I don't see Ann's car at her place, I change my plan.

I leave Ghost Bay behind. The ice scrunches and crackles beneath my snowmobile's skis. I go slowly so that the wind in my face doesn't feel colder. The ice should hold through March, but I don't know that for sure. I see other people riding over it, apparently carefree. What would I do if a crack opened up somewhere? Or if the ice sagged? I haven't got a clue. Nevertheless I drive impatiently toward the Viking house. I can't help it; sometimes it simply grabs me. If I didn't have this obsessive urge, this feeling of being driven, fear would open its jaws. I hope to discover something in the house that I missed earlier. If I'm there alone, I can completely immerse myself in the scene of the crime.

I'm annoyed when I must stop on the ice: my sunglasses keep fogging up and have to be wiped clean. All the same, I feel something like freedom and control on the ice for the first time. The vastness expands my head and lungs and takes a weight off both. Only light and white and sky and horizon. Maybe that's what lures fishermen onto the infinite ocean each year, this lack of any limitation. The ocean is stronger than anything, even when it's covered with ice.

I get moving again. The Viking house comes closer. I steer my machine carefully over the beach and up the snow-covered bank. How different the place seems. Weird. I sometimes wonder if the ghosts of murder victims still hover above the scene of a crime for days on end. But I don't say that to anybody.

I park the snowmobile some distance off; I want to examine the tracks around the house once again. My hopes are dashed. The snow is trampled down almost everywhere. Good that I took pictures when the tracks were still visible. I blink in the sunshine. A lot of people in and around Port Brendan own heavy Ski-Doos with wide skis, not only Hynes and my teammate Sullivan. Checking numerous alibis turned up nothing suspicious. All kinds of people apparently have a key to the Viking house, not merely the fundraisers but also people in the tourist office. And Hynes and his workmen.

Sullivan and Delgado didn't come across any promising angles when interviewing Bakie's friends and relatives. Maybe we're digging in the completely wrong place. Sullivan is still investigating whether Bakie's one-time friend and employee is considered a suspect. And Dennis, Melissa Richards's brother, came up with an alibi for the time of the murder. Unless his mother's lying. Which can't be discounted. Three days have passed since the murder, and there's still no concrete clue as to Bakie's killer. Three days aren't much, but still, things can't move fast enough for me. Hopefully forensics in Happy Valley-Goose Bay will finally come through with results.

I'll work on Bakie's laptop tonight, in peace and quiet. But something's driving me to go back to the crime scene. The way a murderer often returns to the scene where he committed his horrible act.

I slowly approach the sod house. It's so quiet here, after the noise in the village. Suddenly, a large, brown animal stumbles among the trees at the edge of the woods. A bull moose. I freeze. It freezes also, and its dark eyes look at me through long eyelashes. Then it takes two steps toward me and doesn't change direction until I raise my arms, terrified. It gallops along the border of the woods as if on stilts and disappears. My heart is in my throat, beating wildly. I read somewhere that the bull moose is classified as one of the most dangerous animals on earth, especially when in rut. That's in autumn, I know, but the sheer size of the moose was alarming. I stand on the spot for a while as if paralyzed and scour the forest edge for any hint of the moose.

Fortunately, bears are hibernating. But other wildlife—wolves, lynx, foxes, wolverines, coyotes—frisk about in the woods and on the tundra. Polar bears show up at times on the nearby coast. They follow the seals on the ice and go back north in spring. You can apparently see them every winter when they wander through villages. I suddenly realize how reckless it was to come out here alone.

I shiver as I take off my gloves and fumble with the key Meeka gave me a few hours ago. The crime scene tape and the seals on the doors have already been removed, which amazes me. Sullivan and Delgado didn't really take much time to investigate the crime scene. I turn the key in the lock and step into darkness. I have my flashlight on me, but I want to absorb the atmosphere of the room in the dark. That's how the killer—man or woman—must have waited for the victim. In darkness in a windowless room. A glimmer of light, from a flashlight, say, wouldn't be visible from outside. But the killer must have felt safer in the dark. It's quite possible that he parked his snowmobile farther away, as I did. That way Bakie wouldn't have discovered it.

Until now I assumed that Bakie intended to meet somebody here. Maybe that wasn't the case at all. Maybe he wanted to take another look at the room where the banquet was to be held, but all by himself this time; or he wanted to check out his plans on site. But that still doesn't explain how the perp knew Bakie was coming. And why he killed him. Did Bakie surprise him when he was doing something illegal?

Did the perp intend to steal something and panicked?

I've already considered the possibility that there were two perps. A secret meeting nobody was to see. I must go through the photos again more carefully.

I put on my latex gloves by flashlight. Force of habit. I see the chalk lines on the floor where Bakie's body was. I throw light on corner after corner, walls, ceiling, floor; look under baskets and ropes, inspect tools and animal pelts, leather pouches and quivers.

Suddenly I'm seized by a strange feeling.

I'm not alone. Somebody's watching me. I stop; all my senses are sharper. Still, I can't hear, smell, or see anything. I shudder, but not with cold. Maybe terror from meeting the bull moose is still in my bones. I get a hold of myself. Imagine the progression of events. The murderer hides against the wall behind the door, waits until Bakie comes in. Bakie's wearing a thin ski hat on his head; he's pulled back the hood of his green parka. The killer doesn't see his victim's face. Nor his hair, nor the back of his head. He knocks his victim down from behind with a heavy tool or bludgeon. A new scenario emerges in my imagination, still fuzzy, but with potentially grave consequences. I absolutely must talk to Melissa Richards again.

A noise.

I whirl around, flashlight in one hand, pistol in the other.

"Who's there?" I shout.

A movement in the pile of hides lying in the corner on a bunk bed. A leg appears, then another.

"I have a gun," I warn.

A muffled voice. "Don't shoot. It's me."

Two arms scrabble through the hides, pushing them aside until a figure is discernible. Shannon Wilkey.

She stands up and puts a shielding arm before her eyes.

"The light's blinding me," she protests.

I turn the flashlight away. Now she sees my weapon.

"Please put that gun away, Constable. I won't do anything to you." Her voice trembles slightly.

I open the door to let more light in.

"What are you doing here?"

She brushes the dust off her jacket as if that were the most important thing in the world right now. I know that nervousness lies behind this gesture.

"I thought you were the killer coming back. So I quickly went and hid. I could hardly breathe under all those hides. I hoped I wouldn't have to sneeze."

I repeat my question in a stronger tone of voice. "What in the world are you doing here?"

She looks at me, realizing that she has escaped potentially being murdered but is standing in front of a Mountie.

"I lost something, a flashlight, and wanted to see if it was around here somewhere."

The flashlight we found. Now we have its owner. But still no explanation.

"Why didn't you ask the police? This is a crime scene."

"It was sort of on impulse."

We go out into the sunshine in front of the building. The brightness is dazzling after the dark sod house.

"Mrs. Wilkey . . ."

"Please, call me Shannon."

She puts on sunglasses. Nice move—I can't see her eyes anymore.

"Shannon, why didn't you tell us about the flashlight?"

"I didn't notice until today that it was missing and thought it might be here. Or I'd lost it on the way."

"How did you get here?"

"By Ski-Doo. I rented one." She points to the edge of the woods.

What an extravagance to go looking for a small, cheap flashlight. I try to read the part of her face that's uncovered. Something doesn't add up. I apply the screws.

"Shannon, I believe you're misdirecting me. Nothing you're telling me is logical. The Viking house is a murder scene. We're carrying out an investigation. You are bound by law to tell us the truth."

My words don't fail to have their effect; she goes silent for a while. Debating with herself about what to say or what she has to keep quiet.

"Okay, what do you want to know?" she asks at last.

"When were you last in the Viking house?"

"On Wednesday morning."

I think I've misheard.

"On the morning of the murder?"

"Yes. Actually, we were all supposed to meet here. I mean, Kris, Dr. Perrell, Meeka, and me."

"And Ann Smith?"

"Not her, she's kept herself out of it."

"So all the others were here?"

The tracks in the snow say otherwise. And nobody has mentioned anything about this plan to us before now.

"No, only me, as it turned out. Bakie didn't write me until after we were supposed to meet that he couldn't come that morning. Dr. Perrell canceled when Meeka didn't answer his email. He wanted to test the acoustics in the room. What a hoot that is!"

"Why?"

Shannon pouts, expressing her anger.

"We can't hold the banquet here. It simply won't do. You can see for yourself that the tables and chairs aren't even here. A week before the closing ceremonies! No microphone, no electronic equipment. The mobile kitchen isn't ready to go. The generator isn't doable—it's much too loud. This place isn't easily accessible for everybody at this time of year. As a matter of fact, Bakie hasn't wanted any part of this for a long time."

She looked exasperated as hell. I can hear the frustration in her voice.

"What didn't he want to do anymore?"

"This whole business with the Viking house. He's an Inuk. He doesn't give a damn about this place. It doesn't have anything to do with the history of his people. Vikings and Inuit were already bashing one another's heads in a thousand years ago."

I find this fact ironic, given what happened to Kris Bakie. But

Shannon can't actually know that it was a blow to the head that killed Bakie. Or can she?

"You were here alone on Wednesday morning?"

"Yes, and I was pissed off."

"Why did you keep this quiet when you were interviewed?"

"You didn't ask me about it. You only wanted to know where I was in the afternoon."

"You're not stupid. You surely knew that it would be of interest to us."

She takes off her sunglasses and looks me square in the face.

"Constable, I'm here as a foreigner. I'm scared about being dragged into a murder investigation in any way, shape, or form. Besides, I was in shock. Bakie's death really hit me hard."

"How long did you wait here Wednesday morning?"

"A full hour. I almost froze my feet off. I should've known: I should have let the others do it and kept out of the fundraising."

"Did you have anything to do with Bakie's death?"

She puts her sunglasses back on. "No, Constable, you're on the wrong track. I was painting all afternoon."

"But you have no witnesses."

"Oh, but I do," she says, almost triumphantly. "My cleaning lady came by late in the afternoon."

"You didn't tell us that last time, either."

She puts her hood on over her head.

"I really couldn't imagine you'd seriously think I was a suspect, Constable."

"What does your flashlight look like?"

Shannon hesitates before she lets the cat out of the bag.

"It's a SureFire Lawman."

I'm speechless. That's not the small flashlight from the crime scene we sent to the lab. That's a very expensive item. No wonder Shannon's been looking for it. The SureFire R1 Lawman is for pros. For search-and-rescue teams. And for the police. What baffles me the most: the SureFire is like a weapon. A defensive weapon. Its beam can blind an attacker and put him out of commission for a few minutes. And something else flashes through my brain: the SureFire weighs roughly a kilogram; it's heavy enough for a person to strike a serious blow with it.

I immediately see Shannon through totally different eyes.

"Why the heck were you running around with a SureFire Lawman?"

"We're in the wilderness out here, Constable. Not in Canada Place in Vancouver."

I ignore the dig. A certain fact has crystallized.

I believe we've got the second murder weapon. The one that hit Bakie on the head.

That is, we don't have it quite yet.

The killer took it with him.

32

"We have the forensics results for Bakie's corpse and cell phone." Bernard Closs is concealing the feeling that he doesn't have the situation under satisfactory control and isn't making any significant headway. Three days isn't long in a murder investigation. Still, he wishes the noose were tightening around the killer's neck. And not around his own. He faces disappointing four expectant people.

His anger over Calista Gates is still bubbling inside him. He had to make it clear to her that she can't simply disappear by herself to places without taking the station satellite phone and without informing headquarters beforehand. Or him personally. Gates defended herself by saying that she didn't want to tell Wendy because the dispatcher would reveal her location. To his wife Georgina, for example. He secretly had to admit she was right. Wendy ought not to pass on any information, even to his wife. But Port Brendan is a small world with its own laws, and neither he nor Gates can change anything there. Besides, he doesn't want any trouble with his wife. He's got his hands full dealing with the media; they want to see results. To say nothing of his RCMP superiors.

Shortly before the meeting, Gates briefed him on her

encounter with Shannon Wilkey. But he hadn't had time to consider that because he had to concentrate on the team meeting. His information will come first on the agenda; everything else will come afterward. He holds up a sketch outlining a human body.

"The head wounds are external; they come from blows with a blunt object, which were not able to shatter the cranium. The medical examiner assumes there were three blows, the second of which probably knocked the victim unconscious. The head was not protected by the hood on the jacket; the victim was only wearing a thin, synthetic head covering, the kind worn under a helmet. The victim was already unconscious when attacked with a knife. The body does not exhibit any defensive wounds."

He points to a photo.

"Here we see two stab wounds, one under the shoulder blade, one next to the spine. They are not deep and wouldn't by themselves have been fatal. The third wound is on the upper arm, and this one opened up an artery, leading to a great loss of blood. The victim bled out before he could regain consciousness. The murder weapon is the knife we found in the Viking house."

Sullivan stops chewing on his energy bar to interrupt him.

"Just three stab wounds—that doesn't exactly look like overkill. The perp evidently didn't even wait to be certain that Bakie was dead."

Bernard frowns. "We don't know how long the killer stayed with his victim."

He deliberately plays the devil's advocate, arguing in order to illuminate the problem from all sides.

Fred clears his throat. "The killer could have turned his victim over on his back and stabbed him in the heart. But he didn't."

"Maybe he couldn't stomach seeing the victim's face as he killed him. Delgado?"

Frank Delgado makes a face. "Doesn't look to me like he knew the victim, but was rather passive-aggressive. To go at him from behind like that without confronting his victim. A cowardly perp."

"Or he was much too afraid of the victim. Could it have been a woman killer, who could only kill this way?"

"Women and knives. Doesn't happen very often." Sullivan talks with his mouth full.

All eyes turn to Calista Gates, as if she's an expert on female killers. She hasn't said anything up to this point. Bernard would have liked to pump Georgina for her impression of Gates, though he knows that such things are taboo between them. Gates looks tired. But you'd never know once she gets talking.

"I think it's probable that Kris Bakie's the victim of mistaken identity."

He's too surprised to come up with a counterargument.

And the others wait and see for her to set out her reasons.

"My theory is that the killer was ambushing somebody else. He couldn't see who drove up on the Ski-Doo because he was inside the Viking house. Totally dark, and no windows, as we all know. He simply assumed it was his victim because he'd somehow learned that the person was going to show up at that time. When Bakie entered, he was still wearing his thin head protection. His hair and head and most of his face were concealed. The murderer couldn't really see who he was hitting. Only after the stab wounds, which didn't go very deep because of Bakie's thick parka and clothing, did he realize he'd got the wrong person. It's possible that he panicked and took off."

"Or she," Fred notes.

"Or a Viking."

Sullivan's wisecrack makes the men laugh; even Bernard has to grin. He looks at Calista.

Her mien is serious.

"I contacted Melissa Richards today and asked how long Bakie owned that green parka. I thought it looked new. Melissa confirmed that he'd just purchased it online. So the perp—male or female—couldn't identify the person by his parka."

"Doesn't sound plausible to me," Sullivan objects. "In my opinion the murder wasn't planned. The killer used a knife that he found in the Viking house."

Gates is undeterred.

"He could well have brought a knife with him and decided at the scene not to use it so it couldn't be traced to him."

"Tell us about the flashlight," Bernard prompts her. He hopes the SureFire Lawman will bolster her theory.

She recounts in detail what took place late that morning in the Viking house.

Delgado exclaims: "Why is Shannon still running around free? She could have committed the murder."

Gates stays calm.

"She says she has an alibi for the time of the murder, that her cleaning lady was at her place. I don't believe she can knock out a man like Bakie with a flashlight. Even with a SureFire Lawman. But we certainly have to probe some more."

"Gates, with all due respect, your theory is far-fetched."

Sullivan must be frustrated that his own research hasn't been successful, Bernard thinks, and he can empathize with him.

"Why would the perp take the Surefire Lawman with him when he fled?" Sullivan asks. "If he'd left it at the scene, the thing would throw suspicion on the person who owns it. That's Shannon Wilkey. He left the knife there; why not the flashlight as well?"

"Maybe he thought he could use it."

Gates stops, as if something just occurred to her.

"We should turn to the public to look for it."

"How so? Advertise on Facebook?" Sullivan rolls his eyes. "The murderer will definitely hide the thing."

Fred pipes up. "Bakie probably went to the Viking house because he mistakenly supposed that Shannon Wilkey was there. Remember Gates told him that Shannon wasn't home when he came to her villa? He'd called off the morning meeting with the committee and could have wanted to explain himself to her. Probably the two of them were looking for a way to hold the banquet in a more practical location."

It doesn't escape Bernard that Gates casts a thankful eye on her teammate. So they're working together. She obviously feels Fred has backed her up and throws her next words on the table like a challenge.

"If it really was a case of mistaken identity, as I suspect, then the killer is still going to go after his actual victim."

Sullivan and Delgado shake their heads in unison. Fred says nothing. I have to make sure Gates doesn't wrap him around her little finger, Bernard thinks.

He quickly reassumes control of the meeting.

"We'll let that theory hold for now and examine concrete facts. For example, the cell phone. The provider is Telus. Here's the analysis. We can see who Bakie was in contact with in the days before his death."

He distributes the list of phone numbers and text messages.

"Bakie was ready to make a break for it. He'd accepted a job offer from the Hyatt Regency hotel in Las Vegas. But he didn't tell anybody. You see the flight confirmation with WestJet. Las Vegas, one way only. The emails with the hotel."

Delgado is the first to speak up.

"He was on the lam. Somebody must have guessed that he wanted out. Maybe the Richards family. Dennis Richards would surely be furious if Bakie walked out on his sister."

"Dennis also might have poisoned the dog."

All eyes turn to Fred.

"The poison came from Alberta—it's not available here. Dennis boasted that he'd brought rat poison from Alberta and that his mother has had no problems with pests ever since."

"So it's a Richards family vendetta?" Sullivan's fingers drum audibly on the table.

"We know that Dennis Richards invested in Bakie's restaurant," Bernard sums up. "Fifty thousand dollars. No written contract. That's how he got Bakie to get engaged to Melissa. Bakie threatened not to pay him back. We've confiscated a knife and a bone saw from Richards."

Delgado breaks in. "But we've got the murder weapon."

"We're talking about the dog, not Bakie," Bernard patiently explains. "Dennis has an alibi from his mother for the time of Bakie's murder."

"The way the Richardses stick together, the alibi could have been invented."

"I think we shouldn't concentrate just on Dennis Richards," Gates butts in.

"Yeah, sure. The victim was supposedly confused with somebody else," Sullivan says mockingly.

Gates doesn't take the bait. Her years with the RCMP have toughened her up, Bernard thinks. And she knows how to return the ball elegantly.

"How have you progressed with your investigations?" she asks in a neutral tone of voice.

"We haven't gotten much that's useful concerning the victim and his family," Sullivan admits.

So many hours of work for practically nothing. Bernard could tell him that it's often just as important to exclude something as to find something, but that wouldn't fly.

"And you?" Sullivan asks in return.

"The hat from Vancouver was apparently sold in an online auction by the animal rescue group two or three years ago. Too bad I forgot to ask Shannon if it was hers. I'll get back to her. Fred can tell you more about it."

"I've got a list of the seven women who bought the red sweatshirts with the words *Animals Are the Better People* around that time. At least one of the shirts turned up at a yard sale. A member of the group saw it there. Hard to say where it wound up afterward."

"And the ax?"

"Belongs to Gerald Hynes, and he verified it. He claims somebody stole it. And he has an alibi for the time of the murder."

"An alibi from one of his workers who surely doesn't want to lose his job." Bernard can't resist the remark. "We've got to put the heat on a few people. Invite them in for a lie detector test. Let's see how they react."

He savors the astonishment on their faces. At least a few pleasurable seconds for today.

"You're not serious, Sarge," Delgado says.

"No, of course not. Most people won't know we're bluffing. They know about lie detectors from TV and believe everything they see. We'll just apply a bit of pressure and observe their reaction."

"How's this supposed to happen?"

"We'll start with Dennis Richards and Gerald Hynes. Then we'll wait and see. Sullivan has also checked on a former employee of Bakie's who supposedly hates his guts. Bakie fired him because he was on drugs. False alarm, unfortunately. The man has an iron-clad alibi."

"When do we get the dope on Bakie's clothes?" Delgado continues. "We haven't even got the results of the fiber tests. Nothing on blood traces. Let alone DNA. Maybe the perp's in a data bank, but we can't even search that."

Closs feels a stabbing pain in his stomach. "It can take some time." To divert the conversation, he turns to Fred. "What's up with the questioning of Dr. Perrell?"

"I thought someone else was taking care of that," Fred replies.

"He's my doctor," Gates says.

Sullivan laughs. "He's everybody's doctor, unless Dr.

Cameron's on call. So what's that supposed to mean? But okay, we'll contact him."

Fred thanks him, and Sullivan asks: "Something we should shower him with questions about?"

Gates beats Fred to it. "The knife that severed the dog's head might have been a scalpel."

"Well, my dear colleague, you're laying it on pretty thick today. Should we arrest the doc right now?"

Fred reduces the tension with his dry delivery. "Look into who among the fundraisers was planning to meet at the Viking house on Wednesday, and at what time, exactly. And how they communicated. Then we'll know if Shannon's telling us the truth."

"And we'll reexamine all the committee members' alibis," Bernard announces, avoiding Gates's eyes because he knows she isn't pleased with his response. Because she thinks the killer is still after his real victim. Hell, even if she's right—and he hopes not—then he can't do much about it. Happens to a lot of investigators. Murders you anticipate and still can't prevent in spite of all your efforts. Some people can forgive themselves; others let it eat them up inside. Or they bite as tight as an attack dog and never let go. Until they die. Or are murdered.

33

I'm boiling inside. So furious that I almost drive into a snowbank. That farce of a meeting—nothing was really discussed thoroughly. Closs simply cut me off. I know my theory sounds startling, but an investigator must be open to options. Closs doesn't want to come to grips with a potential case of mistaken identity, because it makes him feel powerless. Above all, he doesn't want my assumption to get out to the public and cause panic. Then the Winter Games would be down the drain. As if they're more important than people's safety.

I don't know if my presumption is correct. I just want it to be taken seriously. It can be fatal not to spot a danger. Fatal for innocent people. The way it was fatal for Becca Heyer. And maybe for Kris Bakie.

A husky crosses the street and I brake. It must have gotten loose from somewhere, because he's dragging a chain behind him. Probably one of the dogs in the dog-sled race. I don't have the strength to worry about it. Closs would tell me to get lost if I came in with a stray dog. The sarge is so desperate that he's threatening people with a lie-detector test. Very funny. There's not a machine like that for miles around.

Two murders, no progress. We haven't even been able to clear up the circumstances around the death of Arrow, Bakie's dog. Fred thinks Dennis Richards poisoned it. But that doesn't mean he decapitated the dog. And anyway, what would his motive be? The dog wasn't just Bakie's but Dennis's sister's as well.

At least Fred didn't turn against me. He could easily have exploited the situation. He doesn't think my suspicion implausible. But in doing so, he puts himself directly in his boss's line of fire.

My turn-off comes into view. My anger shifts to Georgina Closs. Good neighbor Rick sent me a text. Georgina has dropped off sleeping bags, pillows, and other things at his place because I wasn't home and the door was locked. She's a busy bee and efficient—you've got to hand it to her. I'm royally pissed off nevertheless because I'm losing my privacy, and during a stressful murder investigation.

Pains in my right leg have come back. Remarkable, the places my brain sends signals to. I knock on the front door at the Stouts' out of habit, although nobody here knocks. The children are all over me at once when they hear me. Nothing beats the sight of a genuine woman Mountie. They want to see my gun, but I fend them off.

Rick appears in the hallway.

"I was on the john," he excuses himself. He looks as if he's just gotten up; his hair is sticking out all over his head. I don't envy him taking care of the kids; I had to take care of my kid sisters for years. Older children condemned to do the same would later either have a huge flock of kids or want to have none at all. I belong to the second group.

Without my asking, Rick informs me that Meeka's gone to the arena for rehearsal. I conjure up three stuffed bunnies from my backpack: white snow hares, the Winter Games mascots. The two boys tear them out of my hand.

Dulcie hugs her stuffed animal very tenderly, with both hands. Her eyes are shining.

"What's his name?"

"You can give him one."

"Arrow," one boy shouts, the one whose name I can never remember.

"No, not Arrow," Dulcie protests. "Not Arrow."

I help her out.

"Maybe Bunnybaby."

"Yes, Bunnybaby." Dulcie beams and trots off with her bunny. "Bunnybaby. Bunnybaby," I hear her sing.

I look at Rick but don't want to mention the dead dog with the children present. It's really peculiar that Dulcie thinks Dr. Perrell did something to the dog. And that the boy said the name Arrow.

"It's all here, downstairs," Rick says as he leads the way. In the basement, I stay rooted to the spot, staring at four bulging garbage bags. They're a sparkling blue.

"Where did you get these garbage bags?"

"Those are Georgina's things."

"I can't believe my eyes!" I exclaim.

Poor Rick. My reaction must absolutely confuse him, but I don't discuss my discovery with him. He helps me load up the sleeping bags.

"Found anything out about Bakie yet?" he asks.

"I can't say because it's an ongoing investigation."

Rick nods in resignation.

"He didn't deserve it. Really didn't. Meeka's crushed."

I didn't get that impression during my last conversation with her, but many people don't show their feelings openly. Rick goes into the house and brings back a plastic container from his freezer.

"Here, for you. Meeka's pea soup's the best, and you surely don't have much time now to cook."

I'm touched and thank him before driving home. I'm barely through the door when I phone Closs.

"Your wife brought me some sleeping bags, and they're packed up in blue garbage bags. Where'd she get them?"

He doesn't seem to understand right away. He's got a press conference going on. Online, conference call.

"Why did she take sleeping bags to your place?" he asks.

Holy smokes! Don't they ever talk to each other?

"For my guests, for some athletes in the Winter Games. The garbage bags are shiny blue."

Now the penny drops.

"I'll call her. She's on the night shift. I'll call you right back."

I drag the bags into the guest room. My leg's throbbing.

As I'm putting the pillow cases on, Closs calls back.

"My wife got them from the clinic," he states. "The bags are used for wet special waste, like after operations."

"And who has access to the bags?"

"The whole staff."

"This means that all the people working in the clinic have to be looked at more closely." I suppress a sigh.

Closs waits a bit before sharing a further complication. "The bags aren't properly disposed of. They wind up in the dump, which is actually not permitted, in fact."

"If I understand you correctly, there are special bags in the clinic for special waste, and they nevertheless wind up in the dump—every last one of them?"

"So it seems."

I think for a minute.

"Somehow I can't imagine somebody going to the dump, emptying a plastic bag with disgusting stuff in it, and then reusing it."

"Unless somebody wants to throw suspicion on somebody else."

"That would be an awful lot of people."

"About two dozen people work in the clinic, not counting the cleaners."

I'd love to say, "Quiz your wife about the folks in the clinic." But I've got to leave that to him. I hope he'll do it.

After our talk, I thaw Meeka's pea soup out, heat it up, and swallow it down boiling hot. I'd never expected a soup to taste so good. Salt beef, yellow split peas, onions, carrots, and turnips. She added bell pepper as well. Sated by a good meal and therefore less angry, I shove the memory stick into the laptop and go through the content of Bakie's emails, hoping to verify my theory of mistaken identity. A few irrelevant emails in the inbox. I go to the trash folder and find the exchange with Dennis Richards. Who thinks like that? Forcing Bakie to marry Melissa by investing in his restaurant? Some marriages don't last long, even with the best of intentions, as I know from my own experience. Martin, my ex, was a fair-weather partner, and I had some really good times with him. But when the going got tough, he left me. Bakie was already out the door; maybe he loved Melissa as well as he could, but he obviously didn't want to chain himself to the Richards family.

I'm astonished to find an email from Ann Smith: *Kris, don't push it too far. Or else it could mean a sudden end for you.*

At first reading, it sounds like a death threat. But I reject the thought after some consideration. It's more probable that Ann was referring to a conflict within the organizing committee. If Kris were to demand impossible terms for his banquet, then the others would drop the whole project.

I look in the photo file. About two dozen pictures of meals beautifully presented on plates. Bakie on a snowmobile trip. Pictures of landscapes. Bakie with sled dogs. A couple of family photos. Then some posed pictures with Melissa, probably engagement pictures taken by a professional photographer. You can tell by looking. But otherwise no personal pictures with Melissa. Maybe she moved them to another electronic device.

I take a second look for deleted files. I find just four photos, apparently of the hospital's committee for fundraising. All of them are the same, but still, one strikes me. It's of Dr. Perrell with

Meeka, Bakie, Shannon, and Ann. The doctor and Shannon placed Meeka in the center. Meeka and Dr. Perrell aren't looking at the camera; their heads are turned to each other—the sun must have blinded them.

Ann is wearing sunglasses and standing closer to Bakie. Rather close, but they aren't touching. She looks serious, as if she had to force herself to pose for the photo. Bakie, on the other hand, is smiling. A head-turner. He's about Ann's height, slim—no muscleman. He looks rather wiry. He isn't wearing his green parka yet but a blue down jacket. Ann's in a white, embroidered parka. I'd love to have one like it.

My leg is relaxed; the pains have almost disappeared. Doesn't mean a thing; they come as quickly as they go away, often in bed as well. Suddenly something hits me. I cover Ann and Kris's heads with a sheet of paper. Then I stare at their height. They're almost the same, and both have a slim build. Of course. How could I miss it. The killer could have mistaken Bakie for a woman. People in the dark, and in voluminous winter clothing and with their heads covered, can hardly be told apart. If my theory's correct, then the murderer could be going after a woman.

Two thoughts flash through my mind: First, should I warn Shannon, Ann, and Meeka? Thought number two: What if one of them is the killer?

I think frantically. As an RCMP officer, I must leave these kinds of warnings to my boss. And I also can't really imagine that one of these three women can knock a man unconscious with a heavy flashlight. Even if the flashlight is perfect for it. Unless the perp is completely out of her mind and prepared to risk everything. Shannon, maybe? But why?

I go through dozens of scenarios in my head, write down names and notes next to them. I don't know how much time has gone by when my phone twitters. The name on the display tells me I have to get ready for a rather long conversation.

"Hello, Mom."

"Hello, my little girl. How are you?"

"Rather well. Just a little tired today. How are you and Dad?"

"He's feeling better. His heart is almost back to normal. I just have to make sure he takes all his medications. And you, are you taking yours?"

I am almost thirty-six and still being mothered. At some point in the future, that will be reversed; I know it from friends with elderly parents. To be sure, my mother will only give up her role with great resistance—I'm convinced of it. I love her, especially from a distance, because otherwise she'd squeeze all the air out of me.

"I certainly do; they really help me."

"Glad to hear it. Do you have a lot of stress?"

Her question tells me she's already heard about Bakie's death.

"Who told you?"

"It was in the paper. A young man, an Inuk, used to be a chef at the Hyatt Regency in Vancouver. How dreadful."

I suspect she thinks Bakie's violent death is dreadful, but for her it's even more dreadful that I must investigate a murder.

I settle her down.

"It happens all over, even in Labrador."

"Calista, I'm worried. That's not normal. You've just arrived in this godforsaken hick town and are supposed to investigate what happened to Lorna Taylor. And now there's another murder. How's that possible? You seem to attract these things."

I tense up. "What do you mean by 'I attract these things'?"

"Disaster follows you around."

"Mom, it's the other way around: I follow disaster."

"Ever since you heard that poor girl screaming back then, these things happen to you."

"They don't happen to me, Mom, they happen to innocent people. Go ahead and call these 'things' murders."

"I know, I know. I often think back to that night, my dear.

Your father and I, we ought to have listened to you. We ought to have—what was her name again?"

"Becca. Becca Heyer. But I don't want to talk about it anymore."

My mother could never be stopped when she got talking.

"If we'd gone looking for Becca right away, if we'd called the police right away, then you'd never have developed this obsession. We—"

"Yes, and the main thing is that maybe Becca would still be alive! That's worth an obsession, don't you think?"

"But you were only twelve years old, Calista. You looked for her everywhere, rang every doorbell. You constantly talked about Becca—nothing else."

"But that's . . . Really, Mother. If Becca had been one of your daughters, would you have called it an obsession?"

"I drummed it into all of you: never to go with strangers!"

"Maybe the murderer wasn't a stranger, maybe he knew Becca very well. That happens more that you think."

"We don't know that; the police never caught him, after all."

"Exactly."

I leave it hanging and unsaid. *Because you didn't believe me, he got away. And Becca lost her life, brutally.*

"You had so many talents. Oh, how you could dance! You used to dance for us in the living room. And such a head for figures. You found math so easy."

"You're saying I should have become an accountant?"

"The RCMP has only brought you misfortune, you have to admit it. That's no way to live."

Mom keeps talking, but my ears are shut. She refuses to acknowledge that I've found my vocation with the police. That I like the work. That I got ahead, moved up. Everything went well. Until I was attacked. But I recovered. I've made some more progress. So says my doctor. Incredible progress. One day everything will be just the way it was before. I have to believe in it. I won't give up. And Becca's murderer—one day I'll find him. I'll find him!

"I hope you will be coming back to Vancouver soon, my darling."

"I hope so, too."

"You're a stranger there, and I know how strangers are looked at in small villages. It was like that in Sophita, too."

Sophita is my mother's native village. It would have surprised me if it hadn't come up in our conversation. Unlike my father, my mother has never cut her ties to Greece.

"Were there no foreigners at all in Sophita?"

"Of course there were, my darling, not many, maybe two or three, who stayed for a few months. Mostly artists from Northern Europe. They didn't come anymore afterward."

"Afterward?"

"After the catastrophe with Ioannis, the fisherman. Have I never told you the story? He lost his boat because he couldn't pay off his debts. It was confiscated. A Swede who came to Sophita every year heard about it. He lent Ioannis his motorboat. A really nice man. But then Ioannis went out in bad weather, the boat tipped over, and he drowned. And do you know what happened? The people in the village said that it was the Swede's fault. That he'd lent him a faulty boat. But it was Ioannis's mistake. He shouldn't have taken it out."

A Greek tragedy. Why is she telling me this? My mother is not naïve. She'll deliver an explanation right away.

And so it is this time, too.

"There are dogs that bite the hand that feeds them."

As always, I can't hold back when mother tosses out bait.

"Mom, only if a dog has been badly treated and is afraid."

"That might be the case," my mother replies, "but they bite the wrong person."

34

Gerald Hynes rides his Ski-Doo to where the shooting contest will take place. He's one of the judges. The fresh air is good for him after working in Dr. Perrell's house, where his thoughts had been racing around in circles. Terrible thoughts. The sky is overcast, which isn't bad. The shooters won't have to squint when looking into the sun. Luckily the wind has died down somewhat, after raging during the night. He can see the large crowd of spectators from some distance away. The shooting contest always attracts a lot of people. Everybody wants to win, and the Hengstridet Corporation has donated the prize money for the hospital. At least twenty thousand. The higher the shooters' scores, the more money is added. To top it off, Hengstridet will double the final amount. The transport company generously stepped in as the sponsor after Bakie's murder. Probably helps its image. So now there won't be a seven-course dinner but a shooting contest instead. Gerald doesn't see the irony of it—that's just the way Labrador is. He's convinced that the contest will bring in more money for the clinic than a banquet would.

Nevertheless, at ten o'clock, he met Dr. Perrell, who was in a bad mood. Although the doctor had the day off and Dr. Cameron had to work this Sunday. Gerald actually intended to hash out details of the renovation, but the doctor was too busy venting his anger over the two Mounties who came to his place to grill him. In the course of the conversation, Gerald found out that it was Delgado and Sullivan, not Calista Gates. They evidently wanted to know who'd been in the Viking house and when, or who'd planned to go there. Dr. Perrell thought they were completely off track. The murder, he said, has nothing to do with Port Brendan. In Perrell's opinion, they should be rooting around in Happy Valley-Goose Bay. The policemen assured him that the local RCMP were doing just that right this minute. But Perrell's mood didn't improve. He kept lamenting: Bakie's restaurant is in Happy Valley-Goose Bay, and Bakie had many contacts there. By "contacts," Perrell probably meant possible enemies as well.

The doctor considers the constables to be amateurs; that's as clear to Gerald as the glass he's installed in the doctor's kitchen cupboards. Perrell claimed many cases haven't been solved because the separate RCMP detachments didn't cooperate. Gerald didn't reveal that the police also had him in their sights and that they were rechecking his alibi yet again. He'd learned this from his foreman. And now he was to undergo a lie-detector test as well. In Corner Brook, of all places. Yeah, they probably don't have all their marbles.

But he still has a grace period. In his opinion, the police can't do anything during the Winter Games. He's fully engaged as a volunteer. He rules on the hits on the targets for the shooting competition. He also arranged to assist the traditional Inuit games of strength; he finds them the most exciting. He's the referee for the seal crawl, the owl hop, and the high jump.

He stops at the tent where the shooters register and pay a small fee.

"How many?" he asks the woman in charge of the paperwork.

"Eleven teams, one hundred and ten shooters total; we've processed about a third of them so far. The best are still to come."

He makes a face. So many participants. That means he'll need to be there for hours.

"Well, then, let's go."

He turns around and discovers Calista Gates a few steps behind the crowd gathered next to the shooting stand. She's observing people. What's she looking for? Or whom? He's got no time for her, which is too bad. He quickly puts on his ear protection.

The banging begins. The fourteenth shooter, a man from Port Hope Simpson, has such a high score that the twenty thousand dollars for the clinic are already secure. It's not only about money but about ego. Gerald runs back and forth, examines the target sheets, enters the results, talks with the shooters who are whining about something or other. After an hour and a half, a young woman from Happy Valley-Goose Bay beats the man from Port Hope Simpson. Almost twenty-one thousand dollars. The spectators' mood is heating up.

Dennis Richards appears. Gerald can't find him on the list of registered shooters.

"Why should I pay a fee when I'm making money for the clinic?" Richards complains.

Gerald scowls and shakes his head.

"It won't kill you. All this costs money. The target sheets and all the administration."

Dennis is irritated.

"Sure, and it's going right into your pocket," he rails.

"Are you with the skinflints or the sponsors?" an onlooker shouts.

"The government should pay for the equipment in the clinic, not us," Richards responds. "That's the last thing we need."

Gerald sees Dr. Perrell in the crowd; he's too far away to hear them arguing, but somebody is sure to report to Perrell what Richards said. Hopefully the doctors will let the idiot wait in the clinic for hours next time when he's caught something.

A cluster of young women shooters hear the quarrel.

"You people always want money from the government," one of them shouts, "but you don't want to pay taxes. Where's the money supposed to come from?"

"So shoot better than me, you goddamn bitches," Richards yells, throwing a bill down on the registration table and picking up his rifle. "I'm on Team Port Brendan."

He demonstrates on this day, too, that he's an excellent shot. His score goes unchallenged for almost an hour, although the young women's scores are hot on his heels. Gerald picks up on the fact that they're in Monday's biathlon.

He's lost sight of Calista Gates, but Perrell materializes beside him and hands him a steaming coffee.

"I hope we make as much as the coffee cart over there," he jokes.

Gerald can imagine the doctor's fingers twitching.

"I can count about five people who can beat Richards," he assures him.

At that moment, he rediscovers Gates. The young women start talking to her at once and drag her over to the shooting stand. Gates goes along with it and laughs. He'd never seen her laugh. He can't tear himself away from watching her face. What a picture!

"She absolutely must take part," one of the biathletes shouts at him. "Cops are good shots."

Gates shakes her head.

"These people are billeted at my place," she explains to him with a wink. "They're going to turn my whole house upside down."

The young women won't give up.

"C'mon, Constable, it's worth a try, it's for the clinic."

Perrell intervenes, and Gerald keeps checking scores but pricks up his ears.

Gates begs off. "It's a shame, but I sprained my right hand

shoveling snow, and it's hopeless. I would disappoint you all."

Dennis Richards comes up and exclaims: "Constable, you can't hide behind that excuse."

"Shut your big trap, Richards!" the same onlooker as before shouts. This time Gerald studies him more closely.

Look at that. Rick Stout. He's usually not this rude. Maybe he wants to impress his neighbor.

Suddenly he hears a clear voice.

"I'll take your place, Constable. If you don't mind. You shouldn't have to shoot with an injury."

Ann Smith is standing next to them. Everyone looks at her in astonishment. She's so stylishly dressed up that she could have jumped out of the pages of a fashion magazine. Gerald often wondered what this exotic bloom was doing here in Port Brendan. She's a bit too exotic for his taste; he's heard she's a vegan and doesn't eat meat or fish—out of respect for animals. She'd head for the hills if she saw his stuffed freezer. And now this lady wishes to shoot. Several of the onlookers grin. Gerald won't stop Ann from shooting. As long as she registers with a team and pays the fee, she's free to enter the competition. She does it in seconds, deciding on Team Port Brendan.

Only Dennis Richards is bad mannered. "Yeah, let the good lady have a gun; we need women who can't shoot."

He laughs, and a few of his friends laugh along with him.

Gerald indicates to Ann her place on the shooting stand. She lies down on her stomach, in her white parka, and takes aim. He realizes at once she's not handling a gun for the first time. She fires speedily, and with concentration.

Those with binoculars react at once, shouting, "Wow!" and "Holy shit!" Their stunned looks say it all. The score leaves no doubt: Ann Smith hit a bull's-eye with every shot. The young women howl ecstatically as if they were in a hockey arena. Masterful—he can't rate it any other way. Ann has clearly left Dennis Richards in her dust.

Dennis stares at the score sheet and doesn't know what to make of it.

"What the hell . . . Is there cheating going on or what?"

"Not with me here," Gerald warns him. "I know what I'm doing."

But he's amazed as well.

Ann has stood up, her rifle still in her hand. Her eyes are shining. She raises the gun higher and higher. The barrel is aimed straight at the doctor standing two meters away.

Gerald is too surprised to step in.

"Dr. Perrell, the money goes to your clinic," she says.

Twenty-six thousand dollars. Doubled, that comes to fifty-two thousand for the hospital. The blood drains from the doctor's face. A barely audible word of thanks escapes his lips; then he turns on his heel and strides off. The rifle barrel still points in his direction. Calista Gates comes over to Ann and takes the gun out of her hands.

"Sorry," says Ann, as if in a trance.

Gerald can't explain how she pulled off a score that certainly no one will beat. But he doesn't doubt for a second that he's witnessed a scene whose significance is known only to Ann Smith and Dr. Perrell. He'd like to see the look on Calista Gates's face to guess what she thinks of it all, but as he turns toward her she's already running after the doctor, trying to catch up with him. People crowd around Gerald, commenting on the perfect result and wanting his opinion. He'd rather have known what the Mountie intends to do with Perrell. He's got no choice but to continue the competition, even if the participants' chances are now zero.

Before he announces the next round, he glances over the crowd, hoping to find Gates and Perrell. All he spots is Shannon Wilkey's face. She looks as if she'd swallowed a dozen hot chili peppers.

35

It's Shannon. I'm in my car. I had to call you immediately. There was an incident today.

What happened?

Ann Smith took part in a shooting competition, a fundraiser for the Port Brendan clinic.

Wow. That's . . . That's not like her.

I don't know why she did it. I'd never have thought it possible. She had the top score with the rifle.

Strange . . . that she'd take that risk. After all the effort she's made until now.

Isn't it? How can she put herself in such a risky situation? She finished shooting, stood up, and threatened Carl Perrell.

How's that?

She raised her rifle and aimed it at him. It's the only way I can describe it.

She aimed it at him?

Yes. I think she wanted to scare him. That's how I interpret it.

Do you mean to say that she knows that Carl Perrell . . . ?

I can't explain it any other way. Maybe he didn't keep his mouth shut.

The man can't be that stupid.

I could say that about Ann. She can't be that stupid.

What alarm level are we at now?

She's got to learn the truth. I'll let you know.

36

I run after Dr. Perrell as well as my boots permit on the trampled-down, icy snow. This is my chance to get something out of him. Several people stare at me, but I don't care. Ann's victory and Perrell's reaction will be the hottest story of the day anyway. I speed up because the doctor is already opening his car door. The motor's running when I knock on the window. He points to the passenger door, and I tear it open.

"Can I have a word with you?" I gasp.

He waves a hand.

"Get in."

I hope Closs doesn't see me, since I declared I don't want to question my own doctor. Sullivan and Delgado would definitely not be thrilled with my butting in. I'll think up an excuse.

"Congratulations on the successful fundraiser," I say, because I don't want to rush things.

Perrell looks at me. His face radiates the boldness of a globe-trotting adventurer. Which he is, of course, in his fashion. An Englishman who has given up his homeland to establish a clinic in a remote region of Canada's north.

Perrell wastes no time on polite formalities.

"Why did you follow me?"

"I'd like to know what was going on between you and Ann Smith just now."

"Constable, I don't have to tell you that because you were there. Anything else?"

"Why did Ann Smith aim that rifle at you?"

"Ask Ann Smith."

"I will. How well do you know her?"

"Do you want to know as a policewoman or as a concerned citizen?"

"Given there's been a murder, I'm both."

The motor has been running all this time; the car is gradually warming up inside. Maybe Dr. Perrell wants it noisy to prevent anybody from listening in from outside. Though that would be difficult with the constant banging away from the shooting area.

"What's that got to do with Bakie's death? I'm afraid you're wasting your time here, Constable."

He's impatient, and I wonder whether Ann's behavior didn't shake him up a little.

"I'd be wasting my time if I did nothing to solve the murder. That's the way you feel too, isn't it? You must also be concerned about Bakie's death."

He says nothing for a few seconds, looks straight ahead. His profile is impressive. Strangers would take him for a man of great decisiveness. He finally speaks.

"Ann and I are both involved in fundraising. As you've just seen."

"How well do you know her?"

"She's a woman who doesn't reveal much about herself."

"Is she your patient?"

"No."

"Is there some reason why she's not your patient?"

More hesitation. I can almost physically feel his resistance. If we were outside, he'd definitely make some excuse to escape. Sitting in a car with somebody makes it hard to hide.

"There was a time when I'd like to have known Ann better. She's attractive, she's mysterious. I'm single. It was only natural that I'd be interested in her. But it wouldn't have gone anywhere if she'd been my patient."

My pulse beats faster. Perrell has opened himself up a bit, a small gap into his inner self.

"Why did you emigrate to Canada?"

"I wasn't happy in England anymore; I was unfulfilled. Though I was perfectly busy. I almost never left the hospital. The constant pressure was destructive. My marriage ended in divorce because I worked so hard. My mother died sometime later, I was free to do whatever I wanted. An acquaintance of mine had emigrated to Canada, so I came here to take a look around."

"But why Labrador?"

"Because of Dr. Grenfell."

"Was that the acquaintance who emigrated to Canada?"

"No, no." Perrell shook his head. "You don't know about Dr. Grenfell?"

"Should I?"

"Yes, of course, he's a legend hereabouts. Dr. Grenfell was an Englishman like me. He came to Labrador at the end of the nineteenth century because there was absolutely no health care here. He had hospitals built, for instance one in St. Anthony in Newfoundland, and one on Battle Island in Labrador. In a hospital ship he sailed along the coast and treated patients. Sometimes he traveled by dogsled. One day he went missing out on the ice and almost died."

"But that was a long time ago."

"Yes, he died in 1940."

"You'd like to be a second Dr. Grenfell?"

"He inspired me. But he had more luck than I had. He married a rich American and lived with her in St. Anthony."

I find the reference to a rich American interesting.

"Do you smoke?"

He twitches imperceptibly.

"Why do you ask?"

"Do you smoke Karelias?"

He arches his eyebrows. "As a doctor you must set an example, as you most certainly know. The way the police must set an example."

That's a non-answer. Was he the one who left the cigarette wrapper in Shannon's bathroom?

I smile politely. "Correct. That does make the search for a suitable partner in a small community difficult."

"Are you talking about Ann Smith?"

If he answers a question with a question, so can I. "How did Ann respond to your interest?"

"She didn't respond. That was clear enough."

"Ann rescued the fundraising event for the clinic. And then pointed a gun at you. Why?"

"Maybe simply out of youthful impetuousness. You explain it to me, Constable, you were there."

"For my part, it looked like a threat."

Carl Perrell whips his head around in my direction.

"What do you mean by that?"

"If somebody aims a rifle at another person, it's either dangerously careless or a threat. Ann Smith doesn't seem to be a careless person to me."

"Maybe she was flushed with victory and wasn't paying attention."

He really doesn't believe that himself. Odd that he doesn't want to acknowledge the threat. Not to me, at least. I dig deeper.

"Is there something I ought to know?"

He rubs his clean-cut jaw. "Don't you want to know why Ann is a better shot than the locals?"

"Yes, of course. Can you explain that?"

He laughs dryly. "The obvious reason is that she's gifted and has practiced a lot."

"That's probably true for many women."

"Not for strangers who spend their summers in Port Brendan."

I think the time has come for a little surprise attack. "The dog's head I found on the ice was probably severed with a scalpel. Can you imagine how that's possible?"

His answer is astonishingly swift. "No. And I didn't put it there, if that's what you mean."

"Can I have a list of all the employees in the clinic? And the part-timers, kitchen staff, cleaning personnel?"

The doctor understands that this is not a question but an order.

"Yes, I'll do it at once. But don't forget the doctor's oath." He puts his hand on the wheel. "I've got to get back to the hospital. Are we done here?"

Most of the time when people want to get away, it's possible to ask one more question.

"So you think that Mrs. Smith has secrets?"

"Sure. Why is a woman like Ann in Port Brendan? What's she doing here? You should pursue that question."

I open the door to signal that he's now released.

"Maybe because of a man." I watch his reaction. "Did Bakie and Ann get along really well?"

He looks at me with a furrowed brow and refuses to answer. Then he reverses his car so fast that I'm just barely able to close the door.

The cold hits me like an ice-cold shower. I pull my hood on, which limits my vision, and look down at the shooting area. I can't see Shannon or Ann. Or the three biathletes. Apart from Gerald Hynes, I don't find a single familiar face. I want to get away from the shooting noise and climb, with some effort, to the top of the hill and to my car. When I arrive, Rick Stout is standing there. I saw him earlier at the firing range.

"Where have all the people gotten to?" I ask him. "Shannon and Ann and my three guests?"

"Ann took the girls with her to the village, probably. Are you going there? My snowmobile is kaput, and Meeka has the car."

"Sure. I have to go there, too."

As we're bumping along in the car toward the main street, I ask: "What happened to your snowmobile?"

"It's an old thing, but I've always been able to patch it up before. Takes a little longer this time, I need a spare part."

Rick looks worried. The Stouts are definitely not well-off. Most people have two cars and two cell phones, but not Rick and Meeka. He fishes near the coast with his brother in summer, in a small boat, he told me. He'd earn a lot more on the big trawlers that travel far out to sea and are gone for weeks or months. But he doesn't want to be separated from his family for such a long time. Not even for money. My father was the same: he could have traveled all over the world as an aircraft mechanic. But he preferred to repair planes for a relatively small company and go home every day.

Rick interrupts my thoughts.

"Well, did the doctor bewitch you?"

I look at him open-mouthed, not knowing which amazes me more: that Rick used the word *bewitched* or that he took the liberty of using it.

"Rick, with all due respect, that's none of your business."

Now it's his turn to look bewildered.

"Okay, okay, I didn't mean it like that."

He'll certainly tell his friends and relatives how piqued the new Mountie was by his joke. And somebody's sure to mention that even though there's a famous nude beach in Vancouver, the people there are nonetheless so terribly uptight.

Rick doesn't seem to hold it against me. He goes on talking: "There's no fooling around with Dennis Richards. He's often intimidated people with his methods."

"What methods?"

"He once drove Jay Bromin to the garbage incinerator and threatened to throw him in."

"What was the reason?"

"He thought Jay had stolen his drug money."

"Dennis deals drugs?"

"Did. Not anymore, as far as I know. That was ten years or so ago."

"How do you know about the thing with the drug money?"

"From a cousin. He was in the car with Dennis when they went to the incinerator."

"What's the cousin's name?"

"I'm afraid I can't tell you that; wouldn't be any use, either. He has a family and has nothing to do with drugs now. It's an old story. They didn't throw Jay into the fire; they just scared the hell out of him. The incinerator isn't working anymore."

Ten years. That was long before Closs. That's why the boss hasn't heard a word about it.

"Thanks anyway for telling me, Rick, I have a better handle on Richards."

"A hard nut, that one."

"There seem to be several in these parts. Somebody opened my door and threw dog poop into my house. Who could it have been?"

"For sure it's the idiots who lived in your house before you. Drunks, they were. Grace Butt finally threw them out. Good riddance!"

"Do those guys still have a key to my place?"

"No. Grace had the locks changed. Why?"

"Because I thought I'd locked the door."

"Go ask Scott Dyson. He worked at your house."

Once again a possible clue leading to Scott Dyson. Maybe the man's not as harmless as he pretends to be.

The first houses of Port Brendan come into view. I change the subject.

"When does the mummers thing start?"

"Tonight. In the arena. Are you coming, too? You really should come disguised as a mummer. It'll be a hell of a lot of fun."

I sidestep the question and just say: "The kids are finally getting their innings. Lilly must be beside herself with delight."

"And how! You should see her, running around in her costume all day."

"Will Meeka perform?"

"Right at the beginning. You can't miss it, absolutely not!"

"Where can I drop you off?"

"At the supermarket. I've got to get some batteries."

"Is Meeka picking you up?"

"I'll find somebody to take me home. Don't forget. It starts at eight."

"Look after your wife and kids," I shout as a good-bye.

He frowns. "Why?"

Because somebody was murdered a few days ago, I want to say. But I bite my tongue at the last second. Nothing's going to happen, I tell myself.

"Just a manner of speaking," I reply, and he shuts the car door.

37

Something's in the air at the station that envelops me at once like a damp mist. Fred's in the office—it's our meeting room as well —looking serious.

"What's the matter?"

"We found the scalpel," he says.

"Where?"

"In our mailbox."

The scalpel is in an evidence bag. A tiny brown spot is visible on the blade.

"This came with it."

Fred holds out a sheet of paper that's in another plastic envelope. Somebody cut letters out of newspapers and glued them on. There are three words on the paper: *REVENGE IS SWEET!*

I shake my head, baffled.

"What in the name of . . . Looks like somebody's read a lot of old mystery novels. Paper and scissors—who ever does something like that these days?"

The corners of Fred's mouth twitch. "I completely agree with you. This is a damn poor joke."

I brush the hair out of my face. Constantly putting on and taking off my hat always loosens strands from my hair knot.

"I'd almost call it a schoolboy prank. But teenagers definitely don't read old detective novels. That's an antediluvian method. What are the others saying? Where are they?"

"Down at the firing range. Dennis Richards and a few of his gang started a fistfight. They don't want to accept the results."

"The bastards. Just because a woman bested them."

"I'm not so sure about that. A local woman probably wouldn't have been a problem." Fred takes the bag with the scalpel off the table.

I dodge any further discussion. My stomach craves something hot.

"Do you believe the dog was dissected with that?" The word *dissected* simply slips out. "I asked Dr. Perrell about the scalpel today. He said it wasn't him. And he pretends to know nothing in other respects."

"Pretends?"

Fred puts the bag back down on the table. I summarize my conversation with Perrell for him, concluding with: "He's not very communicative. Doesn't ask about Bakie. Shows no emotion."

"He's a doctor. Looks death in the face more often than we do. Not always room for feelings there. Still, he talked with you in his car for a long time."

"I hope he'll send us a list of the hospital personnel soon." Then something strikes me. "Who told you I talked to Perrell in his car?"

I specifically hadn't mentioned that detail.

"Closs told me."

"How come the sarge knew?"

Wendy walks in at that moment with two full cups and puts them on the table. I could hug her, but when I see her looking at the anonymous letter, I quickly turn it over. That shouldn't have happened. I reach for the cup and thank her.

"This information mustn't go anywhere," I say emphatically, pointing to the evidence bag.

Wendy punishes me with an indignant look.

"I've been working at this job for twelve years and nobody has ever complained," she says unapologetically before she disappears.

After she's left, I close the door.

Fred looks at me, puzzled.

"What was that all about?"

"Yesterday she told Georgina about my whereabouts. I told the boss I didn't think that was proper."

"Maybe Georgina got it from her husband."

"Not if I'm to believe her words. The sarge apparently doesn't talk with his wife much. He didn't have a clue that the blue garbage bag was loaned from the clinic." I avoid the word *swiped*.

Fred listens with interest.

"I've heard she's often on the night shift."

My phone dings. An email. I check my inbox.

"Perrell sent me the list of personnel. I'll forward it to you right now, Fred. How do things stand with the volunteers in the Salvation Army shop?"

That's where the red sweatshirt with the slogan on it was for sale, but nobody can remember if it was ever sold. Fred ventured a guess earlier that one of the volunteers had snitched it.

"I've got a list of them," he replies. "And the names of the members on the auction page on Facebook where the Olympics cap was auctioned. Just about every woman in Port Brendan is on it."

That's the thing about such small communities. People go along with whatever. Nobody wants to be left out. The lists don't offer us much hope. But we should see if some names are on both lists.

"By the way, I noticed some glossy magazines in Melissa Richards's living room. The letters on the message could have come from them. What about the surveillance camera at our entrance? There must be something on it."

"Hmm." Fred drinks his tea while reading on his phone. "The sarge wants to stick Dennis Richards in a cell. He evidently roughed up Gerald Hynes pretty badly. That's good. Now we don't have to keep an eye on him during the opening ceremonies in the arena."

"Does the sarge think Richards murdered Bakie?"

"Delgado and Sullivan rechecked his alibi. His mother is suddenly not so sure anymore about when her son came home. She got caught contradicting herself."

"Oops!" My head starts working. Did Richards poison Bakie's dog, then behead it, deposit the garbage bag with all those things and the dog's head on the ice, and finally kill the chef? Can't get my head around it all.

"We don't have anything concrete that connects Richards to the murder. Only speculation."

"Closs sees a possible motive. Bakie's debts to Richards. Bakie's plan to leave Melissa in the lurch and take off for Vegas."

Fred doesn't sound very persuaded.

"How could Richards have known about Bakie's plan? And if Bakie's dead, how can Richards get his money now?"

I turn the bag with its colorful letters over again. *REVENGE IS SWEET*. I simply can't imagine that Richards would concoct an anonymous message with cut-out letters. Or anything else. I pace back and forth around the office.

"Richards is a braggart. He would have beaten the hell out of Bakie the way he did Hynes today. Taught him a lesson he wouldn't forget. A frontal attack, with an audience, if possible, not a stab in the back."

Sullivan barges in.

"We're all on night shift today," he shouts. "Boss's orders. We're to mingle with the crowd."

Fred puts down his empty cup.

"Where's the sarge? And Delgado?"

"They're still busy with Dennis Richards. The sarge wants to search his parents' house now. Hynes had to go to the hospital for stitches."

Sullivan looks at me.

"You had a rendezvous with the doctor? Did you get something out of him that we couldn't?"

I explain to him objectively what happened between Perrell and Ann Smith at the firing range.

"Well, she got a bit cocky," is his comment. "I can easily imagine that Perrell has an eye for the ladies. And lately the doctor has been after our constable."

I don't think that's funny. Sullivan is amused.

"Gates, don't take it so seriously. It's the way people talk around here. There's no harm meant by it."

"As you have all my information, my dear colleague, now it's your turn. What did you get out of Dr. Perrell?"

Sullivan turns serious.

"If you ask me, he didn't like Bakie. Kris Bakie was a bit of a star, and Perrell wanted to be a star, too. He had his own ideas, and Kris had different ones."

His opinions are too wishy-washy for me.

"What about the timetable? Who was going to be at the Viking house and when?"

"Perrell corroborated what Shannon Wilkey told you. He originally intended to meet with the whole committee on Wednesday morning at the Viking house. But Ann Smith thought it wasn't necessary for her to be there. Bakie canceled at the last minute. And Meeka never answered Perrell's email. She apparently had never seen it. Only Shannon turned up, if you are to believe her. She hadn't seen early enough, according to Perrell, that he wanted to postpone the meeting."

"Meeka never said anything about a meeting or its postponement. I'll talk to her about it."

Besides, Ann had driven my three young guests to my house in the meantime. A good reason to escape the office and to tell my teammates I'm leaving.

"I'll take care of the lists of names," Fred says.

Sullivan pricks up his ears.

"What lists?"

Fred explains it to him.

"And the anonymous note? Are we talking about a woman here?"

"It might be a man pretending it comes from a woman," I respond.

My answer evidently surprises Fred.

"But you argued against that before. And said a man would never do something like that."

"Changed my mind," I say on the way out.

On the spur of the moment, I go to the hospital. I ask at the reception desk for Gerald Hynes. A different woman is sitting behind the glass than before. Curly hair and painted eyebrows. She must be on Perrell's list.

"Room Eight. Straight ahead and then to the right," she explains.

I knock on Room Number Eight, and when I don't hear anything, I quietly go in. Hynes doesn't even move his head when I approach the bed. He looks terrible. One eye is swollen shut, and two stitches run across his cheek and forehead. Many bruises are scattered around his face and neck.

"Good heavens." It slips out of my mouth. "He beat you up like a madman."

Only Hynes's lips move. "What's the police want with me now? Go after criminals, not me."

"My partners have put Dennis Richards in a cell."

"That's where he belongs, the idiot."

"What was the matter?"

"He tried to tear up the scorecard. But I stopped him in time."

"And then he went after you?"

"Only after I told him I'd shut his mouth for him—he'd spread enough lies."

"What lies?"

"He claimed that Ann Smith put the blue garbage bag on the ice herself. Somebody saw her, according to him. But the police are protecting her, he said, and you can only wonder about the reason why."

"Who said they saw her?" I ask, and a faint suspicion is forming deep inside me.

"Nobody saw Ann do it, Constable. He's just spreading rumors."

Hynes tries to prop himself up and grimaces in pain. "I hope the rat rots in the slammer."

I instinctively reach for his hand. I know what it is to lie wounded in a hospital bed and feel abandoned. The impotence, the helplessness. I'm seeing myself the way Martin saw me back then: limp limbs, straggly hair, dull-eyed, unable to construct a meaningful sentence, unable to eat without help. That wasn't the woman he'd married, who cheerfully jumped into bed with him, who stubbornly persisted through tough times. I'd love to hug and console the woman I was in the hospital at that time and encourage her. Tell her that she's not alone, that things will be fine.

"You're the first person to come visit me," I hear Hynes utter.

I spontaneously stroke his uninjured cheek.

"Kiss me," he asks.

I do it after not giving it much thought. His lips are dry, but the inside of his mouth is warm and enticing. His tongue comes to meet mine, and his hand grasps my hair knot, which gets even more unruly. If Gerald were uninjured, I'd take off my winter jacket and lie on him, just to feel his body beneath me.

When we stop briefly to catch our breath, reality catches up with me. Oh my God, whatever got into me?

At that moment I hear somebody at the door. I whip around. Georgina Closs comes in. She's just as surprised as I am.

"I wanted to check on the patient," she starts off saying.

"I'll wait outside," I answer and walk to safety into the corridor.

"It won't be long," she calls to me. As if she were afraid I'd escape her.

And in fact, she comes back out before I can focus my thoughts and feelings.

Georgina seems very different in her bright blue nurse's uniform. More serious than in civilian dress. One thick braid hangs down her back, replacing her two, smaller ones.

"I've just come on the night shift," she explains, surveying me with her childlike eyes.

Did she see anything? No, that's not possible; I was standing beside the bed when she came in. Close call, though.

"How are my girls?" she inquires.

I need a second to realize that she's talking about the three athletes.

"I assume they're okay. They moved into the guest room at noon and seemed satisfied with it. I met them at the firing range this afternoon—they were very excited."

"They were all in the shooting competition, weren't they?"

"Yes, and they were very good. But Dennis Richards beat them. They're still happy because Ann Smith was better than him and could make more money for the clinic. Who'd have thought it?"

Georgina shows zero enthusiasm. "Yes, who would have thought it. So long as there was nothing fishy about it."

"Do you mean to say . . ."

"Don't you think that's an astounding result? I'm surely not the only one who . . . but I shouldn't say anything. The important thing is that our clinic receives the donation. God knows we need it."

She goes to the door.

"You can go back in."

I look at my watch and decline.

"I've got to go home and see if everything's okay. My guests mustn't feel neglected. Besides, I've got the night shift today—like you."

"Because of the opening ceremonies in the arena?"

"We don't want any more brawls," is all I say. As an RCMP officer's wife, she should actually be able to figure out why the police are more on the alert than usual after there's been a murder.

"Would you mind fetching my hat and gloves from the room? They're lying on the chair."

"Don't you want to say good-bye to Gerald?"

"I've already discussed everything with him I had to, so I don't want to disturb him anymore. He certainly needs peace and quiet."

She blinks but carries out my request. I thank her and head for the entrance. I don't look back, but I know that her eyes are following me.

My car is ice-cold, though I'm burning up inside. I start the motor, turn up the music, and close my eyes. It's working again! My sexual desire is back. I can finally feel it again. A little out of control, but powerfully beautiful. Something that seemed to be lost forever has returned. My damaged brain has restored some cells. Or receptors. Whatever. It retrieved something from its long sleep. I'm no longer like a robot without a sex drive. I don't want to think about my going over the line with Gerald Hynes right now. I push it far, far away from me.

The car takes its time warming up. I start off along the road home. As I open the door, I smell cooking aromas. My sense of smell took weeks to come back after the accident. I'll never again take it for granted. One of the young women is in the kitchen, standing at the stove and stirring a large pot. So much for the community kitchen of the Pentecostal church Georgina talked about. My guests obviously have something else in mind.

"I hope you'll like it," the cook says. She's wearing a short-sleeved T-shirt with white lambs on it. The heating in the house is on full blast.

"Meeka gave us some moose meat, so we added vegetables and made a stew."

The table is set for four. The athletes have made themselves at home. Fortunately, I locked my office and bedroom, out of caution. I'm standing around in my kitchen, indecisive.

"Wonderful," I hear myself say. "Where are the other two?"

"They're still at Meeka's. They've probably lost track of time. They haven't seen one another for a long time and have lots to catch up on."

She loosens the clasp in her hair and rearranges her hairdo, although it all looked perfect. That gesture could have been mine.

"They know one another?"

"Yes, Meeka used to be the leader at our summer camp. She was still going with that idiot from Northwest River. She moved to Port Brendan because of Rick. Then we hardly ever saw her. Dulcie is sweet, isn't she?"

I agree.

"Does Meeka like it in Port Brendan?"

"I think so. Her family lives in Happy Valley-Goose Bay. Rick doesn't want to live there. He needs the open sea."

"Not surprising for a fisherman," I remark. I need the ocean, too. The warm Pacific, not the cold North Atlantic.

She opens the freezer door and finds some ice cubes. Am I seeing things? Ice cubes in winter?

"For a fisherman he's not on the water very often," she says, pouring Coke into a glass.

I've got supplies of both because almost everybody drinks Coke here.

I fill the electric kettle.

"They're not allowed to fish all the time; there are government quotas."

"I'm just saying. Meeka takes these foster kids in so that she can keep her head above water. And she has her hands full with Dulcie. She can't travel around and do her throat singing anymore. That's fine by Rick; he doesn't like it when Meeka's away. But throat singing is absolutely vital for her; he should leave her more room to breathe. She'll wither away otherwise."

Rick's probably doing the best he can. Jobs aren't exactly lying around on the streets of Port Brendan. He helped build the Viking house. So he does earn money apart from fishing. Meanwhile, young women like these athletes have different expectations; many move away in search of a job or a husband. And a more comfortable life.

"Is something not quite right with Dulcie?" I say it in a matter-of-fact voice as I remove a tea bag from a canister.

"She sometimes has medical problems; I don't exactly know what they are. Meeka often has to take her to the clinic. Dr. Perrell has found some medication that's expensive. I think he used it as part of a study. Don't say anything to Rick. Or he'll freak out. They don't have much money."

And yet Meeka gave us some moose meat today. I'm impressed.

"Ah, there they are," my cook exclaims. "I'm as hungry as a wolf."

We're all sitting around the table a few minutes later, and my house is full of chatter and laughter. Naturally all the talk is about Monday's biathlon and race. I used to be a proficient shot, still am with a pistol and sometimes with a rifle, if my right arm is working. But the biathlon is a whole other dimension. You sprint like crazy over the snow on cross-country skis until you reach the shooting stand—and suddenly you've got to be calm and concentrate. All the while, your pulse is racing and your heart's hammering and your breath comes in puffs, like from an old locomotive.

"How do you do it anyway, sprinting and keeping absolutely calm at the same time?" I ask.

The three women laugh, a bit proudly and a little self-consciously. Then they all talk at once and at one another.

"We each have a mantra, words we say to ourselves. My mantra is 'Calm and quick.'"

"Mine is 'Touch and go, and off we go.'"

"I've got a new one: 'I'll hit it every time.'"

Maybe I could adopt a mantra, too: *I never give up.*

"Does that help calm you down?" I inquire.

The cook says: "People think we can slow down our heart-beat, but it isn't so. It doesn't go that fast."

"We control our breath. I shoot between breaths."

"Our trainer taught us how to block out all thoughts while shooting. Then I'm, like, underwater."

They take a break from eating—that's how keen they are about their sport.

I'm captivated, too.

"So it's thought control?" I ask.

"Yes, we try. There are enough things you can't control. The wind, for example. Or the sun."

"Today, for instance. Ann Smith waited for a moment when it was almost calm. And the sun wasn't in her face."

"She really got that right. We should have waited for the right moment, as she did. Then we'd have had a much higher score."

I start spooning up my meal again. Must leave soon.

"I heard that Dennis Richards went ballistic. Did you witness any of that?"

"He didn't catch a good moment they way Ann did. More wind. And the light probably blinded him."

"Ann's really got it. I mean she's really mega good."

I'm a bit jealous of Ann. She's impressed these young athletes. But they're already talking about something else.

"You never know when you're shooting. The best shot can have a bad time of it. You can come third in one race and eighty-seventh in the next. It sometimes seems like a lottery to me."

"Like ten years ago in Vancouver."

"That was at Whistler."

I prick up my ears. Here come the Olympics once again.

"What happened there?"

"Norway and Germany . . ."

"And Russia."

". . . they were the favorites. But an American won."

"The US had never won a gold medal in biathlon before. The Americans went wild with joy when Yvonne Shelcken won."

"Of course, we were very disappointed that Canada didn't win anything."

"But at least it wasn't the Russians."

"Yes, that's right. You never know what's up with them."

I put down my spoon.

"I'm on duty tonight. Do you want me to take you to the opening ceremonies?"

"Ann's picking us up and bringing us back. She doesn't want us wandering around alone at night."

They giggle like young people who think they're never in danger. I'm irritated, against my will, instead of being thankful for Ann's help.

"She's more afraid for us than our parents," the woman on my right jokes.

"My father says Kris Bakie was killed by a jealous person. If somebody's successful, then there are always people who are jealous."

That's apparently the theory most people stick to.

But Bakie was in debt.

I stand up and take my plate.

"We'll take care of that," my guests protest. "We've discovered the dishwasher."

They all laugh.

"We saw the puzzle, too. We could only put in a few pieces."

"Wait, I'll show you."

The cook pushes her chair back and leads the way to the table in the living room. Maybe Ann Smith would have had trouble with a similar invasion of her private space. But in the south of Labrador, the kitchen and living room are treated as public spaces, Closs informed me.

"Here."

The young woman points to a corner of the puzzle. I look at where her finger lies. Indeed, that part of Port Brendan wasn't there before.

"You did a good job," I say appreciatively.

"Pure chance," she replies, flattered.

I've almost finished the built-up area of Port Brendan, with the aid of a magnifying glass. The surroundings, with the monotonous green of the forest and tundra, however, are driving me to despair. There was only one place to latch on to: the log cabins. Just as I am about to turn away, I see something out of the corner of my eye. A little yellow dot on a wooded road. I pick up the magnifying glass. A yellow car.

Only two people in Port Brendan own a yellow car: Georgina and Bernard Closs.

38

Her breath is burning like acid in her lungs. Every stride is an infernal struggle. She takes a quick look around—her pursuers are already there close on her heels. A burst of blood flows through her heart. Her lead has diminished. She pushes more powerfully, her skis flying over the snow.

No longer is her body made of muscle, just determination. The others are faster, stronger, more ruthless. But she will destroy them. Her rifle hangs over her back. Bullets are set. She's waited fifteen long years for this moment. Fifteen years of quarreling, suffering, submitting. Her opponents have tried everything to annihilate her. They've threatened, cheated, and extorted.

Now her time has come. Her goal is very near. She halts her flight, takes her rifle, throws herself onto the snow. Her pulse is racing, her breath turns to gasps.

Then comes an icy calm. It never lets her down. Comes as sure as a faithful dog. A transparent invisible dome sinks over her head, over her hands, the rifle. Leaves everything outside: sounds, people, fear, the struggle, the howling.

She's suddenly in a quiet church, a place of absolute devotion. Her eye seeks out a target. It's very sharp, very clear. Her index finger moves with mechanical precision. The report is a release. And then another pop and another and another.

Every shot hits the mark, every shot is a victory. No one can do it like her. At that moment, she's the Great Destroyer. With each bullet she shreds hopes and danger, ambition and unscrupulousness; she shoots her way out to move upward. To the place where she will stand all by herself. Alone and victorious.

39

His eyes comb through the crowd streaming into the arena. An expectant tension permeates the air. Fred can't understand why the games weren't canceled following Bakie's violent death. It should have been a warning to everybody that a murder's no mere bagatelle. It seems to him that, after the initial shock, people went back to their everyday lives much too quickly. Just as they did after Lorna Taylor's death. He blames it on too much TV. No matter what house he goes into, the TV is constantly blaring in the background. The crime series have taken away the shock of murder. Even if one occurs in the immediate vicinity.

He's jumpy. Keeps looking out for Calista Gates. He's grown accustomed to the daily communication with her, which surprises him. She ought to be a thorn in his side. He actually could have counted on replacing Closs soon. But Closs, whose wife didn't want to leave just yet, must have made some deal with the RCMP brass, and he doesn't have any details. He can't explain what happened any other way. Gates comes to Port Brendan, and Closs stays on. She's killed Fred's plans and doesn't even know it. As a member of the team, Gates is pleasant enough. Better than Delgado or Sullivan. She listens to him and takes him seriously. The job feels different. More diverse. More incalculable. More significant. He's heard about the attack on her in Vancouver, of course, and that she was in the hospital for quite a spell. Nevertheless, it isn't clear to him why she was sent to Port Brendan. She's considered to be an accomplished investigator in spite of being so young. It would have been more logical to send her to Happy Valley-Goose Bay.

So where is she? As a rule, she's so reliable. He thinks about reaching for his cell phone but hesitates. He wants to avoid any appearance of needing her. He knows the area, been here a lot longer than she has. That's an advantage she can't take away from him. Although she's about his age, she's ahead of him in many ways. He joined the RCMP six years ago. Before that, he had a junior position in the economics ministry in Saskatchewan. An eight-to-five job. Not his cup of tea. The police work always fascinated him. He's never regretted his career change—quite the opposite. But his frustration has been growing under Closs. They haven't got to the bottom of Lorna Taylor's disappearance. Now they finally have her remains but still no concrete suspect. And Kris Bakie's murder is a case with enormous question marks. That's one investigation they mustn't screw up.

He discovers Melissa Richards and her mother in one of the rows. Not even a grieving fiancée will skip this event, even though Bakie's dead and her brother is in a police cell. Coming here means everything, apparently. People are standing around the podium, gesticulating, looking worried. The sound system doesn't seem to be working. Maybe all that technical equipment is affected by the ice-cold temperature. Dr. Perrell pops up. He will address the audience after the mayor's speech, probably to promote the clinic. Will he mention Bakie?

Fred goes over to the other side of the arena to have a better view. His annoying vision problems have disappeared since the doctor prescribed some pills for low blood pressure. Nobody's supposed to know about it. Least of all Delgado and Sullivan. They're patrolling the town. So where's Calista? She must be as tense as he is. She thinks Bakie was the wrong target in the murder attack. A mix-up in the dark Viking house. He doesn't rule that out. It would also explain why they're not making any progress in the investigation.

"Can the police finally tell me who killed Kris?" a female voice shouts.

Fred turns around in surprise. Melissa Richards is there right beside him. She spoke so loudly over the noise in the arena that several heads nearby turn toward them.

"I can't talk about it; please ask Sergeant Closs." It's the most convenient answer that occurs to him.

"What are the police doing anyway? What are they doing here? Do you seriously think you'll find the murderer in this arena?"

Fred knows about the emotional state of people afflicted by a tragedy. Even so, he's never been confronted with it in a sports arena. It could very well be that the killer is in the arena, he would like to have replied. Instead, he cops out with a conversational ploy that he learned in training.

"I understand that you'd like some answers. We're working round the clock on the case."

"It's a case to you, Constable, to me it's the lost love of my life." Melissa's voice has grown even louder, like the hustle and bustle in the arena.

He would take her by the arm to calm her down, but a policeman is supposed to avoid that sort of physical contact if at all possible. It could be misinterpreted. He learned that as well. He says instead: "So come to the station tomorrow. We can talk better there than here."

"You just want to get rid of me. Tomorrow you'll say something else to put me off."

She turns away, furious. Looking behind her, he spies Calista at the entrance. She comes in following a bevy of mummers. He guesses at once what she's up to. She's checking the identity of the costumed characters. To see that a potential killer's not hiding behind a mask. That definitely will irritate the mummers. He wonders how she explained it to the children and their parents. Two volunteer organizers take the mummers behind the stage. The program says they'll dance a jig later and shake the Ugly Stick, a broomstick hung with bells, rattling tin cans, and an old boot at the bottom.

His phone rings.

"Where are you?" Calista asks.

He can't understand her very well in the din but describes where he is. She's beside him in less than a minute.

He comes out with his question then and there. "You were checking out the mummers?"

"Yes."

"What reason did you give?"

"You're asking me?" She looks at him, astonished.

"I mean, how did you explain it to people? That you're looking for a killer?"

"Oh, that's it. No, of course not. I happened to have some gold chocolate dollars left over from Christmas in my pack. I said the adults get one and the children two. You only get one if I can have a quick look at your face. They thought it was fun." She grimaces. "I can only get away with this because I'm a stranger from Vancouver."

He has to admit the technique got her what she was after.

"I compared the lists," he says, looking around. He doesn't want anybody listening.

She comes a step closer.

"Shoot."

"I got eight people who work in the hospital and volunteer in the Salvation Army shop at the same time. They also took part in the Facebook auction for the animal rescue group."

He secretly doubts that the result will be of any great help to them. Sweatshirts can be gifts, stolen, or palmed off on somebody. Besides, the eight overlapping names are all women. He thinks none of them is capable of cutting off a dog's head.

Calista doesn't spend much time on the matter.

"Dennis Richards claims that Ann Smith herself was seen on that day with the blue bag on the ice. She's said to have put it there herself. Fred, we should go and ask her."

"Who saw Ann?"

"He didn't say."

He has no trouble understanding her last sentence because the noise level suddenly drops. Port Brendan's mayor is at the microphone, clearing his throat.

"Where's the Sarge?" Calista whispers. She smells of fresh soap. Her hair is tucked under a red wool hat with a pompom. The color suits her. But he can't overlook the tension in her face.

He shrugs. He'd like to know, too.

"We don't need the Olympics; we've got the Winter Games," the mayor shouts, and the audience applauds. Then he says something about "coming together in hard times" and "we'll bounce back." Fred is only half-listening; his eyes are constantly moving back and forth over the rows of seats.

"Is Ann Smith here?" Calista asks.

He shakes his head. "I just see Shannon Wilkey, in the second row."

"Ann brought my guests here. Somebody has to take them back to my place afterward." She whispers in his ear, undoubtedly because she doesn't want to interfere with the speech from the stage. They normally don't come this close.

The mayor closes with an appeal to the legendary Labradorian fighting spirit. The Innu come on stage with drums and invoke the spirits to watch over the games benevolently. After that, four Inuit explain in their native tongue the significance of the games for their tradition. A young nurse—Fred saw her at the clinic—does the translating.

He looks sideways at Calista. Her eyes flit from one corner of the arena to the other and then briefly back to the stage. She's constantly expecting the worst, Fred reasons. When somebody's been beaten up like that, they can never rest. Bakie's murder must only have fueled her obsession.

Loud shouts and whistles from the audience fire up the indigenous performers on stage. They demonstrate feats of strength that have been handed down from generation to generation. Two Inuit women sit down opposite each other on the stage floor with a soft leather lacing around their left ear that they pull on with all their might in opposite directions. Even Calista watches and shakes her head. She's surely seeing this very painful test of strength for the first time. But he, on the other hand, has already witnessed a similar event. He wanted to impress his girlfriend with it, when she was here on her first visit. But she wasn't the least bit interested and never came back to Labrador. She can hardly wait for the day he'll be pulled out of the province. Her family lives in Saskatoon; there's where she grew up, and there's where she wants to raise her children. He hasn't had any sign from the RCMP that they'll transfer him to Saskatoon. He has to earn his spurs first on more isolated rural postings.

His girlfriend was enthusiastic at first, when he became a Mountie. A secure job, a good salary—that pleased her. She wants to have children soon and quit her job in city administration. It was love at first sight when he met her at some friends' barbecue. A bubbly blonde, pretty as a picture, who was always in a good mood. She could have had any guy, but she chose him. He wanted to marry her. But then she refused to move to Port Brendan. That made everything harder. He's aware that he didn't sign up with the RCMP for the job security. He wanted variety, interesting work, not a boring office job; he wanted adrenaline in his blood. He's conflicted. When he's on vacation in Saskatoon, he wants to be with her forever. But doubts always crop up afterward, in Port Brendan. Does his fiancée really know what it means to be married to a cop? And is a woman who's that inflexible really the right one for him?

Loud music tears him out of his thoughts. Mummers stream onto the stage, then keep spinning around and stomping their feet to the rhythmic sounds. They shake their Ugly Sticks and strike the podium with them. The bells and metal cans rattle and clatter.

Calista watches the action on stage with a furrowed brow. Something seems to be on her mind.

"What is it?" he inquires, more loudly than he meant to.

"I can't see Dulcie. Dulcie Stout. My neighbors' daughter."

She no longer whispers. It's just too noisy in the arena for that.

He doesn't understand her concern. They can't really worry about neighbors' children as well.

Calista grabs his sleeve.

"Look, Dulcie's father is getting up."

He does indeed see Rick Stout walking backstage. He knows Rick from the drills with the volunteer fire department. Suddenly a voice like a siren rings out through the arena, and the music breaks off. It's Meeka Stout, standing among the mummers on stage.

"Dulcie's disappeared! Has anybody seen Dulcie? We can't find her!"

Calista instantly runs down the middle aisle to the front. Before Fred can think clearly, she's talking on stage with Meeka.

He hears her voice over the microphone.

"Please, all of you, stay seated. That will help us find Dulcie. Keep calm until we've found Dulcie."

It doesn't help, of course. Some people jump out of their seats, giving in to the impulse to look for the child and not sit there doing nothing. Survival in Port Brendan depends on people helping one another. People there have absorbed that with their mother's milk. Calista isn't aware of that yet. She can't hold back the wave.

Fred runs through the surging turmoil toward the stage. He sees Dr. Perrell out of the corner of his eye talking forcefully at Shannon Wilkey, shaking his head furiously and with anger on his face. Apart from a few elderly people, the whole audience seems to be on their feet. Many are rushing out into the dark.

He makes it to Calista as she's trying to calm Meeka down.

"What do we know?" he yells to counter the cacophony in the arena.

"Meeka saw her backstage about fifteen minutes ago, before she went to get ready for her performance."

"Where's my baby?" Meeka screams. "Please find my baby!"

Dulcie was still backstage fifteen minutes ago. Why the panic, he asks himself. Maybe she went to the restroom. He can't say why, but he's worried more about the chaos than the girl.

Suddenly three young women are beside him, speaking wildly, all at the same time.

"We searched the restrooms—she's not there."

"Can we do something? Where should we look?"

"I've got a flashlight."

Fred turns the trio over to his partner. He wants to talk to the mummers and heads for a teenager who has removed the face covering of his costume and is standing around rather helplessly.

"I'm Constable Fred. Can you tell me when you last saw Dulcie?"

The teen, a youngster with a pimply, sweat-covered face, stammers at first: "I don't know . . ." Then he recalls something. "She was looking for the chocolate."

Fred hesitates for a second before remembering the gold dollars Calista used to bribe the mummers. "Where she looking?"

"She was running back and forth saying, 'Where's my chocolate?'"

"Back and forth where?"

The teenager points to behind the stage.

"Tracy told Dulcie that her dad had put it in his pocket so it wouldn't get lost."

"Who's Tracy?"

"Tracy Wanmore."

One of the helpers.

"Can you show me who she is?"

The teen looks around.

"I don't know . . ." Then he shouts, "There she is."

Fred follows him to a schoolgirl who's dissolved into tears.

"I was keeping a real close eye on her, I was always watching."

An older woman puts an arm around her. Her mother.

"You can't blame my girl for it," she shouts at him.

"I just want to talk with her," Fred responds.

"Why do you want to talk with her? She's done nothing wrong," the mother yells.

Fred looks at the girl, ignoring the mother.

"You can help me find Dulcie. I've heard that Dulcie's chocolate went missing."

"The gold dollar. She was looking for her gold dollar," the teenager repeats; he must have followed Fred.

"What gold dollar?" the mother asks, puzzled.

Bangs go off outside. Fred can hardly believe it. Somebody's setting off fireworks. A car horn beeps like mad. Dogs are barking. Have people gone insane?

The daughter gets a hold of herself and explains more clearly: "Rick took her gold dollar away because he didn't want . . . she would have smeared chocolate all over everything. But . . ."

"The kids lied to her." The teen has got himself going. "They told Dulcie they'd hidden her chocolate."

"What kids?"

Tracy snivels. "The two boys who live with Meeka and Rick. The foster children."

"They're real snotty-nosed brats," her mother grumbles.

Fred pricks up his ears. "What did the kids say to Dulcie —exactly?"

"That they hid the gold dollar."

"Did they say where?"

"I don't know," the teenager says again, and the girl shakes her head.

Only now does Fred realize that people are crowded around and are listening. He hears voices somewhere calling, "Dulcie! Dulcie!"

In all that chaos, he thinks hard.

Then all of a sudden, he suspects where he'll find the little girl.

40

The banging has stopped abruptly. The fireworks shouldn't have started this early at all. I try to convince the three athletes not to go looking for Dulcie in the dark with a flashlight.

Closs looms up beside us.

"What the hell's going on?" he asks, with a peeved look. "This is the very thing we were trying to avoid."

"Rick Stout's daughter has gone missing. She won't know where she is if she's all alone," I reply as I try to get away from the three women. They don't need to hear this.

But Closs doesn't budge an inch.

"It wasn't a good idea to inspect the mummers, Gates. It creates fear, and then we have a situation like this."

Who told him that I wanted to identify the mummers? And where was he when I was doing it? I'm annoyed that he's criticizing me within earshot of my guests.

To avoid a discussion, I simply inform him: "Dulcie's been missing for about twenty minutes. Fred's just now questioning people who were close by."

And I'd be doing it, too, if the sarge weren't holding me up.

"Now we've got all these people wandering around in the

dark." He doesn't stop complaining. "Next thing we know, we'll have an accident or something worse."

Worse? Worse can only be a murder. That's why I checked the mummers, I want to say. But I bite my tongue.

"I ordered the people to stay seated, but they didn't listen," I respond.

Closs just gets even more irritable.

"Are you surprised by that?" he roars.

So where was he for the last two hours anyway? I'm even more irritated.

"We'd like to help in the search," one of the women interjects; they haven't left my side.

"Come with me," he says, ever the good, energetic police officer.

I seize my chance to hurry backstage, on a hunch. Fred's there already. He's lying on the floor, his upper body partly under the stage.

Meeka's crouched beside him.

"Dulcie, come on out. Mommy's here."

I lie down beside Fred and work my way under the podium.

"She doesn't want to come out?" I ask.

I can make out an arm and a leg in the flashlight beam.

"She's shy," Fred grunts.

"Dulcie, angel, come to Mommy," Meeka calls again.

Just the three of us seem to realize that Dulcie's been found. That's good, or else the girl would stay under the stage forever. Without thinking, I reach into my jacket pocket and take out a few gold dollars.

"I've got some chocolate for you, Dulcie," I whisper. "Golden chocolate, a whole lot. Just for you."

Fred aims the light beam on the gold dollars in my hand. Sometimes he does exactly the right thing without being asked. And I do, too. We're not a bad team.

"A whole bunch of chocolate. I've saved it for you."

It works. Dulcie slowly creeps out of her hiding place.

"Look, they're waiting for you." I wave the gold dollars.

The girl crawls toward us, her little face beaming with joy.

"Mine," she says. "All mine."

"Yes, they're only for you. Many, many, many of them."

The minute she's with us, she grabs a gold dollar with her little hand. I pull her the rest of the way out from beneath the stands. Meeka tries to hug her, but Dulcie wants her chocolate and defends herself. I help her gather up the dollars. Fred pulls out a handkerchief to make up a bundle.

I'm just about to praise him for this gesture when he says: "Money is the root of all evil."

"And chocolate is the root of all joy," I fire back.

Meeka holds Dulcie tight. I can't see the two foster boys anywhere. At that point, a scream sounds through the arena. It's so frightening that Dulcie begins to cry.

I rush to the auditorium. One of the biathletes is by the entrance, screaming hysterically. People are already trying to help her, but I push them aside and grab her firmly by the shoulders.

"What's happened?"

Her screams turn into gasps. "He . . . he's lying on the ground," she manages to get out. "He's bleeding."

"Who?" Fred asks as he emerges at my side.

"Where?" I ask.

"He's not moving."

The young woman's in shock, that's obvious.

"A doctor, is there a doctor here?" somebody in the crowd shouts.

"We've got to secure the scene," I say to Fred.

"Where?" I ask the girl again.

Her answer comes out like a groan: "Behind . . . behind the hot-dog stand. He's . . . covered in blood."

Some people move off instantly.

"Back off!" Fred's voice sounds amazingly authoritarian. "Everybody back off!"

Closs heaves into view.

"An injured man, blood, behind the hot-dog stand," I tell him hurriedly. Closs wants to leave immediately, but I push the athlete in his way.

"She's our witness—and your responsibility. And we need an ambulance."

Those words are going to cost me, but at that moment I couldn't care less. I want to secure the scene of the crime before it's ruined.

The hot-dog stand is about a hundred meters away. In the snow, I cannot advance as quickly as I'd like, although the ground around the arena is strewn with gravel. But Fred strides ahead as if he were on skates. He repeatedly shouts to the people following us: "Stay out of the way!"

Many are too curious and ignore him until Fred threatens: "I'll throw you in the lockup if you keep following us!"

We reach the stand, out of breath. The sales window is closed. Nothing to see in front of the stand. We go around to the back with flashlights, avoiding the footprints leading behind it. No tracks will be trampled down this time.

A man's lying in blood-soaked snow. His dark cap's almost fallen off his head. Hair cut short, military style. We carefully turn the body over to see if he's still alive. The left side of his face is covered in blood. A bullet hole is next to his eye.

Dr. Perrell.

Good God. My doctor. A lot of people's doctor.

No time to get emotional.

"A shot to the temple," I observe.

Fred feels the carotid artery for a pulse.

"Nothing, but he's still warm."

He steps aside so I can check his findings. No pulse. None.

It's clear that Dr. Perrell is dead.

I send a silent supplication for him into the universe and take some pictures with my phone.

"Could it be suicide?"

Fred looks at me, but I feel it rather than see it. His flashlight beam is trained on the body on the ground.

"Not if he's right-handed. I don't see any gun."

We follow routine and go through all our options. Who could get close enough to Perrell to shoot the doctor in the temple?

"I saw him fifteen minutes ago," Fred says. "He was talking to Shannon Wilkey. Both looked angry."

"We've got to talk to Shannon. What was Perrell doing behind the hot-dog stand?"

I put on my latex gloves and search Perrell's jacket pockets. I undo the zipper. I find his phone and wallet a few seconds later. Fred shines his light on them. We hear the ambulance siren. The sarge did move fast. I put the wallet and cell phone into evidence bags.

Frantic shouts close by. Sullivan's voice. But it's Closs who comes around the corner. He shudders when he recognizes the doctor. Maybe it was just my imagination; he might simply have slipped on the snow trying to avoid the footprints, as we did.

"Jesus Christ!"

Fred fills him in quickly.

"This time we have a bullett. It's still in the body."

So there is a chance we'll identify the gun.

"Let's get floodlights here," Closs orders.

We need to illuminate the crime scene. I thank the universe that Port Brendan has the appropriate lights.

Sullivan appears with the camera. We make way for him. The sight of the dead man takes his breath away. For once we're spared his sarcasm. A series of flashes brightens the grisly scene. Then he sprays blue paint in the snow to outline the body.

The paramedics arrive at the scene. Closs signals them to remove the body. One of them swears, shocked when he recognizes the dead man. Dr. Triona Cameron will have to officially determine the cause of her fellow doctor's death. There are still onlookers standing a good distance away because Closs has blocked off the area with yellow-and-black tape. Although the populace of Port Brendan doesn't yet know who the dead person is, we won't be able to hush it up for long. Closs has probably directed our witness not to say anything for the time being. Three murders. If that won't jolt the place like an earthquake.

"What's Delgado doing?" Fred asks.

Closs answers: "He's getting everybody to go back home."

"And our witness?" I can't hold back the question, although it will annoy him.

He reacts objectively. "My wife's taking care of her until we can interrogate her."

"We also have to question Shannon Wilkey; she was talking with Perrell fifteen minutes beforehand. And Ann Smith."

"Why her?"

"She pointed a rifle at Perrell during the shooting competition."

Closs frowns. "Probably in fun."

"Then, it wasn't much fun. And it was illegal as well."

A second's pause before Closs hands out our assignments.

"First the crime scene. Gates and Fred, keep working here. Sullivan, you take care of the photos. And please get the lights out here. I'll talk to our men in Happy Valley-Goose Bay and organize transportation. The medical examiner will be amazed to see something coming from us again so soon."

I'm pleasantly surprised. Sarge is giving Fred and me the crime scene. He assigned it to Sullivan and Delgado at the Viking house. What changed his mind? I can't see Sullivan's reaction in the dark; he stomps away without a word. His silence speaks volumes. Closs leaves as well.

Fred squats on the ground. We examine the footprints with

our flashlights. The athlete's shoes are easily recognizable. It's harder with the other tracks.

"Same perp as in the Viking house?" I raise the question.

"Could be the same size. But which are the perp's and which are Dr. Perrell's?"

We'll have to compare the photographs. It didn't escape me that Perrell wasn't wearing his glasses. I can't see them anywhere in the snow. Maybe they were just reading glasses.

"Again, there's no sign of a struggle," I observe and repeat the question: "What was he doing behind the hot-dog stand?"

"The stand is closed, although there are several hundred people in the arena. The owner would have done a terrific business."

"It was open before the opening ceremony started. The operator surely wanted to be in there in the arena."

"Maybe the doctor had to relieve himself fast, and the perp followed him."

"But there are toilets in the arena." I make a stab at a different interpretation. "Let's suppose that Perrell was looking for Dulcie. He looks behind this stand. Somebody follows him, pretending to want to search along with him. The killer has a good flashlight, and Perrell does not."

Fred bites. "A SureFire R1 Lawman?"

Now we're speaking the same language.

"But he doesn't hit his victim with the flashlight. He shoots him."

"And he shoots at close range. A shot to the head is more difficult than to the heart."

"Not necessarily, if there's a lot of thick clothing on the body. Perrell only wore a thin cap."

The right side of my body starts to hurt. I don't know what kicked it off. Maybe the cold. We're barely moving, which doesn't improve the situation. I shift from one foot to the other.

Fred's eagle eye spots my behavior. "We need a hot drink to keep warm. I'll send Sullivan a text."

Suddenly, a light dawns.

"We didn't hear the shot because of the fireworks," I tell him.

"Why did they go off so early anyway? The program said they were supposed to happen much later."

I pull my hood over my cap.

"At nine o'clock. I can only explain it this way: whoever set off the fireworks saw the people pouring out of the arena and thought the ceremony was over."

There's a loud shout for Fred. He runs back to the street. I hear him talking.

"The local rag," he explains when he returns. "Closs is going to have to fight that one. It's going to be all over the country."

It begins to snow. Just small flakes, fortunately. There's hardly any wind. I'm grateful for such things in Labrador.

"Was Perrell well-known across the country?" I ask.

"Not that I know of. But when a doctor is killed . . . Doctors are there to save lives, not to lose their own. You can be sure somebody will draw a parallel with Dr. Grenfell."

Dr. Grenfell. I remember. The British doctor who cared for people here, who had hospitals built in Battle Harbor and St. Anthony, who sailed along the dangerous Labrador coast and took on sick, starving families who otherwise got no medical attention. A hero; a benefactor, a superman.

"At least we can exclude Gerald Hynes and Dennis Richards as murderers in this case," Fred remarks.

His words snap me back to the present with laser-like speed. I'd been able to suppress for several hours what had unfolded in the hospital room. A knot forms in my stomach.

Sullivan saves me. He strides toward us with two large thermoses.

"Tea's in one, coffee in the other. I put sugar in both."

He doesn't even say it sardonically. What's got into him

anyway? Or into Closs? They're both so polite. So assiduous. I choose the tea because I know Fred's totally into coffee. The tea is strong and sweet; I drink it down as if I'm dying of thirst.

We install the floodlights Sullivan brought. The dark blood-stains light up against the white background. We search the surroundings nearby. In a few minutes we stumble across a ball-point pen with the letters *Eagle USA HB2* on the barrel. But the major discovery comes after half an hour. We overlooked it at first because it's white. A pocketknife with a white casing. You don't see that very often. On it are the words *Vote for Pleaman Hick*.

"Who's Pleaman Hick?" I ask.

"An opposition candidate in the last provincial election. An independent." Sullivan gives a low whistle. "Luck seems to be on our side."

I look at him, puzzled.

"Pleaman lost," Sullivan explains, "and everybody said it was because of the white pocketknife. Right, Fred?"

I don't get it.

He tries a second time. "People here think white pocketknives mean bad luck."

"Nice try, my good man, but I don't see why that's funny."

"Trust me, Gates. People here are superstitious, and poor Hick didn't get that until it was too late."

Fred clears his throat.

"Sullivan's right. Fishermen in particular think that way. There was even something about white pocketknives on TV. Nobody wanted one because they're supposed to be unlucky. Because the casing's white."

I stare at them.

"And why the heck is that supposed to bring bad luck?"

Fred shrugs.

"Simply superstition. Why do people think the number thirteen's unlucky? Just as stupid."

I want to put my freezing hands into my jacket pockets, but they're full of evidence bags. I transfer the bags to the box Sullivan brought.

An unlucky white pocketknife. Not one person in Vancouver will believe me.

41

He watches Calista Gates; she's talking almost affectionately to the young athlete who discovered Dr. Perrell. It's good to have a woman on the team in situations like this. Men instill fear in some people, who are much more open with a policewoman. Bernard Closs found that this held especially for women and children. But Gates's gentle persuasion doesn't allay his suspicions. Last night he learned that she can be cold and hard as pack ice. She appeared to be impersonal at the station when she filled in her teammates on the results from the crime scene and their finds. No—he corrects himself—not quite impersonal. He sensed a repressed rage in her when she used the word *murderer* and not *perp*. And later she even used the word *hangman*. He had to order Gates afterward to get a few hours' sleep. He can't afford to have her brain turn to mush because of lack of sleep. He needs her. They're thinking at RCMP headquarters about sending a team of specialists from Corner Brook to Port Brendan and turning over the investigation to them. But what would those people know about life in Port Brendan? He knows the place like the back of his hand. Corner Brook is in Newfoundland, not even in Labrador. It would then appear that, once again, he and his team don't have the ability to bring an investigation to a successful conclusion. So much for his dream of a leadership position in a large city. In a metropolis, where he could live anonymously.

He was able to convince headquarters that morning to give him three more days. That's how long the special unit would need in any case to get to Port Brendan in winter and find their way around the place. He persuaded his superiors with a claim that passed his lips only because of the pressure he was under: "We have Calista Gates from Vancouver here, and she's already made great progress. She's produced a very clear profile of the perp."

With that he was able to come away with seventy-two hours. Now Gates mustn't let him down.

The biathlete gradually responds to Gates's reassuring efforts. His wife had given her a sedative the previous evening, but the effect seems to be wearing off. They're in the guest room in the basement of Gates's house: the other two women are waiting upstairs in the living room. He didn't want to take the three of them to the police station.

Gates asks the woman: "May we ask you a few questions?"

She nods. Her name is Karissa Pardy.

"Can you tell me why you were behind the hot-dog stand yesterday evening? And why your friends weren't with you?"

"I had to pass something on to Dr. Perrell."

Karissa points to a package in the corner wrapped in brown paper.

"What's inside?"

"I don't know. My uncle gave it to me."

"Why didn't you give it to Dr. Perrell in the arena?"

"Dr. Perrell said he wanted to meet me behind the hot-dog stand."

"Don't you think that's a . . . somewhat unusual meeting place?"

Karissa lowers her eyes and doesn't say anything.

She has an idea of what's in the package, Bernard thinks. Something Perrell doesn't want to be seen with in public.

He puts latex gloves on, picks up the package, and carefully opens the paper. A flat box appears. He turns his back to Karissa and opens it. When he sees its contents, he jerks backward. A chain of claws, polar bear claws.

"Take a look at this, Gates."

She stands up and looks over his shoulder.

"Aha," is her sole comment.

She reacts like a pro, he thinks, closing the box back up.

"We have to take your package with us," she explains to Karissa.

"Was Dr. Perrell killed because of the package?" the athlete asks.

"No. What happened to him has nothing to do with you." Gates's voice is amazingly clear.

He looks at her, perplexed. He doesn't share her point of view, at least not at that moment. That's something they'll have to discuss in the office.

"Will the games still go on?" Karissa looks at Gates full of hope. She lives for her sport.

Bernard is familiar with this attitude from his son, who's a hockey player. He weighs in. "No, it's not a good idea under the circumstances."

Karissa starts to cry, and Gates puts an arm around her.

He looks out the window. A storm's coming up. Sheila's Brush. The last big snowstorm until spring. The games would have had a rough time of it even without any murders. In a storm like this, you can't see a target or even a cross-country ski track. But that's no consolation for Karissa Pardy. She rushes to her friends in the living room. Gates waits until they are alone, then goes to the open closet where the athletes' jackets are hanging.

"Look here."

She points to a place on the wall inside the closet.

He comes closer. His eyes need some time before he recognizes anything. A stamp. The Viking symbol with the interlocking triangles. A board like the one used for the crate Lorna Taylor's skeleton was found in.

Gates's cheeks are lightly flushed. "Scott Dyson helped with the renovations on this house; that's what Grace Butt told me."

"Scott was in the slammer when Lorna disappeared."

"But he's sure to know who gave him the board." A note of triumph sounds in her voice.

Later, when she's sitting beside him in the police car, she asks: "Are polar bear claws legally traded?"

"The law only permits Inuit to do it."

"Maybe Karissa's uncle is an Inuit. No reason for Perrell to hide behind a hot-dog stand."

"No. Heaven only knows why a man of forty-two wants to meet a teenager secretly in the dark," he replies and steps on the gas.

"We need to find out why Dr. Perrell left the UK. He told me he felt trapped in the hospital system. Maybe there are other reasons."

"What are you getting at, Gates? Seducing minors? Be careful with things like that. The doctor is virtually a saint in this place."

"What if the murderer was one of the athletes? Or a spectator? They'll all take off, now that the games are over, and we won't have quick access to them anymore."

"Do you really believe the killer's one of the athletes?"

"Hard to imagine. Probably none of them was here when Bakie was killed. Can we get a search warrant for Perrell's house?"

"Already applied. Let's see how fast the judge acts on it. Might take one more day."

He's tired; he's hardly had any sleep.

"It looks to me like someone was settling a personal score. The perp was standing right beside Perrell when he shot him. So we're looking at that old question: Did Perrell have any enemies?"

He's silent.

"When do we expect the lab results?" Gates asks.

He had the evidence bags delivered to Happy Valley-Goose Bay along with the body. He should speak to Georgina about Carl Perrell and find out more about him, but right now she's sleeping after her night shift—thanks to a pill. Perrell's death has truly shaken her. The entire hospital staff is in shock. Talking with his wife will be difficult. Not only because of Perrell.

"And who's looking into the pocketknife?" Gates keeps drilling.

"Delgado."

"Good. I'll go see Shannon and Ann."

He absolutely must have a strong, hot coffee. The steering wheel's so cold that he can only hold it with gloves on. The heater takes forever to warm up the car. He should have left the motor running.

"Sergeant, take a look at this picture."

Gates holds a cell phone up to his face.

"What's this? A jigsaw puzzle?"

"Yes, a Google Earth image of Port Brendan, and a jigsaw puzzle was made from it. Take a close look at this detail shot. What do you see?"

He frowns. What's all this? He should concentrate on the road.

She insists. "That yellow dot. Isn't that your car?"

He brakes carefully and comes to a stop. He can clearly see the yellow dot in the picture. The color stands out against the deep green around it. As a matter of fact, it's Georgina's car. She desperately wanted a Jeep Renegade. He usually takes the police car. The Jeep in the picture isn't standing in front of his house but much farther away. On a road in the woods. He moves forward for a better look. Suddenly, he feels hot.

"When was this picture taken?"

"No idea. It's a present from my brother."

304

That means probably last year. And he hasn't suspected a thing. Now he's even more afraid to talk with his wife.

Did Gates pick up on something? Impossible for her to know anything. She simply thinks it's funny that the Jeep is visible in her puzzle.

He gets the car moving again. On the way to the station, he suppresses any thought that is not related to the murder cases. He learned early on how to create airtight compartments in his head.

His phone rings loudly. Sullivan. He stops in the middle of the road and turns on his flashers.

"Perrell owned a revolver," Sullivan informs him. "He reported it missing three days ago."

Three days ago, dammit.

"How come I didn't know about this?"

"Perrell wasn't sure whether he'd simply misplaced it. His house is being renovated, so that's why he stored some things in places where they didn't normally belong. That's why I waited. We were also so busy with Bakie."

"And you just thought of it now?"

"I had to check my records first. It's a Norinco NP22. Perrell told me he had a permit for it."

The Norinco NP22 is a cheap Chinese revolver. No gun nut would buy a handgun like that, except somebody who wanted it in case of emergency. In Canada most handguns require a special permit. It is no surprise to Bernard that Perrell got the permit from the authorities. A country doctor in the wilds of Labrador—that sounds dangerous. And Perrell had a good reputation.

"Inform forensics. You never know. Maybe Perrell was shot with his own gun."

"I'll call right away." Sullivan pauses. "We definitely need to find the Norinco. Maybe we should put Gates on it."

Sullivan's sulking like a drama queen because it bugs him that Gates and Fred had the crime scene to themselves. Gates reported their results to the team. Murder without a doubt. The angle of the bullet's path. Perrell was right-handed. The wound is on the left. The gun is missing.

He notices two cars are waiting behind him and shouts into the phone, "I'll be in the office in a minute," and cuts the call off.

He gives Gates the latest update. She writes something on a pad.

They arrive at the station to find Sullivan sitting self-importantly on the desk.

"There's more news, Sarge. I found a match between the footprints behind the hot-dog stand and the ones at the Viking house."

He slides off the desk and fans out some photos.

"These winter boots are rather worn down at the heel. That's why the imprint is shallower and not as sharp-edged as new boots. So it could be the same perp. I'm guessing a man."

Gates looks at the pictures and nods.

"I'm off. Want to talk to Karissa Pardy some more."

She's barely gone when Sullivan says: "She's not thinking, like, Karissa's behind the murder?"

Bernard doesn't bother to answer. He really needs a hot coffee and reaches for the steaming cup the minute Wendy brings it in. He's barely felt the caffeine in his veins when disillusionment sets in. Half of Port Brendan's running around in worn-down boots. His hopes lie in the revolver. Hunting rifles can be found in almost every household, but hardly anybody in this town has a handgun. Maybe somebody swiped the doctor's Norinco. Like the theft of Hynes's ax.

Hynes has been crossed out as a suspect in Perrell's murder, unless he sneaked out of the hospital. Georgina or somebody else on the night shift would surely have noticed. Bernard should have another go at Hynes's foreman. And if he isn't the killer, the guy just might have seen somebody slinking around Perrell's house.

"Where's Fred?" he asks Sullivan.

"At the hospital."

"How so?"

"You sent him there yourself. So he can talk to the staff."

Of course. Just now he remembers. Seventy-two hours are what he has. He's got to get through them with or without sleep.

Gates thinks that a personal settling of scores cost Perrell his life. A wicked hunch leads him to hope devoutly that it isn't so.

42

While looking for my guests, I find Karissa Pardy alone in the basement room. She's lying on the lower bunk. I sit down beside her. Her eyes are puffed up from crying.

"Karissa, it will be easier for you if you just tell me the truth."

She turns her reddened face toward me. Her nose is runny. I go into the bathroom for a couple of tissues. She takes them and crumples them in her hand. She must still be in shock.

I hold her hand.

"What exactly did your uncle say to you?"

She sniffs. Her voice sounds as if her nose was plugged up. "He said it was a gift for Dr. Perrell."

"Why did he want to give him polar bear claws for a present?"

She grips the tissues in her hand without looking at me.

My phone vibrates, but I don't want to miss this opportunity with Karissa. She's ready to tell all.

"For drugs?" I push a little.

Karissa shakes her head. "For pills."

Medications.

"My uncle doesn't have much money," she adds.

"Is your uncle ill?"

Karissa nods.

"Mom says it's a rare disease. That's why the pills are so expensive. He has to pay for them himself."

I've been there. My provincial insurance plan doesn't pay for my expensive medication. But I'm lucky that the RCMP covers it with additional insurance.

Not every patient is so lucky. Dr. Perrell looked for a solution. He was king in his realm of patients. A rebel in a white coat. He left the British National Health Service because it was too restrictive for him. He found more freedom in rural Labrador. Here he also had the freedom to assist patients who had little money. What other regulations did he circumvent? I wonder.

"It's good that you told me this, Karissa. You can't be blamed for anything. Neither can your uncle. It was wholly Dr. Perrell's responsibility."

Karissa sniffs again. Her tear-stained eyes make her look very vulnerable.

I hear her friends coming downstairs. They open the door tentatively. They look at me and Karissa.

"Do we have to go home?" one of them asks. "We've trained for so long."

I nod.

"The games are canceled. We have to look out for people's safety. There have been two murders in just a few days. Your coach will organize your trip home and will let you know. You can stay with me until then."

My words come completely spontaneously. Adults need to give these athletes a feeling of security, not anxiety. My instincts tell me that the same murderer from the Viking house waited for Carl Perrell. Bakie was the wrong victim. The series of murders should now be over. Hopefully, hopefully, hopefully.

The trio of guests look at me balefully.

"Maybe you'll catch the murderer today, and then the games can go on."

They don't give up hope so easily, these girls. They must be built that way for a sport like the biathlon.

"We're doing our best. But the games are officially postponed."

Three crestfallen faces by way of response. I understand their disappointment. Everything has conspired against their ambitions.

"I have to leave now," I say. "You have my number. Call me if you need something. You'll find pizza in the fridge." I pause to think for a second. "Lock the door behind me, and don't let anybody in."

"Not even our coach?" one of them pipes up.

"Yes, he's okay. But call me first in all other cases."

I know that instructions such as these aren't very likely to reassure them; two murders are no tea party. Better to be overly cautious than careless.

In the car, I pass on the information I extricated from Karissa to Closs. The motor's running and my seat's getting cozy and warm.

"In your eyes, Pardy is not a potential suspect?" he says.

His words leave me speechless. Does the sarge seriously believe she might have been involved? Karissa's horror cannot have been put on.

"She's a crack shot," he says, breaking my silence.

"With a rifle, not a pistol. I still think the perp was a man."

"We've got to think outside the box, Gates. Have you seen Shannon Wilkey yet?"

"On my way, Sarge."

Think outside the box: okay, that's what he's going to get. I won't tell him I'm planning a quick detour before interrogating Shannon. Might be that nothing comes from my plan. The roads are recently plowed; everything's glistening white, although the sun has not yet broken through the layer of clouds. The Ford Edge effortlessly makes it up the shoveled driveway to a house with a blue facade. How I'll get back down afterward is another matter.

I knock at the door and go in. I only have to call "Hello!" once and an elderly lady appears at the end of the short hallway, dish towel in hand. Her curious expression changes after I introduce myself.

"Leave my son in peace; he's already had a rough time of it," she complains with a look of reproach.

"I live in Grace Butt's house," I explain. "She told me your son did all the carpentry work there. I'm asking about a built-in cupboard."

Scott Dyson's mother listens to me with distrust, then she waves her dish towel.

"He's in the shed next door," she informs me.

I can't believe my good luck. I'll have him there alone, without his mother. I offer my profuse thanks.

Loud drilling comes from the shed. I open the door. A cave for tinkerers. Tools are hanging all over the walls. Clean and orderly. Scott Dyson stands with his back to me and doesn't turn around until I call his name. He looks less jaded than in his photo in the files. And younger than the forty-five years it says there. Maybe it's because of the orange wool cap that hides his bald head. It's not warm in the shed. It also does not smell of hashish. I still can't imagine that he's gotten out of dealing completely. No shop in Port Brendan sells marijuana legally, unlike in some other Canadian cities and towns. People have to get their dope from somewhere. But that's not why I'm here.

Dyson's expression is first one of surprise, then it collapses when he recognizes I'm a Mountie.

"I'm Detective Sergeant Calista Gates," I tell him. "Can I have a few words?"

Dyson doesn't answer but doesn't look aggressive, either.

I decide to home in on my target instantly. I don't have to dish up any fairy tales like I did for his mother.

"I live in Grace Butt's house and found in the guest room a

board with the stamp from the Viking house on it. Can you tell me where it comes from?"

Wrinkles appear on Dyson's forehead. He's clever and has quickly made the connection with the crate that contained Lorna Taylor's skeleton on Savage Beach.

"Not a clue," he answers. But his response is too quick.

"Grace says you did some carpentry work at her place."

I see he's thinking about it.

"You asked Grace?"

"She said she was very pleased with your work. Where did that board come from?"

"Can't re . . . Couldn't Grace tell you that?"

"Did Grace provide the material?"

"I just took what was there." Dyson's face darkens. "You can't pin that Lorna business on me; I was in the slammer."

"And I don't want to, either. We've already counted that out. But when you were adding the boards, you must surely have wondered where they came from. With that conspicuous stamp."

"I just used what was there," he repeats.

"Did Grace provide the material?" I ask a second time.

He doesn't say. That's an answer, too.

"When you found the crate on Savage Beach, you must have noticed the stamp. What did you make of that?"

No answer.

"Do you recall the board in the closet?" I keep drilling down.

"Stuff was lying around everywhere. They also used it for the children's playground."

I was waiting for that answer. I'm just puzzled that it didn't occur to Scott at the outset. Would have been logical. But it came to mind just now. Why? Something stinks. Like the dog shit he probably threw into my house.

"Did you help out with the playground?"

I already know that isn't possible. Scott was still behind bars. I just want to tease him out of his reserve.

"Are you trying to tell me I could have stolen the boards from there? Hate to disappoint you, lady; I wasn't even here when the playground was built."

"Then I'll have to talk to your cousin," I say, backing off.

"Which cousin?"

"Ernie Butt."

Scott shakes his head. "He's not my cousin."

"Oh, no? Ernie told me he was."

I recall that the inspector in Happy Valley-Goose Bay already denied the two were related.

"Did he say that?" Dyson's eyes narrow.

"Yes."

He puts down the drill.

"Is that everything?"

"How well did you know Lorna Taylor?"

"Why do I constantly get asked that question? Do you ask other people, too? Like my so-called cousin?"

"We're asking a whole lot of people. You can surely understand that. I'm trying to find out what kind of person Lorna was. I have to talk to people like you since I never met her."

He bangs the handle of his pliers against the edge of the wooden bench, almost playfully.

"And what have people told you?" he finally asks.

"Was Lorna serious or happy? Was she withdrawn or sociable? Did she have many boyfriends?" is my riposte.

"She liked to flirt, if that's what you mean. She was pretty. She gave lots of the boys the run-around."

"Who, for instance?"

"Not me. I was definitely not good enough for her. I knew it right from the start. She flirted anyway. She could have had me, easy as pie. But she didn't want anybody she could have effortlessly."

Married men, then. My nerves quiver. Scott Dyson, a small-time crook, has ventured out a bit on thin ice. Revealed he's just a little bit short of vulnerable. He wouldn't do that without having a reason to. Must be some cunning behind it.

"Anybody else's hopes she got up, and then gave the brush-off?"

"Dunno. Couldn't be everywhere, you know."

He turns his back on me and pulls out a rusty nail from a board with his pliers. His body language is unmistakable: he's given me all he wants to, won't expose himself any more than that.

I've got one more little query for him. "Do you have a key to my house?"

"No." He doesn't even look up.

I turn toward the door.

"Whatever. I'll change the locks."

With those words, I leave Dyson in his shed. Can't get anything more out of the guy right now. What he's not telling me is in any case more informative than his curt answers. I'm all but convinced he's responsible for the dog crap. And I'm equally convinced I wasn't the target of that dirty deed. It's someone else he despises.

I tramp back to the car. The front door of the house opens. His mother.

"You can't turn around here. You have to back out," she shouts, with a touch of schadenfreude.

I yell over to her, impulsively, "Do you know that Ernie Butt claims your son is his cousin?"

I watch her face. Her lips go narrow, just as Dyson's eyes did.

"Ernie's adopted. Did he tell you that, too?"

"I didn't know."

"Of course he wouldn't tell you. He acts as if he's well-to-do."

I don't think that's unusual. Maybe Ernie struggled with his self-esteem as a child because other people saw him as "only" adopted. The way Dyson's mother referred to it disparagingly. It would almost be natural for Ernie to overcompensate for a thing like that with some ambition or by showing-off.

"So who are his biological parents?"

"His mother is Priscilla Genge. Nobody knows who the father is. Except Priscilla, of course."

"Does she live in Port Brendan?"

"No, she took off when Ernie was a baby, left him behind."

"Where'd she go?"

"Nobody knows."

"Ernie doesn't know, either?"

"Maybe he does. He's got connections. Maybe you should just ask him."

"Did Lorna drive men in Port Brendan crazy?"

I call this type of questioning my Betty's-come-to-visit ploy. Betty was someone my mom knew who'd always show up at our house when least expected.

Scott Dyson's mother probably likes my surprise question as little as Dad did Betty's visits. Nevertheless she responds.

"You can say that again. But the boys here weren't good enough for her." That sounds like an echo of her son. "She only made promises but didn't deliver."

A crude description. Still, it's interesting.

"She set the bait but actually didn't want to catch anybody?" I'm already speaking in fishing metaphors.

"Better ask Grace; she knew Lorna really well. Or Ernie." Scott's mother is almost through the door when she adds: "The less Scott has to do with Ernie, the better."

Then the door is shut.

I stand there for a few seconds, then get into the car and go down the driveway in reverse. I turn onto the street without a hitch and push down on the gas pedal. My hands are tingling, but it's not the cold. I go up the main street to the gas station, park on the edge of the plowed area, and phone Fred van Heisen.

"Where are you?" I ask.

"At the hospital. Trying to question as much of the staff as possible. Not the best place for it. They've got to keep the show going with just one doctor."

"Fred, you have a list with the people who built the playhouse, don't you? Can I have it?"

"Gates, you got a lead?"

"More of a wicked hunch. But I definitely want to check it out."

"I'll send you the list. Keep me up-to-date."

I promise to. Driving through town, I see that it's almost dead compared to the day before. Many of the athletes have probably left by now, and some are waiting. Like my three guests.

My visit to Shannon has to wait. At the station, I run into Wendy.

"They're all out stalking," she declares.

"Wendy, does the name Priscilla Genge ring a bell?"

She nods. "My mother's second cousin."

Cousins. Of course, how could it be otherwise? Everyone's related to everyone in this place.

"What do you know about Priscilla?"

"She had a child by somebody. Then she high-tailed it out of town. She left the child here."

"Was it Ernie Butt?"

"Yes. The Butts adopted Ernie. They didn't have any kids of their own."

"Where did Priscilla go?"

"I can't say. Her parents have heard from her off and on. But they don't say a word about it to anybody. They're ashamed."

"Why wasn't Ernie raised by Priscilla's parents?"

"I've heard they didn't want the child because they couldn't bear the father."

"So people know who the father was?"

"Only rumors. They say he was a bitter enemy of Priscilla's father. But like I said, it was a rumor."

"It's easy to determine paternity with a test."

"Have you spoken with Ernie about this?"

"No, and this must stay between ourselves."

I already regret getting Wendy involved in the matter.

But then she suddenly comes out with an unexpected piece of news. "Mom once told me that Priscilla probably moved to the States. She saw a postcard from San Francisco on Priscilla's mother's fridge. That made Mom curious. But Mrs. Genge didn't say who the card was from."

I feel my hands tingling again.

"When did Priscilla leave? Does your mother know?"

"My parents have passed away. Mrs. Genge, too; her husband has dementia. But just a minute . . . It must have been 1990. Because the Genges took Ernie in that year. He wasn't even a year old at the time. Why not ask Ernie himself? He's sure to know where Priscilla lives."

"No, not yet." I raise both hands defensively. "Don't breathe a word about this."

Wendy looks taken aback. I have to hammer it into her.

"It's very important that nobody knows anything about this, do you understand? We could look foolish if it gets out."

I look a bit like I'm imploring her, and she nods. I've got to act as fast as I can now, before things get out of hand. I close the office door after me and call a former coworker with the Vancouver RCMP.

"I need information on a Newfoundland woman named Priscilla Genge. She might have moved to the United States in 1990 or thereabouts. Maybe San Francisco. I'd like to know where she's living, what she does, whether she's married, and if so, to whom. Can you dig that up for me?"

"For you, I'd do anything," the voice says at the other end of the line.

I sink back in my chair with relief. I still have allies in Vancouver.

43

Wendy's gaze seems peculiar to him when he returns to the station. Bernard wonders if she knows something. Or just has an inkling. She's friends with his wife. And curious by nature. He expects his coworkers to always keep him au courant about where they are. He doesn't always do it himself. Hopefully it will never catch up with him.

"Constable Gates and Constable van Heisen are waiting for you in the meeting room," the dispatcher tells him.

That's not normal. First of all, what she said, and second, the formal way she conveyed it to him. What's the matter this time? He's really had his fill of bad news.

Coming through the door of the meeting room, he already feels the air is filled with tense expectation. He reads it in his team's faces as well.

"You'd better have a good reason to take me away from an interrogation," he begins. "I . . ."

"We do have good reason," Gates says, interrupting him. "Let me explain. First, we discovered that the board with the Viking stamp in my cupboard that I showed you was left over from making the playhouse. You remember that the sawmill donated the material because it was the wrong size for the Viking house.

Ernie Butt was one of the men organizing the construction of the playhouse, and he took the remaining boards with him after it was finished. He could easily have put together the crate with Lorna's skeleton. Second, Ernie . . ."

Gates interrupts herself, goes to the door, and quietly closes it before resuming her report.

"Ernie was adopted by the Butts because his biological mother, Priscilla Genge, abandoned him a few months after he was born. She never revealed who his father was. She emigrated to the US, to a suburb of San Francisco, and married an American. And now the bombshell: her husband is a former American soldier, who was once stationed in Happy Valley-Goose Bay."

Here she pauses. As if he is supposed to see some point to it.

He doesn't quite get it and looks at her.

"You don't mean to say that Ernie . . ." He shakes his head.

"That isn't the whole story," Gates continues. "Ernie knew Lorna. She and his wife, Grace, were close friends, as you know. Grace told me that he was worried about Lorna's relationship with the American soldier. Maybe it was more than worry. Maybe he was mad at Lorna for getting involved with an American soldier, like his mother, Priscilla Genge, who took off and deserted her baby."

He's calmed down. And is disappointed. Calm because there might be something to Calsta's revelations. And disappointed that there aren't more of them.

"Now tell me, Gates, how are we to build a credible case from these paltry pieces of a puzzle?"

"When I spoke to the Butts at my place, Ernie maintained that he always only drove a pickup before he bought his new SUV. Grace corrected him, saying Ernie often took her Hyundai Santa Fe. Ernie wasn't happy about being corrected. I first thought it was because men like Ernie don't like to be contradicted by their spouse. But now I think there's probably another reason behind it."

She looks at van Heisen, who responds immediately. "Ernie Butt wasn't in his office the afternoon Lorna disappeared. Nor during the following days. He called in sick."

"Where did you get that, Fred?"

"In the investigation files, Sarge. Grace told our men in Happy Valley-Goose Bay that she didn't see Lorna the day she disappeared because Ernie had severe stomach pains, and she had to take care of him. It's all in there." Fred hands him some copies. "It's odd that, on the same day, Grace nevertheless went to work. After work—at six—she picked up a snowmobile from the repair shop. That took an hour because she had to wait. This is in the files as well. She needed Ernie's pickup because there wasn't much snow in December three years ago. She couldn't drive the snowmobile. She wasn't at home until seven thirty."

Before continuing, Fred picks up a written page off the table.

"Lorna left the furniture store at five. Ernie knew through Grace what Lorna's plans were for the evening. Therefore, Ernie would have had time and opportunity to intercept Lorna after work and take her to a secret hiding place. And he had Grace's silver Santa Fe at his disposal. Nobody examined it for clues."

"Too late for that now," Bernard remarks.

Gates picks up her narrative again.

"Grace also told me that Ernie always gets mad when her father says that Newfoundland should have joined the United States in 1949 instead of becoming a Canadian province. Maybe Lorna drove him into a blind rage with her needling. She was no shrinking violet and apparently had a sharp tongue. Maybe Ernie acted in the heat of the moment. The repressed anger at his mother, who found an American soldier more important than her own son. And because his mother was out of reach for him, he directed his anger toward Grace's friend, who also chose to be with an American."

Bernard shakes his head again. He needs more from Gates. Much more.

"I've got to solve the murder of a doctor, not to mention Bakie, and you come up with fanciful ideas that nobody can prove. Give me something concrete, Gates, then we can talk."

She sits motionless on her chair, like a cat before a mousehole. Patient. Ready to jump.

"The murderer left the crate on Savage Beach intentionally, so that it would be found. He craves attention; he wants to show off. I strongly suspect he has kept trophies. Even the skeleton is his trophy. We haven't found Lorna's jewelry. Where's the ring from her little finger? And what about her earrings? Maybe he's got some of her clothing, too. I'd like to search Ernie Butt's house and office."

"What? I'll never get a search warrant on the basis of those speculations. You know that better than I do."

Ernie Butt. A government official! Ernie and Bernard are on a first-name basis. This is the last thing he needs. He feels his stomach tightening. If this had to do with a guy like Scott Dyson, a two-bit drug dealer who's done time, then he'd have more elbow room. But now Gates had to go and sink her teeth into Ernie Butt, of all people. The worst of it is that he doesn't completely mistrust her hypothesis. He's always suspected that the perp came from Port Brendan but lives in Happy Valley-Goose Bay. In spite of this, he plays it down.

"Forget it. We'll never get it past the judge."

Gates stays calm. Her calmness irritates him. A thorn in his side. She doesn't have all the pressure on her. If she has something go wrong, she can blame it on the consequences of that assault. Sure he'd like to act. God knows he'd like nothing better than results. A quick success, so he doesn't have to watch his dreams go down the drain. Gates gives him hope but no certainty.

Now he hears her say: "We probably won't get a search warrant for the house. But maybe we'll find something in his car. That would be a good hiding place. He'd have easy access to his trophy when he feels like it. Ernie is still in Port Brendan today. Now's our chance."

She's giving him a way out. Ernie's car. How ingenious. His misgivings collapse like a row of dominoes. Ernie doesn't have to know anything about the search. He could invite him to the station for a chat. Find some excuse. Involve him in a discussion about road conditions and how the police can better control street traffic. Ernie loves to talk. Crow about his job in the transportation office. He thinks feverishly. Best if Ernie parks behind the station where his car couldn't be seen. By anybody. Ernie definitely won't lock the car. Nobody does that in Port Brendan. That gives Fred and Gates time for a quick search. If they don't find anything—and he's afraid they won't—Gates will give up. And he still will have done everything possible.

Unless the judge dismisses a car search out of hand. Which could happen; the judge probably knows Ernie Butt.

He gets up.

"I'll phone the judge."

He doesn't fail to notice that Fred and Gates exchange pleased glances.

And then unexpected things happen. He's put through at once. Explains that it's more a matter of getting as many people as possible off the list of suspects.

The judge listens to his explanation without interrupting. Says at the end: "Send something over to me in writing, Detective Sergeant, but I'm prepared to approve this."

He concludes the conversation and is flabbergasted. Fred and Gates rejoice. He thinks it's premature. "We've got to contact Ernie first."

But even that works. There's no problem enticing Ernie to come to the police station. Bernard takes a deep breath. If only it all goes well.

Ernie parks at the rear of the station after Bernard tells him the front of the station is reserved. When Ernie comes into the office, to Bernard's surprise he doesn't want to talk about street alignment and traffic control.

"What a mess for Port Brendan!" he starts out right off the bat. "Two murders, and in such a short time. Do you have any suspects?"

Wendy brings in two cups of coffee and leaves.

"Ernie, we can't discuss an ongoing investigation—you know that."

"Who'd want to do away with Dr. Perrell? The guy has only done good things for us. People are totally shocked, believe me. They can't get a handle on it at all. We prayed for him in church, but you could have reached out and felt the people's horror with your bare hands."

"His death affects all of us deeply, Ernie, and Kris Bakie's death, too, of course. We're doing our best to catch the killer or killers." He's on edge.

But Ernie doesn't seem the least bit upset. "Were they vendettas? In my opinion, it probably has to do with revenge. With jealousy and resentment. I can't explain it any other way. There were probably people who didn't like Bakie. He . . ."

"Who? We're delighted to have any tips."

"No idea. I don't have any concrete knowledge. But when somebody's successful, there are always envious people around. I can vouch for it from my own experience. I've got a new car, and people are already complaining that the government pays their employees too much and could spend the money on more important things."

Bernard twitches inwardly when Ernie mentions his car. He quickly changes the subject: "We'd like to put a traffic light at the crossing near the supermarket because there are so many near-collisions. Visibility is so poor."

"I'll see what I can do," Ernie assures him. "Maybe the government can free up some extra cash. But that's surely not your biggest worry, Bernard, am I right? How's it look with

Lorna's case? Anything new? Are you still investigating it, or is it just all about Perrell and Bakie now?"

"We're searching everywhere," Closs responds. "If you hear something, report it to us."

"Grace and I, we've told everything we know to Constable Gates. Did she tell you that Lorna threatened poor Bakie about his liquor license?"

"Yes, I'm aware of that. We follow up on every lead."

Wendy reappears, this time with a plate of cookies. The damn door was open the entire time. Gates is right: that mustn't happen.

Wendy puts the plate on the table. "More coffee, Ernie?"

"Please. The sergeant here is letting his get cold."

Bernard attempts a smile. "It's not good for my stomach. I ought to quit."

"What? A little bit of coffee? My stomach takes anything. Never had problems. I've got a constitution like a horse. What's happening with the Taylors, those thugs? Any updates there? The police surely can't allow an innocent man like Scott to be beaten up that way. You put Dennis Richards behind bars because he clobbered Gerald Hynes. The Taylors are . . ."

Bernard doesn't hear the rest. A figure has appeared in the doorway.

"Sarge, can I speak to you for a minute?" Gates asks.

His pulse accelerates.

"Have some cookies," he says to Ernie. "I'll be right back."

Gates walks into the large office ahead of him and closes the door behind them. She takes an evidence bag out of her pocket and holds it up.

Something golden flashes through the transparent plastic.

"Lorna's necklace, a present her parents gave her as a child." Gates's whispering is hoarse with excitement. "Way at the back of the glove compartment."

44

Closs immediately arrested Ernie Butt yesterday. I'd have held off a bit and monitored him, but I'm not the decision-maker here. Actually, I ought to consider the arrest a compliment from the boss. He has confidence in my investigating ability. But we still have a long road ahead of us. Ernie instantly shut up and demanded a lawyer. I harbored the vain hope that he'd defend himself and get caught up in contradictions. Because he so loves to talk. But there's a ray of light: our people in Happy Valley-Goose Bay have searched Ernie's home and his office. They found one of Lorna's rings in a drawer of his desk. The ring she wore over her tattoo on her little finger. At the moment they're securing some evidence in Ernie's cabin in the woods.

Ernie's lawyer isn't all that clever, but he's still able to throw a monkey wrench into the works. He claims to reporters that the gold chain in the glove compartment was planted in Ernie's car by the RCMP, who needed a win; that Lorna gave Ernie the ring as a prize for fundraising for the playground in Port Brendan, and that Ernie kept it because he believed an impulsive Lorna would soon regret it and ask for the ring back. But we have witnesses who saw the ring on her finger during the last days of her life.

The lawyer also stated that Ernie searched for Lorna for days after she disappeared and didn't go to work. Grace could probably give us more on Ernie's whereabouts at the time and what he did exactly. But she won't talk to us since her husband was arrested. She traded in her Hyundai Santa Fe—it's highly probable that Ernie used it for the crime—a year after Lorna disappeared. The Santa Fe was sold for scrap in the meantime. So that lead petered out. I don't think that Grace was involved in Lorna's murder. But for sure she knows more than she's confided to me until now. I can only hope that the preponderance of evidence will induce her to speak and cough up more details. A faint hope, I know.

The available evidence is good but not damning. Not yet. At the present time, Lorna's jewelry is being tested for traces of DNA at the lab. I'm desperately waiting for the results. Grace's family meanwhile has publicly taken Ernie's side. Any minute now, I expect them to throw me out of my house. Which would make me very sad. Especially now, when I have the house to myself. The three athletes have left.

The mood in Port Brendan is bad. The cancellation of the games has angered everybody. And Ernie Butt's arrest hasn't earned the police any sympathy from most of the populace. Ernie is one of their own. If Ernie gets arrested, then it can happen to anybody in town. Nobody's safe from the long arm of the law. That's the way people here think. Not even the Taylors can conceive of Ernie being the guilty party. That's not what a murderer looks like. Thanks to Ernie, Port Brendan had an ally in government when community interests were endangered. It seemed that everybody expected he'd go into politics. Maybe even be premier of the province of Newfoundland and Labrador one day. And now this.

We can't keep Ernie stewing in custody forever. Just twenty-four hours without an arrest warrant. The judge gave us an extension on account of the ring and the necklace. Without a confession, it's still a race against time. Closs's primary aim is to determine whether there's a connection between Ernie and the objects found on the ice. And with the deaths of Perrell and Bakie. I think he's going down a dead end. Ernie Butt was not in Port Brendan when the bag was left on the ice. And neither the footprints nor the snowmobile tracks point to him. And I don't see Ernie having a motive to kill Perrell or Bakie.

I drive to Shannon's house to learn more about that last conversation between her and Perrell in the arena. What made them so mad? The cleaning lady opens the door and tells me that Shannon's at the hairdresser and will be back in two hours. I take a peek in the shed, and her car is indeed not there. Frustrated, I make my way to Crow Point. I pace up and down in my silent house in order to ruminate on the murder cases; it's better here than in the office. I miss the girls' voices. How will Karissa Pardy get over the shock of finding Perrell's body? Or will she be overcome by the memory of it for years to come? Will she get psychological care? I'm not able to talk to her anymore. The doors in the guestroom closet stand open. I squat down and photograph the board with the Viking symbol. It will be part of the evidence against Ernie Butt. When I get up, I feel dizzy. My hand finds support against the wall until I can see clearly again. I must make it through this investigation. I must.

I'm the only one left to cook in the kitchen; I make a coffee and read the text messages on my phone. The first one is from Gerald Hynes. I was able to repress that unrestrained kiss with him, but now it catches up with me again. He tells me that he's no longer in the hospital but at his parents'. And that he has something he must absolutely tell me. I ponder that one. It may have to do with the investigation.

If not, then it's an opportunity to make it clear to him that I intend to maintain professional distance.

He answers my call immediately.

"When were you discharged?" I ask.

"This morning. They've got better things to worry about than a brawler with bruises."

"What's the mood like in the hospital?"

"Muted would be an understatement. Fear. Shock. Nobody can explain why somebody would kill Dr. Perrell. And now there are two murders."

"Who discharged you?"

"Dr. Cameron."

"How is she taking it?"

"She's keeping it together. Many people fall apart in extreme situations, some get stronger."

It's not that simple, I think to myself. Violence and humiliation can destroy the strongest man. Unless he gets help.

"Why do you want to talk to me?" I want to get straight to the point.

"I left a tool at Perrell's house. I wanted to get it before his relatives or somebody else shows up. But not without the police there. Had enough trouble already. Will you come with me?"

"Is there anything there that's relevant for our investigation?" I adopt a more businesslike tone. Hynes has to realize there will be no repeat of the incident in the hospital.

He answers just as dispassionately. "I'll show you something that might be important."

He's crafty, this Gerald Hynes. He's given me an excuse to go into the house and look around a bit. He knows I can't say no. I think hard. I quickly dismiss any thought of informing Closs. Better to present him with a fait accompli. The sarge is under pressure as much as I am. I've got a good hand to play after exposing Ernie Butt. All the same, he told me to go get some sleep before the clock even struck midnight, while the rest of the team kept working. Where did he find out that I can't work all night since the assault? My teammates are sure to have picked up on it. All the more reason to have a look in Perrell's house. It's not so easy to keep me away from a case.

"Where do your parents live?" I ask.

"Across from the old post office."

"Address?"

"Fourteen Pete Road. But you won't find it that way. Go down the street to the harbor until there's a turn. Take it, and it's the third house."

"The first turn—right or left? And what color is the house?"

After some mistakes, I don't trust the locals to give directions.

"First turn to the right. The house is white and a bit brown. You can't miss it."

"Why don't we meet at Perrell's house?"

"Dr. Cameron won't let me drive for three days because of the strong painkillers; then she wants to see me again."

Well, okay. He doesn't want his pickup to be seen in front of Perrell's place.

I'm really supposed to be interviewing Shannon Wilkey and Ann Smith. The side trip with Hynes doesn't have to take long.

"I'll pick you up in fifteen minutes."

I wolf down a muffin in the kitchen and drown it with coffee. When I look out the window, it dawns on me that I've got to drive through the snow storm that's just beginning, although it was predicted for late this afternoon. It's not far to the harbor, but that doesn't mean anything. I'll simply have to drive at a walking pace.

After a few meters on the road, I break out in a sweat, although the heater isn't yet running at full blast. There's not much snow on the road, but the wind blows white flurries from left and right in front of the windshield, and I only have a few seconds between them to take in the surroundings. It has become quite dark, although it's only nine thirty in the morning.

I drive in slow motion. Suddenly headlights loom up out of the blinding white cloud. Shit. I'm in the wrong lane. I'm shaking as I turn off to the side. How can I find the house on Pete Road like this? Somehow I manage to get to the street to the harbor. I recognize the turn by a red rope flapping in the storm. Normally it's tied to wooden posts. I barely make the turn and strain to find the first right. I see from the cars in the harbor that I've missed it. At that moment I hear my phone chirp.

"Where are you?" Gerald asks.

"At the harbor. Are you trying to kill me? It's hell out here."

"Wait. I'll get the Ski-Doo. You can sit behind me."

"I'm not dressed for a Ski-Doo and don't have a helmet."

He hesitates before saying: "I'll bring everything."

I wait with the motor running. Confused thoughts and images flit through my mind. Shannon and her Vancouver cap that she donated to the online auction. The group picture with Perrell, and Ann Smith standing to one side. The dog's head severed by a sharp knife. With the scalpel somebody tossed into the mailbox in front of the police station. A red sweatshirt that disappeared from a Salvation Army shop. Did somebody steal it? Bakie, who'd booked a flight to Las Vegas to begin a new job. Without anybody knowing. Carl Perrell's interest in Ann Smith, who gave him the cold shoulder. What was really going on between those two? The quarrel between Shannon and Perrell a few minutes before he died.

I finally see a shadowy, helmeted snowmobile driver beside my SUV. I unlock the passenger door and lower the window, and Gerald hands me a jacket and helmet. The jacket's too big, but the helmet fits. It's almost impossible to open the door in this wind. I push with all my might against it and force myself outside. How reckless it is to get out in this weather. You'd have to be crazy to even think of doing it. I consign my car to its fate and climb onto Gerald's snowmobile, a rucksack squashed between us.

The wind whips snow in our faces. I hope Gerald sees the dim headlights that appear out of nowhere. How can he drive a motorized sled if his doctor prohibits him from driving a car? But it's too late for such thoughts. I hold on tight to the side bars while the Ski-Doo shakes hard. Suddenly it stops. We've arrived at Dr. Perrell's. I stagger giddily toward the front door, which Gerald opens after several awkward attempts. We bang the snow off our arms and shoulders as best we can. It's surprisingly warm inside; nobody's turned off the heat. What a blessing to escape the storm for a while. Gerald takes off his helmet; one eye is still swollen and black. His scars are awful. I quickly look away and take off my boots. We go into the kitchen, where the renovations are almost finished. Gerald puts his helmet on the marble counter and struggles out of his thick jacket. His face is contorted; it obviously causes him pain.

Feels odd to be alone with him. And in a strange house. I'm on guard. He's planned something for me, but what?

"Come," he says and goes to the living room. I see the couch with mixed feelings. That's where I lay as I woke up from my fainting spell. It seems like so long ago, and yet it's only been a few days. Gerald pushes the couch aside and picks up something from underneath it.

"We had to move the electrical wires in the kitchen and considered our options. We tested the living-room walls and moved the sofa to do it. I found this underneath it."

He has a stack of papers in his hand. They're newspaper articles in a transparent plastic cover.

"I don't like to admit it, but I flipped through all of them quickly. I think they'll interest you." He points to the article on top.

I put on my latex gloves and take the article out of its cover. The headline is short and in bold: *America's Triumph!* Below there is a picture of a woman on skis with a rifle on her back. She raises her arms, still holding her ski poles, to acknowledge her victory. The caption below the picture: "Yvonne Shelcken makes history! The first Olympic biathlon gold for the USA." I sit down on the couch to read.

The article describes how Shelcken won the Olympic gold medal at Whistler in Canada against overwhelmingly strong competition from Russia, Germany, and Scandinavia. She benefited from a rule change, the text says, that gave more weight to the shooting contest in the total score. A result of doping charges against the Russians, who had manipulated the results for years. I recall that the three athletes mentioned Yvonne Shelcken at dinner in the kitchen. A paragraph about Shelcken's life followed. The daughter of a Montana farmer and his wife, her ambition drove her athletic career. She's obviously an incredibly good shot, but a top cross-country skier as well. A small picture shows her during the medal presentation: a healthy, freckled face, blond, short hair —the farmer's daughter bit rings true.

I feel Gerald watching me and look up.

He gesticulates.

"Don't you think it's funny? That he held on to these articles?"

I reflect on what I've just read. Perrell was employed as an emergency doctor during the Winter Olympics. He told me that when I had my hospital appointment. Is that why he was interested in Yvonne Shelcken? Shannon Wilkey was also in Vancouver for the games. And Meeka Stout. Is there any connection there? Now I really would have liked to know what Perrell and Shannon were talking about in the arena just minutes before the doctor was murdered. I look at my watch. Just over an hour to go before Shannon's back home.

I leaf through the rest of the clippings. More about Yvonne Shelcken.

"He seems to have been obsessed with the biathlon," Gerald remarks, somewhat impatiently, because I don't react. I read on. The articles all concern the Olympics in Vancouver and Whistler. He's right: they're all about the biathlon, and Yvonne Shelcken is in all of them. Perrell's name shows up in one of the articles. My pulse quickens.

"Dr. Perrell was working as an emergency doctor during the Olympics," I explain to Gerald.

"Then why did he hide this stuff?"

I have no explanation for him.

Bird calls. My phone. I hesitate. Then I recognize Fred's number. I press the talk button.

45

The lighting in the small canteen is unpleasant. Fred has to suppress a slight chill.

"The women here are all in love with Dr. Perrell," the hospital cook says. A skinny person with a long neck, her voice is as bright as a glockenspiel. The brightest voice he's ever heard in Port Brendan.

The cook is also astonishingly forthcoming, unlike the three employees he spoke with earlier.

"I mean, I should probably say *were* in love with him. Dr. Perrell could wrap them around his little finger."

Lost in thought, the cook falls silent briefly before continuing: "They'd have done anything for him. That's why the place worked so well, though the clinic doesn't have much money."

Fred can hardly concentrate. He can't get Ernie Butt's arrest out of his head. Also the question of how they should nail Ernie down so that he ultimately confesses. Mind you, the necklace in his car and the ring in his office are pieces of evidence that a prosecuting attorney could only dream of. But Ernie will talk his way out of it. He's already mobilized his family and relatives and his friends in government and tried to convince them he's innocent. Fred wishes Calista Gates would keep concentrating on Ernie. But Closs has set her on Shannon Wilkey and Ann Smith, where Fred doesn't see there's anything to be gained.

Ann Smith had definitely allowed herself to play a little bad joke on Dr. Perrell. She must have been so proud of her win in the shooting competition that she tried to unsettle the doctor a bit. Sort of a role reversal between the almighty doctor and the mocked outsider.

And Shannon was sure to have criticized Perrell in the arena for the disaster with the fundraising event in the Viking house. Or vice versa. Bad organization, a quarreling committee, unrealistic ideas. Two alpha animals, each of whom tried to push through their own plan.

He wished Gates were here. She's good at questioning. He could swap ideas with her afterward. Yesterday she'd allowed Closs to send her home without a peep, while everybody else stayed in the office. Sure, they're all exhausted but were working on adrenaline. Maybe Gates is keeping mum and just does what she wants. Like with the Butt investigation. It doesn't take much to see that Calista has a certain something: intuition, acuteness of mind that go beyond normal investigative work. He'd expected a call or text from her today, but she hasn't said anything. That unnerves him. His life suddenly has a new component: with her, an important person has arrived who has influence on his professional everyday life. He doesn't understand yet what he's supposed to think about it.

The cook pushes a plate of partridge berry pie closer to him that he hasn't touched. He doesn't think it proper in this situation to eat, although the pie looks delicious and he'd like to keep the cook speaking freely.

"And that accent!" she exclaims. "Like a British lord. The ladies simply couldn't resist him. They swarmed around him like bees to the hive."

Fred finds the comparison interesting, because he sees bees in Port Brendan rather rarely.

"Did he . . . was one of the women closer to him than the rest?"

"I once heard that he had a girlfriend in Happy Valley-Goose Bay, but nobody could say who it was. Probably just a rumor. People often spread rumors about him. Many say he's gay. But that's just jealousy."

"Did any men have reason to be jealous?"

The cook leans over the table conspiratorially.

"Oh, there are so many jealous people here, you can't even imagine. There are definitely people jealous of you, too. Because of the new policewoman from Vancouver. Such a pretty one."

She points to the pie. "Please do have some!"

That sounds like an order. Fred takes a little piece and slides it into his mouth.

The cook looks at him pleased as Punch.

"Meeka Stout complains that her husband spends hours clearing snow for the Mountie instead of watching the kids so she can get out of the house."

How did we ever come to talk about Meeka Stout? he wonders. *Did I miss something?*

The cook keeps at it.

"Meeka has her admirers, too. That's why Rick won't let her go on tour. Meeka so wants to be a nurse. Preferably in surgery. She'd like to assist with operations. That's what she told my niece. Blood doesn't bother her. She brings Dulcie to the clinic regularly. I think she just loves the atmosphere here. How's the pie?"

"Wonderful," Fred replies, licking his lips.

The cook beams. "Picked the partridge berries myself. I got twenty big buckets last year. I know a few spots where the berries grow real good."

"Is Dulcie sick?"

"I don't exactly know what's wrong with her. Dr. Perrell was very worried. As I said, he had a heart for the poorest people. And now—it's so awful. Everybody loved him, except Georgina Closs, maybe."

Fred helps himself to more pie. He's on thin ice with the cook at this point but doesn't want to stop her.

"Please don't tell her that, Constable, or I'll be in hot water. But Georgina often criticized the doctor. Because of expenses—always expenses. That he gives too much away. That the patients get everything they want. He wasn't strict enough for her. And not punctual enough. She's always bitching. She's not very well liked around here."

"Doesn't she take part in everything?" Fred can't resist the question.

"Yeah, sure, but she fell out with the women in the animal rescue group, too, and so she quit. Best that she did. They keep on going without her. But no one else will ever tell you that because of Georgina's husband."

Fred lets the berries melt in his mouth and says nothing.

"And Georgina always tries to give me less money for the kitchen. She's always talking about the budget. The budget. The budget."

The canteen door opens. A young nurse appears.

"Oh, I . . . I don't want to interrupt," she stammers and disappears.

The cook gets up

"I've got to get back to work, or the patients won't get anything to eat—or the staff, either. I've really told you all I know."

He stands up and thanks her. The cook wraps the rest of his pie in foil, adding another piece.

"For the Mountie from Vancouver," she explains.

As he leaves the canteen for the hallway, he sees the young

nurse from a minute ago standing beside a door. As if she were waiting for him.

"Can I have a word with you?" she asks.

He nods, and she opens the door.

"Best in here."

It's the laundry room. She stands between two irons and piles of freshly washed sheets. He takes note of her name on the collar of her uniform.

"I know what happened to Kris Bakie's dog," she bursts out without further ado. "I was there."

His pulse races.

The young woman smiles in apology, then turns serious. "I . . . people here don't actually talk about it, but . . . after all that's happened, I think I must tell you."

She scratches the back of her hand. "Kris Bakie brought his dog to Dr. Perrell. The animal was dead, and Kris wanted to know what Arrow died of. Dr. Perrell said he'd have to do an autopsy to be sure. Bakie agreed. He didn't attend the autopsy, but I assisted the doctor. He suspected the dog had been poisoned, but he wanted to exclude other causes. Besides . . . he likes to do autopsies." Her face freezes, then she corrects herself. "Liked to, when he was still alive."

Fred just nods silently. But now something combative flashes in her eyes.

"I know that Dr. Perrell really wasn't supposed to do it, but we don't have a vet here, and he couldn't simply watch animals suffer. It's also hard for a pet owner. People don't understand that, if they live just a short hop away from the nearest veterinarian. I love animals, and I'd do anything to help them."

She looks at him defiantly. Fred understands the significance of her words. Dr. Perrell might have lost his license if word got around that he treated animals occasionally. But he understands, too, that a doctor with Perrell's natural disposition couldn't turn people away who came to him with a suffering animal. The nearest vet practice is in Happy Valley-Goose Bay. Four to five hours by car on a dangerous road through the wilderness. Perrell knew Bakie and wouldn't have refused his request.

"What happened to the cadaver?"

"Kris didn't want his dog back after the operation. He couldn't have stood the sight of it. Toward the end of the autopsy, Dr. Perrell severed the head because he wanted to show me a particular part of its anatomy. That sounds terrible, but . . . I'm very interested in anatomy." She presses her lips together and then goes on. "I don't know what went wrong, but the dog should have been disposed of. Along with other . . . special waste." She thinks briefly. "Maybe the doctor was distracted. Meeka Stout had come in with her daughter, Dulcie, who apparently had had a seizure. He had to take care of her immediately."

"Who else was in the hospital during those few hours?"

"Me, naturally. It was late in the evening. The night-shift people were in. I . . . would have to look at the schedule."

"Do you have any suspicion who might have poisoned the dog?"

She shrugs. "All I've heard is that some people were not pleased Arrow ran loose."

"Do you think Dr. Perrell's death might have something to do with the dog?"

"I don't know. I just presume that any information's important."

Her fresh face suddenly seems anxious.

"That is perfectly correct," he assures her. "You did absolutely the right thing. Many thanks for the information."

She seems just as happy as he is to escape the laundry room. He approaches the entrance with rapid steps. Through the glass door, he looks at the snow storm. What drove that young nurse to reveal Dr. Perrell's breach of the law? She obviously worshipped him but also thought it right for him not to stick to the rules if an animal was sick or injured.

Fred has only one explanation. She must suspect who made off with the dog's head. And her anger at that person is stronger than any deference to the deceased Perrell.

But who is this person? And who put the scalpel in the RCMP mailbox with the message *REVENGE IS SWEET*?

46

"I know who cut the dog's head off," Fred says on the phone. "Where are you now?"

"At Perrell's place. Gerald Hynes wanted to pick up a tool. I came with him. He could have gone by himself; he had a key. But he wanted to have me along to avoid problems."

Fred will surely think that now I'm the one who's going to have problems.

"He took me on his Ski-Doo," I add. "My car's stuck in the harbor."

"Can you get rid of Hynes?"

I glance over at Gerald, who's wandering restlessly around the kitchen. He's dragging a leg slightly, like I do sometimes.

"Yes."

"I'll come get you. Take his key and send him home. I thought he was in the hospital."

"Dr. Cameron discharged him this morning."

"Let the boss know. Better he knows about it. He won't whack you in the kisser."

"I'll wait for you."

I put the phone on the table.

Gerald looks at me.

"Everything okay?"

"Fred van Heisen's picking me up. It's best if you leave the scene."

"The scene?" A corner of his mouth turns up.

"Sorry, wrong word. It's crazy right now. So much to think about. But thanks for these papers. They will surely be a help."

He stands indecisively in the doorway. "So I'm dismissed?"

"One more question. Did Lorna drive men crazy in Port Brendan?"

He stares at me. "What—drive them crazy?"

"Did she flirt with them, get their hopes up, and then drop them?"

He shakes his head, half amused, half not comprehending. "Don't all pretty women do that? They know the effect they have on men. They play with it, and men believe in their simplemindedness that they've got a chance."

"So Lorna was no exception?"

"Lorna wasn't shy about her attractiveness. But I'm convinced she didn't sleep with anyone except her boyfriend at the time."

The former boyfriend, who moved across the whole continent to Alberta to work there. Leaving Lorna behind.

"How do you know that?"

"Because the men here really didn't interest her. Very simple. She wanted to get out. She had ambitions. And she made that clear to a lot of guys. That can wound a man's ego really bad."

"Are you speaking from experience?"

He's dumbfounded for a moment, then he responds: "I have to disappoint you, Constable. Lorna might have interested me, but just then she was with her boyfriend. And I hooked up with Melissa afterward. Since we're on the subject: Ernie was mad for Lorna for a while, in case you want to know. Then he fell for Grace."

"Did you ever tell this to the police?"

"No, why should I? Ernie was one of many. Besides . . . who'd have thought Ernie was a murderer?"

Ernie could have been one of the people she rejected. Go ask Ernie, Scott Dyson said when I tried to talk to him about Lorna. And his mother said the same thing. Lorna the flirt. Lorna who flaunted her charms. Who liked to go out. Who cast a spell on Grace. So that's what Dyson was alluding to. Ernie wasn't good enough for Lorna. Probably found him boring and conservative, although he was making a career for himself in Happy Valley-Goose Bay.

And probably not attractive enough as a man. Maybe she let him sense that indirectly. Or directly. Does Grace know about it? But she's not talking to us anymore.

"Can I go?"

Hynes's voice jolts me out of my thoughts.

"Sorry. Yes. Constable van Heisen will drive me to my car. Do you know the Wi-Fi password for this house?"

"Sweet, eight, seven, dreams."

"All lowercase?"

He nods, then limps out the door.

I know the feeling that must be depressing him. His body has got to heal for him to regain his old self-confidence. And when that happens, some people are going to get scared.

Revenge is sweet.

I text Closs about my and Fred's whereabouts and summarize what we've learned. Closs doesn't reply. Maybe he worked through the night and is taking a nap somewhere. Or he's interrogating somebody.

It's still too dark out for this time of year. The storm moves the snow back and forth like white blankets. I switch on all the lights in the new kitchen. Carl Perrell had a number of spotlights built in. It's almost finished, but he'll never see this room again. A life of commitment, senselessly destroyed. With his murder, many patients had their only hopes wiped out. The hope for understanding, healing, help with overcoming bureaucratic hurdles. What murderer would want to do that to his fellow human beings? His hatred of the doctor must have made him blind to everything else. A hatred so great that even his mistake with Bakie didn't hold him back.

During my last conversation with Perrell, I saw his vulnerable side. He was not only a god in white; he was also a human being who needed intimacy and love. Who had to make difficult decisions every day and witness a lot of misery. His murder is terrible enough. But now our team will relentlessly pluck apart his life, because when we apprehend the murderer, then Perrell's private life will be made public at trial and the doctor will be unable to defend himself. He will be punished, again and again, though he's the victim. It makes me furious. Because it also happened to me.

I hear a snowmobile and then noises at the front door. Fred stumbles into the hallway, his helmet still on his head. He frees himself elaborately from his storm protection and lets it fall to the floor, where even more water accumulates.

"Christ Almighty! I thought the squalls would blow me away. I could hardly see a thing."

He runs his fingers through his messed-up hair. The cold air makes his face look good; he doesn't look as tired. He picks up his ski jacket and fishes a package out of a pocket.

"From the cook in the hospital. A present for you."

His eyes are fixed on my rubber gloves.

"Because of the newspaper clippings," I say mysteriously. "I'll explain it all, but first I want to hear what was up at the hospital."

We sit down at the kitchen table. Fred puts the package in the middle and opens the foil. Berry pie!

"What did Closs say?" he inquires.

"I left a message but haven't heard back."

He rubs both hands over his face. Then he begins to speak.

I'm glued to my seat. He spreads out a wealth of information before me. A network of possible connections and clues.

"Interesting that Meeka was there," I remark.

He looks at me quizzically.

"Meeka must have gotten wind of the fact that Bakie had brought his dog to Perrell. And Dulcie found out about it, too. She told me that Perrell hurt the dog. That upset her. She even burst into tears. She must have gotten it from somewhere . . ." I recall my conversation with Meeka. "I asked Meeka what Dulcie meant by that, but she acted as if she didn't have the slightest notion. The question is, why?"

"Maybe because Perrell asked her to say nothing. It could have caused him trouble. In the worst-case scenario, he could have lost his job."

"Then why didn't he keep the incident from Meeka? She surely didn't need to know."

"Meeka brought Dulcie to the hospital in an emergency. The girl apparently had a seizure. Perrell had to attend to her at once and perhaps didn't pay much attention to the dog."

Seizure. Do you still have seizures, Mrs. Gates? I suddenly feel a chill.

Fred toys with the aluminum foil under the pie.

"The cook told me that Meeka wanted to be a nurse. That she was interested in operations."

"You mean Meeka sniffed around in the hospital whenever she was there with Dulcie?"

"Could be a possibility, eh?"

"What more does she know that she hasn't told us? She didn't seem secretive. She even told me that somebody's sending her indecent emails. She didn't have to tell me that."

"Indecent?"

Fred reaches out a hand to attack the pie crust.

"Sexual content. Lewd. As I understood it." I push the pie over to him. "Please eat it."

He breaks off a piece and puts it back. "You really ought to taste it. It's so delicious."

I take off my gloves and begin to eat. Very sweet and sinfully good.

"Other women have gotten emails like those," Fred explains. "They've been going around for weeks. We haven't bothered with them yet."

Not a priority for a purely male RCMP detachment. Doesn't surprise me. By way of an answer, I arch my eyebrows.

"I know, I know," Fred responds. He lowers his eyelids.

Now I notice the lack of sleep in his face. Warmth is his enemy.

"Why don't you lie down for an hour? The boss is probably sleeping, too. He's not answering. I'll tell you more about the clippings later. I need some time to search the internet."

He stands up and indeed wanders into the living room. I watch him lie down. If only this couch could speak.

I take my tablet out of the rucksack. Why was Perrell interested in Yvonne Shelcken? There were hundreds of athletes at the Olympics, after all. Did he treat her when he was an emergency doctor there? Probably not. There's no mention anywhere in the articles of an injury to Shelcken. I first heard of this American woman through my three guests. I don't know much about competitive sports and was just happy ten years ago that the Winter Olympics were over. The one thing I was pleased about was the Canada Line that was built in time for the games. That rapid transit train finally provided a public means of transportation to the airport, as in other big cities. I enter the name of the athlete in the search engine. There are thousands of entries for Yvonne Shelcken. Not only about her sports career. But especially about what happened afterward. That rivets me immediately. A large American rifle organization shows up. Their ads featured Shelcken as their poster girl. Against her will. She sued them for damages. And was awarded them. She gave up her career in sports, went to college, began studying economics. Right-wing conservative groups in the US started to agitate against her. Gun nuts piled on. Then Christian fundamentalists. Then the right-leaning media. Then extremist politicians. Wick Posen, for instance, who made a name for himself with his hate-filled speeches. In an interview, he called her a scandal for the US and said she'd dragged the country's reputation through the mud.

Even though this country girl who'd grown up on a farm, a wondrously talented markswoman, was able to achieve what nobody had before her: the first biathlete to win Olympic gold for the USA.

It has suddenly gone quiet. Only Fred's regular breathing is audible. He's lying on his side, his face turned away. His dark hair is outlined by the bright-colored, decorative cushion his head is on. Funny that I know so little about Fred; I have more trust in him each day regardless. I look out the window. No blowing snow anymore. No howling outside the house! I don't get it. The storm died down practically instantly. How's that possible? Labrador is a riddle to me.

I bite off another piece of pie. Riddles inspire me. Including the puzzle of Yvonne Shelcken. After her Olympic win, the gun nuts must have seen her as one of their own. There are photos of her at the finish line, holding her rifle up in celebration. And then she turned against them. Against the rifle association. Against the gun lovers' pride. And then she just dropped out of a promising sports career.

No more wins for the US. Kiss my ass, she seems to have decided.

I can empathize: Yvonne Shelcken grew up and wanted to go her own way. A life without constraints and daily training. Without public pressure and those never-ending expectations. She began to defend herself. Against sports officials. Against her ambitious father. Against the New Gun Federation. And against the hate of people like the Republican rabble-rouser Wick Posen.

She revealed publicly that Posen had been sentenced for domestic violence. The liberal media jumped on the story.

Then something disastrous happened. Wick Posen was shot. He survived the attack, but ever since, he's only been able to get around with a wheelchair. The right-wing media made Shelcken morally responsible for the attack. She received death threats. That did it: she went underground. These days, nobody knows where she lives or what she does. She completely vanished from the scene.

I study Yvonne's face in the photos. I've never seen this woman before. The Olympics were of no interest to me at the time. Why did Carl Perrell save these articles?

My cell phone startles me out of my ruminations. It's Closs.

"We've got the guy who poisoned Bakie's dog. Joshua Price. A loner."

Sarge says nothing about the fact that Fred and I invaded the privacy of Perrell's house.

"What have you found?"

"He set out poisoned bait because he was annoyed by coyotes."

Fred stirs on the couch. He blinks and stretches his legs.

"And Melissa didn't know about it?" I ask. "That Bakie's dog was poisoned?"

"She and Bakie had a fight. Remember? They didn't speak to each other for days on end."

"Did you see my text messages?"

"I did. Is Fred still with you?"

"Yes."

I'm about to tell him about the press clippings when he says: "I need him at the office. I've got other plans for you."

"Ann Smith and Shannon Wilkey, I know."

He corrects me: "No, there's an ice fishing competition this afternoon on Sataka Lake. I want you to be there. Keep your ears open, and keep an eye on people."

I'm speechless for a second. "This afternoon? We've just had a storm."

I can't think of a better argument on the fly.

"It's over. Good weather today. The competition takes place every year. You can't bar people from holding it. The lake's not far from here. It's not hard to find. Ice fishing starts at one o'clock. You'll have to take the Ski-Doo."

I'm still flabbergasted.

"Is Fred coming with me?"

"No, we need him for something else. We have to stretch our staff somewhat."

He's keeping me away from the investigation. That's all I can think. Why? That's no help to him. I'm supposed to keep my ears open during the ice fishing. As if people would tell me anything. Me, the stranger from Vancouver.

"How long does the event last?"

All is not lost. I can still see Ann and Shannon afterward.

"Probably around two hours. Dress warmly. You won't be moving around much."

That's a provocation. I won't let him treat me like a child. And I'm not letting myself be pushed away from the investigation.

Without missing a beat, I say: "Does the name Yvonne Shelcken say anything to you?"

A long silence.

"Sergeant? Are you still there?"

"Yes, of course. What makes you bring that name up?"

"Carl Perrell collected a dozen or more press clippings about her."

"Where did you find them?"

"Gerald Hynes discovered them. During the renovations."

"Maybe Hynes smuggled them into the house."

What an extraordinary response. He doesn't even ask who

Shelcken is. He must know the name. He's probably more interested in sports than I am.

"I've got a call on the other line. Fred's to bring the articles with him. He can also tell you where Sataka Lake is. We'll take care of the house search."

"Sarge, I have a suggestion. I think it would make sense to go public with some things so we can move ahead."

"Can you express yourself more clearly?"

"I think it would be useful if more people knew about the flashlight and the white pocketknife. Then we have a chance of getting some helpful tips. It's clear to me that you're holding this information back because they're details that only the murderer knows about. But I think the time has come to inform people. Somebody must know more about it and will finally come out with it, now that there's been another murder."

He pauses again.

"I'll think about it."

And he's gone.

Fred's standing up. He sits down at the table with me.

"What was that all about?"

"If I only knew." I shake my head in my cluelessness. "Sarge is sending me to Sataka Lake. To an ice fishing contest. To sound people out. He wants you to go to the office."

I'm so furious that my voice is almost beyond my control.

"Sataka Lake is pretty far away," Fred says. "At least twelve kilometers. I went last year. There's a Ski-Doo trail to it, but you ought to have somebody take you there."

"Sarge claims the lake's not far, and you can explain how to get there."

We look at each other.

"Aha," is Fred's laconic comment as he interlocks his fingers on the table. "What did you find?"

"About what?"

"About Shelcken."

I summarize my discoveries for him. He's now wide awake. I'm glad he's no longer asleep. The situation would have felt too intimate. Shelcken's a good diversion.

"Maybe she moved to Canada," he speculates. "Under a new name. The cook says Perrell's supposed to have had a girlfriend in Happy Valley-Goose Bay. There were rumors. Maybe Yvonne Shelcken is living in Labrador."

"You seriously mean that?"

"Why not? In the States, she'd have to fear for her life. She's safe here . . . as long as nobody knows her true identity."

I'm charged up. "Perrell probably knew her identity because he was a doctor at the Olympics. Maybe he got to know her through that."

Fred folds his arms and leans back. "Did you know that Sarge was stationed in British Columbia at the time?"

I stare at him, open-mouthed. He almost seems a little proud to be able to tell me the news.

And he unpacks some more: "In Kelowna. That's not too far from Vancouver."

"Was he deployed at the Olympic Games?"

"You can go ahead and ask him. Maybe police from all over the province were in Vancouver back then, as reinforcements."

A thought flashes through my mistreated brain. That's why the RCMP hit upon Port Brendan when they were looking for a post for me. Because Closs has connections to the RCMP in Vancouver. That must have been how it worked.

"Then Sarge might know Yvonne Shelcken?"

Fred looks at me without a word.

I jump up and photograph the articles with my cell phone. Who knows if I'll ever get hold of them again, given these omens. My thoughts are racing. It can't be Georgina. It can't be Shannon.

Good Lord! A woman who's an outstanding shot. And who's athletic.

Fred leans forward as if waiting for the answer from me that's been obvious for a long time.

I shake my head.

"Ann Smith doesn't look like Yvonne Shelcken. See for yourself."

But as I place a portrait of her in front of him, an insight takes shape.

The clever makeup. The dark hair. The perfect teeth. The straight nose. That can all be manufactured. That can all be paid for. The perfect camouflage!

"Ann Smith?" The name comes out of my mouth like shocked amazement.

47

I don't want to find anyone in front of my house. Not when I've got so much to think about. I've got to solve the puzzle of Yvonne Shelcken. I don't want any conversation or interruptions. I particularly don't want to deal with Georgina Closs at the moment. And yet she of all people is standing at my front door. How did she find out again where I am at a particular time?

Her yellow Jeep is parked in front of the shed. The only yellow vehicle in Port Brendan. The snowplow has already cleared the streets, and Rick Stout must have removed the snow in front of my house. That means Grace Butt has not instructed him to stop working for me. I can still stay in the house. It's eleven thirty, and almost half the sky is blue. What crazy weather in Labrador. Rays of sunshine break through, and I have to squint in order to see Georgina.

"I'd like to pick up the sleeping bags and pillows. You don't need them anymore, of course," she explains.

"Sure," I respond, and let her in. She takes her colorful pointed cap off inside the house. Her fine, blond hair flies in the warm air from the heating. She looks gloomy. When she sees the guest room, she heaves a deep sigh.

"The girls must have been very disappointed that the games were called off."

"They were inconsolable," I acknowledge. "Have you heard from Karissa Pardy?"

"I've asked her parents about her; she's putting on a brave face, but I'm not allowed to speak with her, officially—my husband wouldn't feel comfortable with it. He considers it a potential manipulation of a witness."

I hear the bitter undertone to her voice. It's certainly not easy being a policeman's wife. Together we pack the bedding into the shiny blue garbage bags Georgina brought. Garbage bags from the hospital.

Maybe I can quiz her about that. But suddenly I don't feel like talking to Georgina. I mustn't rush it.

"I'm sure you were just sympathetic with Karissa and didn't want to do anything illegal when you phoned her parents," I venture to say. "I think it's nice you were concerned about the athletes. Women must support women. Even Ann Smith helped and drove the girls back and forth."

"She really did that?"

The snippy remark reminds me that Georgina doesn't like Ann Smith. Not a good move on my part.

The puzzle crosses my mind; that will interest Georgina.

"Come here, I've got something to show you."

I go upstairs with her to the living room. The puzzle with the bird's-eye view of Port Brendan is still on the table.

"Take a close look. What strikes you?"

She raises a quizzical eyebrow, probably surprised by my request, but she studies the puzzle.

"Is that Port Brendan?"

"Yes, my youngest brother had it made for me as a present. What else strikes you?"

She leans over the table. Suddenly her body goes rigid. She must have discovered the yellow dot. Her Jeep Renegade. She's not smiling as she straightens up and asks: "Did you tell my husband about this?"

"I showed him a picture of it on my phone."

Her lips go thin.

Did Closs not tell his wife anything? It would have been a nice anecdote over supper. For example.

"And what did he say?"

"Not much. I think he wanted to know when the picture was taken."

She receives the information without a word. Her otherwise fresh, girlish face looks infinitely sad.

"Do you like this house?" she asks, looking all around her.

"Yes, very much. I hope I can keep living here."

We've avoided the subject of Carl Perrell until now, but it's the elephant in the room. I can't hold my tongue any longer.

"What's the mood in the hospital like?"

"Everybody's devastated. Nothing and nobody will be able to replace Dr. Perrell."

Her mouth is trembling. She sits down on a chair.

Now it shouldn't make any difference that her last name is Closs. She's a witness like any other, and I'm investigating this matter.

"Weren't you at work that evening when Dr. Perrell autopsied the dog? You do take the night shift. Somebody must have taken the dog's head away. And taken a blue garbage bag. Who could it have been?"

"Haven't got a clue. Maybe Kris Bakie?"

Strange for her to bring up a dead man who can't speak for himself. She certainly knows that Bakie brought in his dead dog and then left without it.

I stick to my guns.

"The contents of the garbage bag were so peculiar. But the things in it definitely have a meaning."

"What meaning are they supposed to have?" She says it almost in resignation.

"To me, they express a threat. The red sweatshirt like the one Lorna Taylor had. The dog's head. The ax. The board with the Viking stamp. The way I see it, that can only mean: the same thing's going to happen to you that happened to Lorna and the dog."

"And the chain?"

The question takes me by surprise. How does she know about the chain? I expected her to leap up and make an excuse and leave. But she stays in her chair.

"Well, I'm not too clear on that. Maybe it was there just to weigh down the bag."

"You've got it all wrong," Georgina declares. Then she brings both hands to her face and begins to cry. It's an abysmally profound, desperate sobbing. It shakes her slim body so powerfully that I'm afraid she'll fall off the chair. It doesn't leave me cold, her despair. I know the feeling all too well. But some hope is mingled in with my sympathy. A dam bursting is usually a prelude to a confession. I hand her a tissue.

She turns her tearstained face toward me.

"He meant so much to me," she gasps. "I don't know how things go on from here."

She means Dr. Perrell—I don't doubt it for an instant.

"And you, what did you mean to him?"

"I don't know. He . . . never spoke about it."

"Mrs. Closs, did you put that garbage bag on the ice?"

She shakes her head. Lowers her eyes. "I just put it outside the door."

"Whose door?"

She says nothing, rolls the tissue between her fingers.

I know the answer.

"What were you trying to tell Ann Smith with what was in the bag?"

She sucks in her lips, wipes her bleary, puffy eyes. "It's nothing like what you said before. I . . . I didn't plan much. I just wanted to scare her."

"Where did you get the ax?"

"I found it in the cellar."

"In your cellar?"

"No, here, in this house. When I was stocking up food for you before you arrived. I looked around the guest room. The ax was in the basement. The board, too. I just took them with me."

My brain's rattling. Scott Dyson. He worked in the house. He must have stolen the ax from Gerald Hynes's pickup.

"Why the red sweatshirt? The cap from the Olympic Games?"

"The animal rescue group didn't want me anymore. So I got rid of the sweatshirt. And the cap . . ." Her troubled face is agitated. Vertical lines appear on her forehead. "That's obvious, isn't it?"

"No."

"Because she was at the Olympics. That's where she got to know him."

"Who? Dr. Perrell?"

She shakes her head again and presses her lips together. A signal that she might clam up, so I change the subject.

"Why the dog's head?"

"I saw it lying there in the clinic. I know that she and animals . . . I thought it would scare the hell out of her."

"And the chain?"

"Because I'd like to put her in chains."

"Why?"

She refuses to answer again. Her tears have ended. She looks completely drained.

"The scalpel and the message?"

"What scalpel?"

"Did you put it in the RCMP mailbox?"

"No."

"Why did you want to scare Ann Smith?"

Georgina gets up. "Ask my husband."

"Does he know? Did you tell him all about it?"

"No, and he doesn't tell me anything anyway."

"Then do it, please, Mrs. Closs, as soon as possible."

She goes into the kitchen.

"I haven't committed any crime," she replies, almost defiantly. "Just done something stupid. Other people do stupid things, too."

I'm about to follow her into the basement, but she wards me off.

"I'll find the way by myself. You surely have other things to do."

I watch her through the little kitchen window as she loads the blue garbage bags into the back of her Jeep. A charming, slender figure with a colorful pointed hat. Georgina revealed her innermost self to me. She fell apart, then straightened herself up again within half an hour. I marvel at how she did it. Will she confess to her husband that she was in love with Dr. Perrell? A love she masked with gruff behavior. And confess that she did something out of jealousy of Ann Smith, something so crazy that people would never have thought it possible? I doubt it. She unburdened herself so that I would tell her husband.

I watch the yellow Jeep drive away. Georgina Closs has put me in an untenable position.

48

Ann stretches her back in the plow position. Yoga exercises always do her good when she's stressed. She survived the worst phase of her life thanks to yoga. But Carl Perrell's murder threatens to turn her carefully constructed life upside down. A second murder in a short time. As to Kris Bakie's murder, she can still delude herself that it had nothing to do with her. Maybe it was an angered acquaintance, a drunken settling of scores. Labrador's a wild part of the country. Many people drink more than is good for them; they carry guns. An argument can escalate very fast. Her lover, whose name she's told no one, had been able to calm her down. You've got nothing to be afraid of, he kept saying. She's got to believe him, because he knows more than most people.

Lorna Taylor's brutal end—that was back in the past. Lorna lived in Happy Valley-Goose Bay. She never met Lorna. Never heard of her until she disappeared.

She tries to keep breathing calmly. Just concentrating on her pose. Don't slip into panic. Yoga has always helped her until now. Yoga and well-meaning people. The police. The Canadian government. Her brother's help. A man's love. She followed him all the way to Labrador. A secret love, but it's strong. It offers her so much support that she's ready to take on a lot.

Winter storms, for example. The locals call it Sheila's Brush. She's experienced it for the first time because she's normally not here in winter. Only her lover knows where she spends the bitter cold season. Winter months, with nothing to do but talk to him on the phone.

Carl Perrell could never have given her what her lover gives her. Perrell was used to having everyone kneel at his feet. He couldn't understand why his charisma had no effect on her. Maybe it would have been different under other circumstances, in another life. Perrell possessed qualities she respected. His commitment to the folks here. His dedication to the clinic. It wouldn't garner him any academic laurels. Perrell was a driven man, a missionary.

Like Dr. Wilfred Grenfell, his role model. Perrell once told her that Grenfell wanted to rush to a patient by dogsled over the ice but got marooned on an ice pan that floated out onto the open sea. It took a long time to find him. He had to kill three of his dogs in order to survive. Wrapped himself in their pelts so he wouldn't freeze to death.

A thing like that impressed Carl. That's the way he saw himself. He took risks. Didn't stick to the rules. Maybe he went too far sometimes.

She hears a motor. Probably the snowplow. Impressive, how quick snow removal is here.

She gets up off the yoga mat and peers out the window. Shannon's SUV. Her pulse quickens. The effect of her yoga has fizzled out. Shannon's already opening the door. If only she'd locked it, as she usually does. But she gets practically no visitors. Certainly not Shannon Wilkey.

"Ann?"

She can't hide, can't pretend she's not home. Shannon is sure to have seen her moving before she came up the path to the house.

The sound of boots being taken off. A zipper pulled down. Firm steps on the stairs. Too late.

Shannon stands in front of her, her blond hair tied back, a bright blue band over her forehead. Her fleece jacket is blue as well, with white stars.

"Forgive my impromptu visit," she says, "but I absolutely must know how you're doing after Dr. Perrell's death." Her voice doesn't sound at all apologetic.

"I'm as shocked as everybody," Ann responds dryly. "You, too?"

Shannon sits down, without being asked, on one of the two living-room chairs, and Ann has no choice but to sit down opposite her. She feels unprotected in her skintight yoga outfit.

But Shannon keeps her eyes trained on her face.

"You know, of course, that he was shot. One of the young biathletes found him."

This was news to her. "Have the police made the cause of death public?"

"No, but everybody in the village is talking about it. What will you say to the police?"

"Me? What have I got to do with it?"

"What will you tell the police when you're asked why you pointed your gun at him at the shooting competition?"

Ann jumps to her feet. "What business is that of yours? Have you come here to grill me?"

Shannon remains seated calmly, her hands held loosely together.

"I'm here to help you, Ann. I'm on your side. You've got nothing to fear from me."

"Oh, no?" Ann folds her arms. "Then why do you attack me with this question?"

"Because I'm worried about you. Because you might be dragged into the murder investigation, and you really don't want that. I'm here because I want to protect you. I know that you're Yvonne Shelcken. Do you need an alibi? I'll give you one right now if necessary."

Ann's heart stops for a second. That name. Shannon knows her name. She slowly sinks down onto the chair again. She mentally slips a glass sphere over her head. Like back then, during a race. Inside that glass sphere there's quiet. Concentration. And an iron will to score a bull's-eye.

She looks straight at Shannon.

"Who are you?"

"I'm not what I seem to be. I fight for democracy. Against the enemies of freedom. Fight against moral disintegration and the destruction of good people. I do it with my own devices and in a way that works best. I've always admired you, and when you were attacked, I helped you from behind the scenes. I'll do it now, too."

"And I'm supposed to believe that?"

"Ask your brother. When you ask him, give him my code word, Herpever 82."

Ann can't grasp what she's hearing. She knows that code word. She and her brother, who lives in Montana, made it up. She knows that she was quickly accepted into Canada thanks to connections with people she does not know. That she got a new identity with the help of influential supporters. That the operations on her face were financed by benefactors. But Shannon's an American. Her husband's a well-known conservative donor. Watch out for Shannon, her lover warned her. Say nothing if she's around.

"Are you spying on me?"

"To a certain extent. But I like this place. And we were concerned about Carl Perrell."

"Who's 'we'?"

"Me. Your brother. People in our circle."

"Why Dr. Perrell?"

"He was too interested in you. And he found out who you are."

Another revelation that spooks her.

"How?"

"We don't know that yet. Somebody must have leaked it to him. Maybe your lover."

Ann freezes.

"Impossible."

"Maybe. Maybe not. We have to consider all options. He knows your identity."

"I trust him one hundred percent."

Shannon does not smile. She also doesn't contradict her.

"Perrell worked briefly as an emergency doctor in a Vancouver hospital. During the Olympics. But we know that he never met you. He came here without any knowledge of your true identity. He actually wanted a position at the hospital in St. Anthony, because of Dr. Grenfell. But then he had the chance to run the Port Brendan hospital. That got him excited." She sighs. "All this wouldn't have happened if he'd moved to St. Anthony."

Ann recorded every detail like an animal looking out for a hunter.

"How come you know all this?"

"We've got friends in Canada. We want to be sure that nobody puts you in harm's way. Now or ever."

"Did you kill Dr. Perrell? Because he was a threat to me?"

Shannon throws up her hands.

"No, for heaven's sake! We don't kill anybody. We're here to protect people. I warned him to leave you in peace. I warned him in a way that showed him we were serious. He didn't like it. In the arena, just before he died, he chewed me out for that reason. But I didn't give in. He was obsessed with you. That was not good."

"And you're trying to tell me that you've come here year after year to keep me under surveillance?"

"And to protect you, is how I'd rather put it. But I like it here. A lot, in fact."

"This is crazy."

"I'd say it's efficient. We fight for people who stand up for their convictions. You opposed the New Gun Federation and paid the price. You had to leave your home country because you feared for your life. Those are the people we fight for."

"Your husband, does he know about this?"

"No, of course not."

"How can you be married to him?"

"He uses me, I use him. It's a wash, right?"

"Why would you take risks like that? What's your motivation?"

"My motivation . . ."

Shannon's face suddenly grows very still; a trace of bitterness plays around her mouth. Her gaze wanders.

Ann's amazed at her abrupt transformation.

The answer comes slowly and haltingly.

"My best friend . . . was killed by a gun nut. And why? Because . . . because she confronted him when he showed up at her house with a machine gun at a party for kids. He . . . was the father of one of the kids who was invited. She told him guns were not welcome in her house at a kids' party. He didn't want to leave at first. Finally . . . finally she threatened to call the police and brought him outside. He shot her at her front door. Just like that. Bruised ego." Shannon stops, breathing audibly. "The executive of the NGF claimed the shooter just wanted to protect his child. Protect him from what? It's absurd. Incredible. The NGF hired a well-known lawyer for him, and he got off with house arrest."

For a few moments there was only the sound of the heating fan. Ann had heard of that incident when she was still living in Montana. There were a lot of people in her home state who thought the judge's decision was a good one. One more reason why she opposed being co-opted by a gun organization.

"Why did you come to me?" she asks.

Shannon draws her arms around her body as if she were shivering.

"We'll help you disappear again if need be. Who knows where this murder investigation's going."

It was a huge mistake, that prank with the rifle, Ann thinks. She ought to have known better: you don't fool around with guns. She was on such a high because she had managed to win even without any practicing. Aim, shoot, win. Maybe she wanted unconsciously to break the chains that her new identity bound her in. Or she wanted to scare Perrell a little. He should have been happy that she was able to bring in a sizable sum for the clinic. But he could only see in her eyes his personal defeat. The woman who would never be his.

"You didn't come to Labrador on my account, Shannon, or you wouldn't have built a house. You know I won't stay in Port Brendan forever."

Shannon smiles again. "I've fallen in love with this part of the country. I found it thanks to you. This is where I overcame my painter's block. My artistic crisis that had paralyzed me for several years came to an end. It's wonderful." She looks at her, eye to eye. "I must have my own four walls. Air to breathe. Light. A beautiful art studio. Or else I cannot paint."

This is how rich people talk. Ann snorted mentally.

"I can't leave now," she says. "Not without him."

"But you leave every winter." Shannon's voice floats softly through the room.

She sighs to herself. Shannon probably also knows where she passes the cold months. Very near the Montana border, so her family can visit her regularly.

"I don't have anything to do with the murders."

"Ann, he won't be able to save you when things get going.

Calista Gates has smelled blood. She'll take it to the bitter end. She's already caught Lorna Taylor's murderer. She'll also discover that you put the garbage bag out on the ice. I saw you do it and didn't tell the Mounties anything. But Constable Gates is a highly intelligent hound dog."

Calista with the lovable face. The black eyes. The melancholy look. Everything just a facade. Maybe she's been play-acting. The way Ann does, too.

"He doesn't have to save me. They've got nothing on me."

"But you don't want to be involved or called as a witness."

No, she doesn't want that. Maybe Shannon's right. He won't be able to prevent it.

Her visitor pulls down the sleeves of her bright blue fleece jacket. "I can take off for the US anytime. But you can't. There are plenty of gun-crazy people there who'd love to put a bullet through your head."

"Somebody did that to Carl Perrell. If it wasn't me, and it wasn't you, who was it?"

"I'm convinced that Calista Gates will soon find out."

49

While I put on my ski pants, Rick Stout never stops talking. I can't really get rid of him because he's taking me to the ice fishing event on Sataka Lake.

"Would never even dream of buying a yellow car. Terrible color. People know right away that a woman's inside."

"Why wouldn't men want a yellow car?" I respond. "It's practical, after all, if you're lost in the tundra. It jumps right out at you."

I tie on my kidney belt. Rick probably thinks that's typical of a woman, too. But he's still going on about Georgina's Jeep.

"She doesn't drive that thing into the tundra. She doesn't do anything but go to the hospital."

That's my cue.

"How did Meeka take the news of Dr. Perrell's murder?"

I've already learned from Rick that Meeka won't be coming with us to Sataka Lake because she's not feeling well. Rick's brother will take the three children on a sled hitched up to his Ski-Doo that he uses for getting firewood from the forest.

Rick's face goes dark.

"She's worried about Dulcie. Dr. Perrell treated her. Have you found out who did it yet?"

I look for my gloves. A pair of thin ones for the first layer and thick ones over them.

"He treated lots of people. I wonder who could have hated him so much. Any ideas?"

He rocks his head back and forth. "Could imagine that not everybody liked him. He sometimes gave it to people straight that they shouldn't drink so much or eat potato chips and watch TV."

"But nobody kills you for that!"

"Maybe he screwed a fisherman's wife."

"Was he a lady-killer?"

"Did he make a pass at you?"

"No."

"He had so many to choose from. Women ran after him in droves."

Women like Georgina Closs. But Carl Perrell might have stayed true to one of them. Ann Smith, who gave him the cold shoulder. And pointed a rifle barrel at him at the shooting competition.

I pick up my helmet.

"I'm ready. Are we going?"

Another snowmobile is standing next to mine outside. I assumed we were going to take mine, but Rick finally got the spare part for his machine and repaired it. Which is a great relief to me. It's no fun on the rear seat, having to put up with the hard bumps and abrupt turns. Like that trip with Gerald Hynes.

I've hardly got the machine going and Rick's already out ahead. He slows down out of deference to me. We cross the main street, go up a slight incline where bushes yield to a snowmobile trail. Soon we've got a couple of hills behind us and jet over the tundra; the vegetation is almost entirely buried under snow. At times an improvised signpost appears. I still lose my orientation quickly and stay right on Rick's heels. The path keeps branching off time and again, and it puzzles me how Rick knows which way to go. I don't see any reference points in the uniform, white wilderness that you can depend on. The glare of the sun is almost blinding; my eyes are burning. I tenaciously follow the blue shadow in front of me that's moving forward. Sometimes Rick glances over his shoulder to see where I am.

After a half hour that seems like an eternity, we go up to a plateau, force the machines through risky curves among low trees, and speed down again onto a white plain. I can make out colored dots on it. The frozen lake! I made it. Rick comes to a stop near a group of people, and I do the same. I get off my Ski-Doo awkwardly; my legs are stiff and frozen through, despite my thermal underwear. When I take off my helmet, I see a dozen pairs of eyes staring at me.

Rick looks like he's enjoying the attention, unlike me.

"No fear, people," he jests. "She won't take the first prize away from you."

"Hey, she's already caught a big fish," one of the bystanders counters. "Unless he jumps off the hook."

He probably means Ernie Butt.

"I hope you'll help us catch Dr. Perrell's killer," I appeal to them. "If you know something, do let us know."

"Do you think you'll find the murderer here?" a woman in a purple ski jacket shouts, and her tone of voice is not friendly.

Of course, what did I expect? People don't think for a second that I'm here to protect them but that I'm here to spy on them. They're not stupid. I curse Closs for dispatching me this gathering.

Rick saves the day.

"I've dragged Constable Gates here so that I don't have to keep giving her salted cod; she should learn to catch her own fish."

Everybody laughs, and I could hug him.

"Well then, we'll just have to see how you do things," a young man teases me, wearing a dazzling orange hunter's cap.

"I'll charge admission," I fire back. I've learned that you only get the locals' sympathy by using humor.

Rick grabs the ice auger and drives it through the ice. A hole opens up in no time in the frozen surface of the lake.

"This is your pathway to Shangri-La," he says with a grin, and I'm surprised again at his choice of words. I underestimate my neighbor; that's now clear. He hands me a rod that looks like a discarded broomstick with a fishing line attached. A small weight hangs from the line about two meters above the hook.

"And now comes the most important thing, the bait," Rick announces. He takes a plastic can from the storage area under his snowmobile seat.

I make a face. "Worms?"

Loud laughter all around the circle. Ironic remarks start immediately.

"Dew worms in winter—that would be something new, eh, Rick?"

"I don't think they've ever seen ice in Vancouver!"

"I hear they heat the soil so they can keep the worms warm."

"The poor beasties!"

I laugh along with them—what else can I do? Rick takes a slab of bacon out of the can and cuts off a corner.

His pocketknife has a white casing.

"I thought white pocketknives are unlucky," I say.

"The lady sure won't catch any fish now, Rick!" the man standing next to me shouts. He's wearing a brown fur cap with ear flaps.

Rick shakes his head, grinning.

"Nonsense, that's all superstition. Do you know what a pocketknife costs in the store? Thirty dollars. Would really be a shame to throw away something like this." He attaches the bacon to the hook.

"Thirty dollars! And Pleaman tried to buy our votes with that.

Didn't help him any." The woman in the purple jacket hasn't gotten any friendlier.

Pleaman Hick. The independent candidate who got next to zero votes in the last provincial election. The unsuccessful politician who gave away white pocketknives to advertise his campaign. I'll have to take a closer look at the knife later. I saw briefly that there were some words on it but couldn't read them. So the knife we found beside Carl Perrell's body can't be Rick's. He's still got his knife. I must ask him afterward whether he knows who else in Port Brendan might still have one like it.

He shows me how to lure fish with my line. A few little tugs, then a yank upward. I lean on my Ski-Doo, because I find standing especially difficult. My right leg hurts from the cold. Other ice fishermen and women are sitting on plastic buckets or folding chairs.

"I'm going to see what the kids are doing," Rick says, handing me a plastic bag. "For the fish. Good fishing!"

"Thanks, but don't get your hopes up. What do you catch here anyway?"

The heckling comes instantly.

"Sharks."

"Twelve-armed squid."

"Moby Dick."

I seem to really inspire mockery.

"Trout and smelt." Rick throws up his arms briefly in feigned despair and leaves without turning around.

"It'll be okay," the young man who'd spoken up earlier yells. His ski outfit resembles a motorcycle rider's.

I wiggle my rod around the way Rick showed me. The group watches me for a while, constantly making comments, then scatters, because I get no bites. My felt-lined boots keep my feet warm, but the cold creeps into the rest of my body. Quickly and relentlessly. I'll certainly not be able to get any relevant information from these people. I'd have to wander around and talk to them one by one. Nobody will say a thing in front of other people.

I look over the frozen lake. Fishing men, women, and children everywhere, patiently sitting beside their hole in the ice. Many are alone, others have company. Bright dots in the black-and-white landscape. People don't feel lost in this vast expanse; I can see that in their behavior. They probably feel a freedom that's important to them. Nothing but nature and an infinite horizon. No fencing them in, no prohibitive signs, no crowding. Only vastness and a wonderful, empty space.

I can see Rick and his kids with a couple, probably his brother and his wife. Meeka's sitting at home, weeping over Dr. Perrell. The doctor who was so vital for Dulcie's well-being. Maybe Meeka did more than revere him, like Georgina. Maybe more women did, too. Did one of his worshippers go crazy with jealousy, like Closs's wife? Did one of them reach for a pistol in her rage? But Bakie's murder doesn't feel right for a woman. Unless she's very strong and has no fear of knives.

"Caught anything?" A clear, high voice startles me. A little boy, maybe seven. He's on a mini-Ski-Doo and is watching me. I didn't hear him coming. I pull hard on the line out of surprise. Something's hanging from the hook. It flops around on the ice. A trout?

"It's big," the boy says in admiration.

I look at the floundering fish.

"What do I do with it now?"

"Take out the hook."

Since I do nothing, the boy jumps off his Ski-Doo, grabs the fish, and pulls out the hook. I hold out the plastic bag for him.

"Do you want the fish?"

"You could win with that one, it's real big," he says knowledgeably.

"I don't care. I'm really not in the competition. I'll give it to you. Do you want it?"

The boy beams and nods. He climbs onto his little Ski-Doo with the fish in the bag and roars away. If only the group that was here had seen that fish, I think, feeling a bit proud.

But I bet they'd hold it against me if I won. As a bloody beginner. And a Mountie on top of it.

I'm all by myself again. Abandoned to the cold. It doesn't seem to bother the others. Just as I'm about to give up fishing and wander around, two snowmobiles come roaring up.

The drivers shout something.

"Polar bear! A mile away." Two teenagers, judging by their voices.

Before I can respond, they drive on. I hear them shout, and people start getting up from their buckets and folding chairs. They climb onto their snowmobiles. Children protest and whine.

I leave the fishing rod on the ice and hop onto my Ski-Doo. Just as I get my helmet on, Rick appears.

He puts up his visor.

"It's best for us to go back. My buddies do have a rifle, but it's better to be safe."

I feel my heart beating.

"Can I follow behind? I don't think I could find the way back."

"Sure. My brother's taking the kids."

He picks my fishing rod up off the ice.

"Ready?"

The polar bear scares me, but I'm also happy to escape the cold. Rick revs his motor and tears ahead. This time noticeably faster than before. I go faster, too, not letting him out of my sight. Not until after a rather long stretch do I realize that he's taking a different trail back. We're the only ones on this part of the trail. Maybe he knows a shortcut. The trails must be connected by loops. He probably wants to avoid the traffic on the other path.

The ground feels wavier. The snow cover over the bushes is not as thick. It's not as easy to stay on your seat. Rick's body oscillates up and down. Suddenly his Ski-Doo jumps sideways and tips over. Rick can just get off in time before he and the machine land on their side in the snow. I cut the motor as fast as I can and slide off the seat.

"Rick, are you hurt?" I help him stand up.

He takes a few steps. "No, don't think so."

He stomps around and investigates the ground.

"A goddamn root," he curses. "Couldn't see it."

He goes back to his Ski-Doo. The bench seat has popped open. Things that have fallen out of the storage compartment under the seat are lying in the snow. I pick up a black plastic bag. Feels heavy. I glance inside. I almost have a stroke. A flashlight. A SureFire R1 Lawman. Quick as a flash, I close up the bag. My eyes wander automatically to Rick's snow boots. Then to his face. He saw me. I hand him the bag.

"This fell out," is all I say. Sounding as normally as possible.

He stuffs the bag under the seat. Then he tries to right the machine. He can't do it. I go at it with him. We groan as we push together and get the heavy vehicle upright. We're both out of breath.

"Don't go that way," he says, pointing to the spot where his machine tipped over. "Who knows what's hidden under the snow." He looks around. "We'll go that way."

He means a wide dip running between bushes sticking out of the snow.

"Isn't that a creek?"

"Never fear, it's frozen. And there's deep snow over it. It will hold."

I don't feel afraid. Cautious, rather. And not only on account of the creek.

It's best not to confront Rick now about the SureFire Lawman, I figure. I'm not going to ask him here whether he stole it from the Viking house. Where Bakie's dead body was lying. I won't ask about the white pocketknife either. First I must safely escape from this icy labyrinth on the tundra and get back to Port Brendan. Maybe I wouldn't make it without Rick. I might keep going around in an endless circle. And freeze to death while doing it.

He must have picked up on my hesitation.

"I've got to turn around. Your machine's in the way. Just move it over the creek, and then I'll lead again."

It all seems logical. Rick sounds the same as always. The helpful neighbor. I didn't see a gun under the Ski-Doo seat. My revolver's in its holster under my jacket. He knows that. He watched me when I put on my winter clothing.

I climb onto my Ski-Doo and head for the broad snow bridge over the creek. I'd prefer to fly over it at high speed, but the bumpy terrain doesn't allow it. I wish I were safely traveling in a column with all the other ice fishermen and women and their children. Too late: I'm already crossing the frozen creek. Suddenly a crackling sound, then splintering. I scream. My Ski-Doo falls in, tips to the right. Falls on top of me. Buries my legs and pelvis beneath it.

I don't scream anymore. The shock silences me.

I'm shaking as I raise my head. The helmet makes it heavy. Everything's okay. My arms, too. When I move my back, the ice under me begins to crack.

I immediately stay completely still.

Then I hear a motor. Rick's coming.

But his snowmobile's going away.

"Rick! Rick! Help me " My voice is muted by the helmet.

I'm still calling when I realize nobody can hear me.

50

Fred can't say what annoys him more: that he can't go to the ice fishing event with Calista or that Bernard Closs is keeping her out of the investigation on some pretense or another. He strongly suspects that the sarge is again making allowances for people in Port Brendan, and he takes great delight in throwing a stumbling block in his way. Displeased, he opens the station door.

Closs intercepts him before he goes into the meeting room; Delgado and Sullivan are already in there.

"How's it going with the newspaper clippings?" he asks immediately.

Without a word, Fred hands over the file with the articles and takes a seat beside his teammates, who are staring at a laptop and ignoring him. Closs comes in seconds later. He lays a writing pad on the table, but not the articles Fred has just given him.

"We've got a new lead in the Perrell case," the boss announces when he's seated. "A witness contacted me to tell me she heard how someone from Port Brendan attacked Dr. Perrell verbally. We're talking about Rick Stout. The incident happened about seven weeks ago. Stout accused Perrell of performing an unnecessary operation on his wife Meeka. It was apparently to remove her Fallopian tubes and uterus. According to the lady who's our witness, Stout yelled at the doctor and alleged the surgery was not necessary—a second doctor advised against it, he said, according to the witness. Perrell seems to have carried out the intervention anyway, and now Meeka can't have children as a result, the witness said. Stout behaved very aggressively, she added. The witness remembers one sentence in particular: Stout shouted that he'd see to it that one of Perrell's body parts was cut off so he couldn't have children, either.

"Who's the witness?" Sullivan interrupts him. "Is she credible?"

"Paula Keyton. A former nurse in the clinic who retired two months ago. The incident occurred in the parking lot in front of the Golden Anchor. She had just driven up to pick up her husband from the pub. She opened the car door to get out when the confrontation started. Afterward Rick Stout went back inside the pub, and Keyton talked for a bit with Dr. Perrell. He said she shouldn't worry about it, situations like this happen to a doctor now and then, you have to understand people, an operation like that one is a drastic matter for a married couple. And, he concluded, the parents are already hard-pressed with Dulcie."

"Is the witness credible?" Sullivan repeats. "I don't know the lady, but we all know how much the people in Port Brendan love gossip."

Fred thinks differently. It speaks for the witness that she contacted the police. The witness has got guts. She's running a risk.

Sullivan doesn't admit defeat. "Sure there are a lot of people who don't agree with doctors' decisions. That doesn't make them potential murderers. Rick Stout was probably a little tipsy and vented his anger."

Delgado goes even further. "Sarge, with all due respect, I can't imagine that Rick Stout's a murderer. Everything I know about him tells me he's a friendly guy who loves his family and is a model father to Dulcie. He sometimes drinks a little too much and gets loud—but who doesn't do that in this town?"

Closs writes on the pad in front of him. "Maybe. We still have to pursue the matter, making as little noise as possible. We don't want people to think we believe they're all suspects."

Aha, Fred thinks to himself, here we go again. Just don't step on anyone's toes.

"Fred?" Closs looks his way.

"I can talk to Rick's wife. He's gone to the ice fishing contest with Gates, and the kids are there as well. Meeka's probably at home alone. That's convenient. Has anybody checked out Rick's alibis at the times of the murders?"

Calista had texted him that Rick Stout was taking her to the lake. Nothing she wrote indicates she might have distrusted Rick.

"Alibis? I thought we weren't supposed to make waves," Sullivan sneers. "Why is Gates out ice fishing? I'd love a fresh trout."

"She's keeping her ear to the ground with the people there," Closs explains.

He sent her. Why doesn't he say so? Fred's mood is getting blacker.

"Can somebody tell me how Rick got Perrell's pistol," Delgado pipes up.

Closs turns to Sullivan.

"Perrell reported the theft of the gun to you. What are the details?"

Sullivan slithers back and forth on his chair. The question appears to make him nervous. He didn't report the theft to the boss right away. Fred knows that much.

"Perrell kept the pistol in the glove compartment of his car. He always kept it locked, he claimed."

"Yes, we know that," Closs mutters, "but how often do people here not lock the glove compartment or even their car. As we found out with Ernie Butt, for instance."

"Has Ernie's guilt been confirmed?" Sullivan exclaims to those around the table. "Or is Gates looking for more evidence at the ice fishing contest?"

Fred sees through Sullivan's demand: he's trying to distract them from the fact that he messed up the report about Perrell's pistol.

"One thing at a time," Closs orders. "Fred, you talk to Meeka Stout. If Rick's done nothing, we'll exclude him as quickly as possible."

"And what about us? Can we go ice fishing?" Sullivan asks.

Delgado shows he's more serious than his teammate. "Ann Smith should be questioned again. I'd like to know why she pointed the gun barrel at Perrell. And I'd like to know what Perrell and Shannon Wilkey were arguing about."

Well roared, old lion, Fred thinks.

Closs gets up.

"We'll review Rick's alibi."

Fred heads to Meeka's. As he's driving along the main street, he ponders how to proceed. He has to act cautiously, or Meeka will clam right up. Something Calista told him comes to mind. The obscene emails on Meeka's cell phone. That furnishes him with a good pretext for his visit.

Five minutes later he drives by Calista's place. He sees a car parked in front of the Stouts' house. That's good; Meeka's at home.

She must see him arrive since she opens the door at once.

"Rick's not here," she says. "He's gone ice fishing."

"I'd like to have a few words with you," he explains. "Some women have received salacious emails, and we're following up. Constable Gates reported that you were one of them."

When she hesitates, he adds: "It won't take long. Just a few minutes."

"Okay."

She goes to the kitchen; he takes off his boots and follows.

Meeka's face is swollen, her eyes puffy. As if she hasn't gotten any sleep.

Since she stays standing, he doesn't sit down, either.

"You're not the only one someone harassed with those emails," he begins. "We want to put the man who wrote them out of business."

She furrows her brow. "You've got time to do this? Aren't you busy enough with the two murders? Dr. Perrell is dead and Kris Bakie is dead. Who's next?"

Careful, now, Fred van Heisen!

"We believe we'll be able to figure out who's behind the emails pretty quickly using the sender's IP address. Can I take a look at your cell phone?"

To his relief she picks up the device that's lying on the table and goes to her messages.

He scans the email she shows him. It's explicit, but not obscene or threatening. Something that lovers would write out of sexual passion.

"Can I forward this email to myself so we can determine the sender?"

She hesitates.

"I've already had enough trouble with them. Rick discovered the messages."

"That's unpleasant," Fred says, "for both of you. Tell him that other women in Port Brendan received emails like these."

"Who?"

"I can't tell you that. We treat all information confidentially. Also, what you tell me in confidence goes no further."

She nods. "I'll be really happy when this is over. Rick was very worked up."

"Well, he's probably not the only one. I'm sure it makes other husbands furious, too."

"Creeps who do something like that . . . maybe they want to create . . . an argument in some families."

"I'm sorry that it's led to disagreements. You really can't do anything about it. If you want, I can explain it to your husband."

Her eyes go damp.

"Rick . . . he thinks it was Dr. Perrell. I told him Dr. Perrell would never do a thing like that. But Rick's convinced of it. Because I'm at the hospital so often. He certainly regrets it now . . . that Dr. Perrell's dead. It's just awful."

Tears run down her cheeks. She quickly brushes them away and leans on the counter.

Fred spies a chink in her armor.

"Believe me, his death shook us all. We're doing everything we can to solve the murder." He scratches his head. "I have to beg your pardon. We should have let you know earlier that you aren't the only woman to get those emails. Your husband might have understood the situation better. When did he accuse you?"

"Three days ago, perhaps. He knew about the emails for a long time, but he never said anything to me. So stupid. Bottled everything up inside. And when he finally came out with it, it was much worse." Her face was agitated. "That's Rick. He thinks because I'm pleasing to him that I'm pleasing to other men as well."

Fred feels something simmering inside him. Does she realize what she's revealing to him? A strong motive. Raging jealousy toward Dr. Perrell. First the operation preventing Rick from having children with Meeka. Then the erotic emails to his wife. Fred looks at her. No, she doesn't know. She's vulnerable, in turmoil, concerned about how things will go now with Dulcie. And he exploits her fragile state. He must. It's a question of murder.

"We also want these emails to stop. So I'll forward them to my account, okay?"

"If that helps." She rubs her face. "But you've really got to find the murderer. That's more urgent." She looks to one side.

"Constable Gates has gone to the ice fishing contest. Do you really think that'll do any good?"

A few minutes later, he's hurtling down the salt-covered street in his police car. Time is of the essence. He parks in front of the station and rushes past Wendy into Closs's office. The detective sergeant, telephone receiver in hand, looks up in surprise. Fred makes a gesture and Closs hangs up.

He delivers a hasty report on his conversation with Meeka Stout.

Closs listens attentively.

"Have you got Meeka's cell phone?" he asks.

Fred says no.

"We need that phone. We have to know if Rick sent Perrell emails using Meeka's name. Or if he sent them to Bakie."

"We can't tell whether it was him or Meeka."

"No, but she'll defend herself if she didn't do it, and those are the contradictions we need."

"So you think . . ."

Closs gets up from his swivel chair.

"I'm not counting it out. We need an impression of Rick's boots. Then we'll see what happens next."

"Where are the others?"

"On the Ski-Doo trail. The game warden called a short time ago. A polar bear's running around near Sataka Lake. The organizers actually had to cancel the ice fishing contest. We want to trap Rick without causing a stir."

Fred's pulse beats faster.

"Heard anything from Gates? Is she still out with Rick?"

"We can't reach her. She didn't take the satellite phone."

As if one of the team would have done it in her situation. Not for ice fishing. But she'll certainly have her firearm on her.

"Meeka's cell phone, is that official, Sarge? I should confiscate it?"

"Use your imagination, Fred. Tell her anything."

This time Meeka will get suspicious. She'll surely see through him. He has to get the phone before Stout gets home.

Fred's already at the door when Closs says one more thing.

"I've issued a press statement. It mentions that a white pocketknife with Pleaman Hick's name on it was found beside Perrell's body. Maybe we'll get an anonymous tip."

Fred puts a hand on the doorknob. Calista Gates will be happy about that.

51

Water bubbles up through the broken ice and soaks my ski pants. I'd never have thought cold could burn this much. How long before my pants are completely saturated? Water's running into my snow boots, too. I try again to lift my head and upper body. The ice cracks as I shift my weight.

I drop the idea immediately. My pulse is hammering. That my legs will be destroyed by frostbite is bad enough. But my head—I repress the thought at once. It's terrifying. I don't feel any pain up there; the helmet cushioned my fall. The snowmobile's whole weight lies on my legs.

Rick Stout. He abandoned me here. If he'd helped me, I would never have believed that he was capable of murder in spite of everything. Of two murders. He showed his hand by fleeing. My death is part of the deal. He thinks I'll slowly freeze to death in the icy water. From where he was standing, he could only see my head. He must have assumed that the Ski-Doo completely buried the rest of my body.

Nobody will look for me here. Rick chose a remote route. The network of snowmobile trails around Port Brendan is enormous. By the time my team misses me, it may already be dark. And I will be dead in an icy grave.

Rick left me behind to cover his tracks. I firmly believe it. He read my eyes and saw that he'd attracted my attention. The Sure-Fire flashlight. The knife with the white casing. My glancing at his boots. Maybe he'll come back to make sure I'm not alive anymore. And if he finds me alive, he's got the SureFire Lawman with him. Or the pistol he stole from Carl Perrell.

How could I not have had the merest hint of this? Rick's constant cracks about Perrell, that he was a womanizer, that he hit on women. Meeka, who went to the hospital so frequently. Who really wanted to be a nurse. Preferably in the operating room.

My legs hurt. The weight of the snowmobile. The icy water.

Then the polar bear crosses my mind. Oh my god! It can smell its prey kilometers away for sure. Which is more terrifying: Being torn to pieces or freezing to death? I've survived a near-fatal attack. Fought my way back to life. And now I must die in this gruesome way.

I think about my parents. First, the assault that almost cost me my life. My mother's back bent with worry. My father fell into a depression. He already had heart problems. They tried to hide them from me, but I picked up on them anyway. The fact that they're about to lose their daughter now on top of it will destroy their lives.

Despair overcomes me.

I pray, plead for my life.

I don't know how much time has gone by. I shiver with the cold. The pain in my legs is stilled. I know precisely what that means. They're freezing. And I can hardly feel my back anymore. Only my hands in the double gloves don't desert me; I stretch my fingers constantly. I also move my face under the helmet, grimace to keep it flexible. My head's still functioning, too. The skull and the soft brain beneath it. It made it through without injury. Of all things.

That thought consoles me briefly. My teeth are chattering until it hurts. I didn't know how awful chattering teeth can be.

Suddenly I hear a motor. A snowmobile.

Rick's coming back. Help!

The motor dies. But there's another motor.

Two snowmobiles. That can't be Rick.

I scream as loud as I can. Open my helmet's visor. Scream again.

Loud shouting: "Calista! Calista!"

My name. Is it a mirage? Visions before I freeze to death?

Footsteps in the snow.

Voices.

"Holy shit!" A stranger's voice. A man.

"We'll get you out, Calista. We'll get you out fast." I know that voice.

A face comes into view.

Gerald Hynes.

I weep tears of exhaustion but don't care. I am saved.

Shouts between the men. I can't see the other one. They slowly push the machine upright.

"Hold on tight," Gerald yells. "Now onto the other side."

I hear the ice crack. The machine was tipped over toward the other side of the creek. Now two men are beside me, raising me up gently, pulling me out of the water.

Gerald's face exhibits total concern. "Are you in pain?"

"No, no," I stammer. "Not anymore."

That's right—my legs have lost all feeling.

They pull me up the slope carefully, like a doll. Once there, Gerald lifts me up under my arms.

"We'll lay you on the sled, okay? We have to take off your wet pants. We'll wrap you up in a heated blanket."

Of course, Gerald's the chief of the volunteer fire department. He knows what to do.

"This is my foreman, Randy."

They take off my boots and socks, my ski pants and thermal underwear. My panties have stayed dry by some miracle.

Gerald wraps me in aluminum foil and a fur blanket. The warmth slowly restores feeling to my legs. It's painful.

I howl.

"Drink this. It'll help with the pain."

Gerald hands me a pill and a hip flask. I smell rum. I grab both of them eagerly.

He talks to me incessantly while taking care of me, probably to keep me awake.

"I read on the internet this afternoon that the police found a white pocketknife with Pleaman Hick's name on it beside Perrell's body. So I tried to contact you but couldn't reach you. I wanted to tell you that you should ask Rick Stout about it. He definitely knows who in Port Brendan owns a white pocketknife. Not many do, definitely not. They're all superstitious. Rick was a Pleaman supporter back then. He distributed the knives to people. In any case—are you comfortable? In any case, I couldn't get you on my cell phone. So I called the station. Wendy said you were at the ice fishing contest and not back yet."

Wendy. Finally her knowing my whereabouts has done some good. How ironic.

Gerald chatters on. "Then I hear that a polar bear's on the move, and everybody's going home from the contest. So I wait an hour, but I still can't reach you. I talk to Wendy again. I ask her if Constable Gates knows the way. And she says you're still not back. I thought, *Something's not right*. I felt it in my bones. So I took off with Randy and sent two other people off on another route. And we drive and drive on, and we're just about to turn around when we see this thing blinking in the bushes."

He holds up an object right in front of my nose. The SureFire Lawman. I stare at the flashlight as if seeing a ghost. Stout must have thrown it away when he fled, but not far enough from the path. And the impact must have accidentally turned on the signaling light function. If it hadn't, Gerald and Randy would never have seen it. It never would have been found. Neither would I. I can't grasp it. Now Gerald's fingerprints are on it. But luckily his foreman is a witness.

"Please stow it away," I beg him. "Please don't lose that flashlight. It's important. Very, very important."

"Don't worry, I'll put the thing beside you under the blanket. Why didn't you go back with the rest of them? To be alone like that, on the barrens, that can be dangerous."

"I was on my way back with Rick Stout," I gasp. "He left me lying in the creek."

The two men stare at me. And exchange glances.

"Did he push you into the creek?" Gerald asks.

He thinks Rick's capable of doing that. He can actually conceive of it.

"He said I should drive over it. But the snow bridge collapsed."

"What an idiot!" Gerald's foreman exclaims. "You only go over a creek if there's a wooden bridge."

"That will have consequences," Gerald mutters. He leans over me. "For the trip back, I'll put the foil and the blanket over your face; we don't want your nose to freeze off. And now we'll stretch the plastic tarp over everything."

I must warn him.

"Gerald, Rick is dangerous. He's got a pistol."

At the word *pistol*, he raises his eyebrows.

"I hear you," he replies. "I'll call the station."

I hear him talking over the satellite phone.

"Yes, she's with us. We're bringing her back . . . Rick Stout was with her. He pushed her into a creek, the ice broke, and the Ski-Doo fell on top of her. Then he simply drove off. She would have died . . . He's got a gun . . . You've already got him? . . . Good, good, good, he's got some explaining to do . . . Sure, we're on it . . . No, no visible injuries. Just bruises on her leg. Definitely hypothermia, but we've packed her up warmly. Randy's with me.

Two more guys are still out and about . . . We've got everything under control for sure. So long."

He phones somebody else, probably the second search party, and talks briefly with Randy. Then he comes back to me.

"Your colleagues have already got Rick at the station. He's apparently got other skeletons in the closet."

I just nod. Gerald gingerly pulls the covers over my face. Then the motors start howling, and the sled glides over the snow.

Gerald's last words spin around in my head. Rick's already at the station.

They must have gotten something on him. Something really conclusive.

52

I'm in Fred's far-too-big ski pants that he brought to me in the hospital. He got Dr. Cameron's permission to take me home. He drives very watchfully, especially around the curves. The hot tea they gave me in the hospital in a never-ending flow rapidly warmed me up. The doctor advised me to have even more.

"You got off with a scare," she stated after examining me.

No broken bones, no muscle pulls, no frostbite, just a leopard pattern decorating the skin on my legs. Black marks from the Ski-Doo lying on top of me. I'm particularly proud of my good old brain, which didn't suffer any new injuries. Dr. Cameron wasn't enthusiastic about my rescuers pouring rum down my throat instead of hot, sweet tea. I won't have a word said against Gerald and Randy; they saved my life. Exhausted as I was, when I got to the hospital, I could see how calmly and sovereignly Dr. Cameron mastered the situation. Perrell's death must have shocked her and everybody else there, but this slight, delicate person seems to have risen to the challenge produced by Perrell's loss.

Fred has the SureFire Lawman that signaled in the bushes and, like the Christmas star, led my saviors to the right place. I'm relieved: we've secured yet another murder weapon. I bombard Fred, who's beside me, with questions. Gerald and Randy are now witnesses against Stout in the coroner's inquiry. Delgado has gone with them back to the place on the barrens where they saw the flashlight blinking. He's hoping to find the pistol there, too. Perrell's own pistol Rick shot him with.

Fred sums up the details for me. After that, he tells me about Meeka's cell phone, which he's confiscated.

"Rick contacted Perrell through Meeka's email address and tried to lure him to the Viking house. Perrell wrote her that he couldn't come. But Rick didn't see Perrell's reply. Meanwhile, Meeka read it and deleted it before he took another look through her phone. It was a second tragic coincidence that Bakie went to the Viking house at the same time, where Rick killed him because he mixed him up with Perrell."

I'm stunned.

"It's awful that Rick hated Perrell so much that he didn't give up his plan even after the mix-up with Bakie; he had nothing against the guy."

"Rick held Perrell responsible for the fact that he couldn't have children with Meeka. And Meeka spent a lot of time at the hospital. Sometimes Dulcie was probably only a pretext for her visits. Rick didn't get it that it wasn't all about Perrell as a man but about Meeka's desire to be a nurse and to help Dulcie."

"A desire that his pigheadedness probably destroyed," I add. "One of the biathletes told me Rick had so restricted Meeka's freedom of movement that she wasn't able to travel and perform her throat singing. She had to constantly look after Dulcie and their foster children, which was obviously just fine by him."

Fred turns up the car heater as he goes on with his report: "Rick didn't want to tell us at what point he conceived of his plan to kill Perrell. We also don't know how and where he stole the pistol. Closs and Sullivan are still interrogating him. But we've got his boots, and as far as we can tell, the soles match the impressions at the Viking house and the hot-dog stand. The tracks from his Ski-Doo as well. Forensics in Happy Valley-Goose Bay still has to confirm that. But we've learned in the meantime from Rick's brother that, contradicting what Rick said, Rick was not cutting fire wood in the forest with him the whole of Wednesday afternoon. He got there later. He had time to go to the Viking house and back. And besides, he had time and opportunity during the search for Dulcie and during the fireworks to shoot Perrell. He followed Perrell behind the hot-dog stand, where the doctor couldn't avoid him."

Rick Stout. It's still unfathomable. I started to mistrust him when he brought out the white pocketknife. He was so obviously unaware that we'd found one exactly like it by the corpse. He must have a number of them left over from Pleaman Hick's campaign.

"Rick was always so helpful to me."

"Until he left you in the ice-cold creek."

"Maybe it was kind of like a hit-and-run. Panic."

"Don't make excuses for him; Rick's a two-time murderer. He kept on going even after realizing he'd killed Bakie instead of Perrell. His mistake must have shaken him up completely, and he still didn't give up."

"I gave it some thought in the hospital. I believe Rick has always had a great fear of being seen as a failure—by others, but by himself as well. He hasn't got much money; he's sort of a casual laborer, and his wife is young and attractive. He's afraid of not living up to her expectations. He can't have children by her. And then he bungles the murder. He's got to make up for it, what-ever it may cost. Because in his eyes Carl Perrell's got to go. Forever."

When we turn into the driveway at Crow Point and roll up to my house, I can't see a light on at Meeka's. Nor is there a car in front of the house.

Fred helps me out of the car. Once in the house, I change my pants and give Fred back his. He's already filling the teakettle.

An unfamiliar feeling for me, to be looked after by men. I

think of Gerald, who went searching for me though he's not in great shape himself. Fred's rooting around for teabags and sugar in the kitchen cupboard. Even Rick was there for me. I'd counted on him. He's done all he can for Meeka, in his opinion. And grown more and more possessive. The blind fear of losing her made him into a murderer.

A thorny question bugs me.

"Do you think Meeka had any idea about this?"

Fred sits down with me at the table.

"I talked to her that afternoon, and she told me Rick was jealous of Perrell. That he thought Perrell sent her erotic emails. She wouldn't have told me if she'd suspected something. She would not have served him up on a silver platter that easily."

Something has changed in the way Fred looks. He seems like he's on alert when his eyes are on me. He looks concerned. And relieved. He looks at me the way a person sees someone who's missed by a whisker never being in this kitchen again.

When he's gone, I lock all the doors. For security. I sleep very soundly, in phases, but wake up repeatedly. In a dream I see myself lying in the ice, a heavy machine on top of me.

I hear nothing from Closs. Until morning.

He texts me at nine: *Up for a visit?*

I'll be ready in half an hour, I write back. I take a long, hot shower and dress warmly.

The sky's gray, but it's not snowing. And there's no strong wind. Who's going to blow away the snow in my driveway in the future? Get firewood for the stove? Grace Butt will have other priorities than thinking about such matters. I'll have to take care of it all myself. Like the Labradorians.

Closs is punctual. Compared to him, I must look like a newly hatched chick. Exhaustion sits on his face like a burial shroud. He plops into the armchair.

"How are you?" he asks.

"Seemingly better then you are, Sarge."

"Rick Stout has confessed. To everything. He fell apart when we confronted him with that huge amount of evidence. The tracks in the snow. The flashlight. The screwed-up alibi. The cell phone records. We found the pistol yesterday, too. Along with the murders, he'll probably be charged with failure to render assistance. And what exactly happened with you?"

I describe the events of the previous afternoon. Closs listens to me without saying a word. He already knows most of it.

"We'll need a written report from you when you're feeling better."

I nod. "Have you questioned Meeka?"

"Yes. She says she didn't send the email to Perrell. She didn't have the slightest idea about it."

"Where's she now?"

"At her sister's in Happy Valley-Goose Bay. With the kids."

"And Ernie Butt?"

"His lawyer claims we never seriously considered Lorna's married, one-time lover in Happy Valley-Goose Bay to be the killer. He had a motive, the lawyer says, to keep her quiet. But our men there grilled the ex-lover thoroughly. There's nothing that would cast suspicion on the guy. Besides, he had an airtight alibi. He was on holiday in Mexico with his family when she disappeared. There's no doubt as to Butt's guilt regarding the killing; he'll be in custody for four weeks. By then, we'll have the whole case cut and dried."

Closs must be rejoicing. Three murders solved. Nevertheless, he looks wiped out. He braces his elbows on his knees, his hands hanging limply, as if all his energy has left him. He looks at me with dull eyes.

"You surely know I'm here for another reason."

My stomach's in a knot. "I can guess."

"My wife told me she spoke to you. About the garbage bag on the ice. She did it out of desperation. It's all my fault. I don't want her to suffer anymore from this situation." He clears his throat.

"Georgina and I, we haven't been in love for years. No bad feelings, no hostility. We decided to stay together because of the kids. Until they could stand on their own two feet. They're important to us. We also agreed to have other relationships. But we have to be discreet; nobody must know about them. Especially the kids. And we don't want to know who the other is seeing, either." He sighs.

I think it's the first time I've ever heard Closs sigh.

"In theory it worked. Actually, in practice as well. Until I fell in love with Ann Smith. And she with me. I met her in Vancouver during the Olympics. She was still Yvonne Shelcken. I was on duty with the RCMP. I can't tell you how we met; all security people are obliged to keep quiet. We had long talks, about anything and everything. There was nothing else between us. But we kept in touch after she went home to the States."

He leans back.

"I can spare you the rest—you know it from the press clippings. When Ann sued the NGF for using her photo illegally in their advertising, the organization launched a smear campaign against her. A right-wing politician, who was also attacking her, was shot. She got death threats. I suggested she emigrate to Canada. With a new identity. She got support from people I can't name. In the US and in this country. When she arrived here, we became a twosome. She comes to Port Brendan every year to be with me. She's agreed to be considerate of the kids until they're bigger. Ann is a remarkable woman."

I suddenly see Bernard Closs through different eyes. He shows me a side of him that I never would have thought possible. He's vulnerable, but courageous.

"Things went well until Georgina fell in love with Dr. Perrell. And learned that he had his eye on Ann. She spied on Ann, and on Dr. Perrell. She was obsessed with Ann—the obstacle to her love for Perrell. But then she discovered that Ann was secretly meeting me."

A thought flashed through my mind. The puzzle. The aerial shot of Port Brendan. The yellow car.

"You realized because of the puzzle that your wife was spying on you?"

"Yes. You showed me the Jeep in it. It wasn't far from the place where Ann and I meet secretly. I figured out the rest. It must be a difficult time for my wife. Ann has become an invincible rival for her. A woman who has not only held Perrell's feelings captive but also gained her own husband's love. Georgina has lost both men."

That's not the only problem here. We're in the middle of a murder investigation. I mustn't lose sight of that.

"Your wife put the garbage bag on the ice," I say.

"Not on the ice. Georgina put it at Ann's front door."

"Why?"

"She freaked out. It was too much for her."

"Then how did the bag wind up on the ice?"

He hesitates before confessing: "Ann put it there. She wanted somebody on the snowmobile trail to find it. So that clues would point back to the person who did it."

"To your wife?"

"To whoever did it—to that person."

"Ann didn't tell you anything about this initially?"

"She's learned there are certain things she can't discuss with a police officer. That's always been a bright red line for her."

I'm slowly getting a headache. My tender brain is working at top speed. Georgina and the garbage bag. At Ann's front door. Ann takes it out on the ice. Georgina and her unrequited love for Perrell. Perrell's unanswered interest in Ann. It doesn't add up.

"Perrell knew Ann's identity. He knew she was once Yvonne Shelcken. He had all those press clippings."

Closs's gaunt frame slumps down even more. "Again, my fault. I kept the articles in my patrol car. In the glove compartment. I was as careless as Perrell was with his pistol. Felt safe—

like him. Or like Ernie Butt. It would be funny if it weren't so serious. I'm a cop. Ernie and Perrell aren't."

"That's where your wife found the newspaper clippings."

"You guessed right, Gates. Georgina began to rifle through my things. To spy on me. Or to put it better, to plot against Ann. That's not like my wife, believe me. I've asked too much of her."

"Did she give Perrell the clippings?"

He nods.

I fold my arms over my chest. I ought to have another hot tea to warm me up. And a painkiller for that headache.

"How could she have guessed it?"

"Because she found a photo in there. Of Yvonne Shelcken and me."

"I didn't see it in the folder."

"Georgina kept it out. She gave it back to me yesterday. And confessed to everything." Closs gets a bit livelier. "I'd like to keep Georgina out of it. Because of the kids. Gates, I'm going to give up this posting and get a transfer. Fred is going to take over the investigation. I'll move away and live with Ann. She needs her new identity; she needs this protection to be secure in her life. Georgina wants to leave, too, because everything reminds her of Perrell. The kids . . . they're old enough to understand that not every marriage is going to last. I'll always be there for them."

I'm sitting in the armchair as if I'm frozen to it. It's perfectly clear what Closs expects from me. He needs my agreement. My silence. My loyalty. I think about it, my temples pounding. The garbage bag has nothing to do with the three murder cases. Quite the opposite: it could distract from them.

I look Closs straight in the eye. "Am I here in Port Brendan because of you, Sergeant?"

He gives a brief start, then sees the bridge I'm building for him to walk over.

"When the position opened up, I was asked if I'd take you. I wasn't pushed to accept you. I immediately agreed. I wanted to give you a chance."

At that moment I decide to make a deal. A swap. I help him, he helps me.

"Here's a suggestion," I offer. "The severed finger. We've kept it secret so far. I'd like to give the information to a specifically targeted person."

He's all ears. Processes it. Then nods.

"I'm sure you know what you're doing."

He gets to his feet.

"I've got to get back to the office. I know Dr. Cameron prescribed a day of rest for you. But . . . we need you, Gates!"

Admitting that must have been tough for him. I'm happy anyway. We need you, Gates!

He found exactly the right words.

The door clicks shut, his car departs. I sit at my laptop and type.

I know this is all very painful for you, but Lorna would have wanted me to inform you. She was murdered and can't speak anymore. We owe this to her. Before Lorna died, someone cut off the little finger on her left hand. Why?

Then I wait.

53

After my fourth cup of tea, my cell phone chirps. I flinch. Go to the bedroom where I left it. An unknown number on the display. An unfamiliar woman's voice. The caller introduces herself as Karissa Pardy's mother. I was actually expecting somebody else.

"How is she?" I ask.

"She wakes up in the night sometimes because she has nightmares about it. It haunts her. She's concentrating on her training right now. She wants to win the junior championship. That helps her."

"I know it must be terrible for Karissa."

And her uncle can't get his expensive medication cheaply from Dr. Perrell anymore.

"I'm also calling because of Meeka," Karissa's mother says. A slight stab to my heart. "She wants to know how you're doing."

I'm floored. How does Meeka know what happened to me? It's clear that word travels fast around here.

"I seem to have survived pretty well," I say, carefully. "Where's Meeka?"

"She's with some relatives. The children, too. Meeka has a large family, a lot of siblings. They take care of her. Family is very important to us."

"Good for Meeka. And good for Dulcie."

Now that Rick's confession is on file, there won't be a trial. Meeka's been spared that. Rick's a double murderer, but he protected Meeka to the bitter end. The human psyche is not always black-and-white; there are many sides to it.

Karissa's mother says good-bye sooner than I thought she would. I'd expected more questions about the investigation that I'd have to deflect. Lost in thought, I look out the bedroom window that's facing the open North Atlantic. The ice doesn't seem as threatening to me as it did in the beginning. It's a surface you can traverse. When you're out on the ice, you get a new perspective on the coast, the land, the woods. So much has changed in the few days I've been here. When Closs leaves, there'll be more upheaval. He plans to have Fred take over his job.

Fred as my superior. The thought makes me uncomfortable. It could affect our collegial relationship. We won't be a team any longer; a new person will certainly come on board. I won't be able to have a say in personnel decisions the way I used to in Vancouver.

Vancouver. Not only one but three solved murder cases in the short time I've been here—that must impress the RCMP brass. Maybe I can use it to bargain for my return. A sudden hope seizes me. I straighten out the sheets and blankets on the bed and go to the kitchen.

Someone's there. I'm rooted to the spot.

"I . . . didn't hear you come in."

"But you're not totally surprised," Grace Butt says, "since you wrote me."

Her smooth, black hair is shiny, but her face is pale, her eyes lifeless.

I gesture toward the armchair, the same chair she sat in when I questioned her for the first time.

"I hoped you'd come for a conversation. Please have a seat."

She sits down ponderously, like an old woman.

"*Conversation* maybe isn't the right word under the circumstances, eh?"

She undoes her zipper but keeps the jacket on despite how warm the house is. She must feel a crushing coldness inside.

"It's your decision, Mrs. Butt," I respond, watching her.

We both know that she's already decided, because she came to me by herself.

I still have my cell phone in my hand and press the record button. This conversation is too important not to be recorded.

Then I sit down and nod to her.

"When . . . when you asked me recently about the tattoo on Lorna's little finger, I didn't tell you the whole truth." Grace speaks in a trembling voice but doesn't avoid eye contact. "There . . . was indeed a small symbol, the three joined triangles or whatever it was. I never asked her about it directly."

She brushes her long hair behind her ear and resumes talking after a long pause.

"Lorna got a second tattoo later on. Just three letters: *USA*. That was when she got to know Guy."

Guy Stravitz, the American soldier who won Lorna's heart. The all-American boy with the open, attractive face.

Grace shifts around inconspicuously as she goes on: "She always teased Ernie with it. Because Ernie allowed himself to be antagonized. She thought his reaction was ridiculous."

Grace suddenly stops.

"How did he react?" I ask.

She folds her hands, pressing them together until some red spots appear.

"He was enraged. He said that as a Canadian she was being unpatriotic; that the United States is not our friend, that the president attacks Canada verbally, and a friend doesn't do something like that."

"Did you know your husband's biological mother is now living in the US and married to an American?"

She nods. "He told me that. When he was an adult, he tried to contact her, but . . . she didn't want to have anything to do with him. That hurt him badly."

"Did Lorna know?"

"He told no one else but me."

I sense she's slowly getting to the heart of the matter she wants to tell me about. The secret she's carried with her for so long.

"There was this incident when Lorna waved her little finger around in front of his face. Bite it off if the tattoo bugs you so much, she taunted him. Not in anger; she was laughing. Go ahead and bite it off. It was fun for her to challenge Ernie. He can be so . . . bigoted. And Ernie . . . he said: Watch out, or I'll cut it off."

We've got him, I think to myself. *Now we've really got him.*

I don't take my eyes off Grace, so that she won't stop talking. My eyes let her know that now is the moment to get it all out.

And she responds. Her voice wavers, and she fights off tears.

"Actually, I'm the one to blame. I wanted to leave Ernie. He thought it was because of Lorna. And it . . . was true. Lorna always did whatever she wanted to. She would have moved to the United States with Guy. She also moved to Happy Valley-Goose Bay before I did. If it weren't for Lorna, I probably wouldn't have gone there. But she gave me courage. I dreamed of staging houses so they would sell faster. I wanted to consult with people about interior decorating. But that's not possible in Happy Valley-Goose Bay. And Ernie would never have permitted it."

Grace struggles to maintain her composure, and I can't help her. Mustn't help her.

"I talked with the pastor of our church, before our wedding," she continues, after taking a deep breath. "I confided my doubts to him about whether that life was right for me. He advised me to postpone the wedding for a little while. Until . . . everything was a little clearer to me. And then Lorna disappeared. I was devastated. That she could just somehow disappear off the face of the earth. I . . . I didn't think at first that something had happened to her. I thought she simply took off. Found something new. Left me behind."

She undoes her tightly locked hands and picks out a tissue from inside her jacket to dab her wet eyes with.

I remember now. Lorna's purse vanished and her cell phone with it. Her ID. Her credit cards that were never activated. Nothing happened to her bank account. Nobody used her phone.

"I thought that perhaps she was in the US illegally. I felt so alone without her. I waited for her to contact me from somewhere. But I never heard from her again. I concluded that Lorna had taken too great a risk. Then I thought maybe something had happened to her. That scared me. And so I married Ernie. Because he meant security."

She pressed both hands to her cheeks. As if to say: Whatever did I do?

"Did you ever harbor any suspicion toward your husband?"

She shook her head.

"Ernie showed . . . he showed great understanding toward me. Because I was so crushed. He said, She'll suddenly show up again. You know Lorna, he used to say, she needs her freedom." Grace looks at me with tearstained eyes. "But she was in love with Guy. Head over heels. He signified freedom to her. A different country. A new life. I could never figure out why she would have left him so suddenly." She wipes her nose before resuming. "Ernie was never impatient when I'd talked about Lorna. He never said, Stop that. He always helped me put up posters of Lorna so that she wasn't forgotten."

She stops, as if abruptly aware of the insanity of the situation.

I say it for her: "But then he lied. Because of the car."

"Yes, he wasn't driving his pickup that day. I had it because I was picking up the snowmobile from the repair shop. A silver

SUV was seen on the street when Lorna disappeared. I had a silver Hyundai Santa Fe. But there are a lot of silver and gray cars in Happy Valley-Goose Bay, of course. Ernie told the police I'd been working that afternoon, and he'd stayed home all day. The next day I found a crumpled-up chewing-gum wrapper in my car, and it wasn't mine. However, he liked that brand. I thought it odd. But I quickly repressed the thought. It just couldn't be. It couldn't . . ."

Her pretty face grows distorted as if a red-hot pain has pierced her body. She hides her face in her jacket. The sounds she emits don't sound like sobs, rather like groans.

Her husband, a murderer. A monster. How is Grace to come to terms with that? We sit there for several minutes, I, the cop; she, my most valuable witness. Then I dare to ask one last question: "Why do you think your husband put the crate with Lorna on the beach so that someone could find it?"

She stares blankly for a while before answering. "I've asked myself that, too. Ernie . . . he was dissatisfied. I remember. He'd hoped for a promotion in the fall, but they passed him over, saying they'd put it off until later. That frustrated him a lot. He ranted like never before."

So, impatience, bitterness. The shame of rejection. Aggrieved self-esteem. I'll show you guys, Ernie must have thought. I'm no loser, *you*'re the losers. You have no idea how smart I am. And you'll never know.

Grace stands up swiftly, a wild expression on her messy face.

"He shoved her into a crate, but he can't do that to me. I will live Lorna's life while he's rotting in prison."

54

Ernie Butt's lawyer is not a happy camper. Fred can smell it a hundred miles away in a wind. The judge denied Ernie bail. Which delights Fred. The tables have turned. Unlike a few days ago, the investigators sitting opposite the lawyer now find themselves in a much stronger position. Fred is almost euphoric over the fact that they've solved a case in the meantime and have the murderer's confession. And that convinces him all the more of his team's strength. Not least because they also found the pistol Rick used to kill Perrell on the tundra, not far from the flashlight.

In contrast to Rick Stout, Ernie won't come clean. He sits with his lawyer across from Fred and Delgado and digs in his heels.

Fred tries confrontation. "Come on, Mr. Butt, the jig's up. The evidence against you is damning. You're only making it worse for yourself if you say nothing."

The lawyer protests: "Mr. Butt has the right to remain silent; you know that better than anyone else. He is innocent, and we will argue that convincingly in court."

Delgado laughs contemptuously. "Lorna's ring in the desk drawer? The necklace in the glove compartment? The material used to make the crate for Lorna Taylor's body? How do you intend to explain all that away? You'd have to be a magician."

"The objects could have been planted there by someone else. My client is the victim of a conspiracy."

Fred ignores the lawyer and focuses on Ernie Butt.

"Now's your last chance, Mr. Butt, to get off with a lighter sentence. Your last chance because . . ."

"Stop harassing my client, Constable. We will come out of this trial the winners. My client is innocent."

Fred almost feels sorry for Ernie. Not only does the evidence look bad for him, but his lawyer is also bad. He leans forward. Time for the explosion.

"If you want a trial at all costs, then be warned: we have an outstanding witness."

He lets the words hang in the air like a guillotine that can drop at any moment.

The lawyer tries to put on a brave face, but his facial muscles go tense.

"Who is the witness you're speaking of, Constable?"

Fred takes his time before speaking. "Mrs. Grace Butt."

"Grace?" Ernie jumps up. "Grace would never testify against me!"

Delgado waves around a stack of papers. "What you see here, Mr. Butt, is the written statement, signed by your wife."

"That's—"

"Do not say a thing, Mr. Butt. It may be a bluff. I shall look into it."

Fred leans back without taking his eyes off Ernie.

"We've got a pretty good idea of the course of events. We know that you intercepted Lorna when driving Grace's car on the day in question; that you offered to take her to the restaurant where she'd arranged to meet her boyfriend. When she got in, you anesthetized her with the ether you'd bought two weeks earlier at the pharmacy. You took Lorna to your cabin in the woods, where you held her captive for several days and checked up on her repeatedly. Witnesses saw the silver Hyundai in the vicinity. You probably cut off her left little finger on the very first day, as punishment. We've seized a knife in your cabin; the medical examiner confirmed Lorna's DNA is on it. You saved the ring as a trophy. After several days you strangled Lorna Taylor with a nylon rope that we also seized in the cabin. You took her body to Port Brendan later, in a crate you built out of boards in the cabin. You unfortunately didn't see the Viking symbol on one of them. You sank the crate on a rope in the water. And you sometimes went back to the spot to enjoy the fact that Lorna was safely inside the crate and could never persuade your wife to leave you."

"Is that all you have, Constable? It is preposterous. Come, Mr. Butt, we have little to fear from these gentlemen."

A really bad lawyer, Fred thinks. And Rick Stout is smarter than Ernie Butt, who now has to go through a trial he'll certainly lose. Rick wanted to spare his wife, Meeka, a trial. Ernie Butt doesn't give a damn about Grace. He'll be staying in pretrial detention. Maybe he'll feel safer there. Lorna Taylor's brothers would probably lynch him if he were running around town.

The lawyer packs his papers into his briefcase. Delgado puts handcuffs on his client and shows the two of them out. Ernie will be transferred to Happy Valley-Goose Bay that afternoon.

Fred remains sitting at the table for several minutes more. He must ask Rick Stout why he committed his deeds when he did, right after Lorna's body was found. Was the trigger anger over Meeka's operation? Did he think the police would connect the murders to Lorna? Did he hope the two murders would put the police on the wrong track? Maybe it was just a coincidence. Rick's hate for Dr. Perrell reached a boiling point, and he had to act to relieve himself of the pressure inside him. Coincidences exist. The pure chance, for example, that Calista Gates came to Port Brendan of all places, and that Closs will give up his position. The sarge has already shared the news with him.

"The post is yours," he informed him.

Fred stands up and leaves the room.

Wendy calls to him from reception: "There are fresh scones!"

He declines. "Thanks, I've got to go out again."

He wants to pay a visit to Scott Dyson, to work on him before Butt's family persuades him not to testify against Ernie. He knows what he can offer Scott in return: to occasionally turn a blind eye here and there.

But before that, he has to go to another house.

He's thinking about Calista Gates while driving through Port Brendan when he suddenly sees her at the gas station. She's talking to a man, Gerald Hynes. The Great Savior. Fred's annoyed that it wasn't him who pulled Calista out of the creek. Now she'll be forever grateful to Hynes for saving her life. A strong bond. Shit.

Should he stop?

He doesn't. After all, he's in possession of information he must keep from Gates until she gets it from somewhere else. Closs sat down with him and clued him in.

RCMP headquarters is going to transfer her to St. Anthony in Newfoundland. A larger town than Port Brendan, with a nearby airport. Gates is to run the post as detective sergeant. And that's not all: there's an internal investigation of Calista's ex-husband going on in Vancouver.

"It's said to be a serious business," Closs told him.

"The guy surely doesn't have anything to do with the assault on Gates?" Fred couldn't resist asking the question.

"You read my thoughts," the sergeant answered. "But I don't know."

If the ex-husband was involved somehow, it would shake the RCMP in Vancouver like an earthquake. And it would be better if Calista were far away from the action.

Fred will feel reluctant to see her move to St. Anthony, but he's also glad. He's been preoccupied with her. That makes him nervous. Having some distance from Calista will do him good. There'll also be distance between Calista and Gerald Hynes. Fine by him, too. But that, however, is something he won't openly admit to himself.

In the rearview mirror, he can see how serious their conversation is. He averts his eyes and goes down a side street to a house with a red door.

Melissa Richards is startled when she opens the door. "You don't have more bad news for me, do you?"

"It depends," he replies.

He's about to take off his boots, but she says: "You can tell me right here, Constable. Let's get it over with."

Her face is haggard, without any makeup. It could be depression; that often happens after the loss of a loved one. How would she have taken Bakie's Las Vegas escape plan? He finds it almost cynical that she was only spared this humiliation because Bakie was murdered before he could flee.

Fred reaches into his pocket and holds out the plastic bags with the scalpel and the anonymous note. The letters from glossy magazines.

"We found your fingerprints on this."

He's bluffing. Melissa's fingerprints wouldn't be in the RCMP data bank. But the surveillance camera in front of the station recorded Melissa at the mailbox. He doesn't want to let her in on it. The fewer people who know about the camera, the better. Or else the day will come when a trigger-happy drunk gets the idea to target it.

Melissa sinks onto the steps leading to the living room. She looks at the floor and says nothing.

He resists the temptation to squat beside her.

"What were you intending to do with this?"

Still nothing.

"We don't have to make a big deal of this. We've got other

things to worry about. Just tell me why you did it. Revenge on whom?"

"Revenge on whoever cut the dog's head off," she mutters.

He's startled.

"But you don't even know that the person used a scalpel."

No answer.

"Where did you get it?"

Then it hits him. Melissa's mother works in the hospital. As a cleaning woman.

"It was your mother's idea, right? She thought it up. Because she was furious that we'd put Dennis in a cell. She wanted to mislead us—intending it as revenge on the police. And you carried it out."

She doesn't contradict him. Keeps her head lowered.

"Didn't you give a damn that you might have steered suspicion to an innocent person with this scalpel?"

Fred puts the evidence bags away. First a mother gives her son a false alibi. Then she concocts an anonymous threat. No wonder Kris Bakie wanted to live very, very far away from the Richardses. He almost made it.

Fred looks down at the hunched figure.

"We'll let it rest," he says, turning toward the door. "So long as there's no more trouble from your family."

Outside, he breathes in the cold air to get rid of the disgust he feels in his mouth.

55

"Are you sure the police haven't made a mistake?" asks the elderly cashier behind the counter at the gas station. "Rick and Ernie, they're no murderers."

My team gets asked the same kind of question; still, it bugs me. The woman doesn't annoy me, but the fact that I can't really defend my job. The two investigations aren't officially closed. We're still checking on details in Rick Stout's confession and gathering further evidence for Ernie Butt's trial.

"We're really working hard," I reply. "Our primary concern is to protect the population."

The woman looks at me as if I've taken her for a fool.

"I've known Rick since he was little; he'd never hurt anybody."

"Apart from the fact that he let Constable Gates almost kick the bucket in the creek," says a voice behind me. I turn around. Gerald Hynes has appeared from nowhere.

"I've heard that story," the gas station owner says. "You should never go on a Ski-Doo all by yourself."

"She wasn't alone. Rick was with her and drove her through the ice. Then he took off and left her lying there, the rat."

I put my hand on his arm. "Just drop it," I say.

It's no use trying to convince people who'd rather cling to their illusions. It would destroy their view of the world, and that's hard to take. I think most people in Port Brendan are in shock. They act as if it's any other day; they go ice fishing, play bingo, go to church—but life is nevertheless not the way it was before.

Gerald goes to the door.

"I'll wait for you outside."

"He's a good man," the woman says. "Melissa Richards jilted him, God knows why. That guy Bakie brought her bad luck. Now she's all alone and has no money. She'd have done better with Gerald. Maybe he's something for you."

I pay for the gas. It doesn't matter one bit what she says. What's important is that there will be justice for the awful crimes against Lorna Taylor, Kris Bakie, and Carl Perrell.

I hurry out of the store. Gerald is waiting beside my pickup, without a hat on despite the cold.

"You'll freeze your ears off," I tease him.

He grins.

"*You*'re the expert in freezing to death."

"I must disappoint you; I've never frozen anything; you saved me just in time."

"Still a ton left to do?"

"It's crazy. Three murders. That's fifty kilograms of files. Heavier than all your tools put together."

"I'd like to take you to Forteau sometime. There's a really good restaurant in the Florian hotel."

"Restaurant owners live dangerously."

I've scarcely gotten the words out when I decide I'd like to take them back. That's how cops speak among themselves, to relieve the pressure, but not in front of outsiders.

Gerald just nods.

"The customers live dangerously, too," he jokes. "You never know what's going to be put in front of you." He looks at me.

"Maybe a drink or two in the Golden Anchor would do you good. As relaxation."

I don't let him know that I'm not supposed to have any alcohol with my medications.

"And you. How's work going? Got any new projects?"

"Now's the time I normally fly off on vacation. Somewhere in the sun. Dominican Republic, Mexico, Costa Rica."

"Or Greece."

"Why do you say Greece?"

"The cigarettes."

He looks at me, confused.

"The pack of Karelias in Shannon Wilkey's bathroom. Remember?"

He laughs and exhales white clouds of breath.

"You're a sly one, Calista, but you're not always right. Those cigarettes were Shannon's."

Now I'm the one who's confused.

"I've never seen her smoke . . . and never smelled cigarettes on her."

"She sneaks them."

Gerald puts his hands in his pockets. His throat is unprotected despite the cold.

"I think she does a lot of things in secret."

"Is that so?"

I don't want to comment on that. Maybe she had a cigarette after a secret rendezvous.

He smiles. "Greece. Why not? It's said to be very beautiful. But I don't want to go there alone."

I can't picture this guy on a beach, lying in the sun, without his heavy winter clothing. Though it would make an attractive image. I'd like to fly away, too. I get wistful.

"I'd like to go back to Vancouver as soon as possible, to see my family, my nieces and nephews." It gushes out of me before I can even give it a thought.

Gerald Hynes gets the message. Calista Gates doesn't want to settle down in Port Brendan. Not in the vicinity. Not in Labrador. Not in eastern Canada.

"You can hardly wait to get away from here," he says. "My tough luck."

His openness is touching. So I open up as well.

"I don't want to leave here with a broken heart, Gerald. My heart hasn't healed completely from the last time."

I don't tell him that I hope to be able to return to Vancouver very soon. Even before the three years are up. Now that I've proved that I'm fully ready for duty again. Three murders solved in two weeks, one of them three years old. Good heavens! What more do they want?

"Do you know what: we can simply practice a little, take it easy; it doesn't have to be so bloody serious." He grins mischievously.

Sure, why not?

"I could call it rehab." Those words slip out, aloud.

We both grin.

"Tomorrow, happy hour in the Golden Anchor?"

"Closer to seven," I answer, climbing inside the car, freezing. It's not much warmer there. With numb fingers, I enter Fred's number on my phone. He answers immediately.

"Where are you?"

"At the gas station. And you?"

"In front of Melissa Richards's place."

I have a present for him. Something to thank him with. He's my bright spot in Labrador. A reliable teammate. Someone who thinks like me. We're a good team. I couldn't have had it any better under the circumstances.

When I handed him the SureFire Lawman recently, he said: "I could use one of these, too."

I tracked down a great flashlight in Happy Valley-Goose Bay, and it came here by truck. It is not a SureFire Lawman: this one is supposed to be even better. I'd like to see his face when he unwraps it.

"Wait for me there, Fred. I'll be with you in five minutes. Don't go anywhere."

He promises her.

He waits for her. Of course he waits for her.

It's a pleasure and scary at the same time.

EPILOGUE

Scott Dyson dips his favorite biscuit in his tea. The small pleasures of the day. He hums an old sea chanty as he chews it. His mother's making a soup of turkey necks. She's cutting up onions, carrots, turnips.

She's just as satisfied with the way events have turned out as he is.

"I told that RCMP lady that Ernie's mother took off. That she simply abandoned Ernie. That he was adopted. He always thought he did better than everybody else. And here he is, a murderer! Not surprised. He thinks he can have any woman he wants, and if one of them says no, he kills her."

Scott doesn't disagree. She constantly talks about Ernie. Ernie, Ernie, Ernie. Now she doesn't have to feel so ashamed that her son was in the clink. Several months. All for a bit of cocaine. Peanuts compared to the murder Ernie committed. Ernie will get the punishment he deserves. Why is it always the little fish that wind up in the clink? Little fish like him. All because of a little bit of coke.

He knew it must have been Ernie when he saw the Viking stamp on the crate. On the crate with Lorna's skeleton. Ernie had taken the rest of the construction lumber from the playground.

And he nattered on about Lorna whenever he came to him to pick up his dose of marijuana. How she made him angry. What a stupid cow she was. Immoral and depraved. Bad company for Grace.

Ernie probably wanted to sleep with Lorna, and she didn't want to, he thought at the time. He himself would like to have had a go with her. An insolent, pretty thing. Perfectly to his taste. But Lorna was out of his league. Even though he isn't stupid. She didn't want to stay in Labrador. He would like to have sold her a bit of stuff. But unlike Ernie, she didn't even smoke. No cigarettes or anything harder.

He'd spotted the gold necklace in her coffin at the last moment. As he was about to go for help on his snowmobile. A flash in the pale winter light. The locket was in a crack between the boards. Stuck in the crate, just like Lorna.

He didn't let the opportunity go by. It was almost an automatic reaction. The nerve endings in his gut told him: this can be useful.

And so it was.

The idea came to him when the cop called on him in the shed. He heard his mother talking with her that day. About Ernie and Ernie's biological mother. Then it hit him like a lightning bolt: *The cops are finally interested in Ernie*. Well, look at that. This bimbo from Vancouver is smarter than he thought. Almost as clever as he is. He knew that she'd show up at his place sooner or later. That the dog shit he tossed through her door would lead to him.

Shit he'd rather have smeared all over Ernie's face. But his time had come when Ernie, bursting with pride, showed off his new jalopy after Lorna's funeral. That's Ernie for you. Swell-headed. Has to flaunt it all. Even Lorna's bones. The idiot puts the crate out on the beach. So that he can prove he's smarter than the police. That he won't get caught like other people. As opposed to Scott, his alleged cousin.

But I'm not a bonehead, Ernie. You're the bonehead.

The moron didn't even lock the glove compartment of his brand-new car. Ernie just needed to be distracted, which really wasn't so hard, and presto! Lorna's gold necklace landed in the compartment behind the manual.

Scott shoves a soaked biscuit into his mouth. His mother babbles and babbles. He only half-listens. She doesn't know what a genius she's brought into the world. Too bad, he'd like to have told her. But it's unfortunate that she can't keep her mouth shut. Which sometimes has its upside.

Lorna and her flirting. Ernie and adoption. The Mountie took the bait right away. She knew she had a clue she had to follow.

She puzzled out the hiding place in the glove compartment quickly.

He always knew: *Crooks think just like cops.*

AFTERWORD

Labrador, a huge, sparsely inhabited region, is part of the Canadian province of Newfoundland and Labrador. Arctic cold influences the climate, especially in winter: the ocean is frozen for several months; in summer, the tundra, dotted with swamps and lakes—and where mosquitoes attack any living creature—is largely impassable. Mighty mountains were shaped by glaciers. Wildlife, such as bears, moose, coyotes, and wolves, roam the dense woodlands. Polar bears wander along the coasts; muskox and caribou graze in the wild, barren vastness. I've traveled several times through the south of Labrador where this novel takes place. I drove the Trans-Labrador Highway from L'Anse-au-Clair through Port Hope Simpson to Happy Valley-Goose Bay before most of this four-hundred-kilometer road through the wilderness had been paved. My companion and I were lucky: a flat tire had to be replaced (it could have easily been two or more) and the wheel bearings were defective—but that wasn't until the end of our trip, so that we were able to take refuge in the repair shop in Port Hope Simpson. Many others weren't so lucky, as witnessed by the wrecks along the highway. A minibus that had passed us halfway down the road had to be towed—a tedious business in such a remote area.

Don't be scared off, dear reader! Labrador is a region you must absolutely visit. Most of the highway from the Blanc Sablon ferry landing to Happy Valley-Goose Bay is now paved. The wild landscape is overwhelmingly beautiful, and hikes through the uninhabited, primeval nature there are unforgettable. So are the inhabitants: Labradorians are kind, helpful, willing to make sacrifices, resilient, and full of warmth and humor. On my trips, they took me in, served as my hosts who shared their everyday lives with me. For this they deserve my first vote of gratitude.

Dr. Wilfred Grenfell (1865–1940) and the brave explorer Mina Benson Hubbard (1870–1956), who are mentioned in this book, are taken from real life. The town of Port Brendan, on the other hand, as well as the people and events there, are entirely fictitious. It is true, however, that American troops were stationed in Happy Valley-Goose Bay, and some still are to this day. There are abandoned radar stations from the Cold War in "Port Brandon." Deserted stations like these can be found in Labrador, in Cartwright and Hopedale, for instance. They were part of the old DEW Line (Distant Early Warning Line), a line of defense in the Canadian North stretching far beyond to Alaska, Greenland, and Iceland that would have allowed Americans to spot and intercept any Russian bombers attempting to fly toward America over the North Pole.

My beta readers dealt with these kinds of details as they critically, meticulously, and attentively read through the German manuscript of *Cries from the Cold*. Their findings, insights, tips, and questions were incredibly valuable and enriched me and the book enormously. Much, much gratitude to you all: Susanne Keller, Helen Radu, Irene Zortea, Hans Kurth, Klaus Uhr, Beny Affolter, Gisela and Koni Dalvit, Ruth Omlin, Karl Uhr, and Regina Thürich. You've all given this book that extra something.

Constable Nicolas Roy of the RCMP served for several years in the northern part of Newfoundland and Labrador and told me about the challenges the police encounter in remote areas. But I did take some liberties, and I am therefore completely responsible for any errors.

It was a joy to hand in my fifth German manuscript to my editor, Gisa Marehn, and, as always, the results exceeded my expectations. She is an incomparable wealth of experience, precision, linguistic knowledge, and investigative skill. I cannot thank her enough.

My translator, Gerald Chapple, who has already translated four of my previous books (*The Zurich Conspiracy, Under Dark Waters, Stormy Cove, The Stranger on the Ice*), mastered his task with aplomb, enthusiasm and incredible workmanship. I am really lucky to have him on board.

I also owe a huge thank-you to copyeditor Lindsey Alexander, who, for the third time, took care of one of my crime novels. After *The Stranger on the Ice* and *Murderous Morning*, she improved and polished this book in a way that is admirable and always to the point.

I was able to count again on the support and keen eye of my wonderful proofreaders in Canada and the United States and Europe: Paula Dunn, Michele Hodder, Constanza Law, Cheryl Shoji, Maureen Matteson and Caroline Huerlimann. You rock!

I'm also thankful for the help of my fellow authors Heike Fröhling, Marion Krafzik and Alec Peche, and to Inca Vogt who did the interior design of this book but is also an accomplished crime novelist.

I have learned many interesting things about the consequences of brain injuries from the gripping book *Prognosis: A Memoir of My Brain*, by the Australian author Sarah Vallance. I was astonished to find how little researchers still know about these injuries and their treatment.

Finally, I would like to thank the man in my life, whose love, patience, and humor carry me over every obstacle when I dive into the wild, cold, boundless Canadian North.

St. Anthony, February 2021
    Bernadette Calonego

P.S. I'm so thrilled I can share another book with you, my dear readers. I would love to hear from you, either on Facebook, Instagram, or through email (you will find the address on my website www.bernadettecalonego.com. If you also like to leave feedback for your fellow readers (and for me, of course), a review on Amazon (https://www.amazon.com/review/create-review/listing? B0924S1964), Goodreads, or another platform would be such a treat! It doesn't have to be long. Even one or two sentences will help readers find my book and will encourage me to keep on writing. I'm very much looking forward to seeing and savoring your thoughts and opinions.

If you like to know more about my daily life and work progress, you can sign up for my monthly author letter on the home page of my website www.bernadettecalonego.com. And don't forget to press the "Follow" button for my author page on Amazon to hear about my new releases. Thank you!

ABOUT THE AUTHOR

Bernadette Calonego was born in Switzerland and grew up on the shores of Lake Lucerne. She was just eleven years old when she published her first story, in a Swiss newspaper. She went on to earn a teaching degree from the University of Fribourg, which she put to good use in England and Switzerland before switching gears to become a journalist. After several years working with the Reuters news agency and a series of German-language newspapers, she moved to Canada and began writing fiction. *Cries from the Cold* is her ninth book and her sixth novel in English. As a foreign correspondent, she has published stories in *Vogue*, *GEO*, and *SZ-Magazin*. She splits her time between Vancouver, British Columbia, and Newfoundland.

For more information, visit: www.bernadettecalonego.com

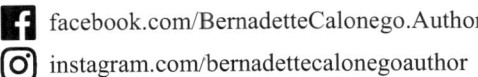 facebook.com/BernadetteCalonego.Author
instagram.com/bernadettecalonegoauthor

ABOUT THE TRANSLATOR

Gerald Chapple is an award-winning translator of German literature. He received his doctorate from Harvard and went on to teach German and comparative literature at McMaster University in Hamilton, Ontario. He has been translating contemporary German-language authors for over forty-five years, especially the poetry of Günter Kunert.

His prose translations include Michael Mitterauer's probing history of Europe from 600 to 1600, *Why Europe? Medieval Origins of Its Special Path*; Anita Albus's wonderfully idiosyncratic book, *On Rare Birds*, and four of Bernadette Calonego's novels for Amazon Crossing.

The Stranger on the Ice being the most recent, as well as four other novels for the same publisher. Since choosing early retirement, he's lived in Dundas, Ontario, with his wife, Nina, an architectural historian. When not translating, he can usually be found studying birds, butterflies, and dragonflies; reading; listening to classical music, or enjoying his children and grandchildren in New York.

ALSO BY BERNADETTE CALONEGO

The Zurich Conspiracy

Under Dark Waters

Stormy Cove

The Stranger on the Ice

Murderous Morning

Made in the USA
Middletown, DE
05 July 2023